IGNAZIO SILONE was born Secondo Tranquilli on May 1, 1900, in a small town in the Abruzzi region of Italy. Like the main character of BREAD AND WINE, Silone led the adventurous life of an underground political organizer. A member of the Communist party for ten years, he risked his life, was smuggled by friends to Switzerland, and went through a painful reevaluation of values that led to his break from Communism in 1931. Silone's own brother, not unlike Murica in BREAD AND WINE, was tortured and beaten to death by the Fascists. Silone adopted his pseudonym when his political activities brought the threat of government reprisal on his family, and continued to write under it for the rest of his life. He completed his famous novels FONTAMARA and BREAD AND WINE while in exile, only returning to Italy in 1944. He died in 1978.

IRVING HOWE has written extensively on politics and literature, and is the author of the Introduction to the Meridian Classic edition of Ignazio Silone's FONTAMARA, also translated by Eric Mosbacher.

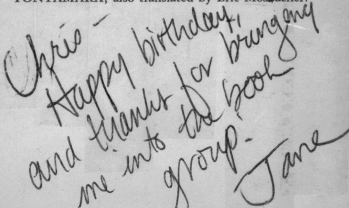

Chris –
Happy birthday,
and thanks for bringing
me into the book
group –
Jane

IGNAZIO SILONE

Bread and Wine

Translated from the Italian by Eric Mosbacher

With a new Introduction by Irving Howe

A SIGNET CLASSIC

PUBLISHER'S NOTE

BREAD AND WINE was first published in 1936, in a Swiss edition (*Brot und Wein*). In the same year, the English edition of the work was published in London. The first Signet paperback edition of *Bread and Wine* was published in 1946. The original text was completely revised by the author in 1955, and published in Italy for the first time as *Vino e Pane*. In an author's note written in 1962 and reprinted here, Silone outlines his reasons for the revision. A Signet Classic edition (translated by Harvey Fergusson II) appeared in 1963; this 1986 Signet Classic edition is a completely new translation (by Eric Mosbacher) of Silone's final version.

SIGNET CLASSIC
Published by the Penguin Group
Penguin Books USA Inc., 375 Hudson Street,
New York, New York 10014, U.S.A.
Penguin Books Ltd, 27 Wrights Lane, London W8 5TZ, England
Penguin Books Australia Ltd, Ringwood, Victoria, Australia
Penguin Books Canada Ltd, 10 Alcorn Avenue,
Toronto, Ontario, Canada M4V 3B2
Penguin Books (N.Z.) Ltd, 182–190 Wairau Road,
Auckland 10, New Zealand

Penguin Books Ltd, Registered Offices:
Harmondsworth, Middlesex, England

Published by Signet Classic, an imprint of New American Library,
a division of Penguin Books USA Inc.

First Signet Printing, March, 1946
First Signet Classic Printing, October, 1963
First Signet Classic Printing (Mosbacher translation), December, 1986
33 32 31 30 29 28 27 26 25

First published in Switzerland in 1936, under the title *Brot und Wein*.
This revised edition first published in Italy in 1955, under the title *Vino e Pane*.
© Arnoldo Mondadori Editore, Milan.
This edition first published in Great Britain by J.M. Dent & Sons Ltd, 1986.
English translation, copyright © Darina Silone, 1986
Introduction copyright © 1986 by Irving Howe
All rights reserved. For information address Mrs. Darina Silone, c/o Russell & Volkening, Inc., 50 West 29th Street, New York, New York 10001.

Cover painting by Anna Demchick

REGISTERED TRADEMARK—MARCA REGISTRADA

Library of Congress Catalog Card Number: 86-062312

Printed in the United States of America

Two encompassing visions held the imagination of Ignazio Silone:
the secular promise of socialist liberation and the Christian
promise of spiritual transcendence. A writer at once sardonic and
kindly, glum and humorous, Silone knew—this knowledge forms
the spine of his work—that even if these two visions might
somehow be yoked through an act of will, they could not settle
into a true harmony, for they pertained to separate realms and
must always be in severe tension. It became Silone's choice as
writer and man to live with that tension, indeed, to leave
himself open to it.

Writing about the desolation of Europe during the decades of
totalitarian power, Silone focussed again and again on political
problems that soon revealed themselves also to be moral
problems—and not in order to offer any programmatic solutions
but to embody human dilemmas in works of fiction. Who,
reading a novel like *Bread and Wine* upon its first appearance in
1936, could suppose that there were any solutions? For a
generation of readers still alive to the call of social idealism yet
grown impatient with party dogmas, Silone's books spoke with
a painful immediacy. Not that we knew anything about the
Abruzzi, that poverty-stricken area of Italy in which his novels
are usually set; we simply felt that the moral–political quandaries
of his characters were ours too. In the years of betrayal and
demoralization preceding the Second World War, a book like
Silone's revolutionary fable *Fontamara* (1930) could bring back
memories of hope and a book like *Bread and Wine*, hope by now
all but lost, could yield a gesture of companionship to friends in
defeat.

The spiritual condition, as Silone once remarked, to which all
his novels kept returning

> resembles a camp of refugees in some no man's land, out in
> the open, existing by chance. What do you expect refugees to
> do from morning to night? They spend the best part of their
> time telling each other stories. The stories are not very
> entertaining, to be sure, but they tell them anyway—mainly,
> to understand what has happened.

From his first novel *Fontamara*, still buoyed by Marxist belief,
to his play *The Story of a Humble Christian* (1968), depicting the
helplessness before the world of a pure-souled Christian who in

the fourteenth century unexpectedly becomes a Pope, everything Silone wrote was motivated by rebellion against social injustice and, as he began critically to examine the terms of his rebellion, by a need to define the condition of humanity for those who had chosen to rebel. What, in this century of the total state, could it mean to be a man? How, in a world of terror and deceit, could one retain a portion of humanity? At what cost, and with what wrenchings of the self?

Silone had once said, "I would willingly pass my life writing and rewriting the same book—that one book which every writer carries within him, the image of his own soul, and of which his published works are only more or less approximate fragments." He did keep writing and rewriting "the same book," for he was fortunate enough to be possessed by a great subject and firm enough to resist the fluctuations of literary fashion which sometimes made him popular but more often did not. His great subject was the relation of corruptible action to absolute principle; of worldly means to transcendent ends; of historical commitment to personal desire.

At the age of fifteen Silone joined the Socialist Youth League of Italy, impelled by outrage over the wretchedness of the peasants. For some fifteen years politics would be his lifeblood. When the Italian Communist Party was formed in 1921, he soon joined it. Later he served as a leader of the antifascist underground. In 1927 Silone journeyed to Moscow with the Communist leader Togliatti, where both rebelled, a little, against a Moscow proposal that they sign a denunciation of Trotsky without even having read the document they were to declare heretical. Togliatti would remain in the Stalinist camp, Silone would leave it forever. Dark years of ill health and exile followed for Silone, with inner moral and intellectual confusion. The rest of his life, until his death in 1978, he devoted to writing, though after the liberation of Italy he participated briefly in the revived Socialist movement of his country.

Silone's fictions are wry, sardonic, weary, and tinged with disillusion, even despair, yet no writer of our time has so stubbornly devoted himself to the theme of human renewal or so persistently refused the lure of nihilism. He knew and loved the Italian peasants, but knew and loved them too well for even a faint tinge of sentimentalism to mar his novels. Educated in Italy, a nation sagging under a culture of high rhetoric, he seemed immune to all vanities of language, all notions that "the word" could ever be self-sufficient. He made of small things—a casual gesture by one of his characters, a sly anecdote told with seeming casualness—tokens of redemptive possibility. His very pessimism could be bracing.

To read Silone's three major books, *Fontamara*, *Bread and Wine*, and *School for Dictators* (1938), a mordant dialogue about the nature of fascism, is to encounter the oldness of things in Europe: all those clever, tormented priests and all those hunted, doubting revolutionists linked in their helplessness. Silone's finest work, *Bread and Wine*, conveys like no other fiction of our time the cowardly surrender of bourgeois Italy to fascism and the sad crumbling of the socialist opposition. A distraught revolutionist, Pietro Spina, puts on the frock of a priest, Paolo Spada, as a disguise for his underground activity (Peter Thorn makes himself into Paul Sword); but then the priest's frock becomes more than a disguise, almost as if he were in quest of a second or renewed being, not to replace his political self but simultaneously to reinforce and oppose it. Silone accepts as a given the conflict between the need for action and the desire for contemplation, the one a striving for worldly power and the second a straining toward individual purity; but he does not posit any facile merger of the socialist and Christian projects. His central theme becomes an effort to hold these two in balance, and the improbability of this effort becomes in his books an occasion for tragedy, yet also an incitement to choice and a kind of freedom.

Let us glance at the main action of *Bread and Wine*. The sick and hunted Spina, as he wanders about the countryside, abandons his doctrinal Marxism—it does not correspond to his perceptions of social reality—but he staunchly maintains his social rebelliousness. The priest's frock he employs as a disguise becomes emblematic of a hesitant and partial transformation of being. He must still bear the responsibilities of a political man, and indeed, as soon as the opportunity arises, he resumes the tasks of the underground leader. ("He was Pietro Spina again.") Yet, with some embarrassment and even guilt, he assumes the semblance of a mundane saint, a revolutionary Christian unburdened by Christian rites or theology. One of the most touching moments in the book occurs in an early chapter when Don Benedetto, the marvelous priest who had been Spina's teacher, reads from an essay Spina had written as a boy: "But for the fact that it would be very boring to be exhibited on altars after one's death . . . I should like to be a saint. I don't want to live in accordance with circumstances, conventions and material expediency, but I want to live and struggle for what seems to me to be just and right without regard to the consequences."

Perhaps it would be more accurate to say that, in his disguise as Spada, Pietro Spina comes to be regarded as a saint by the people around him, though at no time does he invite such a misapprehension. Still, if his task, in Albert Camus' words, is to discover whether it's "possible to become a saint without believing in God," then it is as a human, fallible, even fallen saint.

Part of this stems from political realism. Spina decides, soon after arriving in the Abruzzi, that the usual kinds of political agitation are irrelevant under fascism. People have been misled by slogans too long; they distrust all the phrases of politics; and as for the peasants, they have never trusted anything said by talkers from the cities. Most people understand the truth well enough; it is courage and energy they lack, a readiness to sacrifice themselves. What is needed, Spina concludes, are not political programs but examples of uprightness, a pilgrimage of good deeds. Men must be healed. And this leads, pragmatically, to the idea that in a society as debased as fascist Italy, where no one believes the words everyone repeats, the prime need is an instance of one man speaking the truth without regard to convenience or fear.

For anyone raised in Catholic Italy, there must of course be an ultimate model. Spina comes to believe in the example of Jesus, not in his resurrection but in his agony; Jesus figures for him in entirely human terms. To live as a simple, "primitive" Christian without the church means to shoulder the greatest possible insecurity before man and God. "No word and no gesture can be more persuasive than the life and, if necessary, the death of a man who strives to be free, loyal, just, sincere, disinterested. A man who shows what a man can be."

Yet this yearning for transformed being does not deflect Spina from immediate political action—though in the judgment of his more conventional comrades it may complicate and hinder it. Silone is too shrewd, too experienced for the allurements of moral posturing, or for that charting from secular ideology to religious faith which has become a frequent theme in modern fiction. When Spina goes to Rome and there meets the scattered cadres of the underground, especially the impressive old militant,

Romeo, it is in behalf of political ends. When he talks with the handful of young fascists who naively believe their "revolution" has been betrayed by Mussolini, he deals with them as a political man. And at the book's end, as he flees to the mountains, he weaves an "ordinary felt hat . . . that could equally well be adapted to ecclesiastic or lay purposes, depending on how it was shaped or worn." He is and he is not Paolo Spada, or put another way, Paolo Spada is his doubling possibility, to be assumed, discarded, or partly adopted.

Upon his return to the Abruzzi Spina encounters a disappointment familiar enough to radicals. He comes up against the lethargy of the masses, their deep skepticism about all calls to action, their stubborn belief that somehow misery is an ordained condition. Words alone cannot shake them and only, thinks Spina, the force of one man's example might move them out of their age-old fatalism (a notion, by the way, that bears a curious resemblance to the belief of some anarchists that only feats of violence can "electrify" the masses). Yet, whatever its tactical efficacy, this view of Spina's is also a sign of his genuine if incomplete self-transformation. A Spina who is also a Spada may help break the cynicism that smothers the consciousness of the masses; a new being may hold in check the revolutionist's temptation to manipulate and dominate those he claims to be liberating (this thought is brought home forcibly through Spina's encounter with the anarchistic Uliva in Rome); but whatever else, a new being is necessary in order to survive in the foul atmosphere of fascism. Spina must edge a little into Spada while still remaining Spina.

And here, I think, we reach the intellectual or thematic strength of *Bread and Wine*: that what I've called Silone's two encompassing visions, socialism and Christianity, are brought into a tense connection, not as abstract or inert intellectual systems but as elements of vibrant experience. Spina, and behind him Silone, is obsessed with the problem, how can a decent person act in a terrible time? One answer, not the only or sufficient one, is that he must find a way to live, even if he cannot act, and perhaps with the hope that living well may finally come to be a mode of action. Spina and Spada are two, and then they are one, and then again two, like streams of consciousness joining and parting and finally crossing. The inner clash that Silone's hero undergoes is reflected in the contrast between the two women who are near him, Bianchina, flesh of this world, and Christian, spirit of another. The very title carries this duality: bread and wine as tokens of Christian mystery, bread and wine as substances the peasants need for each day's survival.

A similar tension characterizes the book's narrative. Those segments that are set in the countryside have a way of taking on a semi-allegorical cast, with the peasants speaking at times in emblematic terms, as if they were representative voices rather than individualized figures. I don't mean to suggest that these segments ever become wholly allegorical or depart fundamentally from the norms of realism; only that here we feel the extent to which Silone's imagination is drawn to the fable or exemplary tale. Once, however, Spina comes to the city, the novel settles into a hard and precise kind of realism, a straight rendering of figure and incident.

Silone was a short-breathed writer. One can no more imagine him undertaking the sort of multi-layered, thickly-populated social novel favored by European writers earlier in the century than attempting the experimental structures and dictions of literary modernism. Silone lacked the zest for sheer representation of experience which had characterized the classical nineteenth-century novelists and he showed little concern with niceties or complexities of form. Yet in his own modest (and largely unrecognized) way he was an innovator in the art of fiction, yoking together realistic matter and fablelike modes, and counting heavily on the moral suggestiveness of the anecdote.

The anecdote is the crucial unit in Silone's novels. For him it is the crux of thought and experience, the kernel of inherited wisdom embodied in anonymous voice and skeptical gesture. The anecdote is what remains undefiled in the life of the *cafoni*, the poorest peasants, even after the stupefying rhetoric of bureaucrats and lawyers has become hopelessly corrupt. The anecdote is a last defense of the downtrodden—it is the peasants' "theorizing." What intellectuals freeze into abstraction, the peasants thaw into miniature narrative. The thought behind the anecdote, while often sly and sometimes deep, is seldom developed; it is quick, intuitive, fixed on particulars, like bread and wine.

Anecdotes in Silone's novels serve a function somewhat like dramatic confrontations in conventional novels. The anecdote ties things together, not by "raising" them to generality but by holding them close to the earth. Through his affection for the anecdote, far more than in his sometimes awkward direct statement, Silone declares a stubborn, quizzical and not at all romantic attachment to the folk.

Whenever it appears, the anecdote enriches the texture and speeds the movement of the narrative, warding off that allegorical dryness which is one of Silone's recurrent weaknesses. The pessimistic humor of his main speakers becomes Silone's closest approximation to something like—well, not exactly optimism— but a style enabling resistance to pessimism. A peasant hears that many nations would be "prepared to pay to have [our leader Mussolini] in their country," and then, with a neat bit of slyness, asks, "as he disliked generalities . . . exactly how much other nations would be willing to pay to acquire our leader." At another point a group of peasants is enjoying the "lovely fairy story" about wolves and lambs lying down together so that laws will no longer be necessary, and one of them says that as far as he's concerned, he would "replace all existing laws with one single law . . . It would give every Italian the right to emigrate."

The anecdote becomes a shield against pomposity, against pretentious spirituality, against everything that is falsely pious and official. The anecdote speaks for earth and air, bread and wine.

But it must be asked, does not Silone's method make for a somewhat uneven or bumpy narrative surface? Each segment of the novel, heightened by a supply of anecdote, tends to become self-sufficient, so that we don't get in *Bread and Wine* that accumulating tension, that overarching span of narrative, which we often find, or expect, in realistic fiction. Silone has his own way. Beneath the slow, broken rhythm of his narrative there emerges another and deeper rhythm, that of a man's recurrent effort to discover what he is and why he is here. The growth of Pietro Spina's consciousness, revealed mainly through a series of illuminating encounters with other characters, forms the base line of story and idea, action and thought.

Bread and Wine is a novel deeply entangled with problems and passions of our time—saturated, so to speak, in history. When the book first came out half a century ago, it moved many readers in an especially intimate way, since they too felt themselves to be entangled with these problems and passions. Those of us to whom the book spoke so forcefully were moved not because we saw it as narrowly political but because we felt Silone was a true witness to the turmoil of our moment. When we first read the novel, we could not readily separate its thrust of idea from its artistic substance. History seemed too oppressive for such esthetic luxuries. Nor did Silone invite them. He wrote as a man completely subject to the pressures of his time, utterly indifferent to what posterity (or critics arrogating the voice of posterity) might make of his work.

It was, more or less, in this spirit that we first read *Bread and Wine*, as a work at once true to the claims of fiction and the claims of history. But the decades have passed. I find myself wondering, a half century later, how are we to read this novel once the historical moment it portrays has passed into history? And what can such a work mean to younger readers who have lived through other times, other troubles—readers, say, for whom Mussolini may be just a name and the Second World War not even a memory?

I can only speak for myself. Reading the novel again, I find myself noticing its occasional stiffness of comment, its verbal reticence, its curiously uneven pace. These are all secondary matters. I find myself still moved by memories of my first encounter with *Bread and Wine*, associated with all the terrible events of those years in the late thirties when it really did seem that Western civilization was near collapse. And I find myself moved in a new way, for now this novel of anguish and aspiration seems not just a story about an antifascist desperately searching for a path to effectiveness, but also a meditation—sad, humane, compassionate—on the terms of our life.

Bread and Wine marks out, with a steady truthfulness, the time in which we have lived: perhaps more through Silone's voice than his words. If, as we like to believe, it is true that literature binds us, across the gap of circumstance, to those who came before us, then *Bread and Wine* will speak to anyone, of whatever age, who tries sincerely to reflect upon man's fate in our century.

—*Irving Howe*

A writer frequently has the experience of seeing a stranger reading a book of his. An incident of the kind that happened to me many years ago made an impression on me that I still remember, perhaps because of a combination of circumstances that I did not realise at the time.

I was in a train on the way from Zurich to Lugano, in an empty compartment, when an elderly woman got in. She was modestly dressed, and after a brief nod she sat opposite me, next to the window. As soon as she had settled down she took a book from her travelling bag and opened it at a page marked by a narrow ribbon. As I still had some newspapers and periodicals I wanted to look at I took no more notice of her, but after a while my attention was drawn by the coloured jacket of her book, and I realized that it was the German version of a novel of mine I had written a few years previously, *Brot und Wein*. I put aside my newspapers and periodicals and started observing her with curiosity.

She was neatly and simply dressed, with no ornament whatever about her person, as is still the rural custom in that country, particularly in the Protestant cantons. In spite of her grey hair, her cheeks were pink and her features were regular and fine; her expression was intelligent, open and agreeable, and she must certainly have been beautiful when she was young. I imagined her to be a retired schoolmistress or a doctor's wife; very probably she was a strong, well-balanced woman who had not been spared her share of suffering.

On the pretext of putting away some of my papers I stood up to enable me to see how far she had got in the novel. She was reading a chapter I remembered well, for it had caused me a good deal of trouble. From that moment, though I pretended to be still looking at a newspaper, in my mind I followed her reading page by page, I might almost say line by line.

She remained apparently impassive, though once or twice she shut her eyes for a moment or two, only to resume her reading. It was a strange sensation to be faced with a stranger to whom I was secretly telling a long story. Fortunately that edition of my novel did not include the author's photograph, for if she had recognized me I should have been greatly embarrassed. In fact a strange uneasiness came over me. The page she was reading did not satisfy me at all; indeed, at that moment it struck me as actually absurd. Why had I written it? If I had foreseen that a person like this was going to read the book, I said to myself, I should certainly have cut that page, as well as others, besides giving much thought to certain expressions. Why, I said to myself, do most authors have in mind colleagues and critics who read a hundred books a year instead of strangers to whom the book may have a personal message?

Perhaps I had never before felt so immediately and so acutely the privilege and the responsibility of being a writer, though, I may say, these feelings were not new to me. I recalled the embarrassment caused me a year before by a letter written to me by an Italian worker in the name of a group of his comrades who like him were refugees in Switzerland. They had been discussing a sentence in my book and, not having been able to agree about its meaning, had decided to ask the author. It was a sentence I had written quite casually . . .

The woman got out before I did, and for the rest of the journey I went on thinking about the great worth and power of literature and the unworthiness of most writers, including myself. At any rate my determination to subject *Bread and Wine* to a critical rereading dated from that occasion.

I had written it *ex abundantia cordis* immediately after the Fascist invasion of Abyssinia and during the great Moscow trials staged by Stalin to destroy the last vestiges of opposition. It was difficult to imagine a more depressing combination of negative events. General Graziani's inhuman treatment of Ethiopian soldiers and civilians, the euphoria of many Italians at the conquest of an empire, the passivity of most of the population and the impotence of the anti-fascists were news that filled me with a deep sense of shame. On top of that were my horror and disgust at having spent the years of my youth in the service of a revolutionary ideal that was turning out to be nothing but 'red Fascism', as I then called it. As a result, my state of mind was more inclined to over-emphasis, sarcasm, melodrama than to calm narration. I must add that I was not greatly deceived by the book's exceptional and to me entirely unexpected success, for I was well aware that the success of a book can sometime owe more to its defects than to its merits. But had I the right to go back and revise it? There was no lack of examples, including illustrious ones, pointing to an affirmative answer, but at the time I was inclined to think that a book once published belonged no longer to the author but to the public.

Later, however, I was to see the question in a different light, for after the fall of Fascism it became possible for the first time for my books to be published in Italy. Was I to let slip the opportunity provided for me by a delay that in all other respects had been painful and prejudicial to me? With a clear conscience I took advantage of it to revise the books I had published in exile, *Fontamara*, *Bread and Wine* and *The Seed Beneath the Snow*.

As critics have noted, the structure, the moral essence, the vicissitudes of the characters have remained unchanged; but these books have been stripped of secondary or non-essential material and the basic theme has been deepened. No vanity can prevent me from admitting that my experience confirms the existence of a similarity between writing and the other arts in the sense that the former too is learnt and improved by practice.

In this connection I have also had occasion to confess that, if it depended on me, I should gladly spend my life writing and rewriting the same book: the single book that every writer has within him that is the image of his soul and of which his published works are only more or less rough fragments.

Should I now mention the lessons that it seems to me I have learnt? The first is that a writer with a strong sense of social responsibility is more exposed than anyone else to the temptation of over-emphasis, of the theatrical and the romantic, and of a purely external description of things and facts, while in every work of literature the only thing that matters is obviously the development of the interior life of the characters. Even the landscape and other things by which they are surrounded are worthy of mention only to the extent that they are involved in the life of the spirit. And, since pathos cannot be eliminated from human life, I feel that a touch of irony is required to make it acceptable.

Another thing that has grown in me in the course of years is an aversion to all forms of propaganda. Of all the talk about the so-called commitment of artists, what remains? The only commitment that deserves respect is that of a personal vocation. Besides, everyone knows that the artist cannot sacrifice art to efficacy without also sacrificing efficacy. As for style, it seems to me that the supreme wisdom in telling a story is to try to be simple.

Rome, 1962   Ignazio Silone

CHAPTER 1

Don Benedetto, sitting on the low garden wall in the shadow of a cypress, was reading his breviary. His black priest's habit absorbed and prolonged the shadow of the tree. Behind him his sister sat at her loom, which she had placed between a box hedge and a rosemary bed, and the shuttle bobbed backwards and forwards through the warp of red and black wool, from left to right and from right to left, to the accompaniment of the rhythm of the treadle that lifted the warp cords and of the lamb that lifted the warp.

She interrupted her work to look with ill-concealed anxiety at a vehicle that stopped at the bottom of the hill. But it was only an ox-drawn cart, and she went back to her work, disappointed.

'They won't be long now, you'll see,' she said to her brother.

He shrugged his shoulders, simulating indifference.

On the right were the railway and the Valerian Way that led between fields of hay, wheat, potatoes, beet, beans and maize to Avezzano, then rose to Colli di Monte Bove, before coming down to Tivoli and ending up, like all rivers that flow down to the sea, by leading to Rome. On the left was the provincial road, with vineyards and fields of peas and onions on either side, climbing straight up into the mountains, making for the heart of the Abruzzi, the region of beech trees and holm oaks and the last wild bears, and leading to Pescasseroli, Opi and Castel di Sangro.

The priest's sister kept the shuttle bobbing backwards and forwards without losing sight of the road down below in the valley. But nothing was to be seen except everyday persons and things, and there was no sign of what she was waiting for.

A young peasant woman with a baby in her arms, riding a small donkey, came down the provincial road, which was as stony and winding as the bed of a dried up stream. In a small field behind the cemetery a bare-headed old peasant was tracing

1

brown lines with a small wooden plough drawn by two donkeys. Life seen from the priest's garden was like an ancient, monotonous pantomime.

That day was Don Benedetto's seventy-fifth birthday. It was a warm afternoon at the end of April, the first really warm day after a severe winter. Sitting on his low garden wall, he too raised his eyes from his breviary every so often and looked down at the valley, awaiting the arrival of some of his former pupils. They would be coming separately, from the right and from the left, from the direction of the town and from that of the mountain villages, from where life had scattered them at the end of their student days. But would they be coming?

At that time of day the few houses of the village of Rocca below Don Benedetto's garden seemed uninhabited. In the midst of the huddle of poor houses was a narrow square with grass growing between the cobbles and at the other end of it was the low porch of an old church with a big rose window over it. The houses, the streets, the square itself, looked as if they had been abandoned. A beggar in rags crossed the square and went off without stopping. A little girl appeared in a doorway and stood there, looking. Then she hid behind a hedge and stayed there, peeping out from behind the bushes.

'Perhaps I should have bought some beer,' the priest's sister said. 'And you might have shaved, as it's your birthday.'

'My birthday? It's a fine time for birthdays, to be sure. Tamarind will be good enough for the young men,' Don Benedetto said. 'That is, if they turn up.'

Tamarind came in bottles from town, while Matalena Ricotta, with strawberries, mushrooms and eggs, came from the mountains.

Don Benedetto put his book down beside him on the wall and began looking at the work on the loom. What a disappointment it would be to Marta, his sister, if the young men did not turn up. She had sent out the invitations without telling him, but had revealed the secret to make sure he stayed at home the whole afternoon. But supposing no-one turned up? To disguise their anxiety the two tried not to look at each other.

'Do you know that Sciancalla has gone back to barter?' Marta said. 'He won't take anything for his charcoal but onions and beans nowadays.'

'For several days I've been having heartburn again after every meal,' Don Benedetto said. 'Bicarbonate of soda has trebled in price.'

Bicarbonate of soda came from town, like insecticides and safety razor blades.

'Safety?' his sister said. 'If you shave with one of those things you cut yourself worse than with an old-fashioned cut-throat.'

'Safety is always relative,' said Don Benedetto. 'The Department of Public Safety would be well advised to call itself the Department of Public Danger, after all. When you come to think of it, my former pupils will prefer wine, they're not boys any longer.'

The former pupils whom Don Benedetto was expecting had in fact finished their schooling soon after the Great War, so by now they must be thirty or more. Marta rose from her loom and went to the kitchen to fetch the refreshments she had prepared for the young men and put them on the granite table in the middle of the garden, between the tomatoes and the sage. Her action was perhaps a propitiatory rite, to get the young men to hurry.

'At any rate Nunzio will come,' she said. 'He's bound to.'

'He's a doctor,' said Don Benedetto. 'He's very busy.'

Marta went back to her loom and threw the shuttle full of black wool between the threads of the warp.

'Do you know they've changed the commissioner at the town hall?' she said. 'Another stranger, of course. It seems that there are also going to be other changes because of this new war in Africa.'

'War time is career time,' Don Benedetto said.

Transfers and changes always came from town; commissioners, inspectors, controllers, bishops, prison governors, corporation speakers, preachers for the spiritual exercises, were sent from town with up-to-date 'directives'. Newspapers, popular songs – 'Tripoli bel suol d'amore', 'Valencia', 'Giovinezza', 'Faccetta nera', gramophones, the radio, novels, bromide paper, picture postcards, also came from the town. From

3

the mountains there came the poor Capuchin friar Brother Gioacchino with his bag for alms and Sciatàp for the Tuesday market; and Magascià arrived with salt and tobacco every Saturday, and sometimes Cassarola the wise woman appeared with her herbs and badgers' hair and snakes' skins against the evil eye; and at the end of November the pipers arrived for the Advent novena – 'Ye suffering and afflicted, open your hearts to hope, for the Saviour is about to be born'.

'Have you heard that Clarice has become engaged to a mechanic at the sugar refinery?' Marta said. 'Marrying in wartime is like sowing among thorns.'

The warp cords of the loom got tangled and Marta had to get up to free them.

'There are lucky women who are born with a talent for becoming war widows,' Don Benedetto said. 'Poets are made, but war widows and bishops are born. Mind you, I'm not saying that with reference to Clarice, who seems to be a rather innocent creature.'

'Clarice has a good dowry, good land, hemp land,' Marta said.

'Does the mechanic want to leave the refinery and grow hemp?'

'On the contrary,' Marta explained, 'it's Clarice who wants to sell the land. Hemp is no good any more.'

There used to be a demand for it, but no longer; it was considered expensive, primitive, and crude.

'Cloth made of home-woven wool is no good any more either,' Don Benedetto said. 'Nor are we.'

'Neither are shoes made to measure,' said Marta, 'nor solid wooden furniture. Artisans' workshops are closing down one after the other.'

'And we're not wanted any more either,' Don Benedetto repeated.

Factory products were smarter and cheaper. Those who could shut up shop and went to town, and the old were left alone to wait for death.

Marta had to get up to turn the beam of the warp at the bottom of the loom. That had been exactly what Monsignore had said. 'Your brother's primitive crudity, my dear lady, cannot poss-

4

ibly be tolerated in a school to which the richest, that is to say, the best families in the diocese send their sons,' he had said. There was no denying that Monsignore was neither primitive nor crude and, knowing Don Benedetto to be unambitious and resigned so far as his career was concerned, he had dismissed him on the pretext of poor health.

Since then Don Benedetto had lived in seclusion with his sister in his little house above Rocca dei Marsi, with his old books and his garden. As he was by nature placid and taciturn, there had been little to prevent his rapidly acquiring a local reputation as a misanthropic and cantankerous eccentric and perhaps also something of a simpleton. But the few in whom he sometimes confided knew that his country shyness concealed a liberty of spirit and a liveliness of mind that in his station in life were positively foolhardy. The result was that it was rather compromising to allow it to be known that one was a friend of his. Imagine, then, what his relatives, his brothers, his cousins and sisters-in-law, thought of him. Had all those sacrifices to keep him at the seminary been worth while if he was going to end up like this? They actually hated him for not having the prestige with the authorities that they expected of him and for having been reduced to living like a hermit instead of being able to use influence on their behalf at a time when honest work was of no use whatever in the absence of recommendations and backing in high places. As a consequence of this the last meeting with his relatives in the office of the notary at Fossa had ended with a very painful scene.

'You wretch,' an old aunt called him at one point. 'Don't you realize why we made such sacrifices for the sake of having a priest in the family?'

'Undoubtedly your purpose was to attract the Lord's good will towards you,' Don Benedetto replied.

He should never have said it. That naïve reply sounded deliberately provocative to these worthy Christians, and only the notary's intervention saved him from their legitimate anger. After that he did not see them again. Being deprived of the society of everyone except his aged sister, his affections had settled on some former pupils whose fortunes in the complicated and contradictory vicissitudes of their careers he tried to follow. He had no-one else in the world. Marta had invited some of them, those who lived nearest and those to whom he was most attached, to come to their old schoolmaster's hermitage at Rocca on the occasion of his seventy-fifth birthday. She had asked them to bring others whose addresses she did not know, and she was very worried that the refreshments she had prepared might not be sufficient and that the dozen glasses of different shapes and sizes lined up on the granite table might not be enough. But the opposite possibility, that no-one might come, alarmed her even more. She went on with her weaving, and between one shuttle and the next kept looking at the road in the valley and the paths along which the guests would have to come.

'At any rate Nunzio is bound to come,' she said.

'If those boys are late, it's because the trains and post-buses don't arrive on time,' Don Benedetto said. 'As foreigners don't come to our part of the world, what would be the point of punctuality?'

From Rocca dei Marsi the land sloped gently down to the huge basin of the former lake of Fucino, now reclaimed and the estate of a prince. It was a huge green chessboard of young wheat, cut by canals and long rows of poplars, surrounded by a big circle of gently sloping hills, on nearly every one of which there was a small village, an assortment of houses that looked like a Christmas crib, or a smoke-blackened ancient township with a cluster of towers or surrounded by a high wall or with houses dug into the slope like caves. They were places with ancient names and ancient stories, but many had been destroyed in the last earthquake and badly rebuilt. Behind the ring of hills the mountains rose steeply, furrowed by flood water and torrents, and at that time of year still covered with snow.

Marta stopped weaving and went back into the house.

'Where are you going?' Don Benedetto asked.

'I'll be back in a moment,' she said.

She went up to the first floor and sat by the window overlooking the valley. The confused noises that floated up towards Rocca at sunset only increased the feeling of the village's solitude and remoteness. Some women in black shawls,

6

dirty and old before their time, appeared in the dark doorways of their houses. Others, with handkerchiefs tied under their chins and brass pots on their heads, returned slowly from the fountain. A woman dressed in black crossed the little square and went into the church, holding by the hand, and almost dragging, a little girl in a yellow dress. An old cafone passed by, sitting on a donkey and kicking it. But soon the narrow roads and alleys emptied again and Rocca resumed the appearance of a village of the dead.

'They're coming,' Marta called out from the window. 'Nunzio's coming.'

Don Benedetto promptly rose to his feet, attracted not only by the announcement of his guests' arrival but also by a hubbub coming from the road. It was not easy to see what it was about. All that was visible at first was a long cloud of dust spreading from the road into the neighbouring vineyards and vegetable plots. Then a flock of sheep emerged from the cloud, a little river of yellow waves advancing slowly along the road, and behind it a donkey loaded with the usual equipment of a shepherd; the straw canopy, the saucepan bag, the milk pails and cheese moulds. Behind the donkey came the shepherd himself, surrounded by some big white dogs, and behind him there was a small open car with two young men in it who were shouting themselves hoarse, wanting the shepherd and his flock to move over to the left and make room for them to pass, but with no apparent effect. The shepherd either ignored them completely or gesticulated vigorously, perhaps to indicate that he was deaf and dumb and could not hear them, but at all events that they should leave him in peace. But since even a deaf-mute ought to be able to understand that a car cannot dally for ever behind a flock of sheep, the young men yelled at him more vigorously than ever, and they might easily have passed from words to deeds but for the shepherd's escort of three big, ferocious-looking dogs wearing spiked collars. One of the young men in the car, who was in the uniform of an officer of militia, kept standing up at the driving wheel and threatening the deaf-mute in words and gestures, calling on him to make the flock move over to the right and leave room for the car to pass.

7

The shepherd, surrounded by his dogs, remained unmoved, making equally expressive gestures to indicate his inability to understand what the fuss was about. This had been going on for some time when Don Benedetto advanced to meet the flock, made his way through the cloud of dust, and cordially greeted both the shepherd and the two former pupils of his who were in the car.

'Welcome, welcome,' he called out. Then he turned to the shepherd and said politely, 'These are two friends of mine who are coming to see me.'

The shepherd suddenly regained the power of speech and shouted angrily at the young men in the car, 'Why didn't you say you were coming to see Don Benedetto?'

He gave an order to the dogs, and in a flash the flock had reformed itself lengthwise and moved over to the right, leaving plenty of room for the car to pass. But the two young men had not yet recovered from their amazement at the behaviour of the pretended deaf mute.

'What's the rascal's name?' Concettino insisted, turning to Don Benedetto.

'In spite of his black shirt this young man isn't a coal-heaver, but just Concettino Ragù, remember?' Don Benedetto explained to his sister. 'And of course you know Nunzio Sacca, he's a fully fledged doctor now. They're good lads, both of them.'

To Concettino he said with a laugh, 'I've reached the age of seventy-five and have never yet acted as an informer, and it's too late to start now.' He took his two former pupils by the arm and led them towards his garden.

But the shepherd, no doubt believing himself to be entirely in the right, went on standing in the middle of the road shouting, 'Why didn't you say you were coming to see Don Benedetto?'

'Sit down and rest,' said Marta, to divert the young men's attention from the shepherd. 'The others won't be long now.'

But Concettino could not swallow the insulting behaviour of the phoney deaf-mute. His amazement actually prevented him from being angry.

'What's his name?' he insisted.

'Forgive him,' Marta said with an imploring smile. 'He's not a bad man. He's a poor fellow with an enormous family. Actually he's one of the most decent shepherds in the neighbourhood.'

'My dear fellow,' Don Benedetto, who probably would have preferred to avoid giving this explanation, said, 'there's no need for me, who take no interest in politics, to tell you what your uniform means to the poor. The day on which the tongues of those who pretend dumbness are loosened will be a terrible one, and I hope you will be spared it.'

Concettino looked at Nunzio as if to say: You see, here we are, was it really worth while coming? Nunzio tried to change the subject.

CHAPTER 2

'We came to see you in your retreat,' said Nunzio, 'to show you that you are not alone, that your former pupils . . .'

'*Deus mihi haec otia fecit*,' Don Benedetto replied with a smile, his voice betraying an obvious willingness to respect the conventions. 'Now sit down and rest,' he went on. 'Not there on the ground, that is not grass but thyme; and this is basil, *Ocymum suave*, and further along that is parsley, *Apicum petroselinum*, as you must know, and that at the side is mint. Ancient and honest things. Sit here.'

The three men, slightly embarrassed, sat on a wooden bench under a graceful, silvery olive tree. The old man sat between his former pupils, and Marta asked for permission to return to her loom.

'I still have a few minutes' more work,' she said. 'By the time I've finished perhaps there'll be some more arrivals.'

For a short while the only sound in the quiet garden was the alternating rhythm of Marta's loom, the rhythm of the treadle, the shuttle and the comb. The air was bathed in delicate green light, between the trees it was brightened by beams of gilded dust, and the gentle odours of the aromatic herbs seemed to emanate from that light.

'How peaceful it is here,' said Nunzio.

'Tell me some news,' the old priest said. 'I never see anyone here. What is Luigi Candeloro doing? I haven't heard of him for a long time.'

'He died of typhus in Libya two years ago,' Nunzio said. 'Didn't you know? After he qualified as an engineer he couldn't find a job, and he ended by joining the Corps of Civil Engineers and going to Libya; for the sake of earning a living he would have been willing to go anywhere, even to hell itself, so he told me. He died a fortnight before sailing for home to marry a cousin of mine.'

The old man shook his head sadly. After a short silence he asked again, 'What has happened to Battista Lo Patto? Does he still paint?'

'He plays scopone,'[1] Concettino replied. 'At scientific scopone he's unbeatable.'

'Doesn't he ever vary his programme?' the old man asked.

'Yes, on Sundays.'

'What does he do on Sundays? Does he work?'

'On Sundays he plays billiards.'

'And Antonio Speranza? How is his shop doing?'

'Well,' Nunzio said. 'For ten years he struggled with promissory notes falling due and fines for rotten sardines, rancid olive oil, mouldy pasta and inaccurate scales. In the end he too wanted to make his fortune, so he got into debt on a huge scale and promptly went bankrupt. So now he can't go out in the evening because of the creditors that are after him to beat him up. But he's even more afraid of the carabinieri.'

'And poor Carlo Caione? Is he still ill?'

'He died of tuberculosis and left a wife and two young children,' Nunzio said.

'Has his wife any money at least?'

'No, but she's beautiful,' Concettino said.

The old man fell silent, weary and disheartened. Marta's loom stopped too. The first twilight shadows were gathering on the Fucino. Don Benedetto said almost in an undertone, 'Excuse these questions. It's not inquisitiveness, I assure you. I'm very lonely here, and I often think about you. I never see anyone here.' Then he added, 'Where is Di Pretoro? Still with the railway?'

'He was sacked some time ago,' Concettino said. 'He was the best of us at Latin, that I don't deny, but in my opinion he was always muddle-headed, half a socialist. To be a good socialist, in my opinion, you have to be a millionaire. At all events, he had a casual affair with a poor little seamstress in his village who owned nothing in the world except her sewing machine. I don't blame him in the least for that. Let him who is without sin, as the

[1] A card game.

11

saying is. But the little woman realized the kind of man he was, and very sensibly immediately presented him with a son, and like a fool he married her. She has regularly presented him with a child every year since. So after four years of marriage he has five children, including the one that arrived in advance. Meanwhile he was dismissed from the railway because of his anti-national ideas – another luxury that the idiot permitted himself. Now, anyone who is fired by the railway can't get a job in any other public administration, that's obvious. But as private firms have to recruit staff from public employment exchanges, who are obliged by law to reject political suspects, there could be little doubt about what would happen to him. On the other hand, pride forbids him to do manual work. After all, you don't study for ten years to finish up as a carpenter. So he's permanently unemployed. As for his wife, she's always either pregnant or feeding the latest arrival, so she can't do any sewing. So very often there's nothing for them to eat. Then he can think of nothing better to do than to go to the tavern and drink on credit, and when he's drunk he goes home and beats his wife and children until the neighbours intervene and restore peace. And you know what people say? They say, that's how the pupils of the priest's school end up.'

Don Benedetto looked in turn at each of his young guests, obviously taken aback at the relative indifference with which they related such painful facts.

'Couldn't you help him?' he asked them.

'I saved him from banishment, but perhaps that was a mistake,' said Concettino. 'At Ponza, or wherever it might be, he would at least have been paid an allowance, and meanwhile his wife would have had a rest.'

Don Benedetto struggled to his feet. There was a great weariness in his pale, lean face. He paced up and down in the garden once or twice and then went silently into the house.

Meanwhile Marta had finished her weaving, but she remained bent over her loom as if her back ached. After a few moments she pointed to the work she had done, which was still round the beam, and said to the two young men, 'This rug is my birthday present to Don Benedetto.'

She always referred to him as Don Benedetto, with detachment and respect.

'My dear lady,' Nunzio said, 'you make a present to your brother every day. You made him the gift of your life.'

Marta blushed to her temples and shook her head vigorously.

'No,' she said. 'On the contrary, what should I do without him?'

She was taller and slimmer and rather more bent than her brother, and she actually looked older, though in fact she was ten years younger. Her brow, eyes and mouth still bore the traces of a faded beauty. She rose from her loom and sat on the bench between the two visitors.

'Don't think that we're unhappy because we're lonely,' she said quietly to avoid being overheard by her brother. 'But what makes life bitter is the hostility, the suspicion that surrounds us nowadays.'

'You know very well that that is Don Benedetto's own fault, unfortunately,' said Concettino. 'Do you think there's any hope of a change of heart?'

'Frankly I have no idea,' Marta said. 'Don Benedetto is not a man who confides his sorrows. The little I know I hear from third parties. But what harm have we done to anyone to deserve these tribulations?'

'The past is the past,' Nunzio said. Then, turning to Concettino, he added, 'Can nothing be done?'

'It depends on him,' Concettino said. 'On his good will.'

'Talk to him,' Marta said imploringly. .

Don Benedetto reappeared on the threshold carrying a bundle of yellowed papers.

'Did you receive my suggestion for the blessing of the flag?' Concettino asked him. 'It would be a suitable occasion for remedying past misunderstandings.'

'Yes,' Don Benedetto replied. 'I received it.'

'Do you agree to bless the flag?'

'Of course not.'

'Why? Why insist on your own ruin? Why not take the opportunity to rehabilitate yourself?'

'Rehabilitate myself?' Don Benedetto said in surprise. 'Why

do you address me as if I were a senile delinquent?'

Concettino muttered something inaudible.

'You see,' Don Benedetto said to him, 'I'm a poor old man, full of fears and failings. But also I'm an old-fashioned Christian and, believe me, I cannot act against my conscience.'

'So to you blessing the national flag, the flag of the party in power, is a sin against your conscience?'

'Yes, one of the gravest. It's idolatry.'

'But others . . .' Concettino exclaimed.

'I know what you're going to say,' Don Benedetto said. 'But idolatry is a sin against the spirit, never mind who practises it.'

'Excuse me,' Marta exclaimed imploringly, with her eyes full of tears. 'I don't understand you. Is this friendly behaviour? Is this the way to celebrate a birthday?'

The old lady's bright eyes, which were moist with tears, and her heart-broken voice affected everyone.

'Signorina Marta is right,' said Nunzio, who was the most embarrassed. 'We came here, not to argue, but to demonstrate our affection for our old schoolmaster.'

'Whatever may have been said was of course dictated solely by friendly feelings,' Concettino said apologetically.

'I do not doubt it,' Don Benedetto said with a smile, tapping his shoulder. 'Why should we argue? I often think of you, you know. It's no effort, I have no-one else to think about.'

'What are those old papers?' said Nunzio, thinking he had found a peg on which happy memories could be hung.

Don Benedetto was still holding the bundle of yellowed papers he had brought from his study a short while before, and his hands were trembling slightly.

'They actually concern you,' he said. 'This morning I found the old photograph that was taken when we all said goodbye to one another fifteen years ago, do you remember? I also found the last essays you wrote for me. The subject was "Say sincerely what you want to be and what meaning you want to give to your life"; and I re-read your essays, Caione's and Di Pretoro's and Candeloro's and Lo Patto's and the others' whose sad fortunes you have told me about. Well, I confess in embarrassment and humility that I am beginning to feel completely bewildered. I am

14

even beginning to doubt that it's worth while seeking an explanation. As a nineteenth-century Frenchman, who, like you, was educated by priests, said, perhaps the truth is sad.'

Don Benedetto had dropped his voice, and he spoke gravely and also hesitantly, like someone who is listening in the first place to himself, as if there were a censor inside him, or as if he were a short-sighted man moving about among unknown objects and were fearful of hurting, not himself, but them. He started talking about some of the yellowed sheets of paper he held in his hands.

'In considering such compositions after so many years, all sorts of allowances must of course be made,' he said. 'They are full of literary frills in the manner of Carducci, Pascoli, D'Annunzio. Besides that, there are the naïvetés peculiar to pupils of a school run by priests, and there are the illusions of the age. There are echoes of the tumultuous armistice that had recently been concluded. But, underneath all that, underneath the frills and flourishes and plagiarisms, in several of you there seemed to me to be something vital and personal that coincided with the observations that I had been able to make of each one of you during the years of lower and upper school; and that something was by no means commonplace. Now, what happened to the something later, when you went out into the world? I am referring to the news you gave me just now about some of your schoolfellows and, without wishing to offend you, I am also referring to both of you. You must be between thirty-two and thirty-five if my arithmetic is not at fault, and you already look like cynical and bored old men. Seriously, that makes me wonder what is the point of teaching. You realize that to me that is no idle question. When a poor man who has lived with the idea of making decent use of his life reaches an age such as I have reached today, he cannot avoid asking himself what has been the result of his efforts, what the fruits of his teaching have been.'

'School is not life, my dear Don Benedetto,' Concettino said. 'At school you dream, in life you have to adapt yourself. That is the reality. You never become what you would like to become.'

'What?' Nunzio said ironically to his friend. 'Is that how an activist talks? A Nietzsche fan?'

'Never mind literature, we were talking about serious things,' Concettino said.

Marta was on tenterhooks. She suddenly rose and went towards the table on which there were a number of bottles and a dozen glasses.

'Do you think any others will still be coming?' she said. The poor woman was trembling as if she had a fever.

'They certainly intended to come, but they must have been prevented,' Concettino said evasively.

Marta made as if to take the superfluous glasses back into the kitchen.

'Leave one for Don Piccirilli,' Don Benedetto said.

'We didn't invite him,' said his sister. 'You know very well I left him out on purpose.'

'For that very reason he will not fail to appear,' Don Benedetto said. Then, turning to the two young men, he went on, 'You remember Piccirilli? He was the only boy in your class who wanted to go into the Church. His family were small landowners who couldn't afford to let him go on with his studies, so he had himself accepted without fee by the Salesians, studied theology, and took orders. But no sooner was he ordained than he left the Salesians and went back to his family. That certainly wasn't very handsome behaviour towards his benefactors. Now he has a parish not far from here, but he's not satisfied, he would like to be a teacher at the seminary and a canon. To ingratiate himself with the bishop he acts as his secret informer. "Secret" is just a manner of speaking, because we all know it. He never fails to turn up wherever he thinks something might be said that should be denounced to the diocesan curia. So you can imagine that he does me the honour of frequent cordial visits.'

Meanwhile it was getting dark in the garden, and Marta had difficulty in filling the glasses. Also a cool breeze was coming from the mountains, and Don Benedetto had a fit of coughing.

'We had better go indoors,' Marta said.

The two young men helped her to take the bottles and glasses inside. On the ground floor one big room served as kitchen, workroom and livingroom, as with the peasants. Marta lit a big

16

lamp with a yellow shade and some candles, which she put in the corners of the room. A pleasing odour of apples, quince and walnuts hung in the air.

'It's delightful here,' said Nunzio, looking all round. 'Nothing has changed.'

A yarn windle hung on a nail on the door; a distaff was propped against the doorpost; majolica crockery with a floral design was on the shelves of the sideboard, copper pots and pans hung on the fireplace wall, and red rows of peppers, brown rows of sorb apples and bunches of garlic and onions hung from the huge hood of the fireplace. In what was probably Marta's working corner there was a small recess with a little Madonna made of coloured plaster surrounded by paper lilies.

'Sit down and drink,' Marta said.

There was a knock at the door, and in came Don Piccirilli. Don Benedetto received him standing with his back to the fireplace. The newcomer went towards him and offered him his congratulations. Don Benedetto returned the embrace and invited him to join the others.

'Sit down and drink,' he said. 'There's a glass ready for you.'

Don Piccirilli was plump and well nourished, and he had an expansive and jovial air. He explained that he was late because he had had to finish a little article for the diocesan journal.

'It's called "The scourge of our time",' he explained. 'I don't want to boast, but I think it has come out rather well.'

'I congratulate you,' Don Benedetto said. 'What is it about? The war or unemployment?'

'Those are political issues,' Don Piccirilli replied drily. 'The diocesan journal deals only with religious questions. From the purely spiritual point of view the scourge of our time, in my opinion, is immodesty in dress. Are you not of that opinion?'

'The scourge of our time,' Don Benedetto calmly replied, looking him in the eye, 'is – do I have to tell you? – insincerity between man and man, the pestilential Judas Iscariot spirit that poisons relations between man and man. Forgive me if in speaking like this I am failing in the duties of hospitality.'

Don Piccirilli made a grimace that was intended to be a smile. 'In my parish in recent years, thanks be to God, enormous

17

spiritual progress has been made,' he said. 'Enormous,' he repeated with emphasis. 'The number of confessions has increased by forty per cent and that of communions by thirty per cent. I don't want to boast, but I don't know of any parish that can equal that.'

'But why do you talk of spiritual progress in terms of figures and percentages like a baker?' Don Benedetto said with irony and contempt.

Concettino made a gesture of despair, as if to say, Here we go again; and Nunzio had a violent and very unnatural fit of coughing. But the biggest sufferer in this situation was poor Marta. Her hopes of a reconciliation between her brother and the authorities were collapsing before her eyes, and she could hardly restrain her tears. Hoping to reintroduce at any rate a little conventional cordiality into the occasion, she took from her brother's hand the old photograph in which he was surrounded by his pupils and put it over the fireplace where it was well in the light.

'Do you recognize each other in the photograph?' she asked, trying to speak in as natural a voice as possible. 'I bet it won't be easy.'

The visitors immediately gathered round, each trying first to pick out himself and then expressing surprise at not recognizing one or other former schoolfellow. Don Benedetto stood out in the midst of his pupils like a hen surrounded by her chicks. To judge by appearances, the brood had been pretty heterogeneous. The only thing they all had in common seemed to be the way their hair was cut. The smallest boys squatted cross-legged in the front row and the others were arranged in three rows behind them. Concettino was among the small boys in the front row. His head was shaved, like the others, and he had a small, dark, grey face, with a cat-like expression. After all these years only his eyes were still the same; his quiff and his goatee beard now made him look like a musketeer in a provincial theatre – something that no-one would have expected fifteen years before. But Nunzio Sacca had changed little, apart from the fact that loss of hair over his temples made his forehead look bigger. He was standing behind Don Benedetto in the photo-

18

graph, and he was recognizable by the long thin neck between his rather narrow shoulders, his deep-set eyes and the shy and absent-minded manner that he had preserved.

'Who were your favourite pupils?' Concettino suddenly asked Don Benedetto.

'Those who had most need of me, of course,' Don Benedetto replied without hesitation.

'Names, names, names,' his three ex-pupils demanded in chorus, their curiosity roused.

Don Benedetto looked perplexed. Then he said, 'Where is Pietro Spina now? What has happened to him?'

In the photograph Pietro Spina was standing next to Don Benedetto, who had one hand on the boy's shoulder. Spina had a lean, ashen, sullen look on his face and his tie was askew. After a time, as no-one answered, Don Benedetto repeated his question. 'Does none of you have news of Pietro Spina? Where is he living now?'

The three young men looked at each in embarrassment. Perhaps at the bottom of her heart Marta had still been nursing some illusions, but now she sat down on a stool with the air of someone who has finally abandoned hope. Nunzio went towards her and gave her a smile of brotherly sympathy, while Don Benedetto seemed to have noticed nothing. He turned to Concettino and said, 'If I remember correctly, Pietro Spina was your best friend at school,' he said. 'You admired him so much, you might almost have been in love with him. Where is he now? What news do you have of him? What is he doing?'

'How should I know? Am I my brother's keeper?' Concettino answered, avoiding Don Benedetto's eyes.

At this reply the old man, who was standing by the fireplace, went so pale that he seemed about to faint. Slowly he walked towards Concettino, put one hand on his shoulder and, looking him in the eyes, said in a low voice, almost with tears in his eyes, 'My poor fellow, is this what you have come to? You don't know what a terrible thing you have just said.'

In the painful silence that followed Don Benedetto left the young officer and went and sat in the farthest corner of the room in an armchair under the recesss with the image of the Madonna surrounded by coloured paper decorations.

'Yes, it's true,' he said, 'Pietro Spina was in a way my favourite pupil. You remember him? He was not satisfied with what he found in the textbooks, he was insatiable, restless, and often indisciplined. He worried me, I feared for his future. Was I wrong, perhaps? I don't know if you remember, but the severest punishments he had during his school years were nearly always the result of his protesting at what he considered to be undeserved punishments imposed on one or other of his fellows. That was one side of his character. He was devoted, perhaps too devoted, to his friends. If his superiors made a mistake, he protested. No consideration of expediency could ever make him hold his peace. Isn't that right, Concettino? Wasn't he like that?'

Don Benedetto sought among the yellow papers for the last essay written at school by Pietro Spina.

'Listen,' he said, 'this is Spina: "But for the fact that it would be very boring to be exhibited on altars after one's death, to be prayed to and worshipped by a lot of unknown people, mostly ugly old women, I should like to be a saint. I don't want to live in accordance with circumstances, conventions and material expediency, but I want to live and struggle for what seems to me to be just and right without regard to the consequences." Fifteen years ago, when I read that confession,' Don Benedetto went on, 'though I did not doubt the boy's sincerity, I did not know to what extent he might have been carried away by rhetoric. At the time he was devouring the lives of the saints. He had been an orphan for several years, and family misfortunes had reinforced his tendency to meditation.'

Don Piccirilli had been impatiently waiting for the old man to pause, so that he could interrupt.

'In 1920 Spina wanted to be a saint,' he said. 'Very well. But in 1921 he joined the Young Socialists, who were atheists and materialists.'

'I am not interested in politics,' Don Benedetto said drily.

'You are not interested in atheism, the struggle against God?' the young priest asked curiously.

Don Benedetto produced a slight ironic smile.

'My dear Piccirilli,' he said slowly, almost articulating each syllable separately, 'he who does not live according to expediency or convention or convenience or for material things, he who lives for justice and truth, without caring for the consequences, is not an atheist, but he is in the Lord and the Lord in is him. You can teach me many things, Piccirilli, how to get on in the world, for instance, but I was your master in the use of language, your master in the science of words, and please note that I am not afraid of them.'

He paused, and then added prayerfully, and in a voice that was serene again, 'Can't one of you give me news of Pietro Spina? Where is he now?'

Nunzio eventually decided to tell what he knew.

'He was arrested at the beginning of 1927,' he said, 'and we heard that he was deported to an island, the island of Lipari. A year later he escaped and took refuge in France.'

'That I knew,' said Don Benedetto. 'His grandmother, Donna Maria Vincenza, told me.'

'After about a year he was expelled from France and went to Switzerland,' Nunzio went on. 'There the same thing seems to have happened, and he went to Luxembourg. After some time he was expelled from Luxembourg too, and went to Belgium. How he manages to live I have no idea, but he's probably hungry. I have also heard from an uncle of his that he suffers from lung trouble.'

'What a wretched fate,' Marta said. 'How could he choose it deliberately? Do you think he's mad?'

'He's a puzzle to me, too,' Nunzio said. 'It's a pity, because he really was the best of us all.'

'Can't his relatives help him?' Marta asked again. 'They're rich, after all. Who knows how much his grandmother, Donna Maria Vincenza, must suffer on his account.'

Don Benedetto was staring at the ground.

'Don't imagine it's anything new,' he said. 'On the contrary, it's a boring old story that is repeated over and over again. Vultures have holes, and birds of the air have nests; but the Son of Man has not where to lay his head.'

Marta was trembling, and she looked imploringly at her brother. The three young men rose to their feet.

21

'It's late,' they said. 'We must go.'

The farewells were brief, almost laconic. Marta tried in vain to take Concettino aside.

'It's late,' he said to excuse himself.

Don Benedetto and his sister accompanied their guests to the fork in the road. Don Piccirilli took the track to the left towards the mountains, and Concettino and Nunzio went off in their car along the Valerian Way.

The old man and his sister watched them disappear in silence.

As they left Rocca Concettino muttered to Nunzio without looking at him, 'Pietro's back in Italy. He returned surreptitiously from Belgium. The police have warned us, they're on his trail already. He may have been arrested already. But what can I do if he's mad?'

'Can't you help him? He's one of us, after all.'

'If he's mad, what can I do? He had the luck to be abroad, and he could have stayed there.'

'Can't you help him?'

'How? That's the difficulty. I've got to watch my own step. You're wrong if you think my position is a hundred per cent secure.'

CHAPTER 3

One morning at dawn Dr Nunzio Sacca was called to the bedside
of a sick man. A young man from Acquafredda called for him
with a horse and trap. The doctor was still full of sleep when he
appeared at the door of his house, carrying the bag with his
first-aid kit. After looking at the young man he said, 'We
know each other, I think.'

'I am Cardile Mulazzi of the Mulazzi family of Acquafredda,'
the young man said. 'Yes, we know each other. Forgive me for
coming so early, I'll explain. My grandfather used to have
Monsignore's old mill and land, it was good land, expensive
land. For three years my father rented a vineyard belonging to
your family. Do you remember? Then came misfortunes,
quarrels, illnesses. Two brothers are in Brazil and do not
write.'

'Yes, yes, we know each other,' the doctor said. 'Who's the
patient?'

The narrow, deep-set village streets were still dark; the roofs
were barely caressed by the grey light of dawn. Some peasants
were loading donkeys outside their front doors before going to
work in the country. The wheels of the trap rumbled on the
newly gravelled road. The horse walked; they were going into
the wind, and there was rain in the wind. The doctor pulled his
hat down over his brow and turned up his coat collar. Having
just got out of bed, he felt cold.

'At the end of April rain is good,' Cardile said. 'When I was a
boy you made a speech in the square at Acquafredda, for the
Church and for the people. Do you remember? The word
"Liberty" was on the banner. Our family were on the same side.
It was immediately after the war, and liberty was permitted.
Then the Church was not for the government, but for the
people. We were on the same side. After that the wind
changed.'

The doctor looked at the young man curiously.

'What a strange speech,' he said, but he did not seem to be displeased.

'There's a reason for it,' Cardile said. 'You'll see.'

'What reason?' asked the doctor.

At the fork in the road by the station four carabinieri were waiting. Why so early? One of them recognized Dr Sacca and saluted him. The trap left the village, driving into the rain. The road sloped gently downwards, and the horse began to trot.

'Now,' Cardile went on, 'women and the old are still for the Church and we, of course, look after our own affairs. My father is sixty, and is a prior of the Confraternity of the Holy Sacrament. You can check that for yourself, if you want to. On Sunday mornings he sings at mass, and on Good Friday and Corpus Christi he walks in the procession in a red cassock and makes the responses to the *Oremus*. Every year we give two barrels of wine to the parish for masses. All our dead are buried in the Chapel of the Holy Sacrament in Acquafredda cemetery, on the right as you go in. All this does not mean that we are any better than others, but I have a reason for recalling these things. In short, what I mean is that we are on the same side.'

'We know each other,' the doctor said. 'We know each other. Who's the patient? Someone in your family?'

The trap left the national highway and went up a side road full of puddles between newly ploughed fields. The road wound its way up hill in a series of big zigzags. A light, whiteish mist hung over the skeleton-like branches of the apple trees. The horse resumed walking without instructions from its master.

'Nevertheless there are many ways of knowing one another,' Cardile said. 'We peasants get to know people through the land they own and through testimonials. But is that a way of getting to know people? You work, buy, sell, rent, and you have to have papers and testimonials. If you go abroad to work you have to apply to many offices, and you need recommendations. Is that a way of getting to know people?'

'I agree,' the doctor said. 'But now tell me where you're taking me. Surely you didn't wake me before dawn just to make all these speeches?'

'We shall soon be there,' Cardile said. 'I must ask you to be patient for a little while longer. What I am telling is not just idle chitchat.'

The trap reached the top of the hill together with the first rays of a sickly sun. The horse was sweating, but started trotting again of its own accord. The road had degenerated into a country track overlooking the whole village. Smoke from the chimneys spread a bluish pall over the grey and black huddle of houses.

'I left home at sixteen,' Cardile went on. 'My father would have had plenty of work for me, but I was bored, and I went to France with other young men from the locality. I worked at l'Estaque, near Marseilles, where an underground canal was being excavated. One day someone told me that someone from my part of the world had turned up, an educated person. It'll be someone who wants something from me, I said to myself. My papers were in order, I'd paid what I had to pay, so what could he want? Anyway, the man came to the tavern where we ate, sat down, said he had been away from the Marsica for several years, and started talking about the land and the people here and the way they lived, and about his village in the Fucino. The same thing happened on the evenings that followed. We went out to the wharf at l'Estaque, sat on the ground and talked till late, and it became a habit. I gave up going dancing or to the cinema. I liked his company. I had never had a friend like that. I don't know if I've made myself clear. In the daytime I worked in the tunnel. It was an eight-hour day, but everyone did two or three hours' overtime to earn more. But when the eight hours were up I stopped, knowing that the man whom I enjoyed talking to was waiting for me at the wharf. What did we talk about? We talked about men, and about the land, and about life. We argued, and we also joked and laughed. Here's someone, I said to myself, with whom I have nothing to do, either for work or for papers or testimonials or anything else, who did not approach me as a priest or teacher of a propagandist, people who know everything and are paid to persuade others. Here, I said to myself, is someone who approaches me as a man. Then one bad day he left and I didn't hear from him again. I felt immediately that I was missing something. Then I heard that he had been denounced by the Italian consulate and expelled from France.'

'I can imagine who he was,' the doctor said. 'But why are you talking to me about him?'

'I don't want to be misunderstood,' said Cardile. 'I'm talking about myself. It's obvious that there's nothing special about me. I was born a peasant, and a peasant I shall remain. A peasant lives according to custom, and carrying a knife in one's pocket isn't the only custom, there are also others.'

The horse and trap met two carabinieri coming down from the mountains. They recognized the doctor and saluted him.

At that moment it started to rain again.

'Two years ago,' Cardile said, 'coming back with my barrow from the Feast of San Bartolomeo on the Magliano road, I came across a dog which had been run over by a car and had had its leg broken. It was howling by the roadside in a pitiful manner. I put the dog in the barrow, tied up its leg, and took it home. Two months later a carter from La Scurcola came and took it back, because it was his dog. I mention this to tell you what the customs are. Last summer I found a lame sheep on the road and took it back and put it in the shed between the cow and the donkey; later its owner came and took it back. That is the custom, mine and other people's. Well then, last night that man whom I met at l'Estaque knocked at my door. At first I didn't recognize him.'

'Is Pietro Spina here? Are you taking me to him by any chance?' Dr Sacca asked in alarm.

Cardile drew the trap to the side of the road and stopped, and the two men jumped down. Cardile tied the horse to an elm tree and covered it with a woollen blanket. The doctor looked all round him with a very worried expression on his face. The rain had died down and was moving away towards Tagliacozzo, but big black clouds that had been held in reserve were moving up from Avezzano. The country looked deserted. The two went on talking beside the trap.

'Well then, that man knocked at my door,' Cardile said, 'but he refused to come in, though he was in a pretty bad state and was feverish. So we went for a short stroll. We went down a lane

26

outside the village and sat under a tree. After talking a little about l'Estaque he started telling me that he had returned to Italy surreptitiously and had had a miraculous escape from being arrested by the police in Rome. As a result he had lost contact with his party friends and would not be able to approach them again for some time without risking being caught. He said that for several days he had been wandering in the mountains in the rain but could not go on, because he had a high fever. After a great deal of hesitation he had decided to come to ask me to hide him for a few days until he felt better. He said, "You are a worker, and it is for the party of the workers that I came back to Italy; don't give me away." Last night I hid him in a shed, and now I'm wondering what can be done for him. Can we leave him to die like that?'

'He had only to stay where he was, abroad,' the doctor said irritably.

'But now he's here. I found him on the doorstep, as one might find a dog or a sheep, a dying animal. Can he be allowed to die like that?'

'He has nothing to lose, he's alone. I have a wife and children. Our political ideas are not the same,' replied the doctor.

'But excuse me, this is not a matter of politics,' Cardile said. 'He's a dying man. In the catechism, which they made me learn by heart when I was a boy, it said: The works of mercy are these: to give drink to the thirsty, to clothe the naked, to give shelter to pilgrims and to succour the sick. It did not say: to succour the sick that are of the same way of thinking as you. It just said to succour the sick. I don't know whether I'm mistaken or not.'

'And was it he who sent you to me? Did he tell you he knew me?' the doctor asked.

'He said he was at school with you, but that I was not to fetch you in any circumstances,' Cardile said. 'That's the truth.'

They went on talking for some time next to the horse and trap. A peasant passed with a donkey with a load of wood and eyed them suspiciously. A little later an old woman passed with a goat. Cardile did not know whether to tell the doctor the whole truth. Eventually he made up his mind.

'He didn't want me to fetch you, on my word of honour,' he

said. 'On the contrary, last night he said to me, "I came back to my country for the party of the workers, and if I ask you for help it's because you're an honest worker. But Dr Sacca is an intellectual who has his career to worry about, and on top of that he frequents the diocesan curia and to ingratiate himself with the authorities might be capable of handing me over to the militia." I tell you that though I do not believe it. He was also totally opposed to my getting in touch with any of his relatives. He said he considered himself dead to his family, as if he had entered a monastic order. There was only one person who would not be afraid of helping him, and that was a priest who had been his schoolmaster, but now he was too old, and he didn't want to expose him to any risks. That was how we left things last night. As you can imagine, I couldn't sleep because of him. But at about three o'clock I dozed off and had a nightmare, I thought he had died. I went to see immediately, and found he was worse. So then I came and fetched you without asking his opinion again. It would be our duty to help him even if he were only a sheep.'

The doctor was leaning against one of the shafts and was looking anxiously all round him as if he were feeling sick. Finally he plucked up courage.

'We must make sure he leaves immediately,' he said. 'I'll try to persuade him. If he needs medicine, I'll give you a prescription in the name of some member of your family. May the Lord direct us out of this.'

'He's down there,' Cardile said, 'in the shed behind that walnut tree. It's a shed my father uses in summer. You can go there alone while I stay here on guard.'

In the shed behind the walnut tree the doctor found an old man who looked like a groom huddled on the floor. This upset him, because Cardile had not told him that anyone else would be there.

'Where's the patient?' he asked drily.

'Nunzio, what are you doing here?' the man said. 'Whom are you looking for?'

'Cardile said there was someone here who was ill,' said the doctor, even more upset at being addressed by name.

28

'I'm sorry,' the man said, rising to his feet. 'I explicitly forbade him to send for you.'

Only then did the doctor recognize his former schoolfellow Pietro Spina, and surprise took his breath away.

'Is it you?' he barely managed to stammer out. 'What a state you're in.'

The big, wide-open, deep-set eyes and handsome broad forehead were the only features of his former schoolfellow that he recognized.

'You're my age and you look sixty,' he said. 'What's wrong with you?'

Pietro smiled. No, his premature ageing was not the result of any strange disease, he explained. Must he reveal his secret? Before returning to Italy, to change his appearance and make him unrecognizable to the police, he had for several weeks treated his face with a mixture based on tincture of iodine, thus producing the wrinkles and colouring of premature old age.

'I found the recipe in the life of an old Russian revolutionary,' he said, 'and it's capable of the most widespread application. When the supreme ambition of the average young Italian ceases to be to become the lover of an American or Swiss tourist and he turns to more serious aims, it will perhaps be necessary to open artificial disfigurement parlours for the daintiest dandies to take the place of the present beauty parlours.'

Nunzio gazed at his disfigured contemporary with astonishment and pity. Pietro had never been a handsome youth, but his impetuosity and frankness often caused his face to be lit up by an internal fire that made him attractive to women. How could political sectarianism have driven him to mutilate himself in this barbarous fashion?

'But the police recognized you in spite of the state to which you have reduced yourself,' the doctor said. 'The whole countryside here is being combed by carabinieri and militia who are looking for you.'

'No, the police did not recognize me,' Spina said. 'I was denounced to police headquarters. If I managed to get away it was because they distributed copies of an old photograph of mine everywhere. In any case, I had no intention of staying in Rome, but in some province in southern Italy.'

The resemblance of all this to the plot of a cheap thriller abruptly recalled Nunzio to the childish and dangerous situation in which he had recklessly allowed himself to be involved. The distant sound of a truck on the national road made him start.

'Don't be frightened,' Pietro said to him with a smile. 'Sit down. How are things with you? I've heard some things about you. I know that you're married and have children, that you're a success in your profession and that you enjoy the respect of the authorities. I congratulate you. Are you a commendatore yet? What? No? What an appalling injustice.'

'I'm going,' Nunzio said. 'Why should I sit down? Do you think I want to compromise with you, to argue with you, to listen to your wild ideas?'

Spina motioned to him to calm down. 'I know you've always been a rabbit,' he said. 'Go away, it upsets me to see you quivering with fear. If they haven't made you a commendatore yet, and you're certainly itching to be one, let me suggest to you an infallible method of becoming one. Just hurry away and denounce me.'

'Don't be offensive,' said Nunzio. 'Only a lunatic would mistake common sense for cowardice. Besides, I was sent for as a doctor. I didn't come here to argue with you, but to see what you need.'

'Physician, cure thyself,' said Pietro. 'I assure you that I'm in a better state than you. You may not believe me, but I repeat that it wasn't I who sent for you.'

Nunzio seemed to be seized with sudden compassion and sat down beside him. 'Weren't you safe abroad?' he asked. 'Why did you come back to this dreadful country, into the lion's mouth? If you're in love with freedom, why didn't you stay in a free country?'

'I came back in order to be able to breathe,' Pietro said, making the gesture of filling his lungs. 'You see, even when I was abroad the reality in which I lived my mental life was here, but gradually that reality became a dream, an abstraction. I had a real need to feel the ground beneath my feet again.'

'The greatest revolutionaries,' Nunzio said, 'your masters, Mazzini, Lenin, Trotsky, who plotted for their ideas for decades, spent whole lifetimes in exile. Why can't you?'

'Perhaps you're right,' Spina said. 'I'm a very bad revolutionary. To hell with politics, tactics, strategy. What I mean is, I don't know how to preserve myself in the hope of one day playing a big role. At all events, I'm not going abroad again. You see, Nunzio, I'm just like the wines of our part of the world; they are by no means to be despised, but take them to a different climate and they're no good at all, while other men and other wines seem to be expecially made for export.'

'And if they catch you?' Nunzio asked.

'I admit that prison is rather disagreeable,' Spina said. 'You can take it from me that I shan't go there of my own accord. But if they take me there by force, what can I do about it?'

'In short, ou don't want to go abroad again?'

'No.'

'In that case,' the doctor said, 'it's no concern of mine, I wash my hands of it.'

'I'm delighted to hear you expressing yourself in biblical similes,' Pietro said ironically. 'I see that something remains of your education by priests.'

'What remains with you is the fanaticism,' Nunzio said. 'You no longer believe in God, but instead you believe in the proletariat, and with the same obsessiveness.'

Pietro made a gesture as if to forbid him to speak of things of which he could have not the slightest understanding.

'Yesterday evening,' he said, 'to avoid the carabinieri and militia I walked the whole length of the path halfway up the Monte della Croce, and I saw in the distance the school at which we spent eight years together. The flower beds that we looked after must still be in the garden. Do you remember my geraniums? The big dormitory where we slept in neighbouring beds, so close that we could talk until late at night without the prefect noticing it, must still be on the second floor. Do you remember the fantastic plans we used to make?'

'To me you seem to be recalling prehistory,' Nunzio said.

'When we went out into the world,' Pietro went on, 'we

found ourselves in a society that was totally unforeseen, and each one of us had to make his choice – to submit or to put his life in jeopardy. Once upon a time there may have been middle ways, but for our generation after the war they were closed. How many years have passed since then? Barely fifteen, and anyone who saw the two of us here now would never imagine that up to the age of twenty our lives ran parallel and we nursed the same dreams for the future.'

Nunzio seemed nervous and upset. 'It's true that we now belong to two different parties,' he said.

'Two different humanities,' Pietro corrected him. 'Two different races. I know of no other terms to express what I am trying to say. In my present situation, in which I am practically in your hands, to pretend an esteem for you and those like you which I do not feel would cost me an effort of which I am not capable. Besides, the day of reckoning is not yet. You may go.' ·

'There are many other things of which you are not capable,' Nunzio said. 'You are not capable of understanding that the ordinary person generally doesn't have any choice at all. The conditions in which he lives are prefabricated for him. If they are not to his liking, the best he can do is to wait for them to change.'

'And if they don't change of their own accord, who is to change them?' said Pietro. 'Oh, how pitiful is an intelligence used only to make excuses to quieten the conscience. At least do me the favour of going away.'

Pietro went back into the shed and sat wearily on a donkey saddle. The doctor remained uncertain for a moment, then went up to him and said, 'Let me at least examine your chest. I can get you medicines through Cardile.'

Reluctantly Pietro bared his neck. There was a grotesque contrast between his prematurely aged head, which was the colour of vulcanized fibre, and his slender, clean, slightly bent chest, which was white and graceful, like that of an adolescent. The doctor bent over him, tapped, and put his ear to each of his ribs, checked the frantic hammering of his heart, tried to listen from every side to the painful panting of the lungs. The examination exhausted Pietro's slight physical resistance, and he slowly slipped from the saddle and lay outstretched on the straw-covered floor, shutting his eyes. Nunzio was seized with a sudden feeling of warmth and fellowship.

'Listen, Pietro,' he said, 'let's get things straight, you mustn't die.'

He sat next to him on the straw and started unburdening himself, telling him about the illusions, the disappointments, the miseries, the lies, the intrigues, the boredom of his professional life.

'We live the whole of our lives provisionally,' he said. 'We think that for the time being things are bad, that for the time being we must make the best of them and adapt or humiliate ourselves, but that it's all only provisional and that one day real life will begin. We prepare for death complaining that we have never lived. Sometimes I'm haunted by the thought that we have only one life and that we live it provisionally, waiting in vain for the day when real life will begin. And so life passes by. I assure you that of all the people I know not one lives in the present. No-one gets any benefit from what he does every day. No-one is in a condition to say: On that day, at that moment, my life began. Believe me, even those who have power and take advantage of it live on intrigues and anxieties and are full of disgust at the dominant stupidity. They too live provisionally and spend their lives waiting.'

'One mustn't wait,' Pietro said. 'Those who emigrate spend their lives waiting too. That's the trouble. One must act. One must say: Enough, from this very day.'

'But if there's no freedom?' Nunzio said.

'Freedom is not a thing you can receive as a gift,' Pietro said. 'One can be free even under a dictatorship on one simple condition, that is, if one struggles against it. A man who thinks with his own mind and remains uncorrupted is a free man. A man who struggles for what he believes to be right is a free man. You can live in the most democratic country in the world, and if you are lazy, callous, servile, you are not free, in spite of the absence of violence and coercion, you are a slave. Freedom is not a thing that must be begged from others. You must take it for yourself, whatever share you can.'

Nunzio was thoughtful and troubled. 'You are our revenge,'

he said. 'You are the best part of ourselves. Pietro, try to be strong. Try to live and to endure. Take real care of your health.'

'Nunzio,' Pietro said with difficulty, 'if my return to Italy served only to make you talk like that, I should be satisfied. That is how you used to talk during the nights at school while the rest of the dormitory was asleep.'

Cardile appeared at the door of the shed. He was soaked to the skin.

'It's still raining, and there's not a soul to be seen,' he said.

The doctor and he went aside and conferred for a moment. Then Nunzio said to Pietro, 'For the time being you'll stay hidden here. You must spend the whole day lying down, and Cardile will bring you what you need. Meanwhile we'll find you somewhere more comfortable.'

'I shan't go abroad again,' Pietro said.

'I'm afraid you couldn't even if you wanted to,' the doctor said. 'You're in no condition for a long journey. We must find you a safe and quiet hiding place for a few months. Afterwards you can do what you like.'

When he was left alone Pietro clambered up a step-ladder to the hay loft above the shed. That was his sanatorium.

Chapter 4

At last he could rest, comforted by the warmth of his fever. This was his first chance to relax since returning to his country.

'I feel I'm in a manger scene,' he said to Cardile.

For that idea to have been complete he should have had an ass and a cow for company. The ass and the cow were there, but down below in the shed, as well as a horse, and only at night, because during the daytime they had to earn their hay. When they came back they were tired, and the outlaw upstairs was asleep. The straw encouraged him to sleep. There was no sound to disturb him. Behind the loft there was a brook, and at nights its babbling was his lullaby. Nymphs emerged from it in the dark and told him forgotten stories of his childhood. Memories made him drowsy. When Cardile arrived with food and medicines he opened his eyes, ate, swallowed his pills and then sank back into the straw and dropped off to sleep again. Cardile came twice a day. He would arrive with the ass or the horse, dismount, remove the animal's load, tie it by the halter to a ring fixed in the wall, look round, and then come up to the loft. Pietro recognized every one of his movements. His visits lasted no longer than was strictly necessary.

'Any news?'

'No, nothing. Be patient.'

He was in no hurry. There was a big unframed window in the loft through which the hay was put after the threshing, and he could stay in the shade and see a large expanse of fields through the wide opening; fields of young green wheat, low vines, and apple and almond trees in blossom. He could also see a stretch of the national road in the distance. One evening a long procession of carts passed by with little lights hanging between the wheels, going to some fair. Pietro closed his eyes and went to the fair with them.

'Aren't you bored?' Cardile asked him.

No, he wasn't. He found it difficult to explain his state of mind. He was struck by the naturalness of the things about him, things in their proper place, not in the fictitious world, the fictitious countryside of the haunted imagination of an *émigré*. His own sick body was like a natural object among other natural objects, a thing just like other things, a pile of stiff bones. It was not a central or basic thing in relation to other things, but a concrete, limited thing, a product of the earth. His body lay on the straw between a loaf of bread and a bottle of wine, which was the usual breakfast that Cardile brought him. The straw was yellow, the bread brown, the wine red.

'Bring me some coloured pencils and I'll paint you a picture,' he said to Cardile.

But one evening Cardile arrived panting and out of breath.

'What? Are you still here? Am I to believe my eyes?' he said.

'Where did you think I was?'

'Dr Sacca has just heard you were arrested at a hotel at Avezzano.'

'Well, it depends on whom he got the information from.'

'An officer in the militia, a friend of his.'

'In that case,' Pietro said seriously, 'most probably it's true.'

'To the glory of the militia,' said Pietro, raising the bottle.

'The militia is always right,' Cardile said. 'Have another.'

The bottle was quickly drained.

'Couldn't you bring me a newspaper?' Pietro asked.

'I'm sorry, but I've never bought a newspaper in my life,' said Cardile. 'Newspaper readers in Acquafredda can be counted on the fingers of one hand. I don't want to do anything that might rouse suspicion.'

Pietro did not insist. He had with him some crumpled notebooks containing Lenin's notes on the agrarian revolution. These would have been incriminating if they had been found in the event of a casual search by the militia, but he had not wanted to get rid of them, thinking they might be useful for a closer study of the southern Italian problem, particularly if he were forced to remain out of the active struggle for some weeks. But, leafing through them in his idleness in the hayloft, he found himself unable to go on reading them; they might have been written in Chinese. The fact was that he had always been bored by theory.

One day Dr Sacca made Cardile a speech about vitamins, the conclusion of which was that Pietro needed a more substantial diet. The result was that henceforward he was regularly given two loaves of bread and a double quantity of wine every morning. Every now and then Cardile managed to steal some cheese and salami from home; for Pietro these occasions were Lucullan feasts.

Cardile came to the shed at dawn and sunset to look after the animals or to take them out to work in the fields and bring them back as required. Pietro recognized each of his movements, when he piled the manure or spread the straw, when he only half-closed the door because he would be coming back very soon, and when he shut it. The animals' drinking trough was a short distance away. It consisted of a big wooden tub into which water flowed from an iron pipe fixed to a dry stone wall. The wall served to protect the fountain. Water flowed out of a slit in one side of the tub and continued its way downhill, forming the brook that Pietro heard babbling at night.

One morning, after Cardile's usual visit, Pietro could no longer resist the temptation to take a bath. It was a fine morning, the sun had just risen, and the apple and cherry trees glistened with dew. Down in the plain peasants were busy with the spring sowing and winnowing the young wheat, but on the hillside there was no-one to be seen. Pietro had no difficulty in following the tracks of the animals and finding the drinking trough. The water was light green in colour and very cold. Pietro had just taken off his shirt and was unlacing his shoes when a young peasant woman appeared carrying a pail. There had been no sound of footsteps, as the girl was bare-footed; she had obviously come to draw water. Pietro hurriedly put on his shirt again.

'Excuse me,' he said, trying to smile.

'Are there no fountains near your house?' the girl said disdainfully. 'Why do you trespass on other people's property?'

'I'm on a pilgrimage,' he said. 'I'm simply passing through.'

He tried to placate the girl by politeness.

'Would you like me to help you fill the bucket?' he said.

'Spring has never been a time for pilgrimages,' she said. 'In Christian countries people go on pilgrimages in August or September. In spring they work.'

'I made a vow,' said Pietro. 'You certainly know what a vow is. Actually it's a matter of conscience.'

She was a robust, self-confident young woman, not easy to intimidate; she had thick eyelashes and the strong shoulders, neck and thighs of a woman who does heavy work, but her thin nose, her lively and ironic eyes and her slender ankles meant that she was by no means ordinary in appearance.

'Can't I help you?' Pietro said. 'I'm in no hurry, you know.'

She looked hard at him and supported his gaze without embarrassment.

'Perhaps you live in these parts?' he said. 'I'm delighted to see that you're in no hurry either.'

Her only answer was to plunge the pail into the trough and pull it out full. Before going away she turned to Pietro as if she were trying to think of something to say.

'Good luck,' she ended by saying in a friendly tone that affected him deeply. Why that greeting and that sudden change of tone?

He followed her with his eyes until she disappeared from sight, and then quickly went back to the loft, where he took up a position behind the big window. He stayed there with his eyes fixed on the path down which she had disappeared. The path led through an orchard, and beyond it, above the tree-tops the roof of a farmhouse was visible. Was that where she lived? Pietro stayed motionless at his post all day, and the hours passed without his noticing them. Time stood still. In the afternoon, when he suddenly saw her reappear, carrying a pail in one hand just as in the morning, he thought that perhaps it was a hallucination. All the same, he hurried down the ladder and went to meet her. But he had the sense to arrive at the trough as if he were coming down from the top of the hill.

'Still here?' the girl said, pretending surprise. 'Have you forgotten your vow?'

'I've been waiting for you to come back,' he honestly admitted.

'Were you sure I was coming back?' she said. 'What cheek.'

'No, I certainly wasn't sure. I was afraid you might not come back, but I hoped that you would,' he said. 'I've been thinking about nothing else all day.'

'Where have you been, if I may ask?' she said.

'Up in the woods,' he said. 'I've spent the whole time looking in the direction of your house on the other side of the orchard.'

'Did you spend last night in the woods too?' the girl asked. 'It's not very comfortable at this time of year. What do you do if it rains?'

'I'm waiting for you to offer me a better place,' Pietro said. Now he had laid his cards on the table. The girl did not answer, but waited for him to go on.

'Is there anyone else in the house?' he asked. His voice was trembling, and he tried hard to smile politely to mitigate the crudeness of the question.

'Yes, my mother-in-law,' the girl said.

'At some time of night mothers-in-law generally go to sleep,' Pietro said.

For a moment the girl defended herself by resorting to irony.

'Really,' she said with a laugh. 'That's not bad for a pilgrim.' After a moment she added, 'Also there's the dog. It sleeps in the daytime, it takes it in turn with my mother-in-law.'

'So I'll expect you here, then,' said Pietro. 'It's nice warm weather, but don't keep me waiting too long.'

'Are you in such a hurry?' the girl said provocatively.

'Being alone gets on one's nerves,' Pietro said.

The girl threw caution to the winds and laughed aloud. 'You could tell your beads,' she said.

'I'll expect you as soon as it's dark,' he said. 'Don't keep me waiting.'

How interminable are the hours that precede a romantic appointment.

Cardile was later than usual that evening. A peasant's day is regulated by the weather, and it would have been foolish not to take full advantage of a sunny day in April. Pietro was impatient.

39

'You look much better,' Cardile said. 'I'm delighted that the air in my shed has done you good.'

'Yes, I feel much better,' Pietro said. 'But last night I hardly slept a wink because of a dog's barking. Who lives in that house beyond the orchard?'

'A young woman cousin of mine, with her mother-in-law,' Cardile said. 'Her husband now works at the sugar refinery.'

'What sort of people are they?' Pietro asked.

'Not to be trusted,' Cardile said. 'We're hardly on speaking terms.'

'Excuse me, I'm tired,' Pietro said. 'I hope that dog will let me sleep tonight.'

No sooner had Cardile left than he climbed down from the loft and made straight for the water trough, without worrying about hiding the direction from which he came. The girl was there already.

'You make yourself sought after,' she said.

'I saw a man over there near the shed, and that held me up,' he said.

'That was my cousin,' she said. 'You did well to avoid him.'

'What sort of person is he?' he said.

'Not to be trusted,' said the girl.

'It's just as well that you're different,' he said.

'How do you know I am? Are you sure it'll be all right?'

'Did your mother-in-law give you permission to go out?' he asked.

'I told her I had an errand to do in the village,' she said. 'I mustn't be late; I've got to say goodnight to her when I get back.'

On the ground there was a big bottle, propped up against the tub.

'I've brought you something to drink,' she said.

'Thank you,' he said. 'We'll drink afterwards. It's not wine I'm thirsty for at the moment.'

'Is it a long time since you've been with a woman?' she said. 'Be gentle with me, please. No, don't you see the ground's wet here? It's cleaner over there, under the tree.'

'What's your name?' Pietro asked.

'Margherita,' she said. 'And what's yours? No, don't tell me, please, it would be another lie.'

'Do you think I've been telling you lies already? Do you think I'm a liar?' he said.

'You're not a pilgrim,' the girl said with a smile.

'You're quite right,' he said. 'But that wasn't a lie, it was a manner of speaking.'

The two were lying on the grass, and a little of the warmth of the day still lingered in the air. At the bottom of the hill the village was a cluster of faint lights.

'It's good here,' Pietro said.

'Would you like to bet that I can guess your name?' the girl said.

'Why?' said Pietro. 'If you guess right, it's not worth the trouble, because I know my name already; if you guess wrong, it's a silly waste of time. Do you like wasting time?'

'During the past few days,' the girl said, 'the carabinieri have been to every house and told everyone that there's a fugitive in the area. They said that if he turned up and asked for food or lodging we were to pretend to do as he asked and inform the police immediately.'

'Have you denounced me already?' Pietro asked.

'The carabinieri said that the man is an enemy of the government and that the person who denounced him would get a reward,' the woman went on. 'They talk about you a great deal in the village, your real name's Pietro.'

'Doesn't the reward tempt you?' Pietro said. 'Or do you prefer another one, from me?'

Margherita's reaction was abrupt. She withdrew the arm on which Pietro's head was resting, adjusted her clothing, and sat up.

'Forgive me,' Pietro said. 'I'm an idiot.'

'Do you think,' she said, 'that a woman does not betray a man only if she hopes to sleep with him?'

'You're right,' Pietro said. 'Please forgive me.'

'You may not believe me,' Margherita said, 'but if I had come across a woman who was a fugitive from the police like you I should not have behaved differently.'

'I believe you, Margherita, forgive me,' Pietro said.

'Would you like to know who taught me to be like that?' said Margherita. 'When I was a little girl we hid a man who had escaped from prison in our house for several months. He was a man in distress, a stranger. My father often used to tell us that to honourable people the first of the works of mercy is to help the persecuted.'

She paused for a moment, and then went on, 'You may certainly think it strange to hear me talking of honour at this moment.'

'You talk of it in the sense that I respect most,' Pietro said seriously. 'Every part of the body can be said to have its own honour. But for too long people believed that the most important kind of honour was between the legs.'

'Pietro, let us be truthful,' said Margherita. 'What's the point of fiddling with words? It's better to say nothing.'

Their two faces gradually moved closer to each other.

'Your lips taste like a child's,' said Margherita. 'Is it true you were born near here, in the Fucino area? I've heard it said.'

'What else have you heard?' said Pietro.

'That you come from a well-off family, that you lost your parents in the earthquake, and that you're a bit mad,' Margherita said. 'Why do you lead such a desperate life?'

'Because of what you mentioned a few moments ago, Margherita,' Pietro said. 'I have a certain sense of honour.'

'Would you like to send a message to your grandmother?' Margherita said. 'I could go and see her. They say she's a real lady.'

'I've given up my blood relatives for many years past,' Pietro said. 'It's disagreeable, but I think one must start with that.'

'How can you possibly do such a thing?' Margherita said. 'What a strange idea. You're not a foundling, after all.'

'The only relationship I now respect,' Pietro said, 'is that between minds. Like that which has just been born between us.'

'Pietro, let me think for a moment about what you've just said. Yes, I have the same feeling about you now. Pietro, listen, I want to suggest something to you.'

The girl rose to her feet and tidied her hair. Then she held out her hand to help him to his feet.

'Let us say goodbye without making love,' she said resolutely. 'After what we've just said to each other it seems to me to be the right thing to do. Do you agree? That's how I want it. But what's this?' she exclaimed. 'You haven't tasted my wine yet.'

Pietro raised the bottle and took a long draught.

'It's strong,' he said. 'Have some too.'

Margherita helped herself as generously as Pietro had. The gurgling of the wine mingled with the babbling of the brook. The duet continued until the wine was finished.

'How much was there?' Pietro asked.

'Three litres,' said Margherita. 'Now I must go.'

'I'll come with you as far as the orchard,' Pietro said.

'That wouldn't be wise,' Margherita said. 'Our dog is let off the chain at night and it might go for you.'

They parted without saying goodbye. Only when he saw her disappear at the end of the path was Pietro overcome with sadness; he sat down on the ground and started to weep. His return to the hayloft was difficult for other reasons. In his absence some idiot had changed the whole layout of the place. The door, for instance, had been moved and made smaller, and the ladder was simply impossible to find. Also dawn arrived earlier than usual, before the effect of the wine had worn off. Cardile found him huddled in the manger.

'What on earth are you doing here?' he said. 'Why didn't you sleep up in the loft?'

'A huge rat kept disturbing me,' Pietro said, rubbing his eyes. 'It didn't frighten me, but I didn't want to waste time arguing with it.'

'The bottle I brought you yesterday must have gone to your head,' Cardile said with a smile.

After attending to the animals he went up into the loft to fetch the daily ration of hay. Meanwhile Pietro tried to decipher a very puzzling letter from Nunzio, an almost impossible task in which he was interrupted by exclamations of surprise from the floor above.

'How extraordinary,' Cardile exclaimed. 'I can't believe my eyes.'

He came hurrying down the ladder with the bottle he had brought the evening before. It was full.

'What did you get drunk on last night if this bottle's still full?' Cardile wanted to know.

Pietro's surprise was no less, but it was of briefer duration, because of his innate tendency to remain impassive in the face of the strangest natural phenomena.

'What on earth am I to make of this?' Cardile said.

'Well,' said Pietro, 'it seems to me that this is an obvious refutation of the old proverb according to which it is impossible to have a full bottle and a tipsy wife or friend. All that can be done, it seems to me, is to take cognizance of the fact.'

'I don't understand,' Cardile said.

'Your bewilderment does not surprise me,' Pietro said. 'You are a peasant, and agriculture is based on proverbs. But truth, fortunately, is greater than proverbs.'

Those words served to end the discussion, but not to convince Cardile, who kept looking suspiciously at the bottle and shaking his head. So Pietro was able to go back to trying to elucidate Nunzio's letter. It mentioned in sibylline terms a strange plan for living safely in a mountain village for two or three months, long enough to restore someone's health. What did the person concerned think of the idea? The details were glossed over or incomprehensible, but Pietro decided that a change of air was urgently required and that the burden must be removed from Cardile's shoulders, so he accepted. One of the things he did not realise was that he was to leave immediately.

Hardly had he dropped off to sleep in the straw that evening than he heard a voice downstairs calling him.

'Pietro, Pietro, come down,' it said.

Groping in the dark, Pietro managed to lift the latch in the trap door and look down. Nunzio was down below between the donkey and the cow, holding a lantern and calling him.

'Bring whatever you need,' he said. 'You're leaving immediately.'

As soon as Pietro joined him Nunzio showed him in the

feeble light of the lantern a big bundle of ecclesiastical clothing.

'It's a complicated set up,' Nunzio said, 'and, to tell the truth, it's not really to my taste at all.'

Pietro was speechless. He had not realized from the letter that the plan was that he should disguise himself as a priest.

'I have a horror of carnivals and dressing up,' he said. 'Even when I was a boy I never wore a mask.'

'Given the situation,' Nunzio said, 'we failed to think of anything safer.'

Pietro went on stubbornly shaking his head.

'It's a long time since I left the Church, but disguising myself as a priest is repugnant to me, it's an act of irreverence that is inconsistent with my character.'

This scruple pleased Nunzio.

'If we didn't know you,' he said, 'if we had thought there was the slightest chance of your making improper use of this disguise, we shouldn't have offered it to you.'

The clothing of Pietro in his priestly attire took place immediately in the dim light of the oil lamp. The horse was asleep, and the cow created the impression of not realizing what was happening, for it squatted on the straw and shut its eyes. But the donkey remained on its feet and looked. This attentiveness on its part ended by upsetting the doctor, who took it by the halter and made it face the other way. It allowed itself to be moved, but then turned its head and went on gazing at this strange man who had come down from the hayloft and was now putting on a long, black cassock with a long row of little buttons in front.

'Don't forget that the habit does not make the monk,' Nunzio said.

But Pietro was in no mood for joking and went on muttering incomprehensibly.

To distract him Nunzio improvised a short, semi-serious consecratory speech.

'These garments,' he said, 'are derived from primitive mystery religions, from the priests of Isis and Serapis, as you know. In the Catholic Church they were adopted by the first monastic communities, to try to safeguard Christian values from worldly

45

contamination so that the essential charismatic virtues might be preserved for a minority living outside society and in opposition to society. Thus rites survive the age in which they are born and pass from one religion to another, from one society to another. Now, here are you, a man initiated into the new revolutionary mysteries, into the mysteries of revolutionary materialism, donning the black garments that for thousands of years have been symbols of sacrifice and supernatural inspiration.'

An involuntary smile came into Pietro's eyes.

'Don't talk balls,' he said.

'I don't understand,' Nunzio went on in the same tone, 'why Lenin did not introduce similar clothing, or at any rate the tonsure, for the personnel of the Cominform, to distinguish the agent, depository and interpreter of the sacred texts from the simple proletarian or cafone.'

Time was pressing. Cardile was waiting outside with the horse and trap.

'You will stop at my surgery,' Nunzio said, 'where you will have a bath and have your hair cut, and I shall take an X-ray.'

'Promise to come and see me,' Pietro said.

'All right,' Nunzio said. 'What will you call yourself?'

Pietro thought for a moment. Then he suggested, 'Spada. What do you think of it?'

'All right,' said Nunzio. 'We'll call you Don Paolo Spada.'

'Why Don Paolo?'

'Pietro Spada is too close to your real name. So, reverend Don Paolo Spada, let us go. Have you forgotten nothing? Have you your tricorn, your breviary, your beads, your scapular, the special instructions for your sacred mission?'

'Let us go,' said Don Paolo Spada. '*Procedamus in pace.*'

CHAPTER 5

'The horse doesn't like going out at night,' the driver said. 'I must say I don't blame him.'

'Nor do I,' said Don Paolo. 'But I missed my train. I was delayed by the bishop.'

'Monsignore ought to buy himself a watch,' said the driver. 'How can he send his priests around at night in this appalling weather?'

It had stopped raining a short time before, but it was windy and the air was as cold as in winter.

'Are you cold? Shall I raise the hood?' the driver asked.

'It's all right as it is, provided the rain holds off,' said Don Paolo.

The road was dark and lonely. The sound of the horse's hooves roused the dogs in their kennels. Occasionally an inquisitive face appeared at a window that was still lit. The driver was sitting on his box, smoking his pipe. An occasional shake of the reins was sufficient to keep the horse trotting. The man turned to Don Paolo and said, 'How much do you charge for a funeral service? I'm just asking out of curiosity.'

'Are you thinking of dying soon?' Don Paolo replied.

'Not for the time being,' the man said, and touched a certain part of his body. 'But I should like to know, for purposes of comparison.'

'Forget it,' Don Paolo said. 'Comparisons are odious.'

'Do you know this part of the world?' the man asked.

Don Paolo did not answer. This was the neighbourhood where he was born, from which he had been banished about ten years previously, his native country that was forbidden him. He felt his heart beating, and he was sweating in spite of the coldness of the night. Behind him was Monte Valino, its two summits still covered with snow, and in front of him, covering the whole semicircle of the horizon, was the mountain barrier surrounding the Fucino basin, standing out against the snowy night sky like the gloomy battlements of a closed world. The cab came to a big village in which recently built houses and villas alternated with huddles of muddy huts and piles of rubble. The place was badly lit, and the darkest stretches of roadway coincided with the widest and deepest puddles. At a bend in the road the cab was abruptly halted by two carabinieri, who promptly let it go on when they saw that the only passenger was a priest.

'Good evening, father,' they said.

'*Pax vobiscum*,' the priest replied.

At the end of the village the road was being repaired and the horse started walking. Don Paolo held tight in the jolting vehicle to avoid ending up between the wheels. It was an effort, but it was also a distraction. As soon as the road returned to normal the driver turned toward him and said, 'Do you believe in this new war in Africa?'

'A priest, if he believes at all, believes in God,' Don Paolo replied. 'That in itself is a great deal.'

'What I wanted to know,' the driver said, 'was whether you think the new war will be profitable.'

'Not to those who die,' said Don Paolo.

The driver took this as a witticism, and laughed. But what he really wanted to know was something else, as he explained in different terms. 'Do you think there are plenty of pickings there? Is there gold there? Plenty of gold?'

'So wars are just if there are plenty of pickings, in your opinion?' Don Paolo said.

'In everybody's opinion,' the driver said. 'Do you expect the poor lads to die for nothing? Do only the English have the right to steal?'

'I'm sleepy,' said Don Paolo. 'Leave me in peace.'

The road had been recently gravelled. They were close to Don Paolo's birthplace. The cab jolted in space and time. In this locality Don Paolo knew every bridge, every vineyard, every brook, every tree. At the crossroads before Orta there was an old tavern. Acquasanta, the landlady, was lowering the shutters, and a girl was helping her. Could Acquasanta's daughter have grown that much? The wheels of the cab sank in the gravel and turned with difficulty. They rounded a bend and the first houses of Orta suddenly appeared only a few yards away, there was the electric street lamp on the dark wheelwright's shop at the entrance to the village. Don Paolo shut his eyes. He didn't want to see. The first to notice the cab's arrival was the wheelwright's mastiff. It barked two or three times, as usual, and then listened behind the door, growling to itself uncertainly and interrogatively. The cab passed the shop, nearly grazing the door, whereupon the mastiff let out a protracted, high-pitched howl, to which the bitch guarding the vegetable plot behind the church responded in alarm. Don Paolo kept his eyes shut, but he could tell from the sound of the wheels when the cab reached the cobbles of the small Orta square. The bitch started barking hysterically, woke her young that were sleeping in the kennel together with the puppies and jumped against the gate of the vegetable plot. One by one the other village dogs were roused, including those over by the mill, those at the civil engineers' stores, and those at the carters' stables.

'What on earth is happening?' the cabman exclaimed. 'What sort of a place is this?'

Thirty or forty dogs were howling, growling and barking in every alley and every courtyard. They were still barking when the cab left the last houses behind, and then one by one they fell silent. When Don Paolo opened his eyes again the cab had stopped by a fountain with a big drinking trough for animals. On the fountain there was a bronze plaque with the words: 'Erected at the expense of the Spina family.'

'Wait a minute, I'm getting out too,' Don Paolo said to the driver.

He got out, took some water in the hollow of his hand, and drank. Then he wiped his burning brow with his wet hands. There was no more gravel on the road, and the horse could start trotting again. Don Paolo sat with his back to the driver, so as to be able to see the last village lights. There were still lights in about a dozen scattered windows. Then one went out up on the hill, then another down below near the mill, then another in the direction of the stream, and then another up on the hill. Don Paolo could recognize every house, every chimney, every window, every garden. What had become of his grandmother, old Donna Maria Vincenza? Was she still alive? Did she ever think about him? Had she been troubled by the authorities? What had become of Faustina? Did she remember him? Was she married? He felt like a visitor from another world. The cab passed close to an old pozzolana quarry that had belonged to his father. As a boy he had played hide-and-seek with the children of the men who worked there. Half way up the hill he recognized 'his' vineyard, the last remnant of his father's estate. The fig trees were still in their place, but where were the cherry trees? Where was the walnut tree? His uncle, to whom the vineyard had been handed over, must have had them cut down. Don Paolo's eyes filled with tears. Then the wind rose and turned east, and the trees rustled. Don Paolo bent his head and really went to sleep.

The driver woke him at Fossa dei Marsi, outside the Girasole hotel. He was expected. A woman took charge of his suitcase.

Before taking his departure the driver asked a favour of Don Paolo. 'Couldn't you write me a good recommendation?' he said.

'A recommendation to whom and for what?'

The driver thought for a moment, and then said, 'At the moment I can't exactly say, but there'll be plenty of occasions when it'll be bound to come in handy. You could give me a general recommendation.'

'But I don't know you,' the priest said.

'I didn't know you either,' the driver said, 'but that didn't prevent me from bringing you here.'

'I've paid you for that,' the priest said. 'Goodnight.'

He must have been dazed and exhausted, for he had no memory whatever of his arrival at the inn.

CHAPTER 6

Don Paolo woke early but stayed in bed late.

Nunzio had given him some typed 'Notes on how a priest should conduct himself outside his diocese'. Don Paolo came from the diocese of Frascati and was going to the dei Marsi diocese to convalesce in the mountain village of Pietrasecca. The notes indicated the major difficulties he might encounter and gave instructions on how to cope with them. Don Paolo read and re-read them. The carter who was to take him up to Pietrasecca was coming to fetch him in the afternoon, so he took his time dressing and spent the whole morning in his room. He noted with pleasure that there was a wash-basin. After roughing it in the hayloft a wash-basin in his room offered him real luxury. It also showed the progress that had been made in his country. Over the wash-basin there was a notice in beautiful handwriting saying: 'Gentlemen are requested not to urinate in the wash-basin because of the smell'. In fact the wash-basin stank.

Don Paolo looked at himself in the mirror. His hair had been cut very short in Nunzio's surgery. With his shaved head and in his black cassock he looked grotesque. He almost burst into tears. The cassock had twenty-eight buttons in front. The idea of having to do up or undo twenty-eight buttons every time he put it on or took it off plunged him into despair. Fortunately he discovered that it was sufficient to unbutton it only from the neck to the waist to take it off over his head or to drop it to his feet. These feminine gestures put him in a good humour. But other difficulties arose. He was disturbed at the idea that he would have to raise the cassock every time he wanted to take something from his trouser pockets. Wasn't it ridiculous to have to raise one's cassock in public? But later he discovered an opening near the pockets through which the trouser pockets could be reached. Oh well, being a priest was not so difficult after all. When he went out on to the landing he ran straight into the landlady, the widowed Berenice Girasole. The reception the old woman gave him was rather alarming. She had evidently suffered some sort of calamity; her tearful expression and her sighs boded nothing good for Don Paolo.

'It was Providence that sent you,' she said, kissing his hand.

'No, it was the doctor,' said Don Paolo, slipping away.

Opposite the hotel there was a haberdasher's. To keep himself in countenance he pretended to look at one of the windows, but a burst of laughter from some youths who were standing about drew his attention to the merchandise on display, which consisted of women's knickers and brassières. He fled, and did not stop until he reached a hatter's. His reflection in a big mirror in the window showed him an even more disastrous version of himself than that which he had seen in the hotel bedroom. How horrible. Tired and disheartened, he went back to the hotel. By now it was lunch time.

'Would the reverend father like spaghetti?' the landlady enquired.

'Heaven forbid,' said Don Paolo. 'Anything but spaghetti.'

Fortunately the landlady had other guests to serve.

The diningroom walls were lavishly adorned with coloured pages from a well-known illustrated weekly reproducing stirring incidents such as a train being saved from certain disaster by a signalman's daughter, an aeroplane being attacked by an eagle, cages of a menagerie being broken in the middle of a town, enabling wild beasts to escape and chase terrified passers-by. There were about a dozen other guests in the diningroom, and Don Paolo had the feeling that they were all watching him and talking about him. He tried not to raise his eyes from his plate. When coffee was served Signora Berenice sat at his table to tell him her troubles. She wore no corset, her huge breasts were flopping, and she was perspiring profusely after the hard work of serving lunch. When she mentioned Providence again, Don Paolo rudely interrupted.

'I'm sorry,' he said, 'but I do not belong to this diocese. I came here solely to rest and recuperate.'

The woman was offended and upset, and she fell silent. Don Paolo took advantage of her dismay to go and sun himself in

52

front of the hotel. Five or six youths were sitting round a small table and snoozing, with their hats on and cigarette stubs between their lips. At another table a little farther away other young men were playing cards and scattering yellow spittle like butterflies in the dust all round them. Nearly all of them wore the government party emblem in their buttonholes. Among them an old man in a broad-rimmed hat who looked like a retired actor was playing cards too and was puffing and blowing over his coffee. When he saw the strange priest he gave the signal against the evil eye.

'Iron, iron,' he called out.

The sleepers awoke immediately and they too took the precaution that was called for. Don Paolo recognized the rite and was about to respond with some profanity, but held his peace, because the behaviour of these idlers confirmed him in his priestly role. This gave him pleasure, so he stayed where he was. Opposite the hotel were the beflagged headquarters of the government party and the municipal portico with a medallion of King Umberto with the usual moustache. A lean doorkeeper was seated outside the entrance; he too had an impressive handle-bar moustache. He was surrounded by flies, and every now and then he cleared his throat and spat in a wide arc that reached the very middle of the small square. The strange priest's presence attracted to the hotel a number of beggars escorted by swarms of flies. A cripple who came bounding along on crutches begged for alms in the name of them all. Don Paolo fled back into the hotel where, however, the landlady was on the watch. She seized him by the arm, held him firmly, and started again in a tearful voice, 'In the name of Our Lady of Sorrows I implore you to listen to me,' she said in a heartbroken voice. 'There's a dying girl here, my only daughter, she's dying, don't be heartless.'

'I'm sorry,' said Don Paolo, at the limits of his patience. 'I have already told you, and I now repeat, that I do not belong to this diocese and that I am not authorized to undertake the cure of souls in these parts.'

'Not even in urgent cases?'

'In no circumstances whatever.'

Berenice could no longer restrain her tears. 'Very well,' she said, 'but at least let me talk to you. You might be able to give me some advice. The girl is on the point of death and is not willing to confess to the priest here, because he's a relative. Don't you understand that? When I told her a strange priest had arrived here, she was overjoyed. Jesus Christ sent him to me, she said immediately.'

'I'm sorry,' Don Paolo said. 'If it's so urgent, why don't you send for the priest of a neighbouring parish?'

'It may be too late,' said Berenice. 'And also it would be noticed, and the result would be a scandal. People would ask why the family priest had not been sent for.'

'I'm sorry,' Don Paolo said.

Berenice could not stifle her heart-rending tears. 'How can a girl be left to die without a priest and without a doctor?' she sobbed.

'Why without a doctor?' Don Paolo asked. 'What is this story?'

Berenice was afraid she had said too much, and looked all round her in alarm.

'Can I speak under the seal of silence?' she said.

Don Paolo indicated that she could. Speaking in an undertone, and without ceasing to weep, she told him what had happened.

'The girl isn't married and was going to have a baby. To avoid being dishonoured and dishonouring her family she tried to get rid of it by herself. Do you follow me? The law forbids that, as you know. If a doctor or midwife or anyone else helps a woman to get rid of it, it means imprisonment. That often happens, you have only to read the newspapers. There are some who come to an even worse end. The daughter of the notary at Fossa was four months gone and drank some bleach. A local girl who was in domestic service with the podestà went to Tivoli and drowned herself. My poor girl tried to get rid of it by herself. She had no choice but to risk death or face dishonour. She risked death, and she's dying. Can you imagine a poor mother's situation? I can't tell a doctor, because he'd report it, enquiries would be made, there'd be a trial, and the whole thing would come out. And the girl doesn't want the parish priest to be sent for, because he's a relative. Of course she has sinned, but there is forgiveness for everyone. Didn't Christ die on the cross for everyone?'

Don Paolo was baffled. This was a case not foreseen in the instructions Nunzio had given him.

'I sympathise with you, but I do not know what to advise you,' he said.

The poor priest's eyes were full of tears. Berenice noticed this. She signed to him to come with her as if she wanted to tell him something else, and he obediently followed her. She led the way up to the first floor. Slowly and noiselessly she opened the door of a small room. It was in semi-darkness and smelt of disinfectant. In a corner, under a big black crucifix, there was a small white iron bed.

'Bianchina,' Berenice said quietly. 'Look who has come.'

Something moved in the bed. A thin, pointed, ashen, childish little face, distorted by pain, appeared among the thick black hair scattered on the pillow. When Don Paolo realized that Berenice had gone it was too late. He stayed by the door, rooted to the spot. Several minutes passed like that. He was about to tiptoe out again, but he was stopped by the dying girl's big, wide-open eyes. How was he to explain to a human being on the point of death that he was not like other priests? He was utterly at a loss, he was paralysed. The dying girl went on looking at him with her big, feverish eyes.

'Courage,' he said, trying to produce a smile.

Slowly he tiptoed towards her, bent over her, kissed her hand. Her big eyes filled with tears. The light blanket showed the outline of her slender, dying body, her breasts that stood out like two lemons, her emaciated legs. 'My dear girl,' he said, 'I know everything. Please tell me nothing, don't abase yourself, don't renew your sufferings. You have no need to confess. You are confessed already.'

'Will you give me absolution?' she said.

'You are forgiven,' said the priest. 'Who could fail to forgive you? You have done penance, and it has been too hard.'

'If I die,' the girl said, 'where shall I go?'

'To the cemetery,' said the priest, 'like everyone else.'

'Shall I be saved?'

'Certainly, but don't be in a hurry to go, try to postpone your departure,' he said in a forced humerous tone.

He was holding the girl's hand between his two hands. His hands were burning.

'You're feverish too, are you ill perhaps?' she said.

Don Paolo nodded. 'Yes, I'm ill too,' he said with a smile, 'I too am doing penance.'

At that moment a voice called out from the street, 'Where's that priest who's going to Pietrasecca?'

Don Paolo wanted to go, but the girl held him back with one hand.

'Don't go so soon,' she said. 'When shall I see you again?'

'I shall think about you,' said Don Paolo.

'I don't believe you,' the girl said. 'You have other things to think about.'

'Don't you believe me? Why don't you believe me?' Don Paolo said.

He bent over her and looked her closely in the eyes. Silently the two looked at each other for some moments. Don Paolo was filled with a great pity. 'Why don't you believe me?' he said.

'Yes, now I believe you,' said the girl. 'I've never believed anything so much. You have extraordinary eyes that don't lie. I've never seen eyes like yours.'

'I shall think about you,' Don Paolo said.

The sound of an angry voice came through the window, 'Is that priest coming or not?'

'Now I must go,' Don Paolo said. 'Don't be afraid, you are forgiven. What will not be forgiven is this evil society that gave you the choice between death and dishonour.'

Old Magascià was sitting in the doorway of the hotel. He had finished his soup and was dipping his bread in his wine. He was a big, bearded man, broad-chested and massively built, and his left sleeve hung empty from his shoulder. 'Let us be off,' he said to Don Paolo. 'We have a long way to go.'

He made the priest take his place beside him. The two-wheeled cart moved off slowly, drawn by a donkey that advanced at a walking pace. Magascià was returning to Pietrasecca with the weekly supply of salt and tobacco.

'It's not a vehicle fit for a priest,' he said. 'Still less for a convalescent priest.'

'It doesn't matter,' Don Paolo said. 'How long ago did you lose your arm?'

'Two years ago come Candlemas,' said Magascià. 'But what's the use of complaining? God sends flies to plague old donkeys.' Then he went on, 'Had you met Berenice before? And do you know her daughter? That's a girl who gets herself talked about.'

The priest did not reply.

Magascià tied the reins to the wheel-drag and lit his pipe. 'There's no need to hold the reins,' he said. 'The donkey has come this way once a week for the past ten years and never makes a mistake. She knows where to stop and drink, where to relieve herself, and how long every climb and every downward slope takes.' Magascià had bought a new hat at Fossa, and he was wearing it on top of his old one. 'Her name is Bersagliera,' he went on, indicating the poor, skinny beast that was pulling the cart. 'Bersagliera ought to mean that she moves fast, but she's old now.'

'We all grow old,' said the priest.

'A donkey's a lucky beast,' said Magascià. 'A donkey generally works till it's twenty-four, a mule till it's twenty-two, and a horse till it's fifteen. But man, poor devil, goes on working till he's seventy or more. Why did God take pity on animals and not on men? But He can do what he likes, of course.'

No sooner had they left the town behind than the road started to mount. To the priest the mountains, valleys, hills and streams were old acquaintances. The places they passed through still bore signs of the earthquake; they looked like poor smashed and crumbling beehives that had been only partly reconstructed. On the road they met a small cafone family, husband, wife and baby all on the same donkey; the woman's breast was uncovered and she was feeding the baby.

'What's the crop looking like?' Magascià asked the man on the donkey.

'Bad,' the man answered.

'He's expecting a good harvest,' Magascià whispered in the priest's ear.

'Then why did he say the opposite?'

'To save himself from envy,' Magascià explained.

'And what's your crop looking like?' asked the priest.

Magascià made the sign of the cross. 'Disastrous,' he said.

'Are you afraid I might envy you?' said Don Paolo.

'Envy's in the air here,' Magascià explained.

Every now and then they came across stone-breakers sitting on the ground by the roadside near piles of stones, breaking the biggest stones with hammers. Magascià's cart went through the village of Lama dei Marsi. Ox horns were fixed to the walls of houses and hovels as a protection against the evil eye, and groups of silent old men and women and swarms of half-naked children were at the doorways. As they left the village they passed a chapel dedicated to the Madonna. Magascià made the sign of the cross and said to Don Paolo, 'It's a chapel dedicated to the Madonna delle Rose in memory of a miracle in days gone by. That year roses bloomed, cherries ripened and ewes lambed in January. Instead of rejoicing people were terrified, of course. Were not such blessings the harbingers of disaster? Sure enough, cholera came that summer.'

'Why was the chapel built?' Don Paolo said.

'To keep the Madonna quiet,' Magascià explained. 'You know that better than I do.' Then he went on, 'This years things look good too. Not in my case, of course, I mean it looks as if it's going to be a good year in general, as if other people's crops are going to be good. Who knows what disasters are in store?'

Beyond the chapel the road wound it way between two hills, crossed a bridge and entered the gorge of Pietrasecca, which at first was wide and then narrowed between steep slopes of grey rock. In flat areas formed of alluvial deposits between the rocks were tiny cultivated fields, small farms measured not in hectares but in *canes* or *cups*. More of these tiny fields were to be seen clinging like sticking plaster to the mountain sides. The cart advanced slowly. The road, which skirted a rocky stream-bed, was marked by deep ruts, like railway lines. As they climbed the sides of the valley were more and more rent and riven and poorer and poorer in vegetation. A herd of goats that were nibbling one by one at a few blades of new grass growing between the rocks turned their bearded faces towards the strange priest travelling in the salt and tobacco cart. When the slope grew steeper Magascià got out to lighten the load.

At a bend in the road they came to a small villa in Renaissance style built in a space partly dug out of the living rock. The doors and windows were barred.

'It was built by Don Simone Scaraffa, a local man who made good,' Magascià explained. 'Haven't you heard of him? He spent thirty years in Brazil and made a lot of money as a coffee planter, and he came home to enjoy being envied by us, that's why he had the villa built. But envy prevailed. During the first week he lived in it he went raving mad and had to be sent to Santa Maria di Collemaggio, the Aquila lunatic asylum, and he's still there. Was it worth the trouble?'

Further along they came to a wooden cross planted in a cairn of stones with a date inscribed on it.

'That's where Don Giulio, the Lama notary, was robbed and murdered,' said Magascià. 'At the post mortem they found he had been stabbed in the heart seven times. The person who did him that evil service was never discovered. Don Giulio lent out money at thirty per cent. After his death usury disappeared.'

The first houses of Pietrasecca appeared in the distance.

'It looks like the end of the world,' said the priest, seized with a shivering fit.

'It's a village of adversity,' said Magascià. 'It has twice been destroyed by floods and once by earthquake.'

'How many people are left there?' the priest asked.

'About forty families. Those who can go down to the plain,' said Magascià. 'Those who can, leave.'

They came to another cairn of stones by the roadside with a wooden cross and a date on it.

'That's where . . .' Magascià began.

'I'm not interested,' Don Paolo said irritably. 'It's where some other disaster happened.'

'How do you know?'

'You tell me about nothing but disasters. Are you trying to frighten me?'

Magascià laughed aloud. 'Not even the devil himself could

frighten a priest,' he said. 'Aren't you priests the administrators of death?'

When they reached Pietrasecca it was twilight. Don Paolo saw in front of him about sixty cracked and smoke-blackened little houses, a number of them with doors and windows barred, no doubt having been abandoned. The village seemed to have been built in a kind of funnel dug out of the end of the valley. Only two decent houses were to be seen. One of them, just beyond the bridge, was Matalena Ricotta's inn, where the priest was to stay; the other, at the end of the village, was bigger and older; it occupied a large area surrounded by a low wall and was the patrician home of the Colamartini family, the only old house in Pietrasecca that had survived the floods and the earthquakes. Beyond there was a small church, with a bell-tower and a porch facing the valley.

'Are services held there?' Don Paolo asked.

'There has been no parish priest here for the past thirty years,' Magascià said. 'A priest rarely comes here. It's a poor village. How could we support a priest?'

The little land there was between the rocks round the village was split up into a large number of small fields. The fields were so small and the stone walls that separated them were so numerous that they looked like the foundations of a destroyed town. Immediately beyond the village the gorge closed in to form a barrier, and no road led beyond. Two streams of water that came down the mountain sides met at the bottom of the valley and formed a rivulet that divided the village into two parts connected by a wooden bridge. Don Paolo looked round and could not conceal his alarm.

'You don't like it?' said Magascià.

'I don't understand why villages are built in such stupid places,' said the priest. 'If one had to escape from here, what choice would there be? It's not a village but a trap.'

'It lacks all conveniences,' said Magascià. 'The only advantage is that the authorities take little notice of us.'

Outside the inn there was a spring. A boy with a bleeding nose was bending over it and washing himself, and the water was quite red. Under the bridge a group of women and girls were kneeling at the edge of the rivulet, washing and beating clothes. When they caught sight of the priest they stopped as if they had been put under a spell.

Magascià drove the cart to the front door of the inn, where an old woman, the landlady, was waiting. She was short, thick-set, and wore several heavy petticoats. A very dignified old gentleman with a sporting gun on his shoulder appeared on the scene and welcomed the priest to his poor village. Magascià introduced him, 'This is Don Pasquale Colemartini,' he said.

Don Paolo excused himself, explaining that he was dead tired.

The woman took him straight to the room that had been prepared for him. 'What would you like for dinner?' she asked.

'Nothing,' said Don Paolo. 'All I want is to go to sleep.'

In the darkness of the little room he heard a woman's voice calling her child who was still out playing with other bigger boys.

'I'm coming, mummy, I'm just coming.'

CHAPTER 7

One Sunday morning a young donkey that had been bought at the last fair was christened in the space between the inn and the Pietrasecca bridge just under Don Paolo's window. A young man held the donkey by the halter while an old peasant beat it with a wooden cudgel. After each blow the two men shouted into the beast's ears, 'Garibaldi.'

That was the name that had been chosen for it. To the cafoni the name of Garibaldi meant strength and courage. The christening ceremony was protracted because naturally it took time to convince the donkey that that was its name. The man beat it on the crupper without anger, without impatience, without resentment, but hard, as if it were a mattress, and after each blow he and the young men shouted into the beast's ears, 'Garibaldi.'

The donkey looked at them, and after each blow it shook its head. The man beat it on the crupper, every blow on a different rib, and when he had completed the circuit he started all over again. Dozens and dozens of times the heroic name of Garibaldi resounded in the open space of Pietrasecca, alternating with the sound of the blows on the donkey's crupper. Eventually the man grew tired and said to the youth, 'That'll do. He must certainly know it by now.'

To make sure the youth took a handful of straw, went to the wooden bridge, and called out from a distance, holding up the straw, 'Garibaldi.'

The donkey trotted towards him.

'Yes, now he knows it,' the youth said.

Don Paolo was in bed, burning with fever. The journey had exhausted him. The reiterated invocation of the name of Garibaldi that came to him through the window surprised and alarmed him. Was it possible that the Republican Party could be so strong in such a remote village?

He asked the landlady what was happening.

'Nothing out of the way,' Matalena explained. 'Old Sciatàp is christening his new donkey.'

Old Sciatàp was known by that name throughout the valley. He had been christened by blows, just like his donkey. As a young man in America he had worked as general handyman to a fellow-villager, one Carlo Campanella, who sold coal in winter and ice in summer in Mulberry Street, New York. This fellow-villager, who at Pietrasecca had been Carlo Campanella, in New York had become Mr. Charles Little-Bell, Ice and Coal, and he treated his employee as a beast of burden. Whenever the poor beast complained Mr. Little-Bell shouted at him, 'Sciatàp.'

It seems that in English *sciatàp*[1] means 'be quiet'. When Sciatàp returned to Pietrasecca after several years' residence in America that was the only English word he knew, and he kept repeating it on every possible occasion, irrespective of its appropriateness or lack of it. His wife hardly dared open her mouth, because he immediately put his finger to his lips and shouted at her, 'Sciatàp.'

Thus the word ended by becoming part of the valley dialect. It was the only word of English known at Pietrasecca, the only element of modern and foreign culture that had entered the humble, ancient peasant tradition.

Don Paolo was curious to see the man, so he got out of bed and went to the window. Sciatàp and the donkey were making their way down towards the stream by an alley beside the bridge. At the beginning of the alley there was an old notice board with the words: RUBBISH MUST NOT BE TIPPED HERE. But at that very spot there was a great pile of rubbish, broken crockery, kitchen refuse and other garbage. Don Paolo smiled. Any kind of anti-conformism was pleasing to him, and not everyone could print clandestine leaflets, after all.

Matalena had given him her own bedroom on the first floor. A huge double bed occupied three-quarters of it, barely leaving space for a small table, a chair and an enamelled iron wash-basin. Over the bed there was a crucifix; Christ's limbs were twisted

[1] Pronounced 'Shut up'.

and emaciated, and his face was that of a poor hungry cafone. On the bedside table there was a small blue and white statuette of the Blessed Virgin in the act of crushing the serpent's head.

Meanwhile Don Paolo was no better. The mountain air did not bring about the rapid improvement for which he hoped. He stayed in bed nearly all day without being able to rest properly. The days and nights were interminable. The air was warm and heavy. The smell of cabbage and dried salt cod that floated up from the kitchen made him feel sick. To complete the priestly set-up Nunzio had provided him with some devotional books, a breviary, the *Eternal Maxims* of Sant' Alfonso Maria dei Liguori, the *Introduction to the Devout Life* of St. François de Sales, a *Life of San Camillo de Lellis*, a seventeenth-century Abruzzi saint, a *Life of San Giovanni Bosco*, a Piedmontese saint of the end of the nineteenth century, a *Life of San Gabriele dell' Addolorata*, and a manual of liturgy. To distract himself Don Paolo started browsing in these books, reading passages here and there, just as he would have done with anything else in print, whether it was a thriller or a prospectus for some chemical product. Some of this literature he had read before, either at home as a boy or in his years at school, and many of those pages and illustrations roused long forgotten memories. Symbols and memories of childish terrors slowly re-emerged from the deepest levels of his mind, and so the day came when he felt himself more and more attracted by those sacred books and ended by reading them every evening until his eyes grew tired. That was the state of mind he was in when he wrote his first letter to Nunzio. This was his only way of communicating with anyone without lying, though caution obliged him to sign himself Paolo Spada. 'I'm particularly grateful to you for the reading matter,' he wrote. 'What a strange and haunting impact it makes, I seem to have picked up the thread of my earlier life.'

In addition to the books, the extreme weakness to which his illness had reduced him helped to take him back to his adolescence, when he had been ill a couple of times; as an only son and because of his weak constitution he had always been looked after by his mother, grandmother, aunts and the maid, and had been surrounded by an atmosphere of warm feminine affection.

Though chance had forced him to take refuge in an environment several grades lower, from the social point of view, than that in which he had grown up, all the signs of life that reached him during the day at Pietrasecca between one period of reading and the next came from women and children, since all the grown men were out at work on the mountain or in the valley. Don Paolo had to use the little strength he had left to defend himself against old Matalena's impetuous warmth of heart.

'Saving your reverence, I could be your mother,' she said to him. 'Let me treat you like a son.'

'If you don't stop it, I shall leave,' Don Paolo said. 'I've no intention of returning to childhood.'

Matalena considered the presence of a priest in her inn as a blessing, and she continually found pretexts to come and make a fuss of him. As long as there was a priest in the house it could be considered to be protected against misfortune. Fear of disaster kept her perpetually on tenterhooks. The skull of a cow with two big curved horns was fixed solidly on the roof at the point where the two eaves met.

Don Paolo asked what the horns were for.

'They're a protection against the evil eye,' Matalena explained, making the sign of the cross, 'but only against the evil eye, they're no use against any other misfortune.'

Sure enough, cow's horns had not prevented Matalena's house from collapsing like many others in the 1915 earthquake.

'It was bigger than this house,' Matalena told him several times. 'My husband, God rest his soul, worked in Argentina for six years in order to be able to build it. He sent all the money back to me to pay the builders and carpenters. The house had been finished for barely three months when it collapsed, and I was buried in the cellar for a week. Actually I didn't know it was an earthquake, I thought it was the evil eye, and that only my house had collapsed. You can imagine my despair. When they cleared away the rubble on top of the cellar after a week and made an opening through which I could crawl out, I didn't have the courage. "Let me die here," I called out, "I don't want to go on living." I really had no more desire to live. But they reassured me. "Nearly the whole village has collapsed," they shouted down the hole, "nearly the whole of the Marsica has been destroyed, thirty communes have been razed to the ground and 50,000 dead have been counted so far." It was true. It hadn't been a private evil eye, but a visitation of God. What does the proverb say? Everyone's misfortune is no-one's misfortune. In the meantime my husband, God rest his soul, had had to come back to Italy to serve in the war, and no harm came to him, thanks be to God. After the war he went straight back to Argentina and worked for another five years to save money to re-build the house. Just when it was finished and he was coming back to enjoy it, he stopped writing. After six months of worrying I was sent for by the commune. I thought it was for a new tax. At all events, I went there, and the clerk said to me, "Your husband has been killed in an accident. He was run over by a car." I burst into tears and exclaimed, "There you are, envy struck him because he was coming home to enjoy the new house." '

Every time she told this story the poor woman had a protracted fit of weeping.

'A car accident is a misfortune that can happen to anyone,' Don Paolo said to put an end to it.

'Has it ever happened to you?'

'No.'

'And why not?' said Matalena. 'If you, as a priest, genuinely don't believe in the evil eye, why do you wear black? Why, saving your reverence, do you conceal your legs?'

But Matalena's extravagances were not sufficient to distract Don Paolo from his gloomy mood. Nunzio did not answer his letters, but every two or three days sent him an envelope full of newspaper cuttings with the most important political news. This was not enough to stop him from fretting. How long would he have to remain in this Siberia? Matalena's uninterrupted chatter soon acquired the monotony and naturalness of the sounds of the wind and the stream. Apart from that, Matalena was a pious woman who was proud of observing Wednesdays and Fridays and dedicating March to St Joseph, May to the Blessed Virgin, June to the Sacred Heart, and November to the dead. She had long since passed the canonical age and went about the house unkempt, untidy and with her corset undone. She took great pains over the priest's meals, and after every one of them waited for compliments that never came. Don Paolo had never been a gourmet, and in any case there was not much variety on the Pietrasecca menu; bread dipped in wine was still what he liked best. But every morning Matalena came up to his room to ask what she should cook for him that day, and this was a daily torment to him. One day he lost patience and told her to give him what all the other inhabitants of Pietrasecca generally ate. Matalena was offended by this, and to get her own back did as he asked. For breakfast she gave him a piece of maize bread and an onion, for lunch another big piece of the same bread with raw peppers seasoned with oil and salt, and for dinner a big helping of bean and potato soup. This diet lasted for only two days because, apart from the soup in the evening, Don Paolo's digestion could not stand it. The incident came to the cafoni's ears and caused them a great deal of amusement. It's easy to say that one should live like the poor. Matalena exploited her victory and reverted to the morning consultations. She had inflexible ideas about the treatment and cure of lung trouble.

'The best medicine for it is new laid eggs,' she said.

She kept a dozen chickens in the garden behind the inn, and whenever an egg was laid she took it straight to the sick room. If a chicken was late in laying Matalena would look for it, chase it, grab it and feel it to find out if an egg was really there. After making sure, she called up to the priest from the garden, 'Don't be impatient, it won't be long now.'

Don Paolo's confinement to his bed did not prevent him from following the life of the village. It was a primitive one. In the morning a woman named Chiarina came to the inn with a nanny goat, and Matalena took a bowl and milked it until she had drained it to the last drop. By this time the men had gone to work, and the women combed their hair at an open window or outside in the street, so as to get rid of the lice out of doors. At midday a woman named Filomena Sapone arrived at the inn with lettuce from her garden and a baby in her arms. She sat in the doorway of the inn, uncovered her breasts, and the baby did not wait to be asked. Filomena was the first to ask Don Paolo to confess her, but the priest replied coldly that he did not have permission to do so. This reply became generally known and caused great disappointment. There was a great deal of discussion about it in every family, at the baker's, the cobbler's, the carpenter's and the barber's. Matalena actually went and consulted Don Pasquale Colamartini, but the answer she got silenced her.

'If you annoy him, he'll end by going away.'

In the space between the inn and the wooden bridge the biggest boys practised marching and pre-military exercises. One day a quarrel broke out about who the current enemy was, for everyone complained that the enemy was changed too often. A deputation of three boys came and consulted Don Paolo in his room.

'Who's the enemy now?' they asked.

'What enemy?' the priest said in surprise.

'The hereditary enemy,' one of the boys explained.

The priest did not understand, or pretended not to understand.

'There are two sides in our exercise,' the boy explained. 'The Italians are on one side and the hereditary enemy is on the other. For a long time our teacher said the hereditary enemy was France and Yugoslavia. Then she said it was Germany. Then she said it was Japan. This morning she said, "Children, the new hereditary enemy is England." But in our school book there's a chapter called "The age-long friendship between England and Italy", so we don't know where we are. Which is wrong, our teacher or the book?'

'The book,' Don Paolo said. 'It was printed last year, so it's out of date.'

'Very well, then,' said the boys. 'Let us destroy the English hereditary enemy.'

'The English don't fight on land, but on water,' the priest said.

So the boys decided to fight in the stream. Don Paolo watched the battle from his window. The new hereditary enemy was rapidly defeated, but both sides emerged drenched to the skin.

The village boys constituted a kind of community apart, with its own laws, its own rites, and its own dialect. It had its own champions at stone-throwing, jumping over the stream, lizard hunting and pissing against the wind. Mothers shouted at their sons from morning till night, and the air often resounded with the most terrible curses, but these were so frequent that no-one took any notice.

In the afternoon, if it was fine, the women did their chores in the street. They hung out their washing, or peeled potatoes, or darned or mended, or deloused and scratched their children. The few who had nothing to do came and sat on the stones outside the inn. They were little bare-footed women, dressed in rags and with greasy hair, with the dim-witted expression of milked nanny goats. One of them was an old woman named Cesira, who was worn out with hunger and childbearing and perpetually complained of strange pains. The chief topic of conversation was childbearing. Annunziata was about to have her fourteenth. Lidovina had already had eighteen. The first was always the hardest; the others found the way made ready for them. One of the women, Annina, who was pregnant, touched her belly and said, 'Here's the head, here's one foot and here's the other. It must be a boy, because it sometimes kicks me.'

'That's in the hands of God,' said Cesira. 'God acts in accordance with our sins. Every pain is a visitation from heaven.'

When the women dropped their voices it was obvious that they were talking about the priest. What tales did Matalena make up to satisfy their curiosity? It was difficult to imagine. All the priest could hear was a querulous mumbling. The only thing that changed was the weather. The sultry heat was several times interrupted by short and violent downpours.

Don Paolo vented his ill-humour in the notes he wrote to Nunzio. 'I feel like a chunk of rotten meat surrounded by a swarm of flies,' he wrote. 'I shan't be able to stand this for long.' He could not rest, either sitting or standing or reading or writing.

A swarm of half-naked children completely covered in mud played from morning to night round a puddle created by the overflow from the fountain. They fled only on the appearance of Signorina Patrignani, the schoolmistress.

In fine weather most women, waiting for their husbands to come home in the evening, cooked their soup in the street in a brass pot or petrol can placed on a tripod over a fire surrounded by stones. The smell of beans being cooked filled the whole valley.

As soon as it got dark Signorina Cristina Colamartini arrived at the inn. The deep silence that fell as soon as she arrived indicated the respect in which she was held, and enabled Don Paolo to hear her solicitously asking how he was and making recommendations and giving advice to Matalena on how he should be treated. Then she would hurry away. Don Paolo had not seen her yet, but Matalena had told him that she had studied music for many years in a convent and was about to leave to take the veil.

'She's not a woman, she's an angel,' Matalena said of her, though she did not spare poisonous darts for the rest of the family. At home she had to look after her ninety-year-old grandmother as well as her parents and an aunt who were very old themselves. Her brother, an idler and a good-for-nothing, was nearly always away. 'If you're interested you can ask Magascià,' Matalena said. 'He has the most amazing stories about him.'

'I'm not interested,' the priest assured her.

Cassarola, the wise woman, was a less engaging and more troublesome character. At first she had feared that the priest's appearance on the scene would involve a reduction in her power and prestige, but she was reassured when she heard that he did not have permission to administer the sacraments. One day she presented herself to him to offer him her magic herbs as a cure for the cough. He refused them. She was a revolting hag, with a snub nose and protruding blubber lips. To show the priest how religious she was she started mumbling prayers, exorcisms and responses in barbarous Latin and unbuttoned her blouse at the neck to show him the medallions, scapularies, crosses and rosary that she had hanging from her neck as well as the sacred tattoos with which her arms were covered.

'God rules over good, but not over evil,' she announced with confidence. 'Otherwise why is it that he does not cure his priests when they are ill? Why don't you pray to God and rise cured from your bed?'

To get even with her Don Paolo offered a piece of advice of his own, 'Go to the devil,' he told her.

Fortunately the old woman had other clients. Antonia, the dressmaker, had a little girl who was ill. Cassarola prescribed a glass of wine for her every morning.

'But she's only three,' her mother said.

'Is she three already?' Casserola said. 'In that case you can give her a glass of wine in the evening too.'

Matalena's principal activity in her capacity as the priest's guardian and nurse was to explain to everybody over and over again why he was unable to administer the sacraments.

'Not even if he's paid double?'

'Not even then.'

'Not even if he's paid treble?'

'Not even then.'

'Not even if he's offered his own price on credit?'

'We don't give credit.'

The limited religious needs of the people of Pietrasecca, their baptisms, marriages and funerals were the responsibility of Don Cipriano, the parish priest of Lama, but the older he got the rarer his visits had become, with the result that a tacit compromise had gradually been arrived at between the blind laws of nature and the instincts of the local people, whose religious services had come to be concentrated in short periods of the year.

Marriages were celebrated in October and November, and children were born between May and July. It was a kind of conscription from which there were very few exemptions. Many babies died in the first few months. It was a periodic massacre of the innocents.

On Sunday mornings a number of women went down to Lama for mass. They wore black shawls over their shoulders and black handkerchiefs on their heads, because showing their hair would have been immodest, and black shoes and stockings. From his window Don Paolo watched them going and coming back. The oldest walked with their beads in their hand, letting them run slowly between thumb and first finger. When they were overtaken by the horse and trap in which Don Pasquale and Signorina Cristina went to mass they bowed very respectfully. But there were occasions on which the lack of a parish priest was felt acutely; not even Matalena's watchfulness saved Don Paolo from some disagreeable incidents.

A peasant woman, Teresa Scaraffa, dreamed one night that the baby she was expecting was going to be born blind. Early next morning the poor woman came to see Don Paolo and went down on her knees at his bedside. 'I dreamed my baby is going to be born blind. Only you can save it,' she said.

'I'm sorry, my poor woman, but I can do nothing,' the priest replied.

The woman started weeping and imploring him. 'I don't want my baby to be blind. Why should others be able to see and not he?'

Her round yellowish face made her look like an old sheep. Don Paolo tried to get the idea out of her head, but without success.

'I dreamed it,' she said. 'I saw it with my own eyes. If you don't help me, the child will be blind.'

She would not go away. Don Paolo was very conscious of the fact that if he pretended to say prayers or carry out exorcism in one case the inn would immediately be besieged by other applicants whom it would be impossible to refuse. They would all say that, as he had helped Teresa Scaraffa, he must help them too. The news would reach the villages down on the plain. Apart from behaving like a fraud and a clown, he would end by attracting the attention of the authorities.

So he called Matalena and said to her, 'Please see this woman out of my room, if necessary by force. I'm not interested in her dreams.'

At this Teresa rose like a fury and started yelling, 'Why should my baby be blind? Why should other babies be able to see and not mine?'

Teresa waited for a reply, and Don Paolo coldly repeated that he could do nothing, but in vain. Again the woman went down on her knees with her face on the floor, and she began hitting it with her head and tearing out her hair. She actually pulled out whole chunks of it and screamed the most senseless things.

'Why should he be blind? Why? Tell me why. At least I want to know why. Others will be able to see and he won't. Others will go to school and he won't be able to. Others will rob him and he won't notice it. Others will mock him and he won't be able to see them, and when he's grown up no woman will have anything to do with him.'

Then she rose to her feet and seemed suddenly to have calmed down.

'Now I know what to do,' she said. 'I'll throw myself out of the window, and he'll die with me.'

The woman made for the window, and in her frantic, hysterical state Don Paolo had no doubt that she would throw herself out of it. She was on the window sill when a cry from the priest stopped her, 'I'll do what you ask,' he said. 'What do you want me to do?'

Matalena hurried to fetch the keys of the church, which were kept in the Colamartini house, and then she went to the church and fetched a glass of holy water. Don Paolo was silent and humiliated.

Teresa held out her swollen belly to the priest.

'The head must be here,' she said, 'the eyes must be there.'

At the place Teresa indicated the priest twice made the sign of the cross, once for each eye, and he moved his lips as if he were praying.

'Now he'll be all right,' the woman said with relief. 'It won't happen now. Thank you.'

She went away, but came back a little later with a dead hen.

'You again?' the priest exclaimed angrily.

The woman showed him the hen.

'I can't accept it,' Don Paolo replied. 'Priests cannot accept gifts.'

The woman protested. 'In that case it's no use,' she said. 'If you don't take the hen the grace won't work and the child will be born blind.'

'Grace is free,' Don Paolo said.

'There's no such thing as free grace,' the woman said.

To cut things short she walked out, leaving the expiatory sacrifice on the table.

This happened on a Saturday. That was the day on which Magascià went down to Fossa with his cart to fetch the weekly supply of salt and tobacco. Don Paolo immediately sent for him and gave him a letter to post to Nunzio. 'I've had enough,' he wrote. 'I'm not staying here. I'm leaving for Rome as soon as my temperature's normal.'

Chapter 8

He was sitting on a bench under a rowan tree, writing to Nunzio. Instead of a desk he had on his knees a three-cornered box that Matalena used to avoid wetting her feet and her skirts when doing her washing at the stream. A pleasing smell of fresh bread came from the baker's.

'Though you haven't answered me, I'm writing to you again to save me from talking to myself and making people who see me think I've gone crazy. If this lasts much longer, my lungs may get better, but at the expense of my brain. This is not a harmless bit of play-acting . . .'

A procession of ants was coming down the tree trunk and making its way along the ground. Every ant carried a load. He watched the procession for a time, and then went back to his writing:

'If only I could go to sleep here and wake up next morning, saddle the donkey and go to the vineyard. If only I could go to sleep and wake up, not just with healthy lungs, but with the brain of an ordinary man, free of all abstractions. If only I could go back to ordinary, real life. Digging, ploughing, sowing, reaping, earning a living and talking to the other men on Sundays. Obeying the law that says: Thou shalt earn thy daily bread in the sweat of they brow. When I come to think of it, perhaps the real cause of my distress is my defiance of the ancient law, my way of living in cafés, libraries and hotels, my having broken the chain that for centuries linked my forefathers to the soil. Perhaps I feel an outcast, not so much because of my disobedience to the arbitrary decrees of the party in power, but because of my infringement of the older law that said: Thou shalt earn thy living in the sweat of thy brow. I have ceased to be a peasant, but I have not become a politician. It is impossible for me to return to the soil, but still more impossible to return to the world of illusions in which I have been living up to now. Strange thoughts are coming to me. Please listen.'

He was still writing when a girl from Fossa dei Marsi arrived at Pietrasecca in Magascià's cart.

'The inn's over there, on the right beyond the bridge,' the carter explained.

The girl came hurrying along and said to Matalena, 'Is there a Don Paolo Spada staying here?'

Matalena was jealous of her priest, and before answering the stranger she said, 'Why do you ask?'

'He saved me when I was on the point of death, and I want to thank him.'

'The Don Paolo who's staying here is not a doctor but a priest,' said Matalena.

'Perhaps he's neither a priest nor a doctor but a saint,' said the girl. 'I was on the point of death, he came, he touched my hand, and I was saved.'

Matalena was proud of having a priest at her inn, but the idea of having a saint who actually performed miracles while still living disturbed and upset her.

'Yes, he's a real saint,' she said, to avoid appearing to be unable to recognize a saint when she saw one. 'He's staying here doing penance, like a true man of God. For that reason I'm not sure that he will be willing to see you. You see, he's from a different diocese.'

'Perhaps he's actually more than a saint,' the girl from Fossa said, 'I have an idea he might be Jesus Himself.'

This was too much for Matalena, who sat down on a stool and murmured, 'Are you mad? What makes you think he might be Jesus Himself? Why should Jesus come to my inn? Isn't He in heaven on his Father's right hand?'

Matalena spoke softly, so that her first-floor lodger, if he were really He, should not overhear her doubting words.

'It would not be the first time that Jesus has disguised Himself and come down to earth to see how the poor are living,' the girl from Fossa replied. Then she added in a little trickle of a voice, 'Have you noticed whether his hands and feet are pierced? That is the surest way of telling. Never mind how much he disguises himself, if he is really He, he could not get rid of the stigmata.'

Matalena was suddenly seized with unspeakable excitement. She was not prepared for such a happening. Heavens, what was she to do? His evening meal was ready; it consisted of two eggs and a lettuce salad. She blushed at the sight of that meagre repast. Two eggs and a salad for the Son of God? How disgraceful. One ought at least to kill a lamb. But supposing he was not He?

'What makes you suppose that perhaps it is He? What gave you the idea? Tell me the truth, are you mad?' said Matalena, seized with doubt.

'I recognized him by his voice,' the girl replied. 'When he appeared he took my hand and before I had time to say anything he said, "Courage, I know everything." I realized at once that that was no human voice. I know men, they don't talk like that. I have an uncle who's a priest, he's the parish priest of Fossa, he doesn't talk like that.'

'Tell me what to do if he's really Jesus,' Matalena said. 'Should I warn Don Cipriano? Tell the carabinieri?'

A copy of police regulations was displayed on the inn door, but the arrival of Jesus was not an eventuality foreseen in them.

With bated breath the two women tiptoed up to the first-floor and knocked at the door. There was no answer. Slowly they opened it. The room was empty. Matalena thought she was going to faint.

'He's gone,' she said.

The two women looked at each other in consternation: Then they heard a cough in the garden, and they dashed there immediately. Don Paolo was sitting on a bench under the little rowan tree with some sheets of paper in his hand.

'Who wants me?' he said.

The two women approached timidly.

'I'm Bianchina,' the girl said. 'Bianchina Girasole, from Fossa dei Marsi, Berenice's daughter. Don't you recognize me? Don't you remember me?'

'I'm delighted to see that you're alive,' Don Paolo said, with a smile. 'I've often thought about you.'

'So you kept your promise?' Bianchina exclaimed, radiant with joy.

'Don't you believe me?'

'I believe you,' said Bianchina. 'I was on the point of death and abandoned by everyone, and you came and touched my hand and saved me.'

Don Paolo had another fit of coughing. The sun had set, and the cold shadows of night were mounting from the bottom of the valley. He rose, and the two women followed him to his room. He was tired, and sat on the edge of the bed. Bianchina stayed near the door, but then plucked up courage and said in a tremulous voice, 'Please show me your hands.'

Don Paolo smiled. 'Do you want to tell my fortune?' he asked.

Bianchina carefully examined his hands. There was no trace of stigmata, no trace of the crucifixion. He was not Jesus. He was a saint, but not Jesus.

'All the better,' Bianchina said, looking pleased. 'I prefer you to be a man.'

'Did you think I was a ghost?' Don Paolo said with a smile.

Matalena too sighed with relief and went back to her kitchen. The two remained silent for a moment.

'I see that you're ill,' the girl said. 'Is there anything I can do for you?'

'No, thank you,' said Don Paolo.

The girl's pretty face looked even prettier against the dark rectangle of the door. Perhaps her neck was rather thin, and her red mouth was rather big, and when she laughed it was perhaps rather too big, but the liveliness of her eyes and gestures and her outspokenness and candour gave her an almost childish naturalness and charm.

'My mother wants to throw me out,' she said with a grimace of annoyance.

'Why?'

Bianchina sought for words. 'She thinks I'm the dishonour of the family. Perhaps she's right. If I like a man, I can't resist him. You agree with my mother, of course.'

'I don't know,' said Paolo. 'I've never been a mother.'

Bianchina burst out laughing, but quickly relapsed into gloom.

'Even if my mother were willing to put up with me I couldn't go on living at home,' she said. 'The atmosphere's too stuffy. Didn't you notice it?'

'What do you want to do?' said the priest.

'Isn't there anything I can do for you?'

'It seems to me that you ought to be thinking about yourself,' said the priest. 'What will you do if your mother throws you out?'

'I don't know,' Bianchina said. 'There's nothing I can do. If I knit, I drop the stitches. If I sew, I prick my fingers. If I try gardening I hit my feet with the mattock. The nuns taught me how to make sweets and to do embroidery and the Gregorian chant. Could I go and sing the *Magnificat* and *Salve Regina* on the variety stage?'

'But if there's nothing you can do, what would you do for me?' the priest asked.

'Anything, provided I could stay near you.'

'Meanwhile,' said the priest, 'where are you going to stay tonight?' .

It was an awkward problem. Don Paolo sighed, and Bianchina had tears in her eyes.

'There's an old schoolfriend of mine here at Pietrasecca, Cristina Colamartini. She's a little saint too. Perhaps she'll help me. Do you know her?'

This was just the time when Cristina paid her daily visit to the inn. Matalena told her of Bianchina Girasole's arrival, and she appeared in the doorway of the sickroom, which had been left open. Bianchina fell on her neck and embraced her at length. 'How beautiful you've got,' she kept repeating.

Matalena produced a second chair, and Cristina was able to sit down and tidy her ruffled hair. So far Don Paolo had only heard her voice, and now he was able to note that the rest of her harmonized perfectly with it. She was a really lovely creature. Her face was thin and pointed, but perfectly shaped, and she was tall and slender. She wore a black pinafore with a high neck and long sleeves, like a schoolgirl, an impression accentuated by her jet black hair, which was parted in the middle, slightly waved at the temples and gathered at the back of the neck in a large knot of tiny curls. She said good evening to the priest and apologized for disturbing him.

'What? You haven't met yet?' Bianchina said. 'This is Cristina, and she was my first love. We spent three years together at the same convent school. She was at the top of the class and I was at the bottom, of course, but that was another reason for liking each other.' Then she went on, 'There's always a time in life when you go back to your first love. And this,' she said to Cristina, pointing to Don Paolo, 'is a saint to whom I owe my life.'

Don Paolo took no notice of what Bianchina was saying because he was enchanted by Cristina. A girl like this at Pietrasecca? He could not believe his eyes. Her face and hands had the pallor of white roses, but there was nothing in nature to compare with the light of her eyes and the grace of her smile.

'We're tiring Don Paolo with our chatter,' Cristina said, blushing and rising to leave.

'I'm coming with you,' said Bianchina. 'You wouldn't want to leave me alone with a priest, would you? I'll come back in the morning,' she added, turning to Don Paolo. 'You haven't answered the question I asked you yet.'

Don Paolo's change of mood did not escape Matalena's notice though she did not guess the real reason for it.

'Magascià came and told me some strange stories about that girl,' she said, but she did not go on, because he was not listening.

'I feel much better,' he said. 'It's extraordinary, but I feel almost completely well again.'

However, he hardly slept that night. He earned a severe rebuke from Matalena when she brought him his breakfast.

'You look terrible,' she said. 'People will think I don't look after you properly.'

The priest was staring out of the window.

'I'm surprised Donna Cristina put that girl up for the night after all the talk there has been about her and her brother,' she said.

Through the open window the priest saw Cristina leaving her house. He hurriedly dressed and went downstairs. 'Good morning,' he said with a smile. 'Good morning. You're out early.'

'I'm delighted at having a chance to talk to you for a moment before Bianchina appears,' Cristina said. 'You have no idea of the enormous influence over her that you have acquired.'

'She has too much imagination,' Don Paolo said apologetically.

'Yes, she has had some terrible experiences,' Cristina said. 'She told me some frightening things about herself last night. They kept me awake all night. Believe me, you're the only person who can save her now.'

'Will Bianchina agree to be saved? In what sense?' Don Paolo said.

'You can point out the right path to her.'

Don Paolo did not conceal his doubts. 'Will Bianchina follow that path alone and unaccompanied? I certainly cannot accompany her,' he said.

'You will accompany her with your thoughts,' Cristina said. 'Perhaps that will be sufficient. You have no idea of the impact made on her during her illness by your simple promise to think of her sometimes. She told me that she has lived in the company of your thoughts ever since.'

'I have in fact often thought about her,' the priest admitted. 'But may I go on? You do not know it, Signorina, but my character is already excessively inclined to fixed ideas.'

This confidence visibly embarrassed Cristina. 'What I meant,' she said with a blush, 'was that you should remember her in your prayers.'

Bianchina came hurrying along with her hair flying in the wind. 'What are you two plotting against me?' she said.

'I must go and get breakfast for the rest of the family,' Cristina announced. 'I'll see you later.'

Don Paolo invited Bianchina to keep him company for a while in the garden next to the inn.

'Come and sit here,' he said.

'I hope you have thought about what I asked you,' the girl said. 'Can I do anything for you?' Then she went on, 'I don't want to go back to the empty life I've lived so far. I want at least to

81

see you every now and then. But I don't want to be a parasite.'

'Yes, I need you,' Don Paolo said.

'Really?' Bianchina exclaimed, jumping to her feet. 'Will you take me with you when you go back to your diocese?'

'I need you immediately,' he said.

'Aren't you afraid of scandal? In a little place like this everything is known immediately.'

'I'm not asking you for what you are now imagining.'

'It's all I have,' said Bianchina.

'You have many other things,' Don Paolo said.

'You think so? What, for instance?'

'Listen to me seriously,' Don Paolo said. 'I need to send someone to a friend of mine in Rome on a personal and rather delicate mission. You are the only person whom I can ask to do this for me.'

'Why am I the only person?'

'You're the only one I can trust.'

'Are you pulling my leg? Forgive me, I don't mean to doubt what you say, but look, no-one has ever talked to me like that before. I've never expected anyone to trust me.'

'But I trust you.'

'Is this trip to Rome for something important?'

'Very important indeed,' said Don Paolo. 'But unfortunately I can't tell you what it is. There are secrets about which priests cannot speak. Don't you trust me?'

'I'd throw myself into a fiery furnace for you,' Bianchina said seriously. Then she added, 'Is it a matter of secrets of the confessional?'

Don Paolo nodded.

'Now listen to me carefully, Bianchina,' he said. 'You must tell no-one that you're going to Rome on my account. Not even Cristina or your mother. You must think up some excuse.'

'Making up lies is one of my few specialities,' said Bianchina. 'But it's the first time I've had to do it for a priest. Are there such things as holy lies, then?'

'They're not real lies, but stratagems,' said Don Paolo.

'Will you think about me while I'm away?'

'Yes, I promise,' Don Paolo said.

'You won't be unfaithful to me with Cristina?'

'Don't talk nonsense.'

Don Paolo withdrew to his room to write out the message the girl was to take. 'We can't go on nursing illusions,' was his conclusion.

CHAPTER 9

Don Paolo was torn between worrying about Bianchina, who left unsuspectingly for Rome on the risky business of restoring contact with his clandestine organization, and an ardent desire to see Cristina again, for the girl completely captivated him. To aggravate his anxiety, on the days that followed Cristina did not reappear at Matalena's inn. Had she perhaps realized that she had lit a dangerous flame in Don Paolo? Did she want to resist temptation. He found an excuse to send Matalena on a voyage of exploration. No, Cristina's thoughts were elsewhere, for the day when she was to leave for the convent had been approaching. Her family seemed resigned, her outfit was ready, the Mother Superior had been informed. But on the eve of her departure Cristina's old grandmother, who had always opposed the idea, had succeeded in persuading Don Pasquale to talk to the girl. The conversation between father and daughter had been painful.

'Your grandmother is right,' he said. 'You know the state to which we are reduced. I can't count on your brother. He's an idler and a good-for-nothing, and we don't even know where he is. If you go too I shall be left alone with your grandmother, your mother and your aunt, three old women who are incapable of any kind of work, and we shall be left to end our lives in the care of some servant girl who will rob us of the little we have left.'

After a long fit of weeping Cristina ended by giving in. 'Father,' she said, 'I shall do nothing against your will.'

Her father was very fond of her, and was not irrevocably opposed to her vocation; all he asked her, therefore, was to postpone it.

'If God wants you, He will provide,' he said.

For once the people of Pietrasecca were unanimously on the grandmother's side. The general opinion was that a daughter belonged primarily to her family and only secondarily to the

Church. Don Paolo had already heard strange stories about Cristina's grandmother, who terrorized the Colamartini household. She wanted Cristina to get married. Almost nothing was left of the family heritage, and only a good marriage could save it, but that was an argument that Don Pasquale could not put to his daughter, who sadly and silently and uncomplainingly went on with the housekeeping. She looked after the chickens, made the beds, swept the rooms and the staircase, helped her aunt and her mother in the kitchen, ironed the linen and looked after the bees in the garden. She went out rarely, and then only for a few moments. But one morning, when Don Paolo was in Matalena's garden, she suddenly appeared with a bunch of chives to transplant. Don Paolo was delighted. The morning light wrapped the girl as if in a golden veil. Some bees buzzed round her head as round a flower, and to the priest the flower looked incredibly beautiful, though rather pale. He plucked up courage and said to her, 'Forgive me if I'm indiscreet, but are you perhaps unhappy at not yet having left for the convent?'

Cristina smiled. 'Don't think me discourteous,' she said, 'if I answer you with three words that I was taught as a child and have not forgotten: *Jesus autem tacebat.* Perhaps those words impressed me more than anything else in the Bible. Jesus taught us to be silent under torment.'

'Is secular life a torment to you?' Don Paolo said. 'Cannot abandoning one's family be equivalent to a flight?'

Cristina looked at the priest a trifle uncertainly. Was he playing the part of devil's advocate in order to put her to the test?

'True flight,' she said, 'is distancing oneself from God. Those who are distant from God are distant from their fellows.'

'Cannot one live a decent life with one's family?' Don Paolo asked. 'Cannot one meditate and pray at home?'

'We are not called on to be bold, but to be docile and let ourselves be helped,' Cristina said. 'I read this morning in a book written by a French nun: "Does the newborn babe raise itself to the mother's breast? Or does not the mother take the little one and bend gently over it to feed and comfort it?" We are all like newborn babies of the Church who is our mother.'

These were conventional arguments. Don Paolo and Cristina hardly knew each other. The priest's answer was conventional too.

'I do not propose to embark on a theological discussion with you,' he said. 'But here we are in a country of great poverty in the economic respect and even greater poverty in the spiritual respect. If a cafone succeeds in mastering his animal instincts he becomes a Franciscan friar; if a girl succeeds in freeing herself from servitude to her body, she takes the veil. Don't you think that that is the source of many evils? Don't you think it is better to live and struggle among one's fellows than to shut oneself up in an ivory tower?'

'He who has faith and is absorbed in prayer is never separated from his fellows,' Cristina said. 'Only the soul that does not know God is a leaf detached from the trees, a solitary leaf that falls to the ground, shrivels and rots. But the soul that is given to God is like a leaf attached to the tree. Through the sap that nourishes it it communicates with the branches, the trunk, the roots, the earth. Don't you believe that?'

Don Paolo smiled. Apart from anything else, having to express himself in language compatible with his ecclesiastical habit put him at an obvious disadvantage.

'But you know these things better than I do,' the girl went on with a smile. 'Is the examination over?'

'I assure you it was not intended to be an examination,' said Don Paolo. 'During my first few days here I found the enforced loneliness very trying, but now I'm beginning to endure it. I now have leisure to think about certain things that it is not easy to think about when leading an active life. I should like to discuss them with you.'

'One must let oneself be carried along by the silence,' Cristina said with a smile, 'like an unconscious man carried along by a deep stream. Only then does God speak to us.'

She shook hands with Don Paolo and said cordially, 'I hope we shall meet again. I too like talking to you.'

Don Paolo went back to his room, sat down at the little table, took a notebook, and wrote in it 'Conversations with Cristina'. After thinking for a short time he began to write: 'Never has lying been so repugnant to me as it is now. As long as it's a mere matter of deceiving the police, well and good, it may even amuse me. But what torment it is to deceive Cristina, to engage in play-acting with her, to hush up what I would like to say if I could talk to her freely. My dear Cristina, I shall talk to you freely in this notebook. At least here I shall have no need to pretend.'

Conversation with Cristina was also conversation with himself. 'It seems to me that things have come to a head. I can't go on like this. Perhaps that's why I'm ill.'

The hand with which he was writing stopped. He rose and went over to the window. The Colamartini house seemed uninhabited; its grey, compact outline stood out against the black mountain. It looked like a fortress. Which was Cristina's room? Don Paolo went back to the table and started writing again: 'Staying in this little village, contact with these primitive people, meeting this girl, have taken me back to myself as I was fifteen years ago. In this lovely Cristina I have found many features of my own adolescence, I might almost say a portrait of myself, an embellished and idealized portrait, a female version, of course, but basically a reflection of what I myself felt and thought at that time; the same infatuation with the absolute, the same rejection of the compromises and pretences of ordinary life, even the same readiness for self-sacrifice. When I passed through my native village at night I saw once more the haunts of selfishness and hypocrisy from which I fled. I felt like a dead man revisiting the scenes of his life. The only sound was the barking of dogs, which seemed to me to be a faithful transcription of the thoughts of most of the inhabitants of the village who were asleep at that moment. No, I do not in the least regret having cut myself off from that. The cause of my pain is the question whether I have been faithful to my promise.'

He remembered his first joining a socialist group. He had left the Church, not because he doubted the correctness of its dogmas or the efficacy of the sacraments, but because it seemed to him to identify itself with a corrupt, petty, and cruel society that it should have combated. When he first became a socialist that had been his only motive. He was not yet a Marxist; that he became later after joining the socialist fold. He accepted Marxism 'as the rule of the new community'. In the meantime had that community not itself become a synagogue? 'Alas for all enterprises the declared aim of which is the salvation of the world. They seem to be the surest traps leading to self-destruction.' Don Paolo decided that his return to Italy had been basically an attempt to escape that professionalism, to return to the ranks, to go back and find the clue to the complicated issue.

These thoughts gave him no peace. At meals he was silent and more distracted than ever. Matalena tried talking to him, but in vain, he might have been deaf. To her great offence and sorrow he took not the slightest notice of what he was eating. As soon as he had finished his coffee he went out into the garden, sat on the bench under the rowan tree, and started writing again, with the notebook resting on his knees: 'Is it possible to take part in political life, to put oneself in the service of a party and remain sincere? Has not truth for me become party truth and justice party justice? Have not the interests of the organization ended in my case too by getting the better of all moral values, which are despised as petty bourgeois prejudices, and have those interests not become the supreme value? Have I, then, escaped from the opportunism of a decadent Church only to end up in the Machiavellism of a political sect? If these are dangerous cracks in the revolutionary consciousness, if they are ideas that must be banished from it, how is one to confront in good faith the risks of the conspiratorial struggle?'

Don Paolo reread what he had written and realised that all he had done was to write down a series of questions. Meanwhile a flock of sparrows and some wild pigeons had started hopping and fluttering about him as in an aviary. At one point some women who were watching the scene from a distance decided that he was talking to them; the poor priest, having no-one else to talk to, was in fact talking to himself. The women immediately hurried to the inn to spread the news of this marvel.

'Your priest,' they said to Matalena, 'is talking to the birds, just like St Francis.'

'Yes,' she replied, 'he's a saint, a real saint.'

CHAPTER 10

'We ought to see each other more often,' Don Paolo, over-coming his shyness, said to Cristina. 'Believe me, talking to you does me good.'

'My father has made the same suggestion,' the girl said with a smile. 'He says that so far we have been very inhospitable towards you. If you knew about our family troubles, you would forgive us.'

'So far I've had to spend nearly all my time in bed,' Don Paolo said, 'but during the remainder of my stay at Pietrasecca I shall be very willing to allow myself to be spoilt, if not by your family, then by you.'

Meanwhile the fresh air of Pietrasecca had restored some of its lost naturalness to Don Paolo's face. It was still dark and shadowed, but the wrinkles had vanished.

'I don't want to boast, but you look twenty years younger than when you arrived here,' Matalena said.

Cristina came to an agreement with Matalena about some improvements to be introduced into the care of her guest. The girl had a real genius for creating beauty out of nothing, and it was marvellous to see how Don Paolo's room became cool, fresh and flower-filled at her hands. As Don Paolo's talks with her grew more frequent they became more frank and sincere. At first Don Paolo still felt inhibited by having to avoid rousing suspicion about his identity, but as he became more familiar with Cristina's ingenuousness his worries on that score diminished. He let himself go in stories about his youth, his village, his first studies, his early religious experiences and his first steps in real life, taking care only to make the background of his memories his own diocese and not that of the Marsi. Without realizing it, he ended by infusing life into his ficti-tious role, nourishing it with the still vivid memories of his youth. There was so much spontaneity, sincerity and warmth in his talk that Cristina was quite carried away by it.

Once she said to him, 'If I were to write down what you say and read it to someone without disclosing anything about you, I bet the verdict would be that a boy of eighteen was responsible for it.'

Their liking for each other made them more conciliatory in the arguments that sometimes broke out between them. What Don Paolo dared not say to her he confided to his diary, with tender expressions of love. He often postponed writing in his diary until late at night. He would write a phrase and then cross it out, write it again and again cross it out.

One morning when he opened his window he saw Cristina standing on a little balcony on the second floor of her house. She immediately smiled and greeted him with a slight motion of her head, and then withdrew. He had the impression that she greeted him as if she had been waiting for him to appear. This was the first time he had seen anyone on that balcony, which faced his window and was always closed. But perhaps new life was beginning for it. In fact that morning Cristina had put two pots of geraniums on it. This novelty did not escape the sharp eyes of Matalena, who was openly critical.

'I don't see why she puts geraniums on a balcony that never gets any sun,' she said.

'I expect she's trying an experiment,' said the priest. 'There's no need to discourage her.'

'I didn't think Donna Cristina was a girl who tried experiments,' Matalena said.

But the frequent waterings to which Cristina henceforward subjected the two pots increased Matalena's concern.

'What on earth is the matter with Donna Cristina?' she said. 'With all that water and no sun those geraniums will die.'

She also noticed that Don Paolo's small work table had been moved over to the window. This took her breath away.

'You always used to complain about the draught,' she said. She realized what was up, but did not dare call it by its real name. So she restricted herself to saying, 'I never imagined that a priest would encourage certain whims.'

Matalena was not jealous, but she was upset and alarmed. Her attitude to her priest was of complete traditional respect, and not even in her dreams would she have tolerated any ambiguity in her own feelings towards him. Also she was old, and had accepted the fact. But Don Paolo was 'her' priest, 'her' protector, and not the protector of others, not even of the Colamartini family. She started feeling that a closer friendship with Cristina might induce the priest to accept hospitality in the Colamartini house. Faced with this threat, she defended herself by every means in her power. Thus that very same day she refused a hare that Cristina wanted to give her to cook for Don Paolo. It was a way of telling the girl that her little game had been discovered.

'Thank you, but he doesn't like game,' she said drily, rejecting the gift.

Cristina seemed to fall from the clouds. 'Couldn't you ask him?' she said. 'Perhaps you're mistaken.'

'It's not necessary,' said Matalena. 'Besides, he's my guest, and if he wants anything it's up to me to provide it.'

'He's only your lodger,' Cristina said. 'And my father is perfectly entitled to give a present to anyone he chooses.'

But it probably struck her that it would not be very becoming to continue with that conversation, and so she hurried away before Don Paolo, whose footsteps she heard on the stairs, made his appearance.

Innocent though Cristina was in the matter, it was actually she who was in the wrong. It was not correct to say that to Matalena Don Paolo was an ordinary lodger. Without his realizing it, his importance to her had grown from day to day. To her it mattered little that he refrained from exercising his ministry at Pietrasecca, since that in no way detracted from the sacred nature of his presence. On the contrary, as he did not administer the sacraments the divine investiture that was in him was inaccessible to the other inhabitants of Pietrasecca and remained concentrated and intact, as it were, in his mere presence. As a result his exorcising efficacy could be only reinforced.

She felt differently about him from day to day; sometimes she felt she was his nurse, and sometimes she felt like an orphan or a widow; and, strangely enough, as time passed she felt more and more often like an orphan rather than a widow or a nurse. In his encounters with her Don Paolo prudently adopted the expedient of not understanding.

'I can't imagine this house without you,' she began saying more and more often. 'I couldn't live without your protection, without it the evil eye and envy would afflict the house immediately, while as it is they keep away out of respect for your consecrated presence.'

But she was not naïve enough to imagine that Don Paolo was likely to remain inactive for long in this poor mountain village, and a crazy plan began to develop in her primitive mind; a plan, that is, to keep 'her' priest at Pietrasecca and through him dominate the whole valley.

'Why don't you have yourself transferred here by the Pope?' she said to him on the evening after her breeze with Cristina. 'Do you know the Pope personally?'

'Why should I be transferred here?' said Don Paolo.

'The climate is good, and if you leave you'll be ill again, so it would be much better for you to be transferred here. You could administer the sacraments, hold confessions, conduct baptisms and funeral services. There's no need to worry about the valley being a poor one. If you stayed here, I'd see about meeting your expenses.'

'One more word on that subject,' Don Paolo said coldly, 'and I'll leave at dawn tomorrow morning.'

'You haven't understood,' Matalena said. 'All I'm worried about is your health. We'll discuss it another day; there's plenty of time, after all.'

'There's less time than you think,' said the priest.

This reply left Matalena open-mouthed with surprise and horror.

Next day the arrival of a smart carriage in the space outside the inn roused the curiosity of the whole village. Had someone come to see Don Paolo? No, the visitor was an unknown ecclesiastical dignitary, tall and thin and with distinguished manners, who made straight for the Colamartini house. His uniformed coachman, who stayed behind and guarded the carriage, was immediately surrounded and interrogated by curious villagers, to whom he explained that the prelate had been Signorina Cristina's confessor and spiritual director at school. Had he come to take the young lady away? The coachman didn't know. After a couple of hours the prelete reappeared, accompanied only by Don Pasquale, and he wanted to greet Don Paolo before leaving. The conversation took place at the inn door, while Don Pasquale stood deferentially and silently to one side.

'Signorina Colamartini has talked to me about you with a great deal of respect,' he said to Don Paolo. 'While passing through the Marsica I came up here to Pietrasecca in response to the prayers and entreaties of the mother superior and the nuns who are very fond of Signorina Colamartini and are sad that she is not yet among them.'

Don Paolo was obviously very embarrassed; he stood with his back to the wall, clutching his breviary to his chest. He restricted himself to replying that he had remained completely aloof from any discussions that might have taken place in the Colamartini household.

'Quite right,' said the prelate. 'I too on the occasion of this visit refrained from exercising any pressure on the young lady. I merely thought it my duty to find out why she has postponed following a vocation the genuineness of which is beyond all doubt.'

'Signorina Cristina,' Don Paolo said, 'can also be very useful at Pietrasecca.'

'If one takes account of her purely human qualities, that is certainly true,' replied her spiritual director. 'However, bearing in mind her truly exceptional sensibility and intelligence, I do not see how those gifts can be adequately employed in such a primitive place. But in Signorina Cristina there is also something else. Have you not noticed it? She is one of those predestined creatures who on this earth already bear on their brow, as the biblical phrase has it, the name of the Lamb.'

'Signorina Cristina has made a deep impression on me too,' Don Paolo said. 'Nevertheless I would not say it was wrong for her to remain among such needy people. Nothing would prevent her from devoting part of the day to prayer and meditation. The religious vocation does not necessarily involve living in a convent.'

The spiritual director was touched to the quick and was about to reply, but the coachman respectfully pointed out that it was getting late.

After the prelate's departure Don Pasquale went back into the inn to thank Don Paolo for his sensible remarks and made the mistake of talking to him in Matalena's presence. Among other things, he apologized in genuinely regretful tones for not having invited Don Paolo to his house. 'But if you knew our family troubles . . .' he said. Don Paolo felt obliged to interrupt. 'Your apologies are completely unnecessary,' he said. 'I did not come here on a visit, but on doctor's orders.'

Don Pasquale went on apologizing, however. 'You do not know the tradition in these parts,' he said. 'The custom in the Abruzzi, particularly in small places, is that inns are only for traders. Other travellers, including complete strangers, are generally entertained in private houses.'

'I appreciate that tradition,' Don Paolo said, 'but it really is not applicable in my case. I did not come to Pietrasecca just for a night or two.'

'The difficulty, I assure you, was not the length of your stay,' Don Pasquale replied. 'In the old days guests sometimes stayed for whole seasons. But now we have three ailing old ladies in the house and no servants.'

The conversation continued at the same courteous level and eventually concluded in an invitation to Don Paolo to call at the Colamartini house next day. He accepted with alacrity.

Immediately after Don Pasquale's departure, however, he had to cope with Matalena, whom he had never seen in such an agitated state.

'I hope you didn't believe a single word of what that old man told you,' she said in a voice changed by emotion.

'He created an impression of being a perfect gentleman,' Don Paolo replied.

'That's what he appears to be,' Matalena said, 'but would you like to know what's behind it?'

The priest avoided encouraging tittle-tattle, but that evening

94

it provided a rich and piquant accompaniment to his modest dinner. Of the three old women who lived in the Colamartini house, Matalena told him, the oldest, Cristina's grandmother, was a wicked and unscrupulous tyrant. 'She isn't a woman, she's a she-devil,' Matalena declared. As a young woman she had been the terror of the valley. This was not the first time Don Paolo had heard her talked of in such terms. The second old lady, her daughter-in-law, Cristina's step-mother, was not ill, according to Matalena, but was simply an imbecile. Her intelligence was that of a five-year-old. Don Pasquale had married her after his first wife's death solely for the sake of her dowry, on which the whole family lived. Don Pasquale might perhaps have been telling the truth in saying that the third old lady, his sister, was ill, but in fact nothing had been seen of her for several years; she might have been buried alive. This unfortunate woman was the same age as Matalena, who remembered her as a girl, when she had been very attractive and much sought after. There had been no lack of young men of good family in neighbouring villages who had asked for her hand, but her mother, that she-devil incarnate, had made it a condition that she should have no dowry. She had no intention of allowing the family property, which was reserved for Don Pasquale as the first born, to be divided up. Some suitors would actually have accepted the girl without a dowry, but she had refused to get married on those terms, which her pride would not permit. And so on and so forth. Matalena unburdened herself of all the secret resentments against the Colamartini family that were nourished by the poor. The priest listened in disgust, but did not dare to interrupt her.

'Does Signorina Cristina know all these stories?' he asked at one point.

'I can't say whether she knows every detail,' Matalena replied. 'But the religious little prig breathes that atmosphere, and she must certainly at least know the very unedifying stories about her brother Alberto.'

Cristina's brother had the reputation of being a rogue with no redeeming features. He had not been seen at Pietrasecca since his father had refused to recognize the signature on some promissory notes that the young man had forged. But to Don Paolo not the least curious item in that flood of uncheckable and spiteful gossip was that in the course of it Bianchina's name cropped up. When Signorina Girasole had turned up at the inn and asked for him Matalena had not known who she was. Not till several hours later had Magascià revealed to her that the girl had been Alberto Colamartini's lover. Magascià knew many secrets. It was not surprising if the old sly-boots, going backwards and forwards between Pietrasecca and Fossa and stopping at the Girasole hotel, heard the most shocking stories. According to him, young Colamartini had for some time enjoyed free board and lodging at Berenice Girasole's hotel as well as the use of her daughter. A situation worthy of an oriental potentate. Signora Berenice had persuaded him to marry young Bianchina, but the Colamartini family would not hear of it. Subsequently there had been talk of Signorina Girasole's being gravely ill. When she reappeared after being confined to her bed for some time, she was much thinner.

'That's enough for my headache,' Don Paolo said, rising from his table. 'Good night.'

At the prearranged time he walked hesitantly through the gate of the Colamartini house. Don Pasquale and Cristina received him in a big, half-dark room on the ground floor. Three thin little old ladies in old-fashioned clothes were seated around a heavy walnut table. They had been put on display there for his benefit. An odour of honey and the graveyard hung in the air. Though Cristina smiled at him, Don Paolo was seized with a cold sweat; Cristina did the introducing.

'My grandmother, my aunt, my mother,' she said.

She immediately helped her aunt and her mother into the next room. Her grandmother remained. Under her small white bonnet her head looked like that of a hairless vulture. Her face was shrunken and wrinkled like that of a mummy.

'Where do you come from?' she asked the priest in a shrill, unsteady voice.

'From Frascati,' Don Paolo said with a shudder.

'Have you brothers or sisters?'

'No, I'm an only son.'

'In that case it was wrong of you to become a priest,' the old lady said. 'Very wrong.'

Don Paolo tried to excuse himself.

'My vocation,' he said.

'The Church cannot desire the destruction of families,' the old woman announced. 'Without families there can be no Church or anything else.'

The old lady raised her head in his direction.

'Why don't you say mass?' she asked. 'Have you by any chance been suspended *a divinis*? Don Benedetto was punished in that way too.'

Don Paolo was very embarrassed. Cristina gave him a smile of commiseration, but he took no advantage of her aid.

'What did you say?' the old woman asked the priest.

'Nothing,' he replied.

The old lady made a sign to her granddaughter, who hastened to help her into the next room.

'You must excuse us,' Don Pasquale said to his guest, inviting him to sit in an armchair and taking a seat beside him. 'Ever since we have had no servants,' he went on, 'we have used this room as livingroom, kitchen and diningroom.'

The whole of one wall was covered with copper pots and pans and covers and shapes. There were two big grated windows through which the garden was visible, and at the bottom of the garden there were some beehives.

Cristina brought a tray with a bottle of Marsala and two glasses. At one end of the table she resumed the work that had been interrupted by Don Paolo's arrival. She was ironing tablecloths and napkins, folding them and putting them in wicker baskets.

Don Pasquale poured out the Marsala.

'Last Sunday at Rocca dei Marsi Cristina and I met Don Benedetto,' Don Pasquale said. 'He kept pressing us for news about you.'

'About me?' Don Paolo said. 'Strange.'

'Why are you surprised?' Cristina asked. 'Wasn't it he who recommended you to come and convalesce at Pietrasecca?'

'Of course,' Don Paolo said. After thinking for a moment he

97

added in an embarrassed voice, 'My only surprise, in one way, is that he does me the honour of remembering me.'

'So far from forgetting you,' Cristina said, 'I had the impression that you're his chief preoccupation at present.'

'But not the only one,' Don Pasquale pointed out. 'There were some other visitors there, and the conversation turned to a former pupil of his, a notorious character named Pietro Spina. Well, Don Benedetto actually had the courage to defend him. But, as you know the individual in question, that is something you won't appreciate.'

'He didn't just defend him,' Cristina said, 'he delivered a tremendous eulogy of him.'

'Using the most shocking arguments,' Don Pasquale went on. 'That saddened me greatly, the more so as Don Benedetto is an old family friend and morally is a saintly man.'

Cristina finished her ironing and set about lighting the fire. She knelt in front of the fireplace and blew hard to make it catch. The wood was not seasoned and merely smoked.

Don Pasquale tried to bring the conversation round to Cristina's future. The family point of view, he said, was naturally not impartial, but what would be the attitude of a disinterested third party?

'Certainly not mine,' Don Paolo hastened to say. 'I too have an interest in your daughter's remaining at Pietrasecca.'

Cristina laughed wholeheartedly and, as the fire flared up just at that moment, the reflection of the flames concealed her blushes.

'Even the wolves don't want me,' she said jestingly.

'Real or metaphorical wolves?' Don Paolo said.

Her father then described a curious incident in her childhood. 'Cristina was still in the cradle,' he said, 'and as she was very fond of lambs and it was warm in the sheepfold in winter, one evening we left her alone for several hours in her pram among the sheep. Well, a wolf got into the sheepfold, the whole flock started bleating frantically, and I dashed there with my gun and the dogs, but the wolf had gone.'

'Was Cristina asleep?' Don Paolo asked.

'No, she was sitting up in her pram and calling her mother.

She had not been frightened by the wolf, no doubt taking it for a bad dog that wanted to eat the sheep.'

'Perhaps the wolf realized she was still a baby and decided to come back for her when she was bigger,' Don Paolo said.

'It won't be able to catch me if it waits much longer,' Cristina said with a laugh. 'There are strong iron bars on convent windows.'

This reminder promptly changed Don Pasquale's mood.

'That's how the Colamartini family will come to an end,' he said bitterly. 'A wastrel son and a nun for a daughter.'

The three remained silent for a moment in the half-dark kitchen. Cristina went upstairs to put away the ironing.

'It's sad to be present at the end of one's own family,' said Don Pasquale.

In that room how would it have been possible to think about anything else?

'The fate of the family does not seem to me to depend on Signorina Cristina's decision,' Don Paolo said.

'No, it doesn't, you're perfectly right, of course,' Don Pasquale said. 'At the point we've reached the end is inevitable.'

'One can at least end with dignity.'

'You cannot possibly appreciate what a bad end the Colamartini family is facing.'

'Perhaps it isn't right to talk of good and bad as inevitable.'

'In our case it is. Believe me, even the outward decorum of the family no longer depends on me.'

'There are desperate circumstances in which family decorum should perhaps be cast aside.'

'If I were alone I might well be capable of that,' said Don Pasquale, raising his voice. 'But I can hardly put the three old ladies you met just now out to grass on the mountainside.'

As he said this his eyes filled with tears.

'Forgive me,' said Don Paolo.

'I have four pieces of land left, two planted with vines and two of them arable,' Don Pasquale said. 'Up to a few years ago the wine from the vineyards yielded about 7,000 lire. Now, after the phylloxera and other calamities and restoring the vineyards at great sacrifice and expense, the yield is only a few hundred lire. If I bought wine at market instead of making it from my vines, it would cost me three times less.'

The old man rose and fetched from a drawer a greasy and worn old account book, swollen with receipts and promissory notes.

'Look,' he said, 'the yield from the arable land is hardly sufficient to pay the men's wages, though these have gone down to four or five lire a day, which is not very much. And I have to pay the taxes. For several years I have been wondering why I go on cultivating that land.'

'It's the slump,' Don Paolo said for the sake of saying something. 'Everyone talks about it everywhere.'

'It's bankruptcy,' Don Pasquale said. 'But for the family pride that prevents me from selling land that has belonged to the Colamartini for centuries, I should have got rid of it years ago in my own interest. Land no longer pays. I have an old house near Lama which is now used as a stable, and I've let it. Would you like to know what I've had to spend to fulfil the legal requirement? Exactly six times more than the wretched rent. You think I'm exaggerating? There are no fewer than fourteen charges to be set against it. Here's the list: stamp duty, transcription charge, tax on numbering agreement, notary's fee, registration tax, tax for copying agreement, charge for formal transfer of lease, copies for registrar and parties to the agreement, various costs and postages, receipt stamps . . .'

'What you are saying seems to me to confirm that private property has had its day,' Don Paolo said. 'Are you not of that opinion?'

'I don't know,' said Don Pasquale. 'Before being reduced to this state I resorted to many expedients, some of which were not very dignified, and I've thought about it night and day. Well, father, I don't know what to do.'

'How do smallholders fare?'

'As I do. The difference is that they and their families sweat blood on their plots of land all the year round. That does not prevent every cafone from aspiring to be a smallholder, though the few that achieve it are worse off than the others. Actually land needs an unlimited amount of money.'

'If cultivating the soil doesn't pay,' Don Paolo said, 'why were farm labourers who wanted to expropriate it shot?'

Don Pasquale's manner changed immediately.

'Those shootings were justified,' he hastened to say, 'but that doesn't mean that they were sensible or that they solved anything. The landowners who keep cultivating their land are simply madmen obsessed by a fixed idea. Besides, what else can they do? A farm labourer can become an industrial worker, but for a landowner there's no way out.'

'Are labourers any better off?'

'They are in a bad way too. If they stay here and go on hacking away at the soil it's only because emigration has been stopped,' Don Pasquale said. 'All the same, they're better off than I am. Flesh used to suffering doesn't feel pain.'

'I have the impression,' Don Paolo said, 'that times are getting harder and harder, and that only men of that sort will survive. For the reason you have just mentioned: flesh used to suffering.'

Meanwhile Cristina had finished putting away the linen and came back to keep the two men company. It was Don Pasquale's turn to rise. Behind the house there was a shed with two cows, a heifer and a horse. He excused himself and went to look after the animals.

'Another drop of Marsala?' said Cristina.

'Thank you,' Don Paolo said. 'It's excellent.'

'My father will have told you the landowners' tale of woe,' Cristina said.

'Signorina Cristina,' Don Paolo said, 'I cannot tell you how much it grieves me that your life is so hard.'

'Do you perhaps suppose that that is why I want to take the veil?'

Don Paolo did not reply.

'It isn't,' Cristina said. 'My vocation is real, I assure you. But honesty compels me to add that it is certainly also convenient. But for that special summons from Jesus, how should I manage if I stayed here?'

'You would have the other possibility that life offers most women,' Don Paolo said. 'You could become a good wife and mother of a family.'

'In the state to which good families are reduced,' Cristina said, 'that seems to me to be much more difficult than dying at the stake.'

'You don't have a very high opinion of good families.'

'What I mean is that this seems to me to be a particularly difficult time in which to reconcile the duties of one's station in life with those of one's soul.'

'A Christian woman should not put the duties of her station in life on the same level as those of her soul.'

'If she abandons secular life, she certainly shouldn't. But everyone who remains in the world has a station in life that imposes obligations.'

'But if, as you admit, the duties of one's station become irreconcilable with those of one's soul, surely the only course is to dismiss the former out of hand.'

'Following the example of Pietro Spina, perhaps?' Cristina exclaimed. 'Do you realize that you're repeating the arguments used by Don Benedetto last Sunday?'

'Perhaps it will surprise you, Signorina Cristina,' Don Paolo said in an ironic tone, 'but I do not consider the comparison with Spina outrageous.'

'But the official teaching of the Church seems to me to be different,' said Cristina. 'Social inequalities were also created by God, and we must humbly respect them. . . . But I wonder why our talks always end up in an argument. Undoubtedly it's my fault, I'm obstinate and presumptuous. Let us change the subject.'

The armistice was of brief duration.

'Have you any news of Bianchina?' Cristina asked.

'I heard a curious thing,' Don Paolo said. 'I heard there was a love affair between her and your brother Alberto.'

'Again?' Cristina exclaimed angrily. 'Didn't it end some time ago? It's really scandalous.'

Argument flared up again. Don Paolo had for some time been aware of a sense of irritation, and it now had another excuse to show itself.

'There would be a very simple way of ending the scandal,' he said. 'Let them get married. That would settle everything.'

Cristina's face hardened. 'Impossible,' she said coldly.

The priest pretended not to understand. 'Impossible? Why impossible?' he said.

'My grandmother and my father would consider it a disgrace, not only to themselves, but to their forefathers,' Cristina said firmly. To put an end to the discussion she added, 'Please let us talk about something else.'

'It's not a matter of forefathers, but of Alberto and Bianchina,' Don Paolo insisted. 'If the two are in love, that would be the honourable course to take.'

'Family honour is not a matter for discussion,' Cristina said angrily.

'So even you have these strange medieval ideas?' the priest exclaimed with pretended surprise. 'Even you?'

'Yes, of course, even me,' said the girl, accepting the challenge. 'Who are the Girasole? Where do they come from? As for Bianchina, let me just remind you of the rather special circumstances in which you made her acquaintance.'

'I have not in the least forgotten them,' Don Paolo said. 'But what would you say if your brother Alberto were not entirely extraneous to the girl's illness?'

'How dare you,' Cristina exclaimed, jumping to her feet as if to reject a personal insult.

'I beg your pardon,' Don Paolo said.

Without hesitating he made a slight bow of farewell and walked to the door. Cristina, pale and trembling, watched him leaving and made not the slightest move to detain him.

CHAPTER 11

During the priest's absence Matalena secretly sent for Cassarola, the wise woman, who arrived dragging her feet and complaining about mysterious aches and pains in various parts of her body.

'I urgently need your aid,' Matalena said to her. 'Envy is trying to rob me of my priest.'

'I don't understand,' Cassarola said. 'Do you own a priest?'

Matalena whispered into the woman's ear the cause of her anxieties.

'I don't understand,' the wise woman said. 'Perhaps it's because I haven't had anything to eat yet.'

Matalena offered her bread and cheese and a glass of wine; she waited for a short time and then asked again, 'Is there no sure way of keeping Don Paolo here?'

'Your cheese is salty,' said the wise woman, spitting on the ground.

Matalena hastened to offer her another glass of wine.

'Now please be quick,' she said, 'because he might come back at any moment.'

'Now, let me see,' Cassarola began. 'Do you sleep together?'

Matalena made a display of genuine indignation.

'Is that what you think?' she exclaimed. 'At my age, and with a man in holy orders?'

'That is what I might have thought,' the wise woman said. 'But if you had, he would certainly have left long ago. But why do you want to keep him here? For money?'

'No, for protection. Without him the house will fall down. What am I to do?'

'Be patient, let me think.'

Matalena filled the woman's empty glass and encouraged her to think quickly.

'I can't live without him,' Matalena insisted. 'I'm as frightened as if I were a little girl.'

'Frightened of what?'

'Of everything.'

Cassarola shut her eyes. She breathed with difficulty and complained again about her mysterious aches and pains.

'Give me something to drink,' she muttered. 'My throat's dry.'

'Would you like a glass a cold water?'

'Do you think I'm a cow? Unfortunately I'm not a cow.'

Matalena brought a full jug of wine to the table and put it next to the woman's glass, but she drank straight from the jug. She took several long draughts.

'We'll tie him up like a Bologna sausage,' she announced with a leer when she had finished.

'No, I only want him to stay here.'

'But I tell you he'll obey the two of us as meekly as a child, and through him we'll have control of the whole valley, and the souls in purgatory, and exorcisms.'

'And natural disasters,' Matalena added, 'and subterranean forces.'

'To begin with,' Cassarola said, 'you must put seven of your hairs in every plate of his soup. That's only the beginning. The hairs must of course be black, not dyed.'

'I don't think he'll like them.'

'He doesn't have to eat them, all that matters is to make sure they're cooked with his soup.'

'Are there words to be said during the cooking?'

'I shall say them. Have you a picture of a woman?'

'No. Only of Our Lady of the Rosary.'

Cassarola made a grimace of disgust and resumed complaining about her aches and pains. She picked up the jug and took several more long draughts.

'Then you must take a sheet of paper and draw a picture of a woman yourself. It doesn't have to be complete, it's enough to put in the holes. Listen carefully to what I'm saying and don't interrupt. You must draw nine holes on the sheet of paper to represent the nine holes in the body. Then you must put the drawing under his pillow.'

'But he'll notice it and he'll ask for an explanation.'

'Then you must put it under his mattress. Couldn't you get me some of his hair?'

'I'll try his comb in the morning,' Matalena said.

No sooner had Cassarola gone than Matalena took the additional precaution of lighting an oil lamp and putting it in the presence of Our Lady of the Rosary. While standing on a chair to adjust the lamp she trembled all over with anxiety. Then she spoke into one of the Blessed Virgin's ears, 'Holy Mother of God,' she said, 'I commend this poor priest of mine to you. Make him stay here. If you do, I shall keep this lamp alight for a whole year.'

These precautions served to calm her down a little. She took a chair and put it outside the inn and sat on it to await Don Paolo's return. The heat of the day was beginning to lessen. A pleasant breeze came from the mountain, with a good smell of elder and cut grass. Fortunately she did not have to wait as long as she had expected.

'How was it?' she asked him. Her voice was as timid as if she had been asking for alms.

The priest did not answer. There was a strange expression on his face. He seemed both pleased and upset. Behind him a mendicant friar appeared, covered in dust and mud. The bag on his shoulder was nearly empty.

'Few alms?' Don Paolo said.

'Not even enough to pay for the sandal wear,' the Capuchin replied.

He remained standing humbly by the door. The feet in his worn sandals looked black and deformed because of the scars and swellings. Matalena offered him a glass of wine, but he refused. The priest's presence intimidated him and he did not know what to say, or whether to stay or go. He had several times been reported to the provincial father by parish priests for his familiarity with the cafoni and his fondness for wine.

'Drink, Brother Gioacchino, drink, don't be shy,' Matalena said, but her insistence only increased his embarrassment.

'Everyone serves the Lord as best he can,' he said. 'Some by words, some by charity, some by sanctity. My lot has been having to walk. I'm a donkey of the Lord's, the father superior says.'

Don Paolo smiled. The Capuchin, whose eyes were those of a submissive cafone, hardly dared glance at him.

'Why do people give fewer alms? Are they less religious?' Don Paolo asked.

'Down on the plain they now have insurance, which is an invention of the devil,' the monk said. 'If I ask for something for St Francis so that he may protect the crop against hail, they answer that it's insured already. Then he'll protect you against fire, I say. But they say they already have fire insurance. But how comes it that in spite of all those insurances they still live in fear? What is it they're afraid of?'

'Poor people always live in fear,' said Matalena. 'If you have a house, an earthquake happens. If you're healthy, illness comes. If you have a plot of land, a flood comes. There's envy in the air.'

'Once upon a time every trade had its own saint,' the monk said. 'The cobblers had St Crispin, the tailors St Omobono, the carpenters St Joseph. Nowadays every trade has its own union. But people are no safer than they were before. The fear remains.'

'Is life better in a monastery?' Matalena asked.

'You live badly there to, but you have security,' the monk said. 'You have no family life, but you have no fear either. Also there's hope.'

'What hope?' Don Paolo said.

The monk pointed to the sky.

'It's not a way for everyone,' said Matalena. 'We can't all be monks or nuns.'

'Do you know what holds you back?' the monk said. 'Greed for property. It holds you back like a chain holds a dog. Once upon a time the devil became flesh in women, but now he's incarnated in property.'

'And no longer in women?' Matalena said. 'Brother Gioacchino, there you may be wrong.'

'Woman has lost her power,' the monk said. 'Nowadays it's property that leads to perdition.'

107

'Do the poor get saved?' Matalena asked. 'It doesn't seem to me that they get saved.'

'Those who covet property are not saved,' the monk said. 'They are the phoney poor. Look, I speak out of family experience. After a bad year in which the whole crop was lost my father had to sell a vineyard behind the village castle. He ruined the rest of his life for the sake of buying it back; he grew mean, bad-tempered and quarrelsome, and died without ever managing to buy it back. Then my brother wanted to buy it back, and because of it he committed murder and ended up in prison. My other brother went to Brazil, intending to come back with enough money to buy it back, but he barely succeeded in making a living out there. Meanwhile that vineyard passes from hand to hand. Every three or four years it passes into new hands. How many souls is it sending to perdition?'

'What sort of vineyard is it?' said Matalena. 'Is it a bewitched vineyard? A bad woman vineyard?'

'It's a perfectly ordinary vineyard,' said the monk. 'It's a vineyard just like any other.'

'Does it yield more than other vineyards?' Matalena asked. 'Why does your family want just that vineyard?'

'It belonged to our family for generations,' said the monk. 'Otherwise it's exactly like all other vineyards.'

'In the last resort every woman is exactly like all other women,' Matalena said. 'But if the devil intervenes . . .'

'Nowadays,' the monk went on, 'when my work of collecting alms takes me in that direction and I see that vineyard in the distance, I make the sign of the cross as if I were in the presence of the devil.'

'Do you often go in that direction?' Don Paolo asked.

The monk nodded. 'I know I'm wrong to do so,' he said. 'When one embraces the religious life and abandons the world one should go far away from one's home. It's not enough to change one's name if the water, the stones, the grass, the plants, the dust on the road are those of one's birthplace. One should go far away.'

'I went far away,' the priest confessed in a low voice. 'But I couldn't stand it, and I came back.'

'Perhaps one should go to some place from which one can't come back.'

The monk said this in such gloomy tones that Don Paolo had to restrain himself from flinging his arms round him.

'Drink,' he said, and poured him out a glass of wine. This time he accepted. He drank slowly, after wiping his chapped lips with the back of his hand.

'It must be Fossa wine,' he said to Matalena.

'Yes, it is,' she said.

'It must be from the district half way up the hill, above the pozzolana quarry,' he went on.

'Since you like it, have some more,' said the priest, filling his glass.

'Thank you,' the monk said. 'It's a wine that's worth getting to know.'

Don Paolo felt happy. He found this poor monk very touching.

'Come on, don't stay standing at the door,' he said. 'Come and sit at my table. Matalena, bring us a bottle.'

'A whole bottle?' exclaimed the monk, taken aback.

'Why not? If we feel like it, we'll have another one when we've finished it,' said the priest. 'I'll take full responsibility.'

'Your health,' said the monk, raising his glass. Then, turning to Matalena, he said, 'Couldn't you give me a piece of bread, please? It helps one to drink,' he explained to the priest.

He broke the bread and gave some to Don Paolo.

'There's nothing better than wheat bread dipped in red wine,' he went on. 'But one's heart must be at peace,' he added with a smile.

Don Paolo grew cheerful. Matalena had never seen him like this.

'What are you smiling at?' the monk asked him.

'One day we'll do the devil in,' Don Paolo confided in his ear. 'Yes, one day we'll do him in, that loathsome old enemy of man.'

'How?'

'By abolishing the private ownership of land.'

'Do you mean that land will belong to everyone? Including the vineyards?'

'Land, vineyards, woods, quarries, canals, everything.'

'Do you mean you believe in revolution?'

'I don't believe in anything else,' Don Paolo whispered in his ear. 'Meanwhile drink, Brother Gioacchino, drink and be merry.'

'Do you believe in the Kingdom? In this world?'

'*Sicut in coelo et in terra, amen.*'

'Who will make this revolution in your opinion? The Church?'

'No. The Church, as usual, will bless the revolution, but only after others have made it.'

'Who will make it, then? God Himself?'

'No. You know the old rule: God helps those who help themselves.'

'Who will make it, then?'

'The poor,' the priest said in a serious voice. 'That is, of course, the poor who are uncontaminated by greed for property.'

The monk looked all round and then whispered in Don Paolo's ear, 'Have you by any chance heard of someone called Pietro Spina?'

'Why do you ask?'

'He thinks the same way as you do,' the monk said. 'At any rate, so they say.'

'Have you met others on your rounds who think in that way?' the priest asked.

'Yes,' the monk said in an undertone, 'but secretly.'

'To your health,' Don Paolo said, laughing. 'Drink and be merry, Brother Gioacchino. Let us make a revolution that will do in that loathsome old devil once and for all.'

Matalena listened in open-mouthed astonishment. What strange things to hear from the lips of churchmen. She waited for the two to stop talking before asking the monk whether some natural disaster was in store.

'My husband is dead,' she said, 'and if my house is carried away by a flood, who will rebuild it for me?' Her voice was that

110

of a terrified little orphan girl.

'We shall have worse than that,' the monk blurted out.

His face darkened, and he said no more. Matalena made the sign of the cross and murmured in terror, 'Worse?'

'What shall we have, then?' Don Paolo said in friendly fashion, to induce the monk to speak up.

'One night while I was praying in my cell,' the monk said, without daring to look the priest in the face, 'I looked in the direction of Rome. The horizon was as black as pitch, and there was a red spectre peeping between the clouds.'

'That sounds very plausible,' Don Paolo said with a smile.

Matalena was reassured, for the menace in the sky was directed, not at Pietrasecca, but at Rome. The bottle was now empty, and the monk took his departure, because evening was falling and he hoped to be put up in the Colamartini stable, as on other occasions.

'I hope we meet again,' he said to Don Paolo. 'If not here, up there.'

'Up there? Where? On the mountain? In the woods?' the priest asked.

'In heaven,' the monk said with a smile.

'In case of need I shall get in touch with you sooner,' the priest said.

'You'll find me on the road,' said the monk.

Don Paolo watched him going away. He walked briskly, with a light, dancing stride. The gate leading to the Colamartini house was open. The monk climbed the three steps that led up to the front door and pulled at the bell. As no-one answered it, he sat down at the threshold and waited patiently. A small mouse peeped out of a clump of rose bushes. It was as brown as the monk's habit. For a few moments the mouse and the monk looked at each other in friendly fashion, but their attention was averted by the creaking of the front door.

'I'm sorry,' Don Pasquale said. 'My daughter is not feeling very well.'

CHAPTER 12

The arrival of a letter from Bianchina in Rome put Don Paolo in a state of unusual excitement, though there was nothing sensational in it; the contents were almost commonplace. The trip had gone off well, she wrote. She had had no difficulty in finding the person to whom she had been sent, she had not seen anyone else the whole time, and so she had been able to have a look at the city. She might be coming back very soon, and she would certainly be bringing back plenty of reading matter for him. The effect of this brief message on Don Paolo was almost miraculous. He suddenly felt reinvigorated. The end of his enforced isolation was in sight. He would be having some serious discussions with the party, but discussion was better than soliloquy.

From that moment he tried to get away from the tedious female atmosphere by which he was surrounded; he forgot Cristina, and sought out the company of men. Before leaving Pietrasecca he wanted at least to get to know them better. But during the daytime they were dispersed all over the valley, and they came back only after sunset, in small groups, walking behind their loaded donkeys. From the garden of the inn he watched them climbing up the valley, weary, hungry and ragged, with that typical, forward-leaning gait of theirs that was the result of using the mattock, of working bent over the soil, and also of habituation to servility, to uninterrupted subjection. Now that he felt better, Don Paolo went out to get away from the complaints of Matalena, who was living in fear of his departure, and the complaints of the other women, who darned and mended and deloused themselves outside the inn, and also to get away from the breviary, the *Eternal Maxims*, the ghosts of his youth who, he thought, had vanished, but had gathered round him, taking advantage of his solitude and his physical debility.

One afternoon he crossed the wooden bridge and took the narrow road that led down to the valley. He felt like a machine that had been repaired and was now resuming its usual motion, its usual rhythm. Once more he felt a natural urge that was part of his nature, the urge to be sociable. In his isolation he had been out of his element, a fish out of water. He sat on a wall by the roadside and waited. It was natural for him to wait. As a boy he had waited after catechism in the evening in the square at Orta for other boys, nearly all the sons of poor people, to join him and play games. Later in Rome, when he was a member of a socialist students' group, he had waited for some worker at the gate of the Tabanelli works, outside Porta San Giovanni, or at the gasworks outside Porta San Paolo, to spend the evening with him. At l'Estaque he had waited for Cardile. He knew how to wait.

The first to appear that evening were old Sciatàp and his son, walking a few paces behind their donkey, which was loaded with brushwood. When he saw the priest Sciatàp stopped.

'I've been waiting to talk to you for a long time,' he said, 'but they said you had the cough, and I didn't want to trouble you.'

'The cough's better now,' Don Paolo said.

'I want to talk to you about my son,' the old man went on. 'He wanted to join the carabinieri or the militia, but they turned him down. Couldn't you write a letter of recommendation?'

'Do you really want to be a carabiniere?' the priest asked the young man.

'I certainly do,' he said. 'People speak ill of them out of envy. They don't do much work, and they're well paid.'

'But that's not the point,' said the priest. 'You're a worker. If you become a carabiniere your superiors may order you to fire at dissatisfied cafoni. That has already happened not far from here, at Sulmona, Pratola and Prezza, as you probably know.'

Sciatàp heartily agreed with this.

'Don Paolo's right,' he said. 'If you want to live at all well you have to sell your soul. There's no other way.'

The way his father put it made the boy laugh.

'Is there no other way?' said Don Paolo. 'Is it impossible to live well and stay honest?'

'Do you know the story of the devil and the cat?' Sciatàp said. 'Once upon a time there was a big devil who lived in a cave. He was dressed in black, wore a top hat, and had many rings on his fingers, just like a banker. Three cafoni went to see him and asked him what was required to live well, without working. "What is needed is a soul, an innocent soul," the devil replied. The cafoni went away, took a cat, swaddled it like a newborn baby and took it to the devil. "Here's a soul, a really innocent soul," they said, and in return the devil gave them a book of instructions on how to live well without working. But while they were on their way home the cat started miaowing, the devil discovered he had been cheated, and the magic book went up in flames in their hands. A cat's no use. What is required is a soul, a real, human soul.'

'Very well,' the lad said, 'I'll do what everyone else does, of course. Meanwhile my application has not been accepted. There are too many applications.'

'That's the trouble, there are too many souls,' said Sciatàp. 'The earthquake and epidemics and the war weren't much use. There are still too many souls.'

'What is left to a man who sells his soul?' the priest asked.

The two cafoni looked at him in surprise. What a strange question to come from a priest. As if there were any doubt.

'There's always a way of putting things right while life lasts,' said Sciatàp. 'What's the Church for? Does the Church forbid the carabinieri to open fire? In the procession at Fossa on Corpus Christi day there are always four carabinieri in full dress uniform in the place of honour behind the Sacrament. You said that at Pratola the carabinieri opened fire on poor people. Afterwards they must have confessed. But the cafoni they shot are dead, and who confessed for them? In this world they suffered from cold and in the next they are suffering from fire.'

'I'm sorry,' Don Paolo said, 'but I don't know to whom I could recommend you. I don't know any carabinieri officers.'

Meanwhile the donkey had gone on ahead.

114

'Garibaldi,' the old man shouted angrily after it.

But the donkey took no notice and went on its way.

'It won't listen to me because it's hungry and it's not far to the stable,' Sciatàp explained to the priest. 'When it's hungry it even forgets its own name.'

Sciatàp and his son wished him a good evening and hurried after the donkey, and Don Paolo went and sat down again.

Next to appear was a drunken cafone on a donkey. The man kept slipping from one side to the other, and every time he righted himself he struck and kicked the beast.

'Will you go straight or not?' he kept saying.

Immediately after him came a number of cafoni accompanying Magascià and his cart. Magascià stopped the cart and said, 'We've been to market.'

'Did you get good prices?' asked the priest.

'Prices have fallen,' Magascià said. 'They imposed price control. We didn't want to sell, but we had to, or they would have confiscated our produce.'

'Country prices are subject to price control, but not town prices, which have risen,' said a man standing by the cart.

'Giacinto was arrested by the carabinieri,' Magascià said, 'for rebellion. When he heard about the price control he wanted to go back to Pietrasecca without selling.'

The cart set off again, and Don Paolo joined the men on their way home. Next to Magascià was a man named Daniele, a tall fellow with a big hat askew over his bearded face.

'Daniele had a sick donkey that certainly won't live another month,' Magascià confided in the priest. 'He took it to market and sold it to a Fossa woman as a healthy one.'

'I'll confess next Easter,' Daniel said. 'God will forgive me.'

The whole group laughed with pleasure at Daniele's smartness. A youth named Banduccia who looked as if he were drunk was walking behind the cart, holding on to it in order to keep on his feet.

'Banduccia,' Magascià confided to the priest, 'went to a tavern at Fossa, ate, drank, paid for a round of drinks for everyone present, and then went out into the garden as if to relieve himself, but he jumped the wall and got away without paying.'

'I'll confess at Easter too,' Banduccia said. 'God will forgive me.'

Again everyone laughed. Don Paolo shuddered.

'When Signora Rosa Girasole, the landlady, realized I'd gone,' Banduccia said, 'she tried to make Biagio pay my share, on the ground that he came from Pietrasecca too. Poor Signora Rosa made a bad choice. If other customers hadn't intervened he would have smashed up the whole place. He picked up a log and threw it at her; if it had hit her she would have been done for.'

Biagio was the strongest and most violent cafone in the valley, and Don Paolo had already heard him talked of with great admiration.

'He's been to prison for acts of violence three times already,' another man said approvingly. 'He's a man who makes himself respected.'

'Handing it out's no disgrace, what's disgraceful is taking it,' said Banduccia.

'The first time he went to prison was for breaking his father's arm with a chopper,' said Magascià. ' "He broke my arm, but I'm delighted he's so strong," the old man told me. "He'll make himself respected in life, at any rate by people as poor as himself".'

Other men recalled other brave deeds of Biagio's, but Don Paolo stopped listening. Among the group of cafoni round Magascià's cart there was also a young man of rather strange appearance. He was barefooted, poorly dressed, tall and thin. A big tuft of hair on his forehead gave him a wild look that contrasted with his eyes, which were those of a tame dog. He took no part in his companions' jokes and sallies. Don Paolo smiled at him, and he smiled back and moved closer to him. When the group crossed the wooden bridge and broke up Don Paolo took him by the arm and detained him.

'I should like to talk to you,' he said to him quietly. 'I should like to hear what you think about certain things.'

The young man smiled at him and went off towards the

hovel in which he lived. This was in the farthest corner of the village, among a group of sheds and pigsties. The path that led to it was a foul-smelling ditch that served as a drain for manure. Don Paolo followed the young cafone, who turned every so often and looked at the priest without speaking, but with gratitude in his eyes.

'I should like to talk to you as man to man,' Don Paolo said. 'Forget for a moment that I'm wearing this habit and that you're a simple cafone.'

The young man's home was rather like a pigsty. You had to bend down to get into it; the door also served as chimney. In the darkness and stench inside it was just possible to make out a straw bed stretched out on the cobbled floor and a goat ruminating on some filthy straw. The stench of manure and filthy rags was too much for Don Paolo, who sat at the entrance while the young man prepared his evening meal.

'There's a country,' Don Paolo started saying in an undertone, 'a big country in the east of Europe, a vast plain cultivated with wheat. A vast plain, populated by millions of cafoni. In that country in 1917 . . .'

The young cafone cut a few slices of maize bread, sliced two tomatoes and an onion, and offered the priest a piece of bread with that seasoning. He still had traces of soil on his swollen and scarred hands. The knife with which he cut the bread was obviously used for all purposes. Don Paolo shut his eyes and tried to swallow the food to avoid offending him.

'There's a country,' he began again, 'a big country in which the cafoni in the country struck up an alliance with the workers in the town.'

Meanwhile Matalena had been going from house to house looking for her lodger.

'Have you seen him?' she asked everyone. Eventually she found him.

'Your dinner has been ready for an hour,' she said. 'I was afraid something had happened to you.'

'I'm not hungry,' said Don Paolo. 'Go back to the inn, because I want to go on talking to this friend of mine.'

'Talking to him?' Matalena exclaimed. 'But haven't you

noticed that the poor lad is a deaf-mute and only understands a few signs?'

The deaf-mute was sitting at the entrance to his den next to the priest. Don Paolo looked him in the face and saw realization of the mistake of which he had been the cause slowly dawning in his eyes.

'It doesn't matter,' the priest said to Matalena, 'go back to the inn, I'm not hungry.'

The two stayed where they were, and the one of them that had the gift of speech was silent too. Every so often they looked at each other and smiled. The grey light of evening faded and was followed by the darkness of night. As soon as it was dark torpor descended on the village almost immediately. But for the stench coming from the hovels and sheds the valley might have been uninhabited. After a time Don Paolo rose, shook the deaf-mute by the hand and wished him goodnight. He had to grope in the dark like a blind man.

The only door that was still open and lit was that of the inn. There were always some who came to drink or play cards and stayed late. There was nowhere else to go in the village. The furniture of the bar consisted of two greasy tables, a few chairs with no straw left on them, and a wooden bench next to the fireplace. In a corner under the staircase that led to the first floor were piled provisions for the whole year, consisting of sacks of potatoes, beans and lentils. There was nearly always a saucer of salted roast chickpeas on one of the tables to make the customers thirsty. A picture of Our Lady of the Rosary had been hanging on the wall for so long that it had become part of the place. Customers chewed chickpeas, drank, chewed tobacco, drank again, and continually spat on the floor, so that when Don Paolo came in he had to be careful not to slip.

An old man named Fava was always squatting by the fireplace, staring fixedly at the floor with a sad, stupefied expression on his face. He was perpetually chewing the cud and never talked to anyone. He was the first to arrive and the last to leave, by which time he was so drunk that he could hardly stand. His daughters came to fetch him, his sons came to fetch him, and his wife came to fetch him, but he refused to budge.

'There's wine at home,' his wife said. 'Why don't you drink the wine from our vineyard?'

'I don't like it,' he said with a grimace of disgust.

Matalena had had to exchange some wine with Fava's wife.

'Now we have the wine you like, so stay at home,' his wife said.

'I don't like it,' he said.

And he went back to the inn every night and spent the little money that he earned. His wife ended by holding Matalena responsible.

'You mustn't give him anything to drink,' she said. 'If he wants to drink, let him come home.'

It made no difference. Fava went to the inn every evening, always to the same place.

When Don Paolo arrived after talking to the deaf-mute there were only two peasants playing cards.

'When I saw you talking to the deaf-mute,' one of them said, 'I thought it was a miracle, but it was only a mistake.'

Don Paolo sat down at the table with the two men.

'It wasn't a miracle and it wasn't a mistake,' he said.

'The deaf-mute is very intelligent,' the other man said. 'Perhaps God deprived him of speech and hearing as a punishment.'

The two resumed their game of cards.

That evening Don Paolo was not sleepy. A strange restlessness made him talkative.

'Cafoni have been complaining ever since the world began, but have been resigned to their fate. Will that always be the case?' he said.

'If one could die of hunger we should have been dead long ago,' one of the card players said.

'Don't you think that one day things might change?' Don Paolo asked again.

'Yes, when the patient's dead the doctor arrives,' the other man said.

Don Paolo grew reckless.

'Haven't you ever heard that there are countries in which things are different?'

This time Matalena answered.

'Yes,' she said. 'There are countries that are different from ours, God put the grass where there are no sheep and sheep where there's no grass.'

'I see,' Don Paolo said. 'Goodnight.'

The two men went on with their game. Later one of them said to Matalena, 'Your priest seems a decent fellow, but he's also a bit crazy.'

'You don't understand him,' said Matalena. 'He's too educated for you.'

'Yes, he's educated,' the other man said, 'but also he's a bit crazy. Why doesn't he say mass?'

'He doesn't belong to this diocese.'

'What difference does that make? Mass is the same everywhere. It's that he's a bit crazy.'

CHAPTER 13

Next day was a holiday, and in the evening the bar was crowded with drinkers and card players, as on great occasions. Many stood, because there were not enough chairs, and others played morra[1] outside. Don Paolo stayed in his room, bent over the small table, busy with some sheets of paper that bore the heading: 'On the inaccessibility of the cafoni to politics'. But because of the noise coming up from the bar he could not concentrate. He heard people coming and going, the noise made by the chairs, the calls made by the morra players, the sudden flaring up of arguments followed by shouts, bangs, oaths and the sound of chairs and tables being overturned.

'Please be quiet,' Matalena implored. 'Don Paolo's upstairs resting.'

But her appeals were in vain, for how can one enjoy oneself without making a noise?

A strange squabble arose among three or four young men who were playing settemezzo because of one of the cards. The most important card at settemezzo is the king of coins[2]. Matalena had only two packs, and in both the king of coins was so worn and consequently so easily recognizable that a fair game was impossible. To avoid quarrels Daniele, one of the players, proposed that they substitute another card for it, the three of goblets[3], for instance. The easily identifiable king of coins would have the value of the three of goblets, and the three of goblets, which was indistinguishable from the rest, would have the value of the king of coins.

'Impossible,' another player, Michele, announced.' It would

---

[1] *Morra*, a gambling game played with the fingers only, unlike other games mentioned here which are card games.

[2] *Denari*, a suit in the Italian pack.

[3] *Coppe*, another suit in the Italian pack.

be impossible even if we all agreed to it.'

'Why?' Daniele wanted to know.

'But it's obvious,' a third player, Mascolo, insisted. 'Whatever happens, the king of coins remains the king of coins. No matter how dirty, marked, or worn he may be, he's still the king of coins.'

'But it's enough if we all agree,' Daniele said. 'It'll be a better game if no-one knows who has the king of coins.'

'It's not sufficient for us to agree,' Michele insisted. 'The rules are the rules.'

'You say it would be a better game?' Mascolo declared. 'Perhaps it would be, but it wouldn't be the real game.'

Sciatàp, who was at the other table, the old men's table, and had heard the argument, said, 'Let's ask Don Paolo. A priest knows as much as the devil.'

'You can't,' said Matalena. 'He's resting.'

But Don Paolo, who heard his name being mentioned, appeared at the top of the stairs.

'Did someone ask for me?' he asked.

The argument stopped immediately, and everyone offered the priest a drink. He thanked them all and tried to excuse himself, but in the end he had to agree to go round the room touching every glass with his lips, in accordance with the custom.

'Who wanted me?' he asked at the conclusion of this rite.

Sciatàp explained what the argument was about, and ended, 'Now tell us who's right.'

'It's not a matter of sacred images,' the priest said, laughing.

But Sciatàp cut off his way of retreat.

'A priest knows as much as the devil,' he said.

Don Paolo picked up the king of coins.

'Do you think that this card has a value in itself or just the value that has been given to it?' he asked Michele.

'It's worth more than the other cards, because it's the king of coins,' Michele replied.

'Has this card a fixed or variable value?' the priest asked again. 'Does the king of coins have the same value in all games, at tressette, briscola, and scopa, or does it vary?'

'It varies according to the game,' said Michele.

'And who invented those games?' the priest asked.

No-one replied.

'Don't you think that games were invented by players?' the priest suggested.

A number of men immediately agreed. Games had obviously been invented by players.

The priest concluded, 'If the value of this card varies according to the fantasy of the players and what they agree on, it seems to me that you can do what you like with it.'

'Well said, bravo,' many of those present called out.

Don Paolo was flattered by his success. He turned to Sciatàp. 'Once upon a time there was a man here at Pietrasecca who was called Carlo Campanella, and now there's a man in New York who's called Mr Charles Little-Bell, Ice and Coal. Is there only one of him or are there two?'

'He's the same man,' a number of men answered.

'If a man can change his name, why can't a playing card?' the priest asked.

'A king is always a king,' Michele said.

'A king is a king only as long as he remains on the throne,' Don Paolo said. 'A king who no longer reigns is no longer a king, but an ex-king. There's a country, a big country, from which the sun comes to us, that had a king, let us call him a big king of clubs, who ruled over millions of cafoni. When the cafoni stopped obeying him he ceased to reign, he was no longer a king. Not far away from us, in the direction in which the sun sets, there's a country where another king used to reign, let us call him a king of goblets or coins. When his subjects stopped obeying him he ceased to reign, ceased to be king and became an ex-king. Now he's an emigrant, which is a thing that any of you might be. So play settemezzo in any way you like, and goodnight to you.'

Don Paolo handed back the king of coins to Daniele, said goodnight to everyone again, and went up to his room, followed by the acclamation of the drunks.

But for the next few days the dethronement of the king of coins led to a long trail of comment among the cafoni of Pietrasecca.

The village schoolmistress, Signorina Patrignani, came and complained to the priest in person.

'It was impossible to teach today in the top class,' she said. 'The boys would talk of nothing but that business of the king of coins and the three of goblets, and they kept repeating what you said in the bar last night without having understood it.'

The schoolmistress wore the emblem of the government party on her breast. She sighed deeply between one sentence and the next, and the tricolour emblem tossed about like a small boat on a stormy sea.

'These peasants are very ignorant,' she said, 'and when they listen to educated people such as ourselves they nearly always understand the opposite of what is meant.'

She had just received the latest number of *News from Rome*, the wall newspaper that was intended to be displayed on the school door. It was her custom before putting it up to read and explain the most important items to the cafoni gathered in Matalena's bar. The news spread among the cafoni that the priest was going to attend that evening, and so the bar was fuller than usual. Some of those who turned up the priest had never seen before. In a short time about thirty ragged individuals were squatting in a huddle on the floor. Don Paolo sat at the foot of the stairs leading to the first floor and so could look nearly everyone in the face. The smell of manure and dirty clothing that rose from the throng took one by the throat. They were submissive and diffident people with dazed-looking faces on deformed and contorted trunks, faces misshapen by hunger and illness, and among them were several wild and violent youths. The older men, the notables such as Sciatàp, Magascià and Grascia, stayed standing by the door.

In the strange priest's presence the schoolmistress was unusually nervous and talkative. She told the audience to pay careful attention and not to be afraid to ask for explanations of difficult words. Then she started reading *News from Rome* in a loud and piercing voice.

'We have a leader for whom all the nations of the earth envy us,' she read. 'Who knows what they would be prepared to pay to have him in their country . . .'

Magascià interrupted. As he disliked generalities, he wanted to know exactly how much other nations would be willing to pay to acquire our leader.

'It's a manner of speaking,' said the schoolmistress.

'There's no such thing as manners of speaking in commercial contracts,' Magascià objected. 'Are they willing to pay for him or not? If they are willing to pay, what are they offering?'

The schoolmistress repeated angrily that it was merely a manner of speaking.

'So it isn't true that they want to buy him, then?' Magascià said. 'And if it isn't true, why does it say that they want him?'

Sciatàp also wanted some specific information. Would it be a cash or credit transaction?

The schoolmistress glanced at the priest as if to say: Now you see the kind of people we have to deal with in this village.

The next item concerned the rural population.

'Who are the rural population?' asked one of the throng sitting on the floor.

'You are,' the schoolmistress replied, losing her patience. 'I've told you that hundreds of times.'

Some members of the audience burst out laughing.

'We were the rural population and didn't know it,' they said.

The schoolmistress went on reading, 'The rural revolution has attained its objectives all along the line . . .'

'What line?' someone asked. 'The railway line?'

'Are we the rural population?' Sciatàp asked. 'Is the rural revolution the revolution we made?'

'Exactly,' said the schoolmistress. 'I congratulate you on your intelligence.'

'What revolution did we make?'

'The expression is to be understood in a moral sense,' the schoolmistress explained.

Sciatàp did not want to appear ignorant and pretended to understand, but Magascià was not satisfied.

'That sheet of paper is sent us by the government,' he said, 'and it says that the rural population, that is the cafoni according to what you say, have made a revolution, and that that revolution has attained its objectives. What objectives have we attained?'

'Spiritual objectives,' said the schoolmistress.

'What spiritual objectives?'

The schoolmistress flushed, grew flustered, and there was general confusion. Then she had a brilliant idea, imposed silence and, while you could hear a pin drop, she announced, 'The rural revolution has saved the country from the communist menace.'

'Who are the communists?' said Grascia.

The schoolmistress was safe. She had no more need to think. 'I've told you before, but now I'll tell you again,' she said. 'The communists are wicked people who for choice meet at night in town sewers. To become a communist you have to trample on the crucifix, spit in Christ's face, and promise to eat meat on Good Friday.'

'Where do they get the meat from?' Sciatàp wanted to know. 'Do they get it for nothing or do they have to pay for it?'

'I don't know,' the schoolmistress said.

'So what it boils down to is that, as usual, you don't know the most important thing,' said old Grascia.

The schoolmistress turned to Don Paolo as if to give him a chance to speak and thus come to her rescue, but the priest seemed absorbed in contemplation of the cobwebs on the ceiling.

'As I disagree, I'm going,' Grascia announced.

The schoolmistress invited him to say what he disagreed with, but the old man went off without replying.

Don Paolo overtook him in the open space in front of the inn.

'Well done, I congratulate you,' the priest said to him.

'I only said it to infuriate the woman,' Grascia said. He found it intolerable that a woman should try to instruct men.

'When woman teaches man children are born hunchbacked,' he explained.

It was a sultry night. Gusts of sirocco coming up from the valley along the little stream gave one a slightly queasy feeling.

126

The small crowd had gathered to listen to the schoolmistress and they now quickly dispersed. Near the wooden bridge, where they stopped to talk, Don Paolo and Grascia were joined by Sciatàp, Magascià and Daniele.

'Before going to bed we ought at least to wet our whistle,' the priest suggested.

'If it's a matter of obeying a precept of the Church, we have no possible objection,' said Magascià.

Don Paolo gave Sciatàp some money to pay Matalena for a bottle of wine. Meanwhile Grascia had started inveighing against the schoolmistress again.

'There's nothing worse than a hen trying to lay down the law to a cock,' he said.

'Here, have a drink,' said Sciatàp.

He had brought a glass for Don Paolo, but the priest refused it.

'It's better straight from the bottle,' he said.

Grascia could not get his fixed idea out of his head.

'One of us ought to do her the kindness of giving her a baby,' he said. 'We might even draw lots for the job.'

'Who are you talking about?' asked Magascià.

'The schoolmistress.'

'Leave the wretched woman alone,' Magascià said. 'Everyone earns a living as best they can.'

'Have a drink and pass the bottle,' Daniele said to him. 'We'll draw lots another evening. You're not in a hurry, are you?'

'No, I can wait,' Grascia said.

'Perhaps I may be leaving in a few days' time,' Don Paolo said. 'I'm feeling much better. But before I go I should like to have a better idea of your way of thinking.'

'That's soon said,' said Daniele. 'We're just tillers of the soil and don't have much to think about.'

'Even a cafone thinks sometimes,' the priest said. 'To begin with, why don't you tell me what you think about the situation, Daniele?'

'What situation?' said Daniele.

'The general situation.'

'The general situation of Pietrasecca? Are you asking whether I think Pietrasecca would be better off if it were situated somewhere else? I must admit I've never considered it. This village has always been here.'

'You haven't understood me,' said the priest. 'I was referring to living conditions in general, here and elsewhere in Italy. What do you think of them?'

'I don't think of them,' said Daniele. 'Of course, everyone has his own worries.'

'Everyone is plagued by his own fleas,' said Sciatàp. 'Are you saying we should worry about other people's too?'

'Everyone has his own little bit of land,' said Grascia. 'Everyone thinks day and night about his own little bit of land. If it rains too much, or hails, or doesn't rain at all. Italy is an endless number of plots of land, mountains, hills, plains, woods, lakes, marshes, beaches. If you had to think about them all, you'd go mad. Man's brain isn't big enough. All we can do with our little brain is to think about our own bit of land.'

'And sometimes,' said Sciatàp, 'our brain isn't even big enough for that. And in any case what's the good of thinking? Hail comes just the same.'

'You haven't understood me,' said the priest. 'I want to know what you think about this government.'

'Nothing,' said Daniele.

The others agreed. 'Nothing,' they said.

'What?' said the priest. 'Though you're always grumbling?'

'Everyone has his own troubles,' said Magascià. 'That's all that interests us. At most you worry about your neighbour's. You look at your own vineyard or your own plot of land; you look through the door or the window of your house if the door or the window is open; when you eat your soup sitting at the front door in the evening you look at your own plate.'

'Everyone has his own fleas to plague him,' said Sciatàp, 'and no doubt the government has its own fleas too. Let it do what we do, scratch itself. What else could we suggest to it?'

'You haven't understood me,' said the priest. 'I want to know what you think about taxes, prices, military service and other laws.'

128

'Drink,' Grascia said to him. 'Father, you obviously have time to waste. No, I don't mean to be rude. What I mean is that all these questions are superfluous. Everyone knows what we think about some things.'

'On taxes, military service, and rents we all think the same,' said Daniele. 'Even the most timid and resigned, and even the most sanctimonious. There's nothing new or secret about that. It would be really strange if we thought otherwise'

'Drink and pass the bottle,' Grascia said.

'It's empty,' said Daniele.

Don Paolo offered to pay for another, but the men objected. 'It's our turn,' they said. 'We know how to behave.' They all contributed, and Daniele went to the bar and came back with a full bottle.

'You drink first,' he said to the priest. 'It will serve as a grace.'

'You grumble,' Don Paolo said, returning to the theme, 'but you remain obedient and resigned.'

'We are born and grow up with the same ideas,' said Sciatàp. 'What are our oldest memories? Of our old folk grumbling. What are our children's of their childhood? Of our grumbling. We used to think things couldn't get worse, but they got worse. Even the blind and deaf-and-dumb know it. I've never met anyone who thought otherwise.'

'Even the authorities know it,' said Magascià. 'Do you know what the podestà of Fossa said in his last speech in the square? "I don't ask you not to grumble," he said, "but at least do so at home and not in the public square and not in the corridors of the town hall. At least show a little decency." And in the last resort he was quite right. You must have a sense of decency. What's the use of grumbling?'

'I don't agree,' said Grascia. 'If it doesn't do anything else it at least saves you from exploding.'

'Drink, and pass the bottle,' Daniele said to him.

'But don't you think that one day your troubles might end?' the priest asked.

'Are you talking about the next life, about life after death?' Grascia asked. 'Are you talking about paradise?'

'No, I'm talking about this world,' Don Paolo insisted. 'Don't you think that one day the landowners might be expropriated and their land given to the poor? Don't you think that the country might be run by people such as yourselves? Don't you think that your sons and grandsons might be born free?'

'Yes, we know that dream,' said Grascia. 'Every so often we hear about it. It's a beautiful dream, there's none more beautiful.'

'But unfortunately it's only a dream,' said Magascià.

'A beautiful dream,' said Sciatàp. 'Wolves and lambs will graze together in the same field. Big fish will no longer eat little fish. A lovely fairy story. Every so often we hear about it.'

'So you think that in this world damnation is eternal?' the priest said. 'Don't you think that one day laws might be made by you in favour of all?'

'No, I don't,' said Magascià. 'Don't let's have any illusions.'

'If it depended on me, I'd abolish all laws,' said Grascia. 'That's where all evil comes from.'

'It's a dream,' said Sciatàp. 'A beautiful dream.'

'If it depended on me, I'd replace all existing laws with one single law,' Grascia said. 'There's just one single law that would be enough to stop everyone from complaining, believe me. It would give every Italian the right to emigrate.'

'Impossible,' said Daniele. 'Who would stay here?'

'It's a dream,' said Sciatàp. 'A beautiful dream. It would be like abolishing stable doors.'

'Drink, and pass the bottle,' Magascià said to him.

'It's empty,' said Sciatàp. 'Shall I get another?'

'No, it's late,' Don Paolo said. 'I'm feeling rather tired.'

Back in his room, he took from his suitcase the notebook in which he had written, 'On the inaccessibility of the cafoni to politics' and sat down at the table. He remained sitting there for a long time with his head between his hands. Eventually he began writing: 'Perhaps they are right,' was his first sentence.

Chapter 14

When Don Paolo told Matalena that he was going to Fossa next day she took it as an announcement of impending catastrophe. She barely had the strength to ask him when he was coming back.

'I don't know,' he replied with exaggerated indifference. 'I may come back just to fetch the things I'm leaving here for the time being.'

At that moment Teresa Scaraffa happened to pass by on her way to draw water from the fountain.

'Teresa,' Matalena called out. 'For the love of heaven keep an eye on the place for a few minutes, I'll be back directly.'

'What's the matter with you?' Teresa exclaimed in alarm, but she got no answer.

Matalena, unkempt and in bedroom slippers as she was, started running. Breathlessly she climbed the alley and the steps that led to the cave where Cassarola lived. The wise woman was lying on a sack of maize leaves, complaining about her aches and pains and feeding bits of bread to a goat.

'What's the matter?' she exclaimed when she saw Matalena. 'Is your house on fire?'

'He's going,' Matalena barely managed to gasp with the little breath she had left.

'That's your fault,' the wise woman retorted. 'So I poke the fire and you put it out. Why did you provoke a quarrel between him and Donna Cristina?'

'You know why. It certainly wasn't out of jealousy.'

'Only a hen's brain like yours could entertain the suspicion that Don Pasquale would invite the priest to stay with him. You ought to know who rules the roost in that house.'

Matalena was easily persuaded that she was in the wrong, and she began to snivel.

'What can we do now?'

'We must try to repair the blunder if it isn't too late. If you want to tie someone, it's no use going against nature. Even a priest is made of flesh and blood.'

Matalena hurried back to the inn and smartened herself up. She combed her hair, changed her apron, and put on a pair of shoes.

'Please, please, wait here a little longer,' she said imploringly to Teresa. 'I've got to go and see Donna Cristina.'

To Matalena calling out of the blue at the Colamartini house like this was very much against the grain. Over and above her dismay at the priest's departure, there was a special reason for her reluctance. At her last encounter with Cristina she had been extremely rude, and since then the two had not seen each other. Fortunately it was her father who opened the door. Did he know why the priest wanted to hasten his departure from Pietrasecca? No, he knew nothing about it. Then Cristina appeared; she had been unwell for the past few days, and knew even less.

'I'm going to Fossa tomorrow morning too,' Don Pasquale said. 'Tell Don Paolo I shall be happy to give him a lift.'

Cristina walked back to the gate with Matalena.

'Perhaps both of us have been at fault,' Matalena said humbly. 'Perhaps we both could have done more to keep Don Paolo here.'

'What could we have done?' Cristina asked.

'Perhaps you offended him without meaning it,' Matalena said. 'He was very fond of you, and still is.'

'How is he?' Cristina asked. 'Is he leaving without having completely recovered?'

'During these last few days he has lost all that he had previously gained,' said Matalena.

'I'm very sorry to hear it,' said Cristina.

Don Paolo was punctual for the appointment next morning. It was a fine morning, and the fresh smell of wet grass was coming down from the mountain. There had not been such a bright morning for a long time. While old Colamartini put the mare between the shafts and slowly adjusted the traces, the bit and the blinkers, Cristina came and greeted the priest.

'Are you leaving already?' she said. 'For good?' ·

'I don't know,' said Don Paolo, embarrassed. 'I'm leaving my things here. I may come back, or I may send someone for them.'

His irritation with the girl had vanished, though a certain annoyance and disappointment remained. But the fact of the matter was that his mind was elsewhere. He no longer felt like an invalid. The girl, however, looked run down.

'Donna Cristina has been unwell,' Matalena had told him that morning while he was having his breakfast. 'She has been very ill.'

'I didn't know,' the priest had said.

'She was in bed for a week,' Matalena had added. 'I hope it wasn't your fault.'

'My fault?'

'She's a very sensitive girl, and she was very fond of you. Haven't you noticed that the geraniums on the little balcony have withered?'

Don Paolo received this statement with a certain amount of irritation.

'We're ready,' Don Pasquale announced.

'Bon voyage,' said Cristina. 'I hope we shall see you again soon.'

'I hope so too,' said Don Paolo.

Cristina was going to say something else, but the trap moved off. For a short time the two men remained silent, almost embarrassed.

'The mare's name is Diana,' Don Pasquale said. 'I bought her fifteen years ago to go hunting. Happy times that won't return.'

The shape of the trap, with its high seats and four wheels, the front ones small and the back ones big, the mare's harness, the embroidered cushions on which the two men sat, and even their clothes, also belonged to other times.

A man riding a donkey behind a number of other donkeys approached them from the opposite direction. The donkey the man was riding was small, and his feet nearly touched the ground; he was looking towards the stream and took no notice of the trap as it passed by.

'He leases a small plot of land from me and hasn't paid the rent for three years,' Don Pasquale said to the priest. 'Whenever we meet he looks the other way.'

The trap overtook a cart going down to the valley loaded with sacks of grain. The carter was walking behind the cart; he had applied the wheel drag and was acting as a counter-weight.

'A good crop?' Don Paolo asked.

'This is the whole of it,' said the carter. 'It's all there, and I've got to take it to the landlord before the bailiff comes and seizes it.'

The rusty coloration of the valley gradually turned greyish as they approached the Fucino plain. The stubble of recently reaped fields formed yellow patches on the sloping countryside. Tall cones of hay were visible in the distance, with men moving round them like ants. Women passed with babies in their arms, looking like the madonnas in the churches, dark and ill-tempered madonnas taking their lunch to the men who were busy threshing. The heat of the day began to make itself felt. The horse's head was surrounded by a swarm of little flies. The unmetalled road was bad. In a field a party of militiamen were squatting outside a tent, with their rifles between their knees. All the heat of the midday sun seemed to be concentrated on a small donkey standing motionless in the middle of the road. 'Look, it's just going to burst,' Don Paolo said. Some donkeys loaded with sacks of flour were coming from the Fossa mill. A group of cafoni with bundles under their arms were going in the direction of the station. Even in the midday heat people going away wore everything they had, as if they were fugitives, as if they were never going to return.

Don Pasquale spotted a friend standing at the door of a shop, and he stopped the trap and made him get in. He was Don Genesio, who worked at the tax office.

'That's not an occupation that is generally highly thought of,' remarked Don Paolo.

'That's true,' said Don Genesio. 'To the cafoni, particularly the most backwards ones in the valleys, every official is a big parasitic insect.'

'And they're not entirely wrong,' said Don Pasquale. 'What

does Rome do to remedy our plight? It sets up new offices, and then foreign capitalists infiltrate behind them and act as masters.'

'Priests too are considered more or less to be parasites,' said Don Genesio. 'And that in spite of the fact that people know they can't do without either the one or the other.'

'In what sense do they consider us to be parasites?' Don Paolo asked. 'Do they put us on a par with flies and fleas? If so, they would have no difficulty in doing without us.'

'I can't really say for certain,' said Don Genesio. 'Perhaps they equate us with the cow horns they put on their houses to protect them against the evil eye, or something of the sort. But there's no cause for alarm, they believe they can't do without us.'

Don Pasquale and Don Genesio engaged in an animated conversation about family matters and transfers of property and mortages, while Don Paolo seemed absorbed in his own thoughts. Every now and then the distant sound of liturgical singing came down from the hills. Parties of pilgrims were coming down the mountain roads and joining forces on the national road.

'They're going to the Holy Martyrs at Celano,' Don Genesio said. 'They'll be on the road all day.'

Don Pasquale dropped the priest in the little square outside the Girasole hotel at Fossa and went off immediately, perhaps to avoid meeting Signora Berenice, who hurried forward to greet the priest and kissed his hand with profound respect.

'There's someone waiting for you in the diningroom,' she said.

'Where's your daughter?' Don Paolo asked anxiously.

'I'll send for her immediately,' Berenice said. 'She came back yesterday from Rome, where she found a good job, thank heaven.'

'I'm delighted to hear it,' said Don Paolo.

In the diningroom he found Cardile waiting for him, sitting at a table with half a litre of wine in front of him. They greeted each other cordially.

'I was expecting to see the doctor too,' Don Paolo said.

'I'm sorry, but he couldn't come,' said Cardile.

'Will he be coming this evening? Or tomorrow morning?'

'No, I don't think he will,' Cardile said.

'If he can't come here, I'll go and see him,' said Don Paolo. 'I need his help to find somewhere else to go. If I stay at Pietrasecca I'll die of boredom. I have an idea I want to put to him.'

'Listen,' Cardile said, embarrassed. 'We can't count on him any longer.'

'Why not? Did he tell you that himself?'

'Yes.'

'Is he afraid?'

Berenice brought Don Paolo some wine and went back to her kitchen.

'He's in a difficult position,' Cardile said. 'War to the death has broken out between him and other doctors about the headship of the local hospital. He's not a bad man, but his whole future's at stake. The slightest suspicion would be sufficient to ruin him.'

Bianchina appeared at the door of the inn like a sudden luminous apparition because of her white dress.

'Don Paolo,' she exclaimed joyfully.

The priest went over towards her.

'How are you?' he said. 'How did the trip go?'

'Exactly according to plan,' she said.

Her mother, who was laying the tables, looked pleased.

'Tell me about it later,' Don Paolo said, pointing to the girl's mother, who might have overheard them.

He did not know what excuse the girl had invented to explain her trip to Rome. She had lost the slightly disreputable, gipsy-like look she had had when she came to Pietrasecca, and she seemed better from every point of view. Raising her voice slightly so as to be sure that her mother could hear, she began telling the priest all about the basilicas and museums of Rome. But as soon as her mother vanished into the kitchen she dropped her voice and said, 'I've brought back some papers for you, I've hidden them in the garret.'

'What are they about?' Don Paolo asked.

'I don't know, they're in a closed envelope,' Bianchina said. 'Since you trusted me, for once I respected a secret. I'll bring them to your room.'

'All right,' Don Paolo said. He turned to Cardile and asked him to order lunch for him too. 'But no spaghetti, please. I'll be back in a few minutes,' he said.

On the first floor Bianchina handed him a big yellow envelope. 'Thank you,' he said. 'We'll see each other later.' He went into the room that had been reserved for him and shut the door. His hands trembled as he opened the envelope. This was the first communication from 'foreign headquarters' that had reached him since his return to Italy. The envelope contained copies of three voluminous reports as well as a laconic note asking him to give his opinion of the documents immediately. He restricted himself to reading the titles of the reports. These were: 'The Leadership Crisis in the Russian Communist Party and the Duties of Fraternal Parties', 'The Criminal Complicity with Imperialist Fascism of Oppositional Elements on the Right and on the Left', and 'The Solidarity of all the Parties of the International with the Majority of the Russian Communist Party'. He put the papers in an attaché case and went down to the diningroom. Throughout the meal he hardly spoke.

'Bad news?' Cardile said.

'Very bad indeed,' Don Paolo said. 'Special service from Byzantium,' he added a moment or two later, with a grimace.

'I don't understand,' said Cardile.

'Neither do I,' Don Paolo said. 'But I'm surprised to see that you ordered spaghetti.'

'Do you really dislike spaghetti as much as that?' Cardile said. 'I don't see why.'

The rest of the meal passed off in silence. Only at the very end did Don Paolo say, 'Perhaps I'll go back to Rome tomorrow.'

'So by and large the time you spent here served some purpose,' said Cardile.

'Yes, I think I've gathered a fistful of flies,' Don Paolo said. 'Where did you leave the trap?'

'Quite near here,' Cardile said. 'Unfortunately I have to go back at once to avoid rousing suspicion at home. When shall I see you again?'

Don Paolo accompanied him to the trap. When the time came to say goodbye Cardile embraced him. 'You know where I live,' he said. 'Also you know where my hayloft is.'

The usual idlers were gathering outside the Girasole hotel, as it was coffee time. There were grown men with week-old beards in shirt sleeves and slippers, with their trousers and collars undone, and youths with long, well-oiled hair. Some of the latter were surrounding an elderly man who was gesticulating with the mask-like expressiveness of an aged provincial actor.

'Who's that?' Don Paolo asked Berenice.

'That's our greatest lawyer, Marco Tullio Zabaglia, known as Zabaglione,' she replied.

The priest had heard the name before.

'Wasn't he once the socialist leader in these parts?' he asked.

'Yes, but he's a decent person all the same.'

Zabaglione noticed the priest standing at the door of the hotel and introduced himself.

'I am the lawyer Zabaglia,' he said. 'It's an honour to meet you. Signora Berenice has sung your praises to me. I know all about you. Excuse me, but are you from the curia?'

'What curia?' said Don Paolo.

'The episcopal curia. The reason I ask is that I very much want to know whether the clerical speakers for the departure of the conscripts have been chosen yet, and who will be coming here.'

'They will be chosen during the next few days,' Don Paolo said. 'Who they will be? The usual ones, of course.'

Don Paolo found himself talking to a man whom as a boy he had always heard talked of with hatred by the landowners and admiration and respect by the poor. Zabaglione's local fame was based on his forensic eloquence. If it was known that he was going to plead at a criminal trial the cobblers' and tailors' and carpenter's shops emptied, the concierges abandoned their lairs, and everyone who could went to listen to him. Many of his famous speeches had become proverbial. During the first years of the dictatorship he had had to make tremendous efforts to cause his rhetorical feats to be forgotten. He had transformed his old Mazzini-style beard, which he had worn since he was a young man, into a Balbo-style goatee; and he shortened and thinned his hair, changed the way he knotted his tie, and tried, though vainly, to lose weight. But if these were the most visible and hence the most painful sacrifices to which the former tribune of the people had had to subject himself, there was no counting the minor, everyday mortifications that he had to endure, such as having to sacrifice his ideas, being careful in what he said about the government, and breaking off relations with his suspect friends. In spite of the undeniable determination he had put into all this, he had not succeeded in completely rehabilitating himself, and he was consistently left out in the cold by the new institutions.

What had caused him the greatest suffering in recent years had been having to be silent on the numerous occasions on which he could have stirred the minds of the people, 'raising them to the level of events', as he put it. As a result incidents of historical importance had been utterly wasted, and that was the greatest misfortune that could happen to a civilized country.

'Will you do me the infinite honour of coming to my house for coffee?' Zabaglione said to the priest. 'Some friends of mine would very much like to meet you.'

'Thank you, but I can't,' Don Paolo said. He went back into the hotel, and then abruptly turned and retraced his steps. 'It's not as late as I thought,' he said to Zabaglione. 'I shall be delighted to come with you.'

CHAPTER 15

To reach the lawyer's house they first had to make their way through the old part of the town, with its dark and ancient alleys bearing the names of saints and local benefactors and silent little squares enclosed by stone houses blackened by time. Next they came to the new quarter, built on garden city lines after the earthquake. The streets and avenues were too big for local needs, and the new street names recorded glorious dates in the history of the government party. Heroic slogans, written in charcoal, chalk, tar, or painted in various colours or actually standing out in relief, carved in wood or stone or even forged in bronze, were to be seen on the fronts of houses and on fountains, trees and garden gates.

'Here we are,' the lawyer announced.

Outside his house a party of bricklayers were squatting on the ground, with chunks of bread, knives, and red and green peppers to help it down. They greeted the lawyer cordially. The house was surrounded by a perimeter wall surmounted by glass fragments. In the garden, kneeling on the gravel, a little man was tidying up round a bed planted with flowers in the three colours of the Italian national flag. A refined and attractive lady with hair curled by tongs appeared on the theshold; this was Zabaglione's wife.

'Kiss the father's hand and get us some coffee,' her husband said.

The lady kissed the priest's hand and withdrew to the kitchen. Three skinny girls, dressed in dark clothing and as pale as plants that had grown up in the dark, appeared in the entrance hall. These were Zabaglione's daughters.

'Kiss the father's hand and leave us,' their father said.

The girls kissed the priest's hand, made a slight curtsey and disappeared too.

'I send my daughters to mass every Sunday,' Zabaglione

said. 'If you don't believe me, ask Don Angelo, the Fossa priest. What would become of women without the restraint of religion? Their mother goes with them, of course.'

A sharp smell of cat's urine filled the drawingroom. Worn blue curtains hung from the windows, and the walls were almost completely hidden by shelves full of dusty books. An unidentified plaster bust, perhaps of some ancestor, surrounded by numerous yellowish photographs, presided over the desk.

'Take a seat,' the lawyer said cordially. 'I feel I know you, because, as I mentioned before, I have heard you very highly spoken of.'

Without too much beating about the bush the priest brought the conversation round to the subject closest to his heart.

'About fifteen years ago,' he said, 'I was concerned with the organization of Catholic peasants. Our organizations, like the socialist organizations, were subsequently dissolved. Hence we are in a similar situation from one point of view. What is the present state of mind of former members of the socialist leagues in these parts?'

Zabaglione suddenly became reserved and started tidying the papers on his desk. The silence grew painful.

To encourage him to talk, Don Paolo made up a story about the situation in his own diocese. He talked of a serious crisis in wine production and of growing popular restlessness. The corporations were empty shams in which no-one believed any longer. 'And what is the situation here?' he said. 'What do the former members of the red leagues think? Are they still socialists?'

'They never were,' said the lawyer.

'But most communes were in the hands of your red leagues,' said the priest. 'Or is my memory at fault?'

'Your memory is perfectly correct,' said the lawyer. 'But the point is that those leagues were not political. The poor peasants, the people whom we call cafoni here, joined the league for the sake of company and protection. To them socialism meant getting together. The ideal of the boldest spirits among them was to have work and be able to eat their fill. To have work and be able to sleep peacefully without having to worry about next day. Beside the bearded portrait of Karl Marx in our league premises at Fossa there was a picture of Christ in red clothing as the Redeemer of the poor. On Saturday evenings cafoni came and sang "Brothers arise, comrades arise", and on Sunday morning they went to mass to say amen. The essential task of a socialist leader was writing letters of recommendation. Nowadays the recommendations are written by others; my recommendations have lost their value, because the cafoni no longer take any interest in me. That is what the change of régime means to them.'

'But weren't there any real socialists?' the priest wanted to know.

'The only socialist in this part of the world was, so to speak, myself,' said Zabaglione. 'Yes, there were one or two groups that were a little more vigorous, and they suffered severely as a result. The survivors avoid meeting or being seen together.'

'But grave events such as happened elsewhere did not happen here,' said Don Paolo. 'Why was there so much restraint?'

Zabaglione was silent for a moment. 'Here too shameful things happened,' he said. 'On the 19th of January 1923 – it's a date I cannot forget – a gang of political innovators raided the house of the head of the league at Rivisondoli, and all twenty-two of them raped his wife. It took them from eleven at night till two in the morning. Just an incident. Some of our cafoni took refuge at that time in France or in America. Those who remain, as you know, are no longer called cafoni, but members of the rural population.'

'But oppositional elements must still exist,' Don Paolo said. 'There must be some who look back with regret to the days when it was possible to meet freely.'

'There are not many left here,' Zabaglione replied, 'but I must say I liked socialism myself. As you are a priest, may I confess one of my weaknesses to you? Well, then, socialist theories left me indifferent, but I liked the socialist movement, just as I liked women. The best speeches I ever made were about socialism . . .'

To the priest's intense annoyance, just when the conversation was becoming more confidential other visitors arrived. They were Don Genesio, whom the priest had already met, the chief of the municipal guards, and Don Luigi, the chemist. The chief of the guards wore a magnificent uniform worthy of a pre-war general.

'How many guards do you have under your command?' Don Paolo asked him.

'For the time being only one,' he replied. 'It's a poor commune, you see, and it's growing very slowly.'

Don Luigi was a handsome man, with moustache and hair in the style of King Umberto.

'Father,' he said, 'I assure you that I send my wife to mass every Sunday. If you don't believe me, ask the parish priest. In my opinion religion is to women what salt is to pork. It helps to maintain the freshness and the flavour.'

Don Genesio had smartened himself up; he too was carefully combed and brilliantined. As was to be expected, he too sent his wife to mass every Sunday.

'The news that the bank has closed its doors has begun to reach its customers in the valley,' Don Luigi said. 'Just now I met Don Pasquale Colamartini of Pietrasecca, and he seemed to have gone out of his mind. All that was left of his half-witted wife's dowry was on deposit in the bank, and he didn't know it was sailing through a minefield.'

Zabaglione sighed. 'In the old days the failure of a bank would have led to a magnificent lawsuit,' he said.

'Have you heard of a notorious individual named Pietro Spina?' the commander of the guard asked.

Don Paolo started browsing through an album of picture postcards.

'He belongs to the Spina family of Rocca dei Marsi, and he's a crazy revolutionary,' the man went on. 'It seems that he went abroad and came back to Italy to commit murders. The police have been looking for him for three months. He was reported to our area, for it seems that he wanted to set fire to the sheaves of corn on the threshing floors. But today we had news that he was arrested in Rome.'

'That's another fine trial that will be wasted,' Zabaglione said.

'What do you say?' asked the commander of the guard.

'A little penal servitude will do him good,' said Zabaglione.

'Did you say Spina of Rocca dei Marsi?' Don Luigi asked. 'I know the family. I was at university with Don Ignazio Spina, the boy's father. He was a good man, he died in the earthquake. That's another old family that's going to the dogs.'

'How is it known that he wanted to set fire to the sheaves of corn?' Don Paolo asked. 'Has he been seen in these parts at threshing time?'

'He has never been seen in these parts, either now or in previous years,' the commander of the guard said. 'He has always done his propaganda in towns. But during this threshing season there have been some red inscriptions on walls saying "Long live Pietro Spina". That has never happened before, and it shows that he must have been in this part of the world.'

'Do you think he came here to write his own name on the walls?' the priest asked.

'No, he didn't do it, but his followers did,' said the commander of the guard.

'Oh, his followers,' Don Paolo blurted out. 'Are there any rebellious cafoni?'

He was on the point of forgetting to be cautious when one of the lawyer's daughters came in and served the coffee.

'No sugar for me,' Don Paolo said.

'No, there are no rebellious cafoni, but there's a great deal of unrest among the young,' the commander of the guard admitted. 'The things they say under the pretext of corporativism are enough to make one's hair stand on end.'

'The new generation is the dangerous one,' said Don Luigi. 'How shall I put it? It's the generation that presents the accounts. It takes literally the claim that corporativism means the end of capitalism, and it wants the destruction of capitalism.'

'That's the cause of all the trouble,' said Zabaglione. 'Taking theories literally. No régime ought ever to be taken literally, otherwise where would it end? Have you read today's papers? In Russia the death penalty has been reintroduced for adolescents. Why? Probably because they take the Soviet constitution literally. There ought to be a rule that a country's constitution is a matter that concerns only lawyers and the most trustworthy of the older generation, and that it must be strictly ignored by the young.'

The commander of the guard agreed.

'As you know,' he said, 'I was made responsible for the setting up and supervision of a public library. What need there is of a library here I really do not know. Those who want to read books ought to buy them, in my opinion. But the order was given, the books arrived from Rome, and the library was opened. One might have expected the books to have been properly censored, but instead what happened? Juveniles came and asked for the early works of the head of the government and started saying: "Look, here it says that the Church, the dynasty and capitalism must be overthrown." I tried to explain that those books were written for grown-ups and not for children, and that at their age they ought to be reading fairy tales. But there was no way of putting them off. In the end, with the agreement of higher authority, I had to withdraw those books from circulation and put them in a locked cupboard.'

'Too late,' said Don Luigi. 'My son tells me that someone on his own initiative copied out extracts from those books, which are circulating among the young. Some of them meet at the Villa delle Stagioni on the other side of the stream to read and discuss them. My son says there's going to be another revolution to carry out what those books say . . .'

'Are they young peasants?' Don Paolo asked.

'No,' said the commander of the guard, 'they are three or four young students. The authorities know all about them, and when the right time comes they'll put a stop to their little game.'

Zabaglione shook his head.

'The greatest of evils is when the young start taking seriously what they read in books,' he said.

Don Paolo and the chemist left Don Zabaglione's house together.

'You said you knew Pietro Spina's father in his student days,' the priest said. 'Was he as mad as his son?'

'We met at Naples,' Don Luigi said. 'We were Republicans, like most students at that time. Giuseppe Mazzini was our god, and Alberto Mario his living prophet. Then we returned to the Marsica, and he married very soon after. He came to see me a few years later, and he had changed out of all recognition. I shall never forget what he said. "The poetry has finished and the prose has begun," he said. I'm genuinely sorry about his son.'

'Did you also know Don Ignazio's wife?' the priest asked.

'I met her a couple of times with her husband,' said Don Luigi. 'She was an excellent lady.'

'What was it that your friend complained about, then?'

'Certainly not his wife,' Don Luigi said, 'but all the petty rivalries, jealousies, envies and self-interest of provincial life.'

'It seems to me,' the priest said with a smile, 'that you are justifying the rebellion of that young man, what's his name? I mean young Spina.'

'No,' Don Luigi said. 'His revolt is illusory and is therefore to be deplored. I can feel nothing but compassion for the unfortunate young man. Now the authorities complain that my son Pompeo is inciting his friends and talking about another revolution. I certainly don't approve of what he says, but neither do I want him to be taken seriously and mishandled. Now he's at the poetry stage, I say, and later on he'll have a regular job and he'll marry and settle down and he'll reach the prose stage.'

'What would happen if men remained loyal to the ideals of their youth?' Don Paolo asked.

Don Luigi raised his arms to high heaven as if to say that it would be the end of the world.

'The time always comes,' he said, 'when the young find that the bread and wine of their home have lost their flavour and they look elsewhere for their nourishment. Only the bread and wine of the tavern at the crossroads of the great highways can

146

assuage their hunger and their thirst. But man cannot spend all his life in taverns.'

CHAPTER 16

The priest saw in the distance an old gentleman leaning against a street lamp as if he had been suddenly taken ill, and then he recognized him as Don Pasquale Colamartini. Quickly he said goodbye to the chemist and hurried to his assistance. The old man seemed to be semi-conscious and hardly recognized the priest until he collapsed in his arms.

'Courage,' Don Paolo said to him. 'Courage.'

The old man was gasping for breath, his pallor was corpse-like, and he was unable to speak. The priest helped him, one step at a time, as far as the trap, and it was even more difficult to help him on to the box and put the reins in his trembling hands.

The old man's eyes were full of tears. 'It's the end,' he managed to say.

'Isn't there anyone here who could go back to Pietrasecca with you?' Don Paolo asked. 'Haven't you a friend here who could go with you?'

The old man shook his head. 'There's no-one, no-one,' he whimpered.

Don Paolo followed the trap until it disappeared round the bend in the road. Outside the Girasole hotel a number of people were talking about the failure of the bank.

'As for Don Pasquale,' Berenice was saying, 'it's a well-deserved chastisement of heaven. He took a half-witted old woman as his second wife so as to be able to lay his hands on her money without having any children, and now he's lost the money, the children by his first wife are leaving home, and he's left with the old idiot.'

Don Paolo was about to protest when someone took him by the arm. It was Bianchina.

'Come away,' she said. 'Don't get upset.'

'How can your mother be so spiteful?' said the priest.

'Perhaps she feels it to be her duty because of me,' Bianchina said. 'Perhaps she feels it to be her duty as a good mother. At all events, that's what the poor thing believes herself to be.'

'Good mothers, what a disastrous institution,' the priest said. Then he added, 'I'm sorry I didn't get on the trap and go back with Don Pasquale. I'm very worried about him.'

'Poor old chap,' said Bianchina. 'But for the fact that he might misinterpret the gesture, I might try to catch him up and help him, and Cristina. But it's impossible to do so much as draw a breath here without being misunderstood. Listen, Don Paolo, you must take me away from here, please, I implore you, I can't go on living here.'

'We'll discuss that another time,' Don Paolo said. 'Do you know the son of Don Luigi, the chemist?'

'Pompeo?' said Bianchina. 'He's a friend of mine. I'm glad you're interested in him. I've already talked to him about you. If you'll come with me to the Villa delle Stagioni, I'll introduce him to you.'

The Villa delle Stagioni was an old country house that had come down in the world and was now a farmhouse. Once upon a time it had been the holiday home of a baron who had subsequently died in Rome, riddled with debts.

On the way Bianchina said, 'Alberto Colamartini, Cristina's brother, will probably also be at the villa.'

'At Pietrasecca I heard some talk about the two of you,' Don Paolo said.

'From Cristina?'

'No, you know how discreet she is.'

'I should have preferred it if you had heard it from Cristina,' the girl said. 'She wouldn't have embroidered any gossip.'

'But she too was opposed to the idea of your getting married,' Don Paolo said.

'So was I,' said Bianchina. 'Alberto made the mistake of talking to his father without telling me first. Do you know I wrote to Don Pasquale on that occasion? Didn't he tell you? I told him I hadn't the slightest intention of getting married, but that if in a moment of weariness I ever resigned myself to the idea I should put his son Alberto last on the list of young men to be made unhappy by me.'

'Are you as fond of him as that?' said the priest.

'No,' said Bianchina. 'He's too like me.'

Meanwhile they had reached the perimeter wall of the villa. The two leaves of the main gate through which one entered the park had been taken from their hinges and were leaning at an angle against the wall. Stinging nettles and poppies grew freely along the main drive. An ivy-covered, Renaissance-style pavilion had been turned into a barn, and the peacock cage was being used as a hen-coop. The villa consisted of two wings set at right angles. The ground floor of one wing housed horses and cows, and human beings inhabited the others. The unframed windows of the upper floors created the impression that the latter had either been abandoned or were used to store wheat. There were four empty niches on the façades between two balconies. On the walls, which were cracked and lined with damp, the words LONG LIVE CORPORATIONS WITHOUT BOSSES and LONG LIVE THE SECOND REVOLUTION had been painted in big letters. In one corner a young man was playing alone with a leather ball.

'Alberto,' Bianchina called out. 'That's the famous Alberto,' she said to the priest.

'Did you come down from Pietrasecca today?' Alberto asked Don Paolo. 'How's Cristina?'

He had a boy's slim figure and immature eyes and voice; his face was open and yet stubborn at the same time.

'I'm worried about your father,' Don Paolo said to him gravely. 'You know about the failure of the bank in which he had all his money? The news may have struck him a fatal blow. I had to help him into his trap just now. I fear the worst may happen.'

'The person you call my father threw me out,' Alberto said. 'He no longer considers me his son.'

'If you had seen him just now,' Don Paolo said, 'I'm sure you would have forgotten all that. He was a poor old man who could no longer stand on his feet, a poor old man who had been struck a fatal blow.'

'Won't you go to Pietrasecca at once?' Bianchina said. 'I could get you a horse.'

150

'If he were still alive when I got there, the mere sight of me might be fatal to him,' Alberto said. 'If I arrived too late my grandmother would throw me out. Have you met that terrifying old fury? I'm only sorry for Cristina.'

Another young man arrived; he was about the same age as Alberto, but stronger and more robust, and he wore a sports vest and shorts.

'This is Pompeo,' Bianchina said.

'Bianchina has talked to us about you,' Pompeo said.

'I think you're made to understand one another,' Bianchina said.

'We are probably in agreement on essentials,' said Don Paolo. 'I'm referring not so much to political theories as to the use to be made of our lives. But it's the kind of agreement that is difficult to describe.'

'Why?' said Pompeo.

'We are divided by superficial things,' said Don Paolo. 'In order to understand one another we should not be afraid of discarding commonplaces, symbols, labels.'

'We are not afraid,' said Pompeo.

'We have reached a point,' Don Paolo went on, 'at which a sincere fascist should not be afraid of talking to a communist or an anarchist; and an intellectual should not be afraid of talking to a cafone.'

'Are you perhaps saying that all divisions between men are artificial, and that struggles are useless?' Pompeo asked.

'Certainly not,' Don Paolo said. 'But some divisions are artificial, deliberately created to conceal real conflicts. There are divided forces that ought to be united, and artificially united forces that ought to be divided. Many present divisions are based on verbal misunderstandings, and many unions are verbal only.'

'Let us sit down,' said Bianchina. 'One thinks better sitting down.'

Two wooden benches were fetched from somewhere on the ground floor and put against the wall. At that moment a young peasant arrived and let out the cows. They came out slowly, two by two, and went over to drink at a trough in a corner of

151

the yard. They were thin, black and white, working cows, with big curved horns, and they drank slowly, looking askew at the persons sitting on the benches. The cowman shut the door of the shed and came and sat with the others.

Pompeo was saying, 'There was a man who saved the country from ruin and pointed the way to regeneration. His words were plain and left no room for doubt. When he came into power we were surprised that his actions conflicted with his promises. We wondered whether he had betrayed us. Someone came to these parts a few weeks ago and told us what had happened. The man was a prisoner of the bank, he said. That's what he told us. But what did he mean? Is the man really chained up in a bank vault, or was that just a manner of speaking?'

'What do you think?' the cowman asked the priest.

'I cannot say positively whether it's true that the man of whom you speak is really imprisoned in a bank,' said Don Paolo. 'Some believe it. But in any case it's not a matter of one man only. What is certain, as anyone who keeps his eyes open can see for himself, is that the whole country is a prisoner of high finance.'

'So what must be done?' said Bianchina.

'I too believe that a second revolution is necessary,' Don Paolo said. 'Our country must be freed from imprisonment by the bank. It will be a long and difficult enterprise and full of pitfalls, but the effort will be worthwhile.'

Don Paolo spoke calmly and without emphasis, but with a firmness that left no doubt. Bianchina flung her arms round his neck.

'Whoever would have supposed we had a priest with us for the second revolution?' Alberto said with a laugh.

'Don Paolo is not a priest but a saint,' Bianchina said. 'Didn't I tell you?'

'In every revolution there have been priests who sided with the people,' Pompeo said.

'I must tell you that I do not attach much importance to my priestly habit,' Don Paolo said.

'It will be more prudent if you remain a priest,' said Pompeo.

'Let us respect prudence,' the priest said with a laugh.

'But what are we to do immediately?' the cowman asked.

'That is a matter that I should prefer to discuss with Pompeo alone,' Don Paolo said.

The priest and the chemist's son went off on their own. They left the park, jumped a brook and took a path flanked by tall whitethorn hedges.

'We belong to different generations, but to the same species of young man, recognizable by the fact that we take seriously the principles proclaimed by our fathers or schoolmasters or priests. Those principles are proclaimed as the foundations of society, but it is easy to see that the actual functioning of that society conflicts with or ignores them. The majority, the sceptics, adapt themselves, the others become revolutionaries.'

'The sceptics,' Pompeo said, 'maintain that the discrepancy between doctrine and reality is an ineluctable fact of life. What is the answer?'

'It may be. But revolutions are also facts of life,' Don Paolo said. 'Everyone must make his choice.'

'You're right,' Pompeo said. 'What matters is the use one makes of one's life.'

The path continued along a row of almond trees between fields of burnt stubble. It was very hot. There were some isolated clumps of ripe blackberries, and the two stopped to pick some. Further on the path came to the national road, which at that time of day was crowded with donkeys, carts and cafoni coming back from work.

'What are we to do?' Pompeo asked.

'Let us think about it together,' Don Paolo said. 'We'll discuss it again when we've thought about it.'

'I'm delighted to have met a priest like you,' Pompeo said. 'I have friends in all these villages, and I'll introduce them to you.'

'It seems to me,' Don Paolo said, 'that the troublesome illness that forced me to leave my diocese and come here is only now acquiring a meaning.'

Before returning to Fossa the two friends separated to avoid being seen together.

The guttural voice of a sound film at the local cinema filled the principal street of Fossa, which was crowded with boys, and followed the priest all the way to his room. He was tired but happy. Before undressing he packed his bag in preparation for his departure next morning. He put the papers he had received from Rome the day before in the fireplace and burnt them without hesitation. No sooner had he taken his shoes off than he heard a rustle outside the door.

'Can I come in?'

It was Bianchina, cheerful and heavily scented.

'Do you know that Pompeo's enthusiastic about you?' she said.

'I very much hope we shall be friends,' Don Paolo said with a smile. 'I'm grateful to you for having introduced him to me. To me it was an event.'

'Really?' said Bianchina. 'Love at first sight?' She looked at him with a smile. 'The more I see of you, the more likeable and strange I think you,' she said.

'You shouldn't observe me too closely,' Don Paolo said. 'It frightens me and it might force me to do more pretending than is necessary.'

'May I confess a suspicion of mine?' Bianchina said. 'I'm not at all sure you're a real priest.'

'What do you mean by a real priest?'

'A boring person who has the *Eternal Maxims* in the place where his head ought to be. In other words, a person like my uncle, the parish priest of Fossa, and a lot of others besides.'

'You're right, I'm very different from that kind of priest,' Don Paolo said. 'Perhaps the biggest difference is that they believe in a very old God who lives above the clouds sitting on a golden throne, while I believe He's a youth in full possession of His faculties and continually going about the world.'

'I prefer your God,' Bianchina said with a laugh. 'But can you guarantee that He too won't age eventually?'

'No, alas,' he said. 'How can there be a guarantee against such a disaster? All the young eventually grow old.'

'Well, don't let's get depressed about it,' said Bianchina. 'Let's hope that the youth of the gods will last longer than ours.

When are you sending me to Rome again?'

'This time it's my turn,' said Don Paolo. 'I'm taking the first train tomorrow morning. I've told your mother already.'

'And you're leaving me here?' Bianchina protested, her eyes filling with tears.

'You'll stay here to help Pompeo,' Don Paolo said. 'Contacts with neighbouring villages must be restored immediately. Perhaps the time for action will come sooner than we think. I'll leave you some money for expenses.'

'Will you be coming back soon?' said Bianchina. 'You won't forget me?'

'Stop asking silly questions,' said Don Paolo. 'You know very well that I often think about you.'

'I'll set the alarm clock and come with you to the station,' said Bianchina.

'You'll do nothing of the sort, for heaven's sake,' said the priest.

'Why not? Are you ashamed of me?'

'It's the sort of thing married couples do, and it would be quite inappropriate in the case of a priest.'

CHAPTER 17

In the train Don Paolo quickly discovered how disagreeable it was to travel in disguise, surrounded by strangers who seemed to scrutinize him and seized every opportunity of striking up a conversation. He thought he had extricated himself from this by standing in the corridor with his face to the window, but hurriedly moved away at the first stop when he spotted familiar faces on the platform. He ended by huddling in a corner of the compartment, pulling his hat down over his eyes and reading his breviary, holding it close to his face as if he were short-sighted. He read at random; psalms, litanies, stories of martyrs and saints, checking the situation in the compartment after every stop. Fortunately the journey was not a long one.

His priestly clothing enabled him to make his way safe and sound through the close police surveillance at the Termini station. As an additional precaution he fell in with a group of foreign priests who got out of another train. When he reached the square outside he made straight for an underground public bath-house.

'A bath,' he said to the girl cashier.

The girl was called to the telephone and gave him his change without looking at him.

The corridor between the cubicles was long, low and wet. The old woman attendant who made his cubicle ready for him looked at him with curiosity and said something that Don Paolo did not understand. He gave her a substantial tip. In his suitcase he had a jacket, a hat and tie, the minimum required for transforming himself into a layman. He took the bath seriously, for he needed it, and he lingered for a long time in the warm water. Before emerging from the cubicle he spent some time listening to the voices in the corridor, and as soon as he was sure that the old woman was cleaning the inside of another cubicle he made his exit unobserved. He was Pietro Spina again. He went back to the station to put the suitcase in the left luggage office, but how strange it felt to be walking in the street without a cassock. He felt everyone was looking at his legs. He started walking quickly, almost running, and several times he looked to make sure his trousers were properly buttoned. Eventually he jumped on a tram that took him to the Lateran quarter. The big sun-baked square between the basilica of San Giovanni and the Scala Santa was full of fairground swings and roundabouts that were being dismantled. They had already been stripped of their night-time attractions; carpenters were knocking down the timber framework, and tents, pasteboard, lamps, wooden horses and tin swords were being piled onto lorries. Plaster trophies, a ghost ship painted on a stormy sea and the fur of a Bengal tiger were lying on the ground.

Pietro crossed the untidy square and made for the cool shadow of the Scala Santa church. A number of women in black were climbing the stairs in the middle of the church on their knees. They stopped on every step, practically collapsed, sighed painfully, and said interminable prayers. Pietro stopped next to a marble group representing Pilate showing the scourged Christ to the people. On the pedestal were the words: *Haec est hora vestra et potestas tenebrarum*. Pietro did not have long to wait. A man who looked like an unemployed worker approached and looked at him with curiosity.

'Excuse me,' he said, 'but are you the pilgrim from Assisi?'

'Yes,' said Pietro. 'And who are you?'

'I'm a friend of the driver.'

'I have a message for you,' said Pietro, handing him a letter.

'Do you know where to go this evening?'

'Yes,' Pietro said. 'I shall try to manage.'

He went to the Porta San Giovanni and then continued along the Via Appia Nuova. Then he went down a side street and crossed a district that centred round some film studios and a new church. Beyond it was a huge expanse that was a domain of cats, stray dogs and down-and-outs. It was cut up by ditches and trenches and also served as a dump for scrap iron, timber, tiles, pipes and sheets of corrugated iron.

A few months earlier, fleeing from the police, he had taken refuge here in the hut of a former fellow-villager of his named Mannaggia Lamorra. As a boy Lamorra had been a servant in the Spina household at Orta, and later he had emigrated in search of fortune. He had sold fizzy drinks in the La Boca quarter of Buenos Aires and worked as an unskilled labourer in a brickworks at St André, near Marseilles, and after several years he had returned to Italy as poor as when he left it, which made him ashamed to go back to his village. He was now working as a navvy in a pozzolana quarry near Rome. Pietro had no difficulty in finding his wooden hut with its corrugated iron roof. Lamorra, cheerful and ready to oblige, came forward to meet him.

'Back again in these parts, sir?' he said.

'Yes, for a day or two,' said Pietro. 'Why aren't you at the quarry?'

'It was closed down,' Lamorra said. 'I shall have to find another job.'

'Well, for a day or two you can work for me,' Pietro said. He gave him an address, and said, 'Go and find out if a bricklayer named Romeo is still living there; and find out if he's working, and if so where, but do so naturally, without rousing any suspicions.'

Lamorra went off immediately, and Spina went into the hut, which was as hot as an oven. While waiting he dropped off to sleep.

Lamorra came back late and drunk, but with precise information. Meanwhile Pietro had made two beds inside the hut, but Lamorra, seized with sudden respect, refused to enter.

'It's a small hut,' he said, 'and how can I sleep by my master's side?'

'Don't bore me,' Pietro said. 'Here you're the master and I'm your guest.'

'All the more reason why it's impossible,' said Lamorra. 'If destiny sends me my master as a guest, how can I possibly sleep beside him?' He looked back on the past without resentment. 'Your father was a good man,' he said. 'When he was in a bad

158

temper he'd beat me, but he was a good man. One Easter he gave me a suckling kid.'

Pietro lay on a folding bed inside the hut and Lamorra lay on the ground near the door. The bed was swarming with lice and fleas. Pietro twisted and turned but did not complain, for fear of offending Lamorra. But the latter noticed it.

'There must be insects in the bed,' he said. 'If you take no notice of them they'll leave you alone.'

'Goodnight,' said Pietro.

Under the influence of the wine he had been drinking Lamorra began recalling the happiest times of his life.

'Once,' he said, 'your father gave me a Tuscan cigar. What a cigar. It was a Saturday night, and I smoked it on Sunday morning in the square outside the church while the women were coming out after sung mass. They don't make cigars like that any mc.e.'

Pietro dropped off to sleep while Lamorra went on recalling outstanding events in his long life.

'At Buenos Aires there's a sheet of water that's called Riachuelo,' he said. 'The Italians, who are called *gringos* and also *tanos*, live round it. Once upon a time there was a fine fat Negress there . . .'

Next morning Pietro got up early and waited at one side of the Porta San Giovanni. It was not long before Romeo appeared but, as he was with other workers, Pietro did not approach him, but followed at a distance. Workers arrived in crowds from all sides. Pietro was affected by the beauty of the scene, the beauty of Rome at dawn, when the streets were crowded with people going to work, talking little and hurrying. Romeo went down the Via delle Mure Aureliane, left his companions at Porta Metronia and went on alone along the Via della Ferratella. Pietro followed him, and whistled a song that Romeo used to sing on the island of Ustica when they were both deported there:

> Never a rose without a thorn,
> Never a woman without a kiss . . .

Romeo turned, pretended not to recognize him and went on

to a building site where he was foreman. Bricklayers and their mates were already waiting for him. The building on which they were engaged was still in the early stages. The wall came up to the bricklayers' chests, and it was now necessary to put up scaffolding. Romeo gave the necessary instructions, and when Pietro approached Romeo called out to him at the top of his voice, 'Are you the owner of that terrace to be repaired?'

'Yes. I want to find out what it's going to cost.'

The two left the tool shed to discuss the question. Pietro drew the plan of a terrace on a piece of paper, and then said, 'I've arranged to meet Battipaglia this afternoon. But for the practical work in the Fucino region I need to find a trustworthy person, if possible a worker who comes from that part of the world and is still in contact with his home village. I want him to go back to it straightaway and to work in contact with me. It will be difficult for me to build up anything lasting without a working class helper.'

'You're asking for too much,' said Romeo.

'He has got to be found,' Pietro insisted. 'The prospects in the Fucino are very favourable, but the people available to me are young and inexperienced. I can't do anything without some more trustworthy person. But it must be someone born in the area.'

Romeo thought for a moment. 'You're asking for too much,' he repeated. Then he explained the situation. 'The persecution of people from Apulia, the Abruzzi or Sardinia who were among us has been ferocious. The police, as you know, nearly all come from the country, and you can't imagine their fury when they lay their hands on a subversive who is not a townsman but a countryman. If a townsman is for liberty, they certainly regard it as a grave crime, but if a working man who is a former cafone is against the government it amounts to sacrilege. He's nearly always killed. If he manages to get out of prison alive he's a shadow of his former self, and even his fellow-villagers are terrified and avoid him.'

'What has become of Chelucci?' Pietro asked.

'They caught him again last month after the distribution of an anti-war leaflet, and now he's in Regina Coeli. He's nearly blind.'

'What about Pozzi?'

'There are suspicions about him,' Romeo said. 'No-on can explain why Chelucci was arrested and he was not, as the police found them together. But the police may have done it on purpose, to discredit and isolate him. How can one find out the truth? There are a number of cases resembling his, and they're the saddest.'

'Are there no others from the Abruzzi?'

'There used to be Diproia before he married. As soon as he married he refused to have anything more to do with us. Now he goes to mass with his wife every Sunday morning. There was also a student named Luigi Murica, but he has completely vanished. I had several attempts made to find him, because he was an excellent young man, but we never managed to track him down.'

'What about the seamstress, Annina?'

'She joined up with Murica.'

'I know, that's why I asked.'

'She may still be with him. You might try at the place where she used to live. If she has moved, they may know her new address. But what do you want her for? She's not from the Abruzzi.'

'She may know where Murica is.'

'Come back here tomorrow evening when we knock off,' said Romeo. 'I'll see what I can do on my own account.'

Pietro walked away down the Via della Navicella and the Via Claudia, intending to make for the centre of the city for the sake of seeing it again, but its beauty had already faded. No-one was to be seen in the streets but men in uniform, civil servants, priests and nuns. It was an entirely different place. But between ten and eleven o'clock, when the big parasites, tne members of the hierarchy, the higher civil servants, the monsignori in their violet hose began to appear, he once more found Rome nauseating. He turned down the Via Labicana and made for the outskirts again, not before buying a tin of insecticide.

'What's it for?' Lamorra asked him.

Pietro explained.

'If you show the insects you think them so important,' Lamorra said, 'it'll turn their heads and they'll never go away.'

'Would you be willing to go back to Orta?' Pietro asked him. 'I'd give you a confidential little job.'

'I'd go anywhere except Orta,' Lamorra replied. 'I'd go back to Orta only if I'd made money and could buy a house and land. But as it is . . .'

'But you wouldn't do anywhere else, you see,' Pietro tried to explain. 'If you went to Orta I'd bear all the expenses, of course. Think about it.'

'I'm not going back to Orta,' Lamorra said, putting an end to the discussion.

In the afternoon Pietro went to meet Battipaglia, the inter-regional secretary of the party. The appointment was in a little church on the Aventine.

When Pietro got there his comrade was there already, pretending to read a notice on the wall near the door. Pietro had not seen him for many years. He was rather bent and his hair had turned grey. Prison had aged him. To make him aware of his presence Pietro stopped for a moment beside him, standing right up against the wall to read the notice as if he were short-sighted. Then he went into the church. He had not been inside it before. Two rows of arches divided it into three. The arches rested on trunks of ancient columns of different sizes that rose from the floor without pedestals and with rough and differently decorated capitals. The stone floor was almost completely covered with memorial tablets. At the other end of the church the big altar looked like a simple stone tomb with a wooden crucifix, painted black, and four candlesticks. The church was half dark and deserted. There were only two women kneeling in front of the lamp lit at the altar of the Sacrament. Pietro waited by the door, near the font. Battipaglia came in and walked slowly round the church. Eventually he came and talked to Pietro.

'I've had money waiting for you for a month,' he said in an undertone. 'I also have a new passport for you. How are you?'

'I've no use for the passport at present,' Pietro said. 'I'm not going abroad again.'

'That's your business,' said Battipaglia. 'It's no affair of mine, as you know, it came straight from headquarters abroad. I'll send it to you through Fenicottero. What you do with it is entirely up to you. Who's the person you sent recently from Fossa with your news?'

'Her name's Bianchina, she's the daughter of an hotel keeper.'

'Is she a comrade? How long has she been in the movement?'

'She's not a comrade, but she can be trusted. She doesn't know who I am or what the purpose of her trip was.'

'Isn't that risky?'

'Even if she found out who I am she wouldn't give me away.'

'That's your affair, it's no business of mine to lecture you. Is she your lover?'

'No.'

'That's your business, it has nothing to do with me, as you know. The girl talked about a revolutionary priest said to be in your mountains, one Don Paolo, do you know him?'

'No,' said Pietro.

'You ought to get hold of him, he might be useful. Your report has been forwarded to headquarters abroad.'

The sacristan had come in through the little sacristy door and had lit two candles on the big altar. A priest in sacred vestments emerged from the sacristy, announced by the ringing of a bell. He stopped and prayed in front of the first step of the altar. The sound of footsteps outside the church door heralded the arrival of other worshippers. These were a number of nuns. They dipped their fingers in the holy water, made the sign of the cross, and hurried towards the altar.

'Were you able to do any work?' Battipaglia asked.

'It's difficult to do anything with the cafoni,' said Pietro. 'They're more open to Gioacchino da Fiore than to Gramsci. Meridionalism is a bourgeois Utopia. But I discussed all that in my report.'

'Because they had no direct contact with you,' Battipaglia said in an undertone, 'headquarters abroad have asked me to press you for a reply to their request for comment on their latest political decision. As you know, it's a formality more than anything else.'

'I've no head for formalities, as you know,' said Pietro.

'Nobody of course believes you have the slightest hesitation about declaring your solidarity with the majority of the Russian Communist Party,' Battipaglia said. 'You're an old comrade, a rather strange one, but everyone has a high opinion of you.'

'To tell you the truth,' Pietro said, 'I know nothing about the issue. If I find it so difficult to understand, I don't say my native region, but my native village, how do you expect me to have an opinion on Russian agricultural policy, to disapprove of some views and approve of others? It wouldn't be serious, would it?'

'Did Bianchina bring you the three reports?'

'Yes, but I haven't read them yet.'

'When will you read them? Headquarters insist on having your reply as soon as possible.'

'I don't know when I shall be able to read all that stuff,' Pietro said. 'I don't even know if I'm in a position to understand and form a genuine opinion about it. I've other things on my mind, I mean the situation here.' Then, making an effort, he went on, 'I don't want to pretend, I'll tell you the truth, I burnt those papers. Bringing them with me would have meant taking a useless risk. And besides, frankly, they don't interest me.'

'What you have done is very serious,' Battipaglia said. 'Do you realize that?'

'What it boils down to,' Pietro said, 'is that I do not feel able to form opinions on matters outside my experience. I cannot stoop to any kind of conformism, to approving or condemning things with my eyes shut.'

'How dare you describe our condemnation of Bukharin and other traitors as conformism? Are you mad?'

'Always declaring yourself to be on the side of the majority is conformism,' said Pietro. 'Don't you think so? You backed Bukharin as long as he was with the majority, and you would still be backing him if the majority supported him now. How can we hope to destroy fascist subservience if we abandon the critical spirit? Try and answer me that.'

'Do you claim that Bukharin was not a traitor?'

'I genuinely don't know,' said Pietro. 'All I know is that now he's in the minority. I also know that it's for that reason alone that you dare oppose him. Answer my question if you can: would you be against him if the majority were for him?'

'Your cynicism is beginning to pass all bounds,' said Battipaglia, barely restraining his indignation.

'You haven't answered my question. Give me an honest answer if you can.'

'If it depended on me, I should expel you from the party immediately.'

Battipaglia was trembling with indignation, but the place they were in imposed restraint. After a long silence he went away without saying goodbye. Pietro stayed where he was, leaning with his back against the font. The service continued. The faint light of the candles made the gold of the monstrance in the middle of the altar glitter and created a luminous halo around the priest's white hair. Then the service came to an end, and the small congregation moved towards the exit. When one of the nuns dipped her fingers in the holy water to make the sign of the cross she was struck by Pietro's appearance. She stopped beside him and looked at him for a moment. 'Don't despair,' she murmured with a smile.

'What do you want?' said Pietro.

'Courage,' she repeated. 'Refuse to despair.'

'Who are you?' said Pietro. 'What do you want of me?'

'Courage,' the nun said. 'The Lord tries no-one beyond his strength. Can't you pray?'

'No.'

'I shall pray for you. Do you believe in God?'

'No.'

'I shall pray to Him for you. He is the Father of all, even of those who don't believe in Him.'

The nun hurried away to rejoin her companions. After a while Pietro left the church too.

Evening had fallen. He had been intending to go to the

cinema, but gave up the idea. His fellow-villager Lamorra was waiting for him outside his hut, where he had prepared something to eat. Pietro's appearance alarmed him.

'What's the matter with you?' he asked. 'Has something serious happened?'

'Yes,' said Pietro in a voice that discouraged further questions.

'Aren't you going to eat?'

'No.'

That night Pietro did not sleep and Lamorra noticed it.

'May one ask what happened to you?' he asked. 'Is it a disappointment in love?'

'Yes,' said Pietro. 'Leave me in peace.'

'Has a woman let you down?'

'Yes.'

'One shouldn't love too much,' Lamorra said. 'Your father was a passionate man too.'

Next morning Pietro was late for his appointment with Romeo. His face was like an old man's and his eyes were swollen. The building site was deserted. Romeo was waiting for him behind the toolshed, and a boy was with him. He obviously knew nothing about the previous day's clash with Battipaglia.

'This is Fenicottero,' Romeo said.

'Money and a Czechoslovak passport for you arrived from foreign headquarters a month ago,' the boy said.

'How do you know it's a Czechoslovak passport?'

'I opened the envelope.'

'That was wrong of you,' Pietro said.

'We distributed the anti-war leaflet at San Lorenzo yesterday,' the boy said to change the subject.

'What does the leaflet say?'

'I haven't had time to read it,' the boy answered.

'You helped distributing leaflets?' Romeo asked.

'Yes, I did. There are few of us left, and we all have to do a bit of everything.'

At this Romeo lost his temper.

'What?' he said. 'Your job is liaison and you do propaganda

166

too? Don't you know that every time the two things have been combined the whole thing has gone up in smoke?'

The boy was embarrassed and confused.

'What trade have you learnt?' Romeo asked him.

'A bit of everything,' the boy replied. 'I don't have a real trade.'

'That's the trouble,' said the builder's foreman. 'A man who doesn't have a proper trade can't do conspiratorial work. A builder who puts up scaffolding first of all puts up the spars and then connects them with the horizontals and then fixes them to the walls with crosspieces. A builder knows that a spar can't be used as a crosspiece. And it's like that in every trade. The conspiratorial trade has its rules too, and those who don't know them and don't respect them pay for it with years of imprisonment and sometimes with their lives.'

Romeo's indignation was not yet exhausted. He too was now a partisan.

'I haven't the slightest desire to go back to prison because of you,' he went on. 'From today you will no longer do liaison work. Do you understand? Don't show yourself in this neighbourhood again. If we meet you'll pretend not to know me.'

The boy left with his tail between his legs.

Romeo gave Pietro the addresses of some people from the Abruzzi who had left the cells for some years.

'You should be the best person to try to bring them back into the movement,' he said. 'But is it prudent? Decide for yourself.'

'That's not the difficulty,' Pietro said. He was going to say something else, but changed his mind. 'Perhaps we'll discuss it another time,' he said.

CHAPTER 18

Pietro followed up the clues given him by Romeo and tracked down an old friend, a violinist named Uliva. They had not met for years, since they were both members of a communist students' cell, and all Pietro knew about him was that he had spent several months in prison. After that, like so many others, he had kept away. He lived with his wife on the fourth floor of a house in the Via Panisperna in the Viminal quarter.

A young woman in a very obvious state of advanced pregnancy showed Pietro to his room. Her eyes were red and swollen as if she had been weeping the whole morning. Uliva received his old friend with indifference, showing neither pleasure nor surprise. He was a lean and slender little hunchback, and the dirty black suit he was wearing gave him a sad, neglected appearance. Even after Pietro came in he remained lying on a couch, smoking and spitting on the ground. The spittle was aimed at a wash basin but more often than not missed it, for yellow stains were to be seen all over the place, on the fringes of the rug, the desk and the walls. The room was untidy, smelly, and in semi-darkness.

'It's a long time since we saw each other,' said Pietro. 'I didn't expect to find you in this state.'

Uliva replied with a short, ironic laugh. 'Did you suppose I'd become a civil servant? Or an officer in the militia? Or a commendatore?'

'Is there no other choice?'

'I don't think so.'

'It's sufficient to look about you,' said Pietro. 'Perhaps you're living too isolated a life. There are those who resist, who struggle.'

'That's an illusion,' said Uliva. 'Do you remember our students' cell? Those who didn't die of hunger or in prison are even worse off.'

'The worst thing that can happen to anyone is surrender. One can accept the challenge; resist, struggle against it.'

'For how long?'

'Ten years, twenty years, two hundred years, for all eternity. There's no life without struggle.'

'Do you think that ventriloquism is struggle?' said Uliva. 'What's the point of inflating yourself with empty phrases? I've lost my taste for that sort of thing, I tell you. After spending ten months in prison for shouting "Long live liberty" in the Piazza Venezia I spent some time sleeping in winter in public dosshouses and in summer under the bridges of the Tiber or the colonnades of the Esedra or on the steps of churches, with my jacket rolled up under my head as a pillow. Every now and then there was the nuisance of the night patrol coming and asking me who I was and what my job was and what I lived on. You should have seen them laugh when for lack of anything else I showed them my academic diplomas, my degrees from St Cecilia's academy of music. I actually tried going back and living in my native village in the province of Chieti, but I had to make a getaway at night. It was my relatives who imposed banishment on me. "You're our ruin, our disgrace," they said.'

'All the same we mustn't capitulate,' said Pietro. 'We must remain united with the workers' cells.'

'Don't talk to me about that,' said Uliva. 'I used to know some printers. They have all come to terms with the situation. The working masses have been either nationalized or brought to heel. Even hunger has been bureaucratized. Official hunger entitles you to the dole and state soup; all that private hunger gives you is the right to throw yourself in the Tiber.'

'Don't let yourself be taken in by appearances,' said Pietro. 'The strength of the dictatorship is in its muscles, not its heart.'

'There you're right,' said Uliva. 'There's something corpse-like about it. For a long time it has no longer been a movement, not even a Vendéean movement, but merely a bureaucracy. But what does the opposition amount to? What are you? A bureaucracy in embryo. You too aspire to totalitarian power in the name of different ideas, which simply means in the name of different words and on behalf of different interests. If you win, which is a misfortune that will probably happen to you, we subjects will merely exchange one tyranny for another.'

'You're living on figments of your imagination,' said Pietro. 'How can you condemn the future?'

'Our future is the past of other countries,' Uliva replied. 'All right, we shall have technical and economic changes, that I don't deny. Just as we now have state railways, state quinine, salt, matches and tobacco, so we shall have state bread, shoes, shirts and pants, and state potatoes and fresh peas. Will that be technical progress? Certainly, but it will merely serve as a basis for an obligatory official doctrine, a totalitarian orthodoxy that will use every possible means from the cinema to terrorism to crush heresy and terrorize over individual thought. The present black inquisition will be succeeded by a red inquisition, the present censorship by a red censorship. The present deportations will be succeeded by red deportations, the preferred victims of which will be dissident revolutionaries. Just as the present bureaucracy identifies itself with patriotism and eliminates all its opponents, denouncing them as being in foreign pay, so will your future bureaucracy identify itself with labour and socialism and persecute everyone who goes on thinking with his own brain as a hired agent of the industrialists and landlords.'

'Uliva, you're raving,' Pietro exclaimed. 'You have been one of us, you know us, you know that that is not our ideal.'

'It's not your ideal,' said Uliva, 'but it's your destiny. There's no evading it.'

'Destiny is an invention of the weak and the resigned,' said Pietro.

Uliva made a gesture as if to indicate that further discussion was not worthwhile. But he added, 'You're intelligent, but cowardly. You don't understand because you don't want to understand. You're afraid of the truth.'

Pietro rose to leave. From the door he said to Uliva, who remained impassively on the couch, 'There's nothing in my life that entitles you to insult me.'

'Go away and don't come back,' Uliva said. 'I have nothing to say to an employee of the party.'

Pietro had already opened the door to leave, but closed it and went back and sat at the foot of the couch on which Uliva was lying. 'I shan't go away until you have explained to me why you have become like this,' he said. 'What happened to you that changed you to this extent? Was it prison, unemployment, hunger?'

'In my privations I studied and tried to find at least a promise of liberation,' Uliva said. 'I did not find it. For a long time I was tormented by the question why all revolutions, all of them without exception, began as liberation movements and ended as tyrannies. Why has no revoluton ever escaped that fate?'

'Even if that were true,' Pietro said, 'it would be necessary to draw a conclusion different from yours. All other revolutions have gone astray, one would have to say, but we shall make one that will remain faithful to itself.'

'Illusions, illusions,' said Uliva. 'You haven't won yet, you are still a conspiratorial movement, and you're rotten already. The regenerative ardour that filled us when we were in the students' cell has already become an ideology, a tissue of fixed ideas, a spider's web. That shows that there's no escape for you either. And, mind you, you're still only at the beginning of the descending parabola. Perhaps it's not your fault,' Uliva went on, 'but that of the mechanism in which you're caught up. To propagate itself every new idea is crystallized into formulas; to maintain itself it entrusts itself to a carefully recruited body of interpreters, who may sometimes actually be appropriately paid but at all events are subject to a higher authority charged with resolving doubts and suppressing deviations. Thus every new idea invariably ends by becoming a fixed idea, immobile and out of date. When it becomes official state doctrine there's no more escape. Under an orthodox totalitarian régime a carpenter or a farm labourer may perhaps manage to settle down, eat, digest, produce a family in peace and mind his own business. But for an intellectual there's no way out. He must either stoop and enter the dominant clergy or resign himself to going hungry and being eliminated at the first opportunity.'

Pietro had a fit of anger. He took Uliva by the lapels of his jacket and shouted in his face, 'But why must that be our

171

destiny? Why can there be no way out? Are we chickens shut up in a hen coop? Why condemn a régime that doesn't yet exist and that we want to create in the image of man?'

'Don't shout,' Uliva calmly replied. 'Don't play the propagandist here with me. You have understood very well what I have said, but you pretend not to understand because you're afraid of the consequences.'

'Rubbish,' said Pietro.

'Listen,' said Uliva, 'when we were in the students' cell I watched you a great deal. I then discovered you were a revolutionary out of fear. You forced yourself to believe in progress, you forced yourself to be an optimist, you forced yourself to believe in the freedom of the will only because the opposite terrified you. And you've remained the same.'

Pietro made Uliva a small concession. 'It's true,' he said, 'that if I did not believe in the liberty of man, or at any rate in the possibility of the liberty of man, I should be afraid of life.'

'I've ceased to believe in progress and I'm not afraid of life,' said Uliva.

'How were you able to resign yourself? It's frightening,' said Pietro.

'I'm not in the least resigned,' said Uliva. 'I'm not afraid of life, but I'm still less afraid of death. In the face of this pseudo-life stifled by pitiless laws the only weapon left to man's free choice is anti-life, the destruction of life itself.'

'I'm afraid I understand,' said Pietro.

He had understood. An expression of great sadness appeared on his face. There was no point in going on with the discussion.

The young woman who had opened the door to Pietro came in to fetch something. Uliva waited for her to go out again and then went on, 'I have a certain respect for you, in spite of everything. For many years I've seen you engaged in a kind of chivalrous contest with life or, if you prefer it, with the creator; the struggle of the created to overcome its own limitations. All that, and I say so without irony, is very fine, but it requires a naïveté that I lack.'

'Man really exists only in struggle against his own limitations,' said Pietro.

'You once told me about a secret dream of yours,' said Uliva. 'You expressed it in country terms. You wanted to turn the Fucino plain into a soviet and appoint Jesus president of the soviet. That would not be a bad idea at all if the son of the carpenter of Nazareth were still really living on this earth and could hold that office in person. But, if He were appointed and His absence duly noted, would you not be obliged to appoint a substitute? Now, we in this country know very well how the representatives of Jesus begin and how they end. Oh, how well we know it. The poor blacks newly converted by the missions do not yet know it, but we know it, and we cannot pretend that we do not know it. What became of your historicism, Pietro?'

'I gave it up,' said Spina. 'If Jesus ever lived, He is still alive now.'

Uliva smiled. 'You're incorrigible,' he said. 'You have a prodigious capacity for self-deception. I'm incapable of it.'

Then he went on, 'Listen to me. My father died at Pescara at the age of forty. He died of drink. He left me nothing but debts to pay off. One evening a few weeks before he died he sent for me and told me the story of his life, the story of his failure. He began by telling me about his father's, that is, my grandfather's death. "I die poor and disappointed," he told my father, "but I place all my hopes in you; may you get from life what I failed to get." When he felt his own end approaching, my father told me that he could only repeat what my grandfather had said to him. "I too, my son, am dying poor and disappointed, but you are an artist, and I hope and pray that you may get from life all that I vainly hoped for." So it goes on from generation to generation, illusions are passed on together with debts. I'm now thirty-five, and I've reached the same point as my grandfather and my father. I'm already a conscious failure, and my wife is expecting a baby. But I lack the folly to believe that the unborn child will get from life what I have failed to get. Either he'll die of hunger or he'll die in slavery, which is worse.'

Pietro rose to leave. 'I don't know whether I shall come back,' he said. 'But if you or your wife have need of me . . .'

'Don't bother,' said Uliva. 'We shan't be needing anyone.'

In the Via Panisperna an uproar was being made by about fifty young men wearing students' caps who were carrying a big tricolour flag and a board with the words HURRAH FOR THE WAR. They had an escort of a few policemen, and shouted and yelled and called out to passers-by and sang a new song that said: 'We'll make hairbrushes of the Negus's beard'. People at shop doors and windows looked on curiously and made no comment. In the Via dei Serpenti Pietro came across another party of students with a similar flag and a similar board, singing the same bootblacks' song and with a similar police escort. Among the throng hurrying home or going about their business Pietro recognized the uncertain footsteps of the unemployed, of those who had nowhere to go and ended up following in the students' wake.

Near the Colosseum Pietro stopped to watch some young Avanguardisti exercising with guns and machine guns. Boys of from fifteen to seventeen were being instructed in how the various parts of these weapons fitted together, how to strip and reassemble them, and how to pass from marching order to readiness for action. They were serious and attentive, like little men, and carried out the drill with great speed. Pietro's appearance attracted the attention of an old woman.

'Why are you weeping?' she said to him. 'Are you feeling ill?'

Pietro nodded as if to say yes and took to his heels. He spent the whole afternoon aimlessly wandering about. He was obviously a soul in torment.

His appointment with Romeo was in a tavern in the Via degli Ernici in the Tiburtine quarter, next to the Acqua Marcia viaduct and the railway. The rust of the railway sidings and the smoke of the locomotives gave their colour to the whole street, and the walls were impregnated with the smell of coal and heavy oil. The tavern was nearly empty when Pietro walked in. In one corner a carbiniere was eating spaghetti and tomato sauce with a mournful and ferocious air, as if he were making a meal of an anarchist's guts. The floor was thickly covered with sawdust to receive the spittle. The only picture on the wall was of a majestic transatlantic liner crossing the ocean at night under a full moon with its cabins illuminated. Later porters and labourers turned up, ordered their half-litres, drank them, casting oblique glances at the liner so that the carabiniere should not notice them secretly embarking for America. Then they paid for their wine, disembarked, spat on the ground and went off home in a bad temper.

Romeo turned up late, drank a quarter of a litre at the counter, coughed and left again without approaching Pietro. Pietro went out after him and followed him at a distance, and had some difficulty in doing so because Romeo kept changing direction at every corner, obviously to make sure he was not being trailed. Eventually he slowed down in the Vicolo della Ranocchia and let Pietro catch up with him.

'Have you heard about the explosion in the Via Panisperna?' he asked.

Pietro had not.

'Uliva's flat was blown up, burying him and his wife and the tenants on the floor below. The press has been ordered to say nothing about it, but it happened in the middle of the city and the news spread in a flash. Uliva seems to have been preparing to blow up the church of Santa Maria degli Angeli in a few days' time during a service to be attended by the whole government. A fireman friend of ours who helped clear away the rubble told us that a plan of the church with a great many technical notes was found among Uliva's papers.'

'I went to see him this morning,' Pietro said. 'I had the impression he was preparing a big funeral.'

'If the concièrge saw you going in, he'll certainly remember you,' Romeo said. 'You have a face that isn't easily forgotten. That's another reason for you to leave.'

In the Piazzale Tiburtino a big crowd had gathered round groups of soldiers, militia and carabinieri.

Pietro asked some bystanders what was happening.

'Mobilization is being announced tomorrow,' someone said. 'The new war in Africa begins tomorrow.'

Tomorrow? There had been talk about it for some time, but just because there had been so much talk about it the idea had become improbable and strange. But now the improbable was going to happen, in fact it was already there, behind the scenes, and tomorrow it would make its entry on the stage.

'I forgot to tell you that that liaison lad had been arrested,' Romeo said. 'They'll certainly beat him to get him to talk. In these cases the wisest course is to expect the worst, so be on your guard. Here's the money that came for you a month ago, and the passport. We must avoid seeing each other for a few weeks.'

'I've no more time to waste,' Pietro said firmly. 'I've been back in Italy for six months. I've done nothing yet, and I'm tired of waiting. I need a reliable colleague to work with me in the Marsica.'

'An illegal organization is a web that's continually made and unmade,' Romeo said. 'You know that better than I do, and it's a web that costs blood and patience. Our organization in Rome has been smashed and rebuilt from the ground up several times. How much work is required to re-establish contacts, and what a short time they often last. I've seen many friends go to prison, and others have disappeared without trace. Some we had to get rid of because they became suspect. But we have to stick to it.'

'Very well,' Pietro said. 'I'll manage by myself.'

'There's also something else,' Romeo said with obvious embarrassment.

'What?'

'I've seen Battipaglia, the inter-regional organizer.'

'What did he tell you?'

'He told me you might be expelled from the party.'

'It doesn't depend on him.'

'If that were to happen, I should be very sorry,' Romeo said. 'Do everything possible to avoid it. Don't be obstinate.'

'Let them leave me in peace,' said Pietro. 'Don't let them ask me for the impossible. I can't sacrifice for the party's sake the reasons for which I joined it.'

Romeo insisted. 'Breaking with the party means abandoning the idea behind it.'

'That's not true,' Pietro said. 'It would be like putting the Church before Christ.'

'All right,' Romeo said. 'I know your way of thinking. But don't be obstinate.'

The two firmly shook hands and went off in opposite directions.

CHAPTER 19

Before returning to the Marsica Pietro wanted to try again to find at least one experienced comrade to take back with him to help him. He wanted to avoid the risk of leaving Pompeo and his young friends to their own devices in the event of his being caught. So he told Lamorra that he would be staying in his hut for a few days longer. His former fellow-villager took advantage of this to make a proposal of his own.

'I can't go back to Orta,' he said. 'I've already told you why. It's the only place in the world in which I refuse to set foot. But you're not going to Orta either. So why don't you take me with you? I'm sick and tired of digging pozzolana.'

'What would you do with me?' Pietro asked.

'I'd do anything for you, even the humblest jobs,' Lamorra said. 'I'd carry your bags. Do you shave yourself? I'd take letters to your girl. And I'd hardly cost you anything. I'd eat your left-overs.'

'You're crazy,' Pietro said. 'I can't stand servants.'

Lamorra was disappointed. 'Don't imagine I'd say this to anyone else,' he said. 'You're my master's son, and I don't say this to criticize you, but it seems to me that you're still a child.'

'Don't waste time in idle chatter, but try and find the person I told you about,' Pietro said.

Lamorra did not find Murica, but Annina, his girl, who had moved to a big council building in the Via della Lungaretta in Trastevere that exuded poverty and filth. Pietro went there immediately. He found the girl bent over her sewing machine in a small untidy room that was both workroom and bedroom.

'Romeo will have mentioned me to you,' Pietro said. 'I've come to ask for news of him.'

The girl received her importunate visitor with obvious disappointment. She was still very young with an elfin-shaped face and regular features, and in spite of her hostile expression her eyes were beautiful. Pietro, embarrassed, stood by the door until she offered him a chair. When he sat beside her Annina looked at him with a smile veiled with sadness.

'Do you know there's a strange resemblance between you and the person you're looking for?' she said. 'Even the arrogant way in which you call on people resembles his. Also he was born at Rocca dei Marsi, which is not far from where you were born, I think. He talked to me about it once.'

'It's about five miles away,' Pietro said. 'Where is he now? I need to see him urgently.'

'He often used to talk to me about you,' Annina said. 'He was sorry he did not know you personally. But the life of the cells was very isolated, it was difficult for comrades to get to know one another.'

'How long is it since you saw him?'

'Nearly a year. Several people have come and asked for him.'

'Might he be in prison?'

'No,' the girl said with confidence. 'He was picked up with others in the May Day round-up last year and was in prison for a couple of months. When he came out he swore he would kill himself rather than go back.'

The sound of footsteps came from the stairs outside. A little girl came in, handed in a dress to be repaired and went away again.

'Had you know him for a long time?' Pietro asked.

'Why reopen old wounds?' Annina replied.

'Forgive me,' Pietro said. 'I didn't ask out of curiosity. If you knew me better you would know that I deserve your confidence.'

'I know that,' Annina said.

She tidied up the table and fiddled with her sewing machine.

'We met in the cell about three years ago and liked each other immediately,' the girl said, blushing. 'It was not a flirtation, but a real love affair. I was still living at home at that time, and my mother kept scolding me for forgetting everything else and taking no interest in anything but him. He was my first young man, and to me he was son, brother and lover all at the same time. He was very fond of me too.'

The girl rose, and turned her back to her visitor to hide her tears. When she sat down again her eyes were red.

'I don't want to revive sad memories,' Pietro said.

'It's not a matter of reviving forgotten memories, alas,' said Annina, 'but of a living, painful reality that is always before my eyes and dominates my life.'

'Conspiratorial life is hard,' Pietro said. 'To hold out and not allow ourselves to be crushed we have to be pitiless.'

'Our affair did not in the least diminish our activity in the cell,' the girl said. 'On the contrary, we were more active because of it. We organized outings and reading evenings, and sought out social novels to discuss and comment on. To give more time to the party we even renounced getting married, setting up a home and having children.'

'How did the idyll end?' Pietro asked. 'Forgive me, but what most surprises me is that the break was so complete, both personal and political. I heard so much about you, and, if you allow me to say so, I always wanted to meet you. But the rules of conspiratorial life forbade it. You were talked about as a person in whom we could have complete confidence and actually with admiration. Everyone said you were a real comrade. And now? Don't you miss taking part in the struggle? I don't understand you. How can you resign yourself to ordinary life?'

Annina fell silent. Eventually she seemed to make up her mind. 'There are some things that it's difficult to talk about,' she said. 'But perhaps it's my duty to tell the story, and perhaps you are the best person to whom to tell it. You come from the same part of the world, you're like him, you probably think the same way as he does, and perhaps you have the same faults. Also you represent the party.'

The girl had another fit of weeping and then, with difficulty, she began her story.

'When he was arrested last year,' she said, 'he was beaten a great deal, but what had a greater effect on him than the beating was the moral maltreatment, the slaps and the spitting. He came out of Regina Coeli upset and depressed. I attributed this to physical weakness, but with the passing of the weeks his fear

180

of the police and the possibility of another arrest did not diminish. "Rather than go back to prison I'll kill myself," he kept telling me. The police had warned him to break off his old contacts and not to see me again, as I too was politically suspect. So when he was with me he was always ill at ease. The sound of a truck would make him grow pale. We no longer knew where to meet. He still loved me, he wanted to be with me a great deal, he was very jealous if he did not not see me every day, but when he was with me he felt he was in danger, and as a result he almost hated me. The old carefree spontaneity had gone, and every meeting became a torment. "The police may catch me at any moment," he used to say. Also there were all sorts of physical effects; he had heart trouble, his digestion was irregular and he had attacks of asthma. A policeman often came to see me to ask about him. He was from Apulia and had red hair and was particularly hateful, and he would come at the most improbable times, preferably at night when I was in bed. I soon realized that it was not so much Luigi as me that he was after, and several times I had to defend myself by force; and eventually I persuaded a girl cousin of mine to come and stay with me so that I should feel safer.'

'On Christmas Day last year,' Annina went on, 'I had lunch with Luigi in a restaurant outside the Porta San Paolo. That day he was in an unusually calm, cheerful, almost carefree mood, just as in the old days. We hadn't been alone together for some time, so I asked him to come back with me to the small flat I then had in the Via del Governo Vecchio to spend the afternoon together. On the way we bought flowers, fruit, sweets and a bottle of Marsala. He was helping me to arrange the flowers in a vase when there was a knock at the door, which we had locked. "Who is it?" I called out. It was the police. Luigi started trembling, and to avoid collapsing he sat on a chair; he signalled to me not to open the door. But the knocking grew more and more insistent. "I shan't go back to prison," he muttered. "I'll throw myself out of the window, but I shan't go back to prison." Meanwhile the police had nearly broken down the door. Now, at that flat there was a small balcony from which it was easy to climb up on to the roof, so I signed to

Luigi to go and hide there. As soon as he disappeared I opened the door and two policemen came in, the man from Apulia and another, younger one whom I didn't know. It was no good denying it, they knew Luigi was with me, they had seen us coming back together. They looked under the bed and in the wardrobe. The man from Apulia said that if he wasn't in the room he must be on the roof. I barred the way to the balcony. "Don't arrest him," I said. "Arrest me, but not him." They tried to move me out of the way by force, but I fought them with my fists and kicked and bit. "You won't arrest him," I kept telling them. "All right, but on one condition," the policeman from Apulia replied. "On any condition," I said. I would have gladly given my life to save Luigi from prison, but the two policemen wanted something else. I don't know how long they stayed. I only remember much later hearing Luigi's voice behind the half-closed shutters of the balcony. "Have they gone?" he said. He came into the room. "What are you doing, are you asleep?" he said. He went over to the window and looked out to see whether the house was being watched. "There's no-one in the street," he said with satisfaction. He picked up a biscuit from the table and ate it. He went to the door and listened, to make sure there was no-one on the stairs. Then he came towards me. "What are you doing, are you asleep?" he said again. I had a sheet over me, and he removed it. He saw that I was naked, and on the sheet he saw traces of the two men. He made a grimace of disgust. "Whore," he shouted at me, and spat on the bed and flung to the ground all the things that we had bought to celebrate Christmas. He upset the sewing machine, flung the bottle of Marsala at the big mirror and smashed it, and walked out, slamming the door behind him. I did nothing and I said nothing. What had happened had happened.'

That was the end of Annina's story, and she fell silent. There was the sound of a man's footsteps outside the door.

Pietro sprang to his feet.

'If that's the policeman from Apulia,' he said, 'this time you'll hide and he'll have to settle accounts with me.' Instead it was merely a postman, who handed in a parcel and went away again.

182

'That policeman,' Annina said, 'had the sense not to be seen again, and so had his colleague. Once or twice in the street I thought I saw them in the distance, but they slipped away immediately.'

'What do you think has happened to Murica?' Pietro asked.

'He has probably gone back to his people at Rocca dei Marsi,' Annina said.

'Haven't you ever thought of talking to him?'

'What for? What happened, happened.'

'I'll go and talk to him.'

'I couldn't live with him again,' Annina said resolutely. 'Not with him or with anyone else. The whole thing disgusts me now.'

'Annina, thank you for giving me your confidence,' said Pietro. 'Perhaps it will not have been to no purpose. I hope to see you again.'

CHAPTER 20

The carriage was crowded with young men who had been called up, and two gentlemen wearing the party emblem were talking about the war. The other travellers listened to them in silence.

'With the devices at our army's disposal, you'll see that the new war in Africa will be over in a few days,' one of them said. 'Our death ray will carbonize the enemy.'

To illustrate how the hostile forces would be scattered, he blew hard into the palm of one hand as if to blow away some dust.

'Did you see in the newspaper that the men called up at Avezzano are to be blessed by the bishop today?' the other man said. 'The death ray will of course also open the way to the missionaries.'

Among the young men who had received their call up papers was an old peasant with a mouth organ. His son was sitting with his head on the old man's shoulder and was fast asleep. 'Give us a tune,' his neighbours said, but the old man shook his head. Perhaps he didn't want to miss what the two gentlemen were saying about the war that was just going to begin and the mysterious death ray. The two gentlemen were armed with hunting guns, the cartridge cases on their belts were full, and they were going to the Fucino to shoot migrating quail.

'They arrived late this year,' one of them said, 'but this year they're fatter than last year.'

'There's always a compensation,' the other one said, and laughed.

Their neighbours, not wishing to seem stupid, started laughing too, though a little late.

Other young conscripts got in at every station. Nearly all smelt of grappa and the stable. Those who couldn't find a seat squatted on their bundles. Others took chunks of maize bread from their knapsacks and started eating. The old man with the mouth organ passed round a bottle of wine. 'Give us a tune,' his neighbour said again, but he shook his head, he didn't want to.

Don Paolo huddled in a corner. His worn, shapeless hat, his worn and threadbare cassock, made him look like a poor priest from a mountain parish. By many small signs he could tell the mountain villagers from those of the valleys and those who were coming down from the sheepfolds; they were poor people whose capacity for suffering and resignation had no real limits, and they were used to living in isolation, ignorance, mistrust, and sterile family feuds.

Whenever Don Paolo thought he recognized anyone from Orta he hid his face behind his breviary and pulled his hat down over his eyes. Even the landscape had put on uniform. The train, the stations, the telegraph poles, the walls, the trees, the public lavatories, the bell-towers, the garden gates, the parapets of bridges, bore inscriptions exalting the war.

He arrived at Fossa without incident. What with its multicoloured adornment of orders for meetings, garlands, flags and inscriptions on the walls in whitewash, paint, chalk, tar and coal, the place was unrecognizable. The Girasole hotel seemed to have been turned into a mobilization centre.

Berenice, untidy and dishevelled, was dashing about in a state of great excitement. But she had time repeatedly to kiss Don Paolo's hand and bid him welcome.

'What good fortune to have you here with us on this glorious day,' she said. 'What good fortune.'

'Where's Bianchina?' the priest asked. 'Where can I find Pompeo, the chemist's son?'

But by this time Berenice was far away.

There was a continual coming and going of men and youths in the diningroom and on the stairs. A group of men wearing the party emblem, already hoarse from talking too much, were sitting round a table, discussing the details of the spontaneous demonstration due to take place in the afternoon. The strictest precautions were to be taken to ensure the enthusiastic participation of the whole population of Fossa and the surrounding areas. Fossa must at all costs be prevented from making a bad impression.

'Must we send trucks as far as Pietrasecca?' someone asked.

'Of course, they must be sent everywhere,' was the answer. 'But carabinieri must go with the trucks so that people will see the necessity of coming here of their own accord.'

At another table a number of landlords and merchants, big, strong, plump men carefully oiled and greased and presided over by the lawyer Zabaglia, had been furiously discussing for several hours past the menu for that evening's banquet. Zabaglione was so carried away that he did not notice Don Paolo's arrival. Serious disagreement had arisen on a matter of principle, and Zabaglione had ended up as usual by making it a matter of personal prestige. The issue was which was to be served first, white wine or red.

The committee for the reception of applications for voluntary enlistment was in session in Berenice's bedroom on the first floor. Those for whom there were no chairs were sitting or lying on the landlady's bed. The words 'Happy Dreams' were beautifully embroidered on the pillows. Over the head of the bed there was a chromolithograph representing a guardian angel caressing a dove. The haberdasher who had a shop in the town hall square facing the Girasole hotel had gone bankrupt and had had to close down, but the shop had reopened that morning. His wife, Gelsomina, was sitting behind the counter and there was a notice on the door saying 'Creditors are advised that the proprietor of this establishment has enlisted voluntarily'. After looking through the list of volunteers Don Genesio, the clerk in the registrar's office, had exclaimed, 'This will be a bankrupt's war.'

This remark enjoyed an enormous success and was repeated to everyone who appeared on the scene. Don Luigi, the chemist, was looking everywhere for his son, but couldn't find him. He was desperate. Everyone else's sons were volunteering, and was his to be the exception? He too was in business and had promissory notes falling due. 'Have you seen Pompeo?' he anxiously asked everyone he met. 'If I find him and he doesn't volunteer I'll shoot him as sure as God's in His heaven.'

Don Paolo too was anxiously looking for Pompeo, but for different reasons. Without saying anything to his father he went to look for him at the Ville delle Stagioni. It was silent and deserted. Near the cows the priest found Bianchina. She was alone, singing softly to herself and playing with a rubber ball. She was delighted to see Don Paolo and flung her arms round his neck.'

'Where's Pompeo?' he asked.

'He's gone to Rome,' Bianchina said. 'He was sent for.'

'By whom?'

The girl didn't know. 'It must be for the second revolution,' she said.

'Where's Alberto?'

'At Pietrasecca, he's returned to the nest. His father's dead. He left me because he was jealous of Pompeo, and of you, and everyone.'

'What's the cowman doing?'

'I don't know, he's engaged, he wants to get married.'

'I have an urgent favour to ask you,' Don Paolo said.

Bianchina made a curtsey and replied, '*Ecce ancilla Domini.*'

'I want you to go to Rocca dei Marsi and find a certain Luigi Murica. All I want you to tell him is that an acquaintance of his from Rome would like to see him, and can he come? You mustn't say anything else to him even if he presses you.'

'I'll go by bicycle,' the girl said.

The bicycle was in a room in the villa reserved for sporting equipment. Don Paolo watched her leaving in the direction of Rocca and went back to the hotel.

As the time for the declaration of war on the radio approached the crowd in the streets grew thicker. Motor-cycles, cars, trucks loaded with police, carabinieri, militiamen and party and corporation officials arrived from everywhere. Donkeys, carts, bicycles and trucks arrived bringing cafoni from the valleys. Two brass bands marched through the streets, playing the same anthem over and over again *ad nauseam*. The bandsmen's uniforms were like those of animal tamers at the circus or porters at grand hotels, with magnificent gold braid and double rows of metal buttons on their chests. Outside a barber's shop there was a big placard showing some Abyssinian women with breasts dangling almost to their knees. A dense group of youths had formed in front of it, gazing at it goggle-eyed and laughing.

At the bottom of the square, between the party premises and the town hall arcade, a radio set had been hoisted, crowned by a trophy of flags. It was from this that the voice proclaiming war would emerge. As the poor people arrived they were herded beneath this small object on which their collective destiny depended. The women squatted on the ground, as in church or at market, and the men sat on their knapsacks or donkey saddles. They had only a vague idea of why they were gathered there and kept glancing surreptitiously at the metallic radio box. Finding themselves all together like that, they were ill at ease, sad, mistrustful.

The small square and the adjacent streets were packed, but the influx from the surrounding countryside continued remorselessly. The halt arrived from the quarries, the blind from the kilns, the lame and the bent from the fields; the vine dressers came from the hills with hands worn by sulphur and lime, and the inhabitants of the mountains with legs bent by the labour of scything. Since their neighbours had been willing to come, they had been willing to come. Should the war bring misfortune, it would be misfortune for all, in other words only half misfortune; but should it bring fortune you had to try and make sure of your share of it. And so they had all come. They had left the pressing of the grapes, the cleaning of the barrels, the preparation of the seed, and had hurried to the local town by order. Eventually even the inhabitants of Pietrasecca arrived and were packed in next to the Girasole hotel. 'Don't move from here,' the village policeman advised the newcomers.

Signorina Patrignani, the Pietrasecca schoolmistress, kept explaining to those in her charge how they were to behave, when they were to shout and when they were to sing, but her voice was lost in the general hubbub. Magascià lost his temper.

'Leave us in peace,' he called out. 'We're not children.'

Don Paolo talked to Magascià and old Gerametta about what had been happening at Pietrasecca since his departure. Magascià told him the sad news of Don Pasquale Colamartini's death. 'It was on the day he took you down to Fossa,' he explained. 'That evening he came back dead. The mare brought him right to the front door. On the way a number of people met him and greeted him, but no-one realized he was dead or dying. He was sitting on the box slightly crookedly and with his head on his chest just as if he were asleep, and he was still holding the reins. Donna Cristina has asked me about you several times,' Magascià went on. 'She wanted to know when you were coming back. Alberto is at Pietrasecca, but he's no help to her.'

The Pietrasecca men waited quietly for the ceremony to begin, but the women were more curious and impatient. Cesira suggested that they should go to church 'before the machine starts talking', but Filomena and Teresa were against this, because they were unwilling to lose their places. But as the others went, they went too. Meanwhile the men passed round a bottle of wine.

'When is it going to speak?' Giacinto asked Don Paolo, pointing to the magic box.

'At any time now, I think,' the priest said.

This piece of news was passed round and revived the general anxiety.

'It may speak at any moment,' people said to one another. Only Cassarola the wise woman had been unwilling to get down from Magascià's cart. The women came back from church and tried to make her get down. 'Come with us,' they said. 'Come and sit with us.'

The wise woman did not reply.

'What do you want?' one woman asked her.

The old woman looked at her mistrustfully. 'There's a yellow comet in the air,' she finally announced. 'There will be war and then there will be pestilence.'

The other Pietrasecca women could not see the yellow comet, but they made the sign of the cross all the same.

'What saint should we pray to?' asked Cesira.

'Prayer's no use,' the wise woman announced. 'God reigns over the earth, the waters and the sky, but the yellow comet comes from beyond the sky.'

Sciatàp offered her the bottle of wine. She drank, and spat on the ground. Magascià climbed into the cart and whispered in her ear, 'Tell me the truth, what do you really see?'

'A yellow comet,' she replied. 'A yellow comet with a long yellow tail.' She turned to Don Paolo and said, 'For you I see something else.'

'What do you see?' the priest asked curiously.

She waited to make sure that no-one else could hear, and then she said in an undertone, 'Up on the mountain there's a white lamb, and a black wolf is looking at it.'

Meanwhile some pale young ladies with baskets of tricolour rosettes were circulating among the submissive and anxious crowd. Don Paolo recognized them as Zabaglione's daughters. They came towards him and pinned a rosette on his breast. They were extraordinarily excited and out of breath.

'Oh, father,' they said, 'what a marvellous day. What an unforgettable day.'

The priest handed back the rosette. 'I'm sorry,' he said. 'I can't.'

A surge in the crowd caused by new arrivals who wanted a place from which they could see the loudspeaker carried the girls away.

The roar of a motor-cycle drowned the general hum; the new arrival was Don Concettino Ragù, in the uniform of an officer of militia. To avoid meeting him Don Paolo took refuge in his room. He took up a position behind the curtains of his window on the second floor. From this observation post the assembly round the loudspeaker looked like a gathering of pilgrims round an idol. Over the roofs he could see tall bell-towers, the tops of which were crowded with boys like dovecotes packed with doves. Suddenly the bells started ringing clamorously. Party notables made their way through the throng and surrounded the destiny-laden loudspeaker with patriotic fetishes – tricolour flags, pennants and a picture of the

190

leader with exaggeratedly projecting lower jaw. Shouts of 'Eia, eia,' and other incomprehensible cries came from the group of notables while the rest of the throng remained silent.

The inevitable 'mothers of the fallen' were ushered to the post of honour immediately beneath the loudspeaker. Their presence was obligatory. They were an assembly of poor little women who had worn mourning for fifteen years, had been awarded medals fifteen years before, and in exchange for a small allowance were condemned to be at the disposal of the warrant officer of the carabinieri whenever public ceremonies required their presence. Near the 'mothers' and surrounding Don Angelo Girasole, the parish priest of Fossa, were the parish priests of neighbouring villages: old, shy, good-natured priests, gloomy priests, athletic and impressive priests, and a canon who was as pink and white as a well-nourished wet-nurse.

'What a lovely celebration,' the canon exclaimed. 'What a magnificent celebration.'

A number of well-nourished landowners, heavily bearded men with fierce eyebrows and wearing sportsmen's velvet, were drawn up under the town hall arcade. The bells went on pealing loudly, with boys taking turns at the ropes. At one point members of the group of notables in the square signalled to them to stop, because the speech on the radio was about to begin, but the boys either didn't understand, or pretended not to. Altogether there were about a dozen bells the continuous ringing of which made a deafening din. Militiamen appeared at the top of the nearest bell-tower and made the boys leave the ropes, but the other bells went on ringing, with the result that the first hoarse muttering that came from the loudspeaker went unnoticed. Then loud shouting arose from the group of notables and militiamen, a rhythmical, impassioned invocation of the leader, 'CHAY DOO! CHAY DOO! CHAY DOO! CHAY DOO!'

The invocation slowly spread, was taken up by women and boys, and then was repeated by the whole crowd, even by those farthest away as well as those at the windows, in an anguished, religious, rhythmical chorus. 'CHAY DOO!

CHAY DOO! CHAY DOO! CHAY DOO! CHAY DOO! CHAY DOO!' Those nearest the loudspeaker signalled to the crowd to be quiet so as to allow the speech to be heard, but the crowd massed in the adjacent streets continued to intone the redeeming invocation, went on crying aloud to the leader, the magus, the great wizard who held sway over the blood and future of them all. The shouting of the throng mingling with the continued pealing of the bells made the speech coming over the radio completely inaudible to the majority, and the repetition of those two syllables ended by losing all meaning and becoming a kind of exorcistic formula mingling with the sacred music of the bells.

At one point those nearest the loudspeaker indicated by signs that the broadcast was over.

'War has been declared,' Zabaglione called out.

He indicated that he wanted to speak, but even his voice was lost in the clamour of the crowd that went on invoking grace and salvation. The spell was broken only by the loud roar of petrol engines. The cars and motor-cycles of the authorities began moving through the throng and going away in all directions. As soon as Don Paolo saw Don Concettino disappearing he abandoned his refuge and came down into the street. Zabaglione received him with open arms. 'Did you see my daughters?' he exclaimed with pride. 'Did you see them distributing rosettes? They were completely transfigured by patriotic ardour.'

'They were as lovely as angels,' said Don Paolo.

Zabaglione was deeply affected by this compliment.

Don Paolo added, 'I have spoken about you to the bishop. I hope I may have helped you.'

Zabaglione wanted to kiss him, and in spite of the priest's resistance he actually succeeded. 'My dear friend,' he said. 'I have heard you talked of as a saint, but I didn't know that the Church had such obliging saints.'

The lawyer took the priest's arm and led him to his house through the beflagged streets. 'Hurrah, hurrah,' he shouted to every group of people he met. His wife opened the door, pale and trembling.

'Kiss the father's hand and leave us alone,' Zabaglione said.

The lady bent and kissed the priest's hand, but before withdrawing she said to her husband, 'The girls haven't come back yet.'

Zabaglione raised his eyebrows. 'Send the maid to look for them immediately,' he ordered.

In the diningroom Zabaglione offered Don Paolo a drink. 'The Lord wanted to chastise me,' he said. 'Why did he give me daughters and not sons? At this hour they would already be in Africa. For lack of sons I have made my clients who are awaiting trial volunteer. Most of them will not be accepted, but the gesture remains.'

The priest looked at him benevolently, as if to say that between friends one could talk more freely. Why, after all, had he come home with him? 'The war will be a hard one,' he began.

'It doesn't matter,' said the lawyer. 'At worst we shall always gain something. Don't you agree? Our country has grown greater after every war, and in particular after every defeat.'

'After the broadcast you wanted to make a speech,' the priest said.

'It was on the programme, but the enthusiasm of the crowd made it impossible,' said the lawyer. 'In any case, I was only to have introduced the official speaker, one Concettino Ragù, who was to have spoken on "The revival of the rural masses and the Roman tradition".'

'The Roman tradition is a lot of nonsense in that context,' said the priest with unusual frankness. 'If the cafoni allow themselves to be mobilized for war, it is certainly not out of deference to a Roman tradition of which they know nothing.'

His not having been chosen as the official speaker still rankled with the lawyer, so he was glad to have someone to whom he could unburden himself. 'You're quite right,' he said. 'It's absurd to talk about the Roman tradition at the present time. Our tradition goes no further back than the Bourbons and the Spaniards, against a background of Christian legends. Besides, even in Roman times there was no Roman influence here. The people here differed from the Latins in religion, language, alphabet and customs.'

'Do you think there is any opposition to the war among the cafoni?' Don Paolo asked.

'They don't have enough to eat, so how do you expect them to take an interest in politics?' said Zabaglione. 'Politics is a luxury of the well fed. But there are some disloyal elements among the young.'

Don Paolo quickly said goodbye and went back to the Villa delle Stagioni. When he was inside the perimeter wall he thought he saw a girl lying on the straw behind the peacock's cage, and he slowly approached. Too late he saw that it was not Bianchina, but one of Zabaglione's daughters in the company of a soldier. Warned by experience, when he saw two girls on intimate terms with two other soldiers on the other side of the small temple of Venus, he had no need to approach to realize that they were the lawyer's other two daughters. But the Villa delle Stagioni was deserted. Swallows were flying about in the big, empty courtyard, keeping close to the ground. They too were about leave to spend the winter in Africa.

Don Paolo, disheartened and with his nerves on edge, went back to the town. There was great animation in the streets, particularly round the taverns.

Berenice had put a roast sucking pig for sale outside the hotel. It lay on a table, pierced by a spit from its tail to its neck. Through the rent in the belly you could see it was stuffed with rosemary, fennel, thyme and sage. A small crowd had gathered round it but, apart from soldiers who had received their first pay since mobilization, customers were few. Some young cafoni gazed at it open-mouthed, showing their fangs like hungry wolves. A sergeant in the militia had a big helping and was cutting it up with a new knife, one of those instruments with blade, punch, potato-lifter and scissors that roused the admiration of the whole crowd.

Under the arcade of the town hall a stall had been erected offering enlarged and coloured views of Abyssinia. You had to pay ten centesimi to see them. Who could not afford ten centesimi? Don Paolo paid up, queued with the others and filed past a series of apertures equipped with magnifying lenses. Putting one eye to the latter enabled one to see Abyssinian women with bare hairy legs and protruding breasts. The last picture showed the Empress of Abyssinia. The queue of viewers moved much more slowly than Don Paolo would have liked, but there was no help for it. Some of those ahead remained absorbed for a long time in front of every picture, and a timid invitation to them to hurry attracted protests and jibes from the whole queue. When at last he was able to get away from this artistic spectacle he had reached the limit of his patience. He wandered this way and that, feeling exhausted and discouraged. Twice he returned to the Villa delle Stagioni, and on both occasions he made out the white underwear of Zabaglione's daughters between the straw and the grass, but there was no trace of the cowman or the other young men. By now Bianchina should have returned from her search for Murica.

That was how the afternoon passed. Local high society gathered at Berenice's hotel for the celebratory dinner while the artisans, petty bourgeoisie and cafoni of Fossa, as well as those from villages in the neighbourhood who had stayed behind, gathered in a field next to the Buonumore bar on the banks of the stream. The host had put a great many benches outside for the occasion and was selling off black wine from Apulia at a reduced price. He had set up a big barrel under a poplar tree near the path that ran along the bank of the stream, and it was from this that he poured the wine, filling half bottles that young barmaids took to the improvised tables. Among others Don Paolo came across a party from Pietrasecca, including Magascià, Sciatàp and others, many of them already drunk.

'Have you understood anything of what is going on?' the priest asked his acquaintances.

'What a thing to expect,' said Sciatàp. 'No-one told us there was any need to understand.'

'Things take their own course,' said Magascià. 'Like water in the river. What's the use of understanding?'

'If you fall in the river, do you let yourself be carried along by the stream?' the priest asked.

Magascià shrugged his shoulders. A man named Pasquandrea said the only thing that mattered was that soon it would be possible to emigrate again. Another, named Campobasso, said that horses and mules were sure to be requisitioned, but those who had only a donkey had nothing to fear, so he was all right. Sciatàp asked the priest whether the 'death ray' could destroy seed in the ground. The others listened and drank, bewildered, stupefied and silent.

'You'd do better to drink and not waste time asking us things we don't understand,' Magascià said to the priest. 'You see, at Pietrasecca a joke or a play on words lasts for many years, it's handed down from father to son and repeated an endless number of times, always in the same way. But here you hear so many novelties in a single day that you end up with a headache. What is there to understand?'

'Things take their own course whether you understand them or not,' said Sciatàp.

Don Paolo saw Zabaglione approaching along the path beside the stream. He looked pale and distressed and took Don Paolo aside.

'Have you by any chance seen my daughters? I fear something may have happened to them,' he said.

The lawyer was immediately recognized by many of the drinkers by whom he was surrounded. They offered him drinks and began shouting, 'Speech, speech, we want a speech.'

The crowd demanded a speech as they would have demanded a song or a tune or a mazurka, depending on the performer's speciality. Zabaglione refused, resisted, but ended by giving in. Some youths lifted him almost by force on to a table next to the barrel. He preened himself, smoothed his moustache, smoothed his hair, looked round the crowd, and smiled. His face was transfigured. He raised his arms towards the starry sky and began in his warm baritone voice, 'Descendants of eternal Rome, O you my people.'

The orator addressed the drunken artisans and cafoni as if they were an assembly of exiled kings, conjuring memories of ancient glory out of the fumes of wine.

'Tell me,' he said, 'who carried civilization and culture to the Mediterranean and to Africa?'

'We did,' some voices answered.

'But the fruits were gathered by others,' the orator declared.

'Tell me again, who carried civilization to the whole of Europe, as far as the misty shores of England, and built towns and cities where primitive savages pastured together with wild boars and deer?'

'We did,' a number of voices answered.

'But the fruits were gathered by others. Tell me again, who discovered America?'

This time they all rose to their feet and shouted, 'We did, we did, we did.'

'But others enjoy it. Tell me again, who invented electricity, wireless telegraphy, all the other marvels of civilization?'

'We did,' some voices replied.

'But others enjoy them. And lastly, tell me who emigrated to all the countries of the world to dig mines, build bridges, make roads, reclaim swamps?'

Once more they all rose to their feet and shouted, 'We did, we did, we did.'

'And there you have the explanation of all our ills. But, after centuries of humiliations and injustices, Divine Providence sent to our country a man who will recover everything which is ours by right, everything of which we have been robbed.'

There were shouts of, 'To Tunis, to Malta, to Nice.'

Others shouted, 'To New York, to America, to California.'

One old man shouted, 'To São Paulo, to the Avenida Paulista, to the Avenida Angelica.'

Others shouted, 'To Buenos Aires.'

Sciatàp who was sitting near Don Paolo, was seized with wild excitement and tried to climb on to a small table, though he could hardly stand because of the wine he had drunk. He imposed silence on his neighbours and started shouting, 'To New York, to 42nd Street, take my advice, I beg you, I implore you.'

People were crowding around Zabaglione to get him to continue, but in the distance he had seen three girls arm in arm with three soldiers walking down the path along the stream. He jumped down from the table, forced his way through the throng and went off in pursuit. After the orator's departure it was just as it is when a pleasing concert has come to an end and everyone repeats on his own account the tune that he liked best.

'In New York,' Sciatàp was telling his neighbours, 'in Mulberry Street, there's a shameless person who calls himself Mr Charles Little-Bell, Ice and Coal. He must be the first to get his deserts. Everyone is entitled to his own opinion, of course, but my idea would be . . .'

Campobasso drew him aside and asked him, 'What is there at 42nd Street?'

'It's the entertainment quarter,' said Sciatàp. 'The entertainment quarter of the rich. There are beautiful women there, perfumed women.'

He half closed his eyes and sniffed at that distant feminine perfume. He said no more because his son had arrived, comically arrayed in an ill-fitting uniform, with his sleeves folded over his wrists and his trousers coming down only to his knees.

'Have a drink,' his father said to him. His son drank. 'Have another drink,' his father ordered, and his son obeyed. 'Now listen to me,' his father said. 'Don't forget what I'm telling you in front of everyone. If the government decides to send soldiers with the death ray to New York, step forward and volunteer. Tell the government that your father has been there and explained the layout to you. Well then, as soon as you disembark at Battery Place turn sharp right . . .'

His son laughed open-mouthed, looked gratefully at his father, and nodded his head in agreement at everything he said.

Meanwhile a group of drunken cafoni had gathered round the barrel of wine and started singing an old emigrant's song:

> Thirty days in the steamship
> And we got to 'Merica . . .

At this point a row broke out because some soldiers left without paying. The waitresses shrieked and the landlord threatened them with a big kitchen knife.

'Get the money from the government,' the soldiers shouted from a distance.

By now the barrel was nearly empty, but about a dozen cafoni went on singing the emigrant's song. Some of them were clinging to the barrel, holding tight, like men in a boat on a rough sea, and singing:

> We found neither straw nor hay
> We slept on the bare earth
> Like beasts of the field.

They sang out of tune, their voices were strident and tipsy, they prolonged phrases till their breath ran out and accompanied their singing with grotesque imitations of travellers embarking and leaving.

CHAPTER 21

Magascià was the only one to notice that Don Paolo was weeping.

Wearily the priest rose and walked slowly back into the town. By now it was dark. He wanted to go back to the hotel, to go up to his room and lie on his bed, but at the hotel entrance there was a group of laughing, guffawing people. He stood a little to one side, confused and undecided, until someone noticed him and called Berenice.

'Come to the dinner, come along,' she said. 'There are a number of gentlemen who want to meet you.'

'Thank you, I've already eaten,' Don Paolo said. 'Is Bianchina at home?'

'She hasn't come back yet,' Berenice replied. 'I don't know where she is.'

Don Paolo went away without knowing where he was going, but then he once more made for the Villa delle Stagioni. When he left the last houses behind the darkness was complete. He stopped and walked on, not knowing what to do. He crossed the bridge over the stream and went down a path flanked by vegetable plots. Snatches of the emigrants' song reached him.

> And 'Merica is long and wide
> Surrounded by rivers and mountains

Near the perimeter wall of the villa he was suddenly attacked by a big dog that leapt from a hedge. Fortunately a peasant came to his assistance. He was the cowman, Pompeo's friend.

'What are you doing in these parts at this time of day?' he asked in surprise.

'I'm looking for Pompeo,' Don Paolo said.

'He's been called to Rome,' said the cowman. 'He hasn't come back yet.'

'And where's Bianchina?' Don Paolo asked.

'I haven't seen her,' the cowman replied. 'Goodbye, I must go.'

'Haven't you got a moment for me?' Don Paolo said. 'I should like to talk to you.'

'I'm sorry,' the cowman said. 'My girl's waiting for me.'

Slowly and reluctantly the priest turned back to the hotel. The streets of Fossa were almost deserted and were dimly lit. The flags, the trophies, the arches, the streamers created the impression of a carnival evening. Don Paolo was exhausted from walking, his feet were dragging, his cassock was dirty and dusty. But at the entrance to the hotel he hesitated again. The sound of voices and singing was still coming from the dining-room. The last guests at the patriotic banquet were still there, and he could not go up to his room without going through the diningroom. To avoid being greeted and talked to by those odious people he walked round the back of the hotel and tried the kitchen door. He found it at the bottom of a yard crammed full of boxes, vine cuttings and piles of charcoal. The sound of washing up came from the kitchen.

The charcoal roused the priest's interest. It was soft wood charcoal. He picked up a few pieces and filled one of his pockets with them. Then he tiptoed back, forgetting his tired-ness, and set out on a short reconnaissance of the neighbouring streets. The street leading to the station was deserted, and no sound came from the station, where a beggar with a dog was sleeping in the waitingroom. The last train had gone. Over the ticket window Don Paolo wrote in charcoal: DOWN WITH THE WAR and LONG LIVE LIBERTY. He crossed the small station square and went back into the old part of the town, by way of a dark and twisting alley that took him to the church of San Giuseppe. The walls were cracked and unsuitable for charcoal graffiti, but the three wide steps leading up to the church door were smooth and polished. Excellent, Don Paolo said to himself. It was as if generations of Christians had day by day for centuries been keeping them clean in expectation of his arrival with his bit of charcoal. He wrote in big block letters: LONG LIVE LIBERTY and LONG LIVE PEACE. When he

201

had finished he moved away and looked back two or three times to admire his handiwork. He was well satisfied. It really created an excellent impression at the foot of the church. In the lunette of the doorway there was a picture of San Giuseppe with his flowering stick. Don Paolo smiled, raised his hat to him, and went on with his walk. At a bend in an alley he came across a drunk advancing in zigzags. The man was taken aback, but then burst into idiotic laughter and started following the priest, murmuring, 'Wait a minute, don't be in such a hurry, darling.'

The priest hastened his stride but, as the drunk persisted in following him, he let the man catch him up under a lamp post and was ready to give him a couple of slaps. But the drunk realized his mistake, made a comic gesture of astonishment and began muttering apologies, 'Oh, what a mistake,' he said, 'what sacrilege I was about to commit.'

Don Paolo went on with his walk and reached the tax office. A government coat of arms was on the door and the windows were solidly barred. Expensive and totally useless ornaments. But the façade had been recently whitewashed. Had the men who did this realized what they were doing? At all events, Don Paolo carefully wrote in big letters on the white wall: LONG LIVE THE INDEPENDENCE OF THE PEOPLES OF AFRICA and LONG LIVE THE INTERNATIONAL.

More drunken voices reached him, and to avoid any more encounters he went back to the hotel, using the back door, as the kitchen was now deserted. In his room he was surprised to find Pompeo, sitting on a chair and waiting for him.

'I came back from Rome by the last train this evening,' he said. 'As soon as I heard you were here I came to see you, I've been waiting for you, because I've got to talk to you.'

'I've been looking for you too and have been waiting for you all day,' Don Paolo said, and went on, 'Pompeo, this infamous war has begun, the war of the bank against the poor, and what are we doing?'

Pompeo went pale. 'No, Don Paolo, you're wrong,' he said. 'This is a war for the people and for socialism.'

'Are you mad? How can you believe that?'

Pompeo described what had happened on his trip to Rome, where he had gone with a friend who, like him, believed in the second revolution. They had spent the evening with rich friends, and the conversation had naturally turned to the war. Pompeo had been greatly surprised to hear a banker who was one of the guests expressing reservations about the new war in Africa, which he considered a very expensive political enterprise. Others who were present shared this feeling. So what was the reason for this war? the two young men had asked. The first answers had been uncertain and vague. No-one dared mention a certain man's name, still less criticize him, but eventually the banker, after a great deal of cautious beating about the bush, had frankly expressed his opinion. He said that every war in modern times inevitably led to state socialism and the destruction of private property. That's good enough for me, Pompeo had replied. If that was the case, he would volunteer immediately to fight for the new social empire.

Don Paolo was about to reply, but hesitated. The hand in his pocket was still dirty with charcoal.

'The war will gain us fertile land for our unemployed,' Pompeo went on. 'They will be the free owners of that land.' He took a piece of paper from his wallet and showed it to the priest. 'I enlisted voluntarily today,' he said.

'In that case we have nothing more to say to each other,' Don Paolo muttered.

But Pompeo, after some hesitation, still had something important to say to him. 'Promise me that you will do none of the things that we agreed on,' he said.

Don Paolo did not reply immediately. Perhaps he did not want to lie.

'Promise me,' Pompeo insisted.

'I promise you,' Don Paolo said. He added, 'Bon voyage. I sincerely hope you will return from the war safe and sound. Then we shall discuss things again.'

Pompeo embraced him affectionately.

'I'll write to you from Africa,' he said, and left.

Don Paolo washed the charcoal from his hand. The wash-basin stank disgustingly of urine. He looked at himself in the dirty, tarnished mirror. He had aged greatly that day. His black clothing made him look dismal. While he was undressing he had a nasty coughing fit, and some light reddish foam appeared between his lips. He spat into the washstand. There was no doubt about it, it was blood. Slowly he lay down on the bed.

He was still lying there, dressed and awake, when he heard someone tiptoeing to the door and stopping and listening. 'Come in,' he said. It was Bianchina.

'I saw the light, that's why I came,' she said. The girl was made up and smelt of grappa. 'The declaration of war was celebrated at Rocca too,' she said with a laugh. 'Some friends of mine there insisted on entertaining me, of course. But that Murica of yours is an idiot. I went all over the place before I eventually found him on a vegetable plot where he was growing I don't know what. I did exactly as you said, and told him that a friend of his had sent me especially to tell him that he would like to talk to him, and that he would come and see him if he agreed. He didn't even thank me or offer me so much as a glass of water. He replied coldly that he didn't want to see anyone.'

Don Paolo was breathing with difficulty and was afraid he might be going to have another coughing fit.

'Why don't you say anything?' Bianchina asked. 'Why aren't you in bed yet? You haven't even taken off your shoes. What's the matter? Are you depressed?'

The priest nodded.

'Why are you depressed? Are you in debt? Are you in love?'

The coughing returned to shake him. His head fell on to his shoulder and from one side of his mouth a thin trickle of warm blood flowed on to his chin. He saw Bianchina grow pale, and she was on the point of hurrying to get assistance. But he managed to seize her by the hand and stop her. He smiled and muttered, 'Don't be afraid, it's nothing. It's not the first time. It stops by itself.'

Bianchina wetted some handkerchiefs in cold water and put them on his brow and his chest.

'The important thing is to keep calm,' she kept telling him.

She took a dark blue veil from her waist and wrapped it round the electric lamp to dim the light. Every so often she renewed the cold compresses.

'I had an aunt who had this illness, so I know what to do,' she said. 'The important thing is not to be afraid. Leave everything to me.'

Slowly, without his having to rouse himself or make an effort, she undressed him, put a sheet over him and made him comfortable. Carefully she wiped away the traces of blood on his mouth and chin.

'You'll see, it won't be anything serious,' she told him several times.

She forbade the patient to talk, and gave him a pencil and a sheet of paper in case he wanted to ask for anything.

'Now it's time to go to sleep,' she said finally. 'Good night.'

She lay on a quilt stretched out on the ground beside the bed. But neither of them managed to go to sleep.

Later on the sick man said to her, 'Did you too celebrate the declaration of war?'

'Yes.'

'Why?'

'I did what everyone else did. Does that displease you?'

'Yes.'

'Go to sleep and don't worry about it,' Bianchina said.

In the morning she went and told her mother about Don Paolo's illness, but came back to his room straightaway and told him that there was great excitement in the town because of some disgraceful anti-war slogans on a number of public buildings. They had been written in charcoal during the night. While Bianchina was cleaning the room she discovered some big black stains in the washbasin, as if a charcoal burner had been washing his hands.

'What's this?' she asked. But instead of waiting for a reply she quickly cleaned the washbasin. Then she went over to Don Paolo and said reproachfully, 'You really are a baby. An incorrigible and reckless baby.' But Don Paolo's appearance roused her to sympathy, for she immediately added, 'But you're a nice person all the same.'

'Bianchina,' Don Paolo said, 'how lucky it is that the human race includes women, it doesn't just consist of calculating males.'

Bianchina thought for a moment. 'Perhaps you say that out of pure calculation.'

'Of course.'

'And how do you know that I too am not acting out of calculation?'

Don Paolo watched the girl scrubbing the floor. Her ankles were perfect. Her bosom was like a well-filled bread basket. The first time he saw her her breasts were like little lemons; now they were like fine, ripe apples.

CHAPTER 22

'As soon as I'm fit enough to travel I'm going abroad,' Don Paolo told Bianchina. 'I can't go on living in this odious country.'

'Find me a job and I'll come with you,' the girl said.

The idea of meeting Bianchina abroad amused Don Paolo.

'If you go abroad,' he said, 'I'll tell you a secret that will make you laugh.'

'Couldn't you tell me now?'

But Don Paolo was not to be persuaded.

Berenice looked after the priest in accordance with the advice of the Fossa municipal doctor. In particular, he told her to do everything possible to distract the patient from melancholy thoughts, a task that was conscientiously taken over by Bianchina. Because of the patient's condition the girl was obviously somewhat restricted in her choice of means; she had to renounce a whole series of forms of entertainment that Don Paolo would certainly have enjoyed, but at the expense of his health. But she was a bright and resourceful girl, and she recalled a number of harmless pastimes from her school days that distracted him from his black mood. One of these was fly racing. At Bianchina's school this had been practised chiefly in class. The object was to catch flies in flight, without hurting them and without being seen by the sister in charge. A pin or small feather would be inserted into the flies from the rear and then they would be lined up on the bench and encouraged to engage in what was called a towing race. Bianchina acquired quite a reputation at this, but when she tried catching flies in flight now she sometimes damaged them. Her excuse was that she was out of practice.

'You learn so many things at convent school, but later in life when you need them you find you've forgotten them,' she said.

The towing races took place on Don Paolo's bed. The black

leather binding of his breviary served as the track. Some flies started out at once and made straight for the finishing line, while others went off at an angle and left the track or stopped after the first few steps.

'Those that won't go are the wives,' Bianchina explained. 'They slow down to let their husbands win, the silly idiots.'

Don Paolo discovered that, apart from the difference in scale, fly racing, when watched at close quarters, was full of surprises and distractions, just like ordinary horse or motor racing. In spite of Bianchina's precautions, echoes of the excitement produced in the town by the charcoal anti-war slogans frequently reached the sick room.

'So many policemen have never been seen here before,' Berenice said. 'Anyone would think Fossa was a den of crooks.'

Bianchina said nothing, or tried to change the subject.

Gelsomina, the haberdasher's wife, who had taken her husband's place now that he had volunteered, stood in the doorway of the shop and stopped passers-by. 'Have you heard anything new?' she asked. 'It must certainly have been a stranger.'

Outside the hotel door there was a permanent group of people talking about nothing else. What the bigwigs said was repeated and commented on from one household to the next.

'It was such a delightful celebration, everyone was so happy, and everything was so harmonious,' Berenice said. 'Who could have had the idea of writing that nonsense on the walls?'

'What it amounts to is that envy is present among us too,' said Don Luigi, the chemist. 'Someone who cannot enlist and has no sons whom he could send to enlist relieved his feelings by doing this.'

'Never a funeral without a jest, never a wedding without a grumble,' said Zabaglione. 'Come, come, don't let us exaggerate.'

'Night birds are birds of ill omen,' Don Genesio proclaimed. 'Appearances are never to be trusted.'

'Quite right,' said Berenice. 'Fire is smouldering among the cafoni. We must be on our guard, you don't see fire in day-light, but at night it glows.'

'Cafoni? Rubbish,' said the chemist. 'Cafoni can't read or write, and the anti-war slogans were written in block letters. Cafoni, my foot.'

'It must be admitted that there are some young people who have lost their heads,' said Zabaglione. 'I'm not referring to anyone in particular, of course.'

But Don Luigi caught the insinuation and retorted with venom. 'For your information, my son has volunteered,' he said. 'The honour of a volunteer is unimpeachable. Apart from that, while we're on the subject, neither I nor my son have ever been socialists.'

This was Zabaglione's Achilles' heel. The shaft went home.

'That repartee leaves me unaffected,' he said, pale with anger. 'Everyone knows that I gave up my ideas long ago. Who has never been a socialist? Even the head of the government was once a socialist.'

'Why all the excitement?' Bianchina said. 'Just because of a bit of charcoal on the wall? What a lot of fuss about nothing.' In this case the girl's naïveté was genuine. 'I really don't under-stand why people make such a fuss about a few words scrawled on a wall with charcoal,' she said to Don Paolo.

Don Paolo, however, seemed pleased at the fuss, which showed no sign of abating, and he tried to explain the reason for it.

'The dictatorship is based on unanimity,' he said. 'It's sufficient for one person to say no and the spell is broken.'

'Even if that person is a poor, lonely sick man?' the girl said.

'Certainly.'

'Even if he's a peaceful man who thinks in his own way and apart from that does no-one any harm?'

'Certainly.'

These thoughts saddened the girl, but they cheered Don Paolo.

'Under every dictatorship,' he said, 'one man, one perfectly ordinary little man who goes on thinking with his own brain is a threat to public order. Tons of printed paper spread the slogans of the régime; thousands of loudspeakers, hundreds of thousands of posters and freely distributed leaflets, whole armies of speakers in all the squares and at all the crossroads, thousands of priests in the pulpit repeat these slogans *ad nauseam*, to the point of collective stupefaction. But it's sufficient for one little man, just one ordinary, little man to say no, and the whole of that formidable granite order is imperilled.'

This frightened the girl, but the priest was cheerful again.

'And if they catch him and kill him?' the girl said.

'Killing a man who says no is a risky business,' said the priest. 'Even a corpse can go on whispering no, no, no, no with the tenacity and obstinacy that is peculiar to certain corpses. How can you silence a corpse? You may perhaps have heard of Giacomo Matteotti.'

'I don't think so,' Bianchina said. 'Who's he?'

'A corpse that no-one can silence,' Don Paolo said.

Berenice burst into the room in a state of high excitement.

'At last, at last,' she exclaimed.

'Have you won the lottery?' Bianchina asked.

'Pompeo knows who did the writing on the walls,' Berenice said. 'He's on is way to Avezzano to tell the authorities.'

'How does he know?' the priest asked.

'He has just told the haberdasher's wife himself.'

Bianchina hurried to her room to fetch her hat and dashed to the station.

'Don't meddle in affairs that don't concern you,' her mother shouted after her down the stairs. 'Don't go on being our ruin.'

But Bianchina was far away.

Don Paolo jumped out of bed to pack his bags and flee. He had had no fever for several days and his cough was better, but he could hardly stand. Besides, where was he to go? There was only one railway line, and if he took the train it would be easy to catch him. And if he went up into the mountains and spent a few days in the woods? In his condition that would be madness. So he unpacked and went back to bed. Everything considered, being arrested here in Fossa, in a place already in a state of ferment, might be more useful than being arrested at the station in Rome. Orta, his birthplace, was a few miles away.

Don Benedetto was a few miles away. Schoolfellows of his lived in every village in the neighbourhood. News of his arrest would reach the cafoni. During the long nights of winter poor hungry people sitting round the hearth would remember his gesture.

Once more there was a protracted wait for Bianchina.

After a first quick check through his belongings to eliminate all traces of anything that might compromise others, he had plenty of time to repeat the process several times more. At every sound of wheels outside he dashed to the window, but his anxiety remained unassuaged. The time the girl took was incomprehensible. Avezzano was barely an hour away by train. Why were the police so slow?

Bianchina and Pompeo came back late that evening. The endless wait had left Don Paolo exhausted.

'We ate and drank,' Bianchina told him, laughing. 'We were just coming back when we passed a cinema, and Mickey Mouse was on the programme, so of course we went in.'

'Is that all?'

'No, it isn't.'

'Didn't Pompeo go to Avezzano to denounce someone?' the priest asked.

Bianchina smiled. 'What an amazing memory you have,' she said. 'I'd forgotten all about it.'

'Well, then, what happened?'

'By the time we got into the train Pompeo had told me that he knew for certain who did the writing on the walls. In the train we had an argument, we nearly tore each other's hair out. When we got out at Avezzano the chief of police was waiting to hear what Pompeo had to say, but by then he'd changed his mind.'

'Whom did he denounce, then?'

'A cyclist coming down the road from Orta,' Bianchina said. 'Pompeo saw him in the distance, but wasn't close enough to identify him. I confirmed what he said. That night I myself saw a cyclist coming down the road from Orta.'

Bianchina had told her mother the same story immediately she got back.

'From Orta?' Berenice exclaimed. 'So Gelsomina was right, it was a stranger.'

Berenice hurried over to the haberdasher's.

'Gelsomì,' she called out. 'We were right. It was just as we said, it was a stranger, a man from Orta, who tried to compromise the people of Fossa.'

The news spread through the shops and bars in a flash, and of course it turned out that many others had seen the cyclist from Orta that night. But he was not one of the men who came to Fossa regularly for the market; he was a stranger.

'The usual Mystery Man,' the warrant officer of carabinieri exclaimed furiously.

Now that the danger was over, Don Paolo cheered up again. His spirit of adventure was revived.

'I'll take you abroad with me,' he said to Bianchina, 'and I'll tell you stories.'

'Where will you take me?' the girl wanted to know. 'To a mission station among unbelievers in the colonies?'

'Yes, among unbelievers, but in Paris or Zürich,' Don Paolo replied.

CHAPTER 23

Next day Don Angelo Girasole, the parish priest of Fossa, appeared at his sister's hotel to renew his invitation to Don Paolo to visit the parish church. The strange priest could no longer extricate himself from a social duty that hitherto he had found various excuses to postpone.

Don Angelo was barely sixty, but looked much older. His hair was white, his face was lean and yellowish, and his back was bent. On the way he told Don Paolo that he was the oldest of ten brothers and sisters of whom the only survivors were Berenice and himself. His duties kept him busy from dawn to late at night. He had no-one to help him, and the parish was big. Apart from masses, confessions, funerals, novenae and tridua, rosaries and services of all sorts at which he had to officiate or attend, there were the new lay duties imposed by the state, the baptisms and marriages and the illiterate mothers who came to him to ask him to read the letters sent them from America, there were the Children of Mary, the San Luigi Youth Club and teaching the catechism at elementary schools, there were the children who had to be prepared for confirmation and for their first communion, and there were also the Congregation of Charity, the Confraternity, and the tertiaries of St Francis.

'If I am to say my breviary and retire into myself a little and prepare myself for the death that I feel to be approaching, though so slowly, I have to take advantage of odd moments of leisure,' he said.

Every evening he felt so tired that he could hardly stand. Yet sometimes, even in the worst season of the year, he would be woken in the middle of the night to go to the bedside of someone who was dying. But he did not complain. On the contrary.

'A man of God must always be tired,' he said. 'For idle

thoughts come in idle moments, and behind them the evil one is always on the watch.'

In the little square outside the church a crowd of boys were kicking a football about. They stopped to let the two priests pass.

'Don't forget that catechism begins in a quarter of an hour,' the parish priest reminded them.

On the steps of the church Don Angelo stopped for a moment to recover his breath.

'You will probably have heard of the sacrilege that took place here,' he said to Don Paolo. 'One night a stranger with a mask over his face came here, to the threshold of the church, and scrawled the most crazy things.'

'By the way,' Don Paolo said, 'what do you think of this new war?'

A woman was waiting for the priest at the door of the church to arrange the date for a baptism.

'A poor country priest,' said Don Angelo, 'has a great deal to do and little time to think. For the rest,' he added with a smile, 'there are the Old Testament and the New, and the Pastor of the Church to guide us.'

'I expressed myself badly,' Don Paolo said.

The interior of the church seemed dark at first, but one's eyes quickly got used to it. Part of the uneven, disjointed stone floor was occupied by women, all dressed in black, who were praying and whispering among themselves, squatting in the oriental manner as a sign of humility and familiarity with the house of God. One old woman was crawling on her hands and knees towards the chapel of the Blessed Sacrament with her face to the ground, licking the floor and leaving behind her on the old stones an irregular trail of saliva that looked like the silvery trail of a snail. A young man in soldier's uniform walked slowly by her side, looking awkward and embarrassed.

Don Angelo genuflected before the tabernacle, and Don Paolo followed suit. On the altar there was a picture of the body of Christ on the knees of his Mother, who was dressed in mourning. Christ looked like a cafone who had been killed in a quarrel and whose body was already decomposing; the wounds in the hands and feet and the deep rent in the breast looked as if they were in an advanced stage of gangrene, and the red hair was probably full of dust and vermin. But his Mother looked like the widow of a rich merchant who had been overwhelmed by misfortune. Two paraffin tears shone on her handsome pale cheeks; her black eyes looked upwards, as if to avoid seeing the son of whom she had had such high hopes but who could not possibly have come to a worse end; her finely embroidered veil covered her waved hair and came down half-way over her brow; a smart lace handkerchief was tied to the little finger of her right hand, and on the pedestal at her feet the woeful words *Videte si dolor vester est sicut dolor meus* were carved in letters of gold.

The neighbouring altar of San Rocco was adorned with the usual variety of polychrome votive gifts put there by those of the faithful who had been granted miracles. They varied according to the grace received: hands, feet, noses, ears, breasts and other parts of the body were represented, some in natural size.

The soldier's mother had now completed her ordeal. 'Please find out whether we can get the allowance at once,' she said to Don Angelo. 'Otherwise, how are we to live?'

'What allowance?'

'The mother of every conscript is entitled to four lire a day,' the soldier said. 'It says so in today's paper.'

'To whom should we apply for it?' another woman came and asked the parish priest. 'The podestà? The town hall? The carabinieri?'

Another woman whose small boy was ill with erysipelas was waiting in the sacristy. She wanted permission to dip a small piece of cloth in the oil of the lamp that was burning at the side of the tabernacle so that she could lay it on her dying child's heart. Don Angelo gave her permission.

'Do you see? A country priest has little chance to think of the war,' he said to Don Paolo. 'Now we shall be having prayers for dependents' allowances, later there will be prayers for the safe homecoming of prisoners of war and prayers for the missing, and then there will be prayers for leave to be granted for those required to work on the land, and prayers for pensions and prayers for orphaned children.'

'Aren't there government offices to provide those things?'

'Yes, but the poor mistrust them and are generally rudely treated when they go to them, so they come and shed tears in the sacristy.'

'Many years ago, in Rome, on the occasion of a jubilee, I met one Don Benedetto de Merulis who came from this part of the world. If I'm not mistaken, at that time he taught Greek and Latin at a diocesan school, I think. Is he still alive? Do you ever see him?'

'Come this way,' Don Angelo said.

He wanted to show Don Paolo the parish treasure. He went to a cupboard that occupied the whole of one wall and with some difficulty opened its two enormous, inlaid wooden doors. He showed Don Paolo the jewellery and enamel work on the top shelves, the silver bust of a martyrd saint in a special niche in the middle, and a large number of chasubles, dalmatics and richly embroidered stoles hanging, as in a wardrobe, at the bottom.

The sacristan came in with two glasses of wine for the priests.

'You asked about Benedetto,' Don Angelo said. 'Yes, he's still alive. He is a very reckless man of God. For many years he lived an exemplary life, and in learning and virtue he was the master of us all. But now, on the brink of eternity, his contempt for the opinion of men and his excessive confidence in God prompt him to utterances that border on heresy.'

'That is a risk that saints have often taken,' Don Paolo remarked.

'It is not up to me to distinguish between virtue and indiscipline,' said Don Angelo. 'I cannot tell you how much I suffer on his account. When he was ordained I was still a seminarian, and I was full of admiration for his sober and dignified tranquillity, the stainless purity of his private life. He insisted on celebrating his first mass in a prison chapel and his second in a hospital. You can imagine how shocked his relatives were, for a first mass is generally a social event.'

'I hope you do not share the relatives' point of view,' Don Paolo said.

'No,' said Don Angelo, 'but even at that time his brusque way of flying in the face of public opinion worried his superiors. For that reason they avoided entrusting him with a parish and directed him towards teaching. Study of the classics and the company of the young seemed to have a modifying effect on his character, but his relations with his superiors and the authorities did not improve. He had no feeling whatever for social conventions.'

'I do not know to what divine commandment you are now referring,' Don Paolo interrupted. Don Angelo went on as if he had not heard.

'Eventually he was suspended from teaching. I always tried to maintain my friendship for him in his solitude, but now I can really do so no longer.'

'Is he so dangerous?' Don Paolo asked.

'Judge for yourself,' Don Angelo replied. 'Let me tell you the most recent incident. A man from Fossa, a parishioner of mine who worked for some days in his garden, told me that he had heard him say that the present Pope's real name was Pontius XI. At Rocca dei Marsi, where Don Benedetto now lives, this was widely repeated. In their naïve ignorance and because of the respect they have for him many took what he said literally and believed it. That parishioner of mine was stricken with doubt and came here to the sacristy to ask me whether it were really true that the Church had fallen into the hands of a descendent of Pontius Pilate, he who when he had to deal with any grave matter washed his hands of it.'

'And what did you tell him?' Don Paolo said. 'I'm interested.'

The parish priest looked at his guest in surprise.

'Forgive me,' Don Paolo said. 'I expressed myself badly. You naturally believe that the Church does not wash its hands of those things.'

The sacristan came in and told Don Angelo that the women were waiting in the church for the rosary and that the boys had started arriving for the first catechism class.

'Don Benedetto's case is now actually being investigated by the provincial committee for deportations,' Don Angelo went on. 'That is the pass he has come to. A former pupil of his who has a good deal of influence in the government party and I intervened on his behalf and went to see him. We wanted to suggest that he should sign a brief statement of loyalty to the present government and of acceptance of the present policy of the Church. That would have sufficed. He received us politely, but as soon as I started explaining that to avoid greater evils the Church often had to make the best of a bad business he interrupted me. "The theory of the lesser evil may be acceptable for a party or a government, but not for a Church," he said coldly. I tried to avoid getting involved in an abstract argument with him, because in the abstract the worst heresies always present themselves in seductive guise. So I replied, "But do you realize what would happen if the Church openly condemned the present war? What persecutions would descend upon it, and what moral and material damage would result." You will never imagine what Don Benedetto replied. "My dear Don Angelo," he said, "can you imagine John the Baptist offering Herod a concordat to avoid having his head cut off? Can you imagine Jesus offering Pontius Pilate a concordat to avoid the crucifixion?" '

'That reply does not seem to me to be anti-Christian,' Don Paolo said.

'But the Church is not an abstract society,' Don Angelo said, raising his voice. 'The Church is what it is. It has a history of nearly 2,000 years behind it. It is no longer a young lady who can permit herself acts of foolhardiness and indiscretion. She is an old, a very old, lady full of dignity, respect, traditions, bound by rights and duties. It was of course founded by the crucified Jesus, but after him there came the apostles, followed by generations and generations of saints and popes. The Church is no longer a small, clandestine sect in the catacombs, but has a following of millions and millions of human beings who look to it for protection.'

'Sending them to war is a fine way of protecting them,' said Don Paolo, seeming to forget prudence for a moment. 'In the time of Jesus,' he went on, 'the old synagogue was an old, a very old, lady with a long tradition of prophets, kings, law-givers and priests and a large following to protect. But Jesus did not treat it with much respect.'

Don Angelo was still sitting in front of his glass of wine, which he had not yet touched. He closed his eyes, as if seized with a sudden dizziness, and remained like that for a few moments. There was a blue transparency and a slight nervous tremor in the eyebrows that surmounted his deepset eyes. 'My God, my God, why do You frighten me?' he murmured.

The sacristan returned and told him that the women were still waiting for the rosary and that the catechism boys were kicking up an infernal din. The parish priest rose to his feet.

'Excuse me,' he said, and followed the sacristan.

Don Paolo went back to his hotel.

Outside the town hall a noisy crowd had gathered. Two cafoni who had come to the local magistrates' court because of a lawsuit had been recognized as coming from Orta and attacked by a mob that appeared out of the blue with a most unlikely collection of weapons. The two unlucky scapegoats, who were of course quite unaware of why they were the objects of such hatred, had with difficulty been saved from lynching by a party of carabinieri and locked up in the police station. They continued to be the object of the most violent threats. The carabinieri appealed to the lawyer Zabaglia to try and calm the mob, but his most strenuous efforts failed. The excitement died down only when it was announced that the two unfortunates from Orta were to be officially declared to be under arrest and taken to prison on a charge of having aided and abetted the writing of seditious slogans on the walls of Fossa.

'Why only aiding and abetting?' someone objected.

'Because they're both illiterate,' the warrant officer of cara-binieri explained. 'I appeal to your commonsense.'

The invitation to commonsense, if the truth must be told, was not without its effect. The crowd calmed down and split up into groups. To enter the hotel Don Paolo had to force his way through a group of men and young mothers with babies in their arms who were arguing with Berenice.

'I'm leaving tomorrow,' Don Paolo said to Berenice. 'Where's your daughter? I want her to do me a favour'

Pietro immediately sent Bianchina to Rocca dei Marsi with a note to Don Benedetto, signed with his own initials, asking whether he could come and see him.

'Please don't keep me waiting twenty-four hours for an answer this time,' he said to the girl.

'How old is this Don Benedetto?'

'Seventy-five.'

'Don't worry, I'll be back right away,' Bianchina said with a laugh. She jumped on her bicycle and was off in a flash.

Within an hour she was back with a note written in small, clear, regular, slightly tremulous handwriting:

> *. . . tibi*
> *non ante verso lene merum cado*
> *iamdudum apud me est; eripe te morae.*[1]

This was the first time Pietro had seen his former teacher's handwriting since he had left school many years before. It was like being confronted with a school task again, but it was an easy one and the invitation was cordial.

[1] 'There has for a long time been in my house for you a cask of old wine not yet opened. Do not delay.' Horace, Book III, Ode XXIX, to Maecenas.

CHAPTER 24

'Perhaps he'll be late,' Don Benedetto said to his sister. 'Perhaps he won't come till after dark.'

'Don't you think that having him here might be dangerous?' Marta said.

The way her brother looked at her made her correct herself immediately. 'What I meant was that it might be unwise for him.'

'By now he must be pretty expert in these matters,' Don Benedetto said. 'He has been doing nothing but hiding and getting away for years. At all events, you had better leave us alone,' he went on. 'He might want to tell me things it's wiser to confide to one person only.'

'I shan't disturb you,' Marta said. 'But what I've been wanting to say is that he can't remain an outlaw for the whole of his life. Don't you think we ought to tell his grandmother? She and his uncle are rich, they might be able to get him a lawyer and have him pardoned by the government.'

'I don't think Pietro would want to be pardoned.'

'But there's no disgrace in a pardon. Why should he refuse one?'

'The point is I don't think he feels guilty. Only those who repent are pardoned.'

'But he won't be able to live in the woods for the rest of his life,' Marta repeated. 'He must still be young. How old is he?'

'The same age as Nunzio, thirty-four or thirty-five.'

'But ruining your whole life just for a political opinion isn't right, it isn't decent. You were his teacher, you ought to tell him that.'

'I don't think he does it just for politics,' Don Benedetto said. 'He has seemed to me to have been picked for a hard life ever since he was a boy.'

'But if he's persecuted it's because of his political opinions.'

'Do you remember when he came to see us here immediately after taking the school leaving exam? It was the summer after the earthquake.'

'Yes, he was wearing mourning, his parents had been killed.'

'Well, I remembered the occasion a short time ago,' Don Benedetto said. 'He told me something in confidence that must have been very important for his future development. His parents' death had affected him deeply, as was natural enough, but something else happened in those terrible days after the earthquake, when we were all wandering about among the rubble and taking shelter where best we could, something that actually shattered him. I don't think I've ever mentioned it before, because Pietro himself asked me not to tell anyone. But now a long time has passed. Well,' Don Benedetto went on, 'he had the misfortune to see, without being seen, a monstrous incident that filled him with horror. He was the only witness, and he kept the secret. He didn't tell me exactly what it was, but it was obvious from what he said that the person concerned was a relative of someone from his immediate environment.'

'Crimes have always happened,' said Marta.

'The person concerned enjoyed universal respect and after the crime he went on living as before, honestly, so to speak and enjoying general esteem. That was where the monstrosity of the thing lay.'

'Can't you tell me what sort of crime it was?' said Marta.

'It was robbery with violence at the expense of an injured or dying man who was still half buried in the rubble,' Don Benedetto said. 'The criminal was not in need, the crime was committed at night and, as I said, Pietro witnessed it by chance. He was fifteen at the time. He fainted out of sheer horror. When he told me about it some months later he was still trembling. The killer was a neighbour and acted in the certainty of not being discovered. He was what is called a decent, respectable man. Thinking about it now, I feel that Pietro's fugue began at that time. At one time I used to think that he would end up in a monastery.'

'Didn't you hear a noise?' Marta said. 'Someone's knocking.'

Marta hurriedly withdrew to her room. The expected guest was at the threshold. He was in lay clothing and without a hat, but a black garment he was carrying on his arm like a coat might have been the cassock he had taken off just previously. Pietro and Don Benedetto greeted each other and shook hands. Both were embarrassed by emotion.

'Did you come on foot?' Don Benedetto asked.

'I left the carriage down in the village,' Pietro replied.

Don Benedetto pointed to a big armchair and sat beside him on a stool that was rather lower. As he was bent with age, this made him seem smaller than his former pupil. Pietro tried to react against the emotion of the scene and to appear perfectly at ease.

'Behold the lost lamb returning to the shepherd of its own accord,' he said with a laugh.

Don Benedetto, who was looking with surprise at the young man's precociously aged face, failed to see the joke and shook his head. 'It's not easy to tell which of us is the lost lamb,' he said sadly.

'Many people talk about you in the villages round here,' Pietro said. 'What I've heard has been enough to convince me that you're the only person who keeps Christian honour alive in these parts.'

'That is not at all my opinion,' said Don Benedetto with bitterness in his voice, 'and I assure you that that is not false modesty. The truth of the matter is that I know I'm useless. I have lost my teaching job, and I have no cure of souls. It's true that I have the reputation that you mention, but if someone comes here to tell me about some wrong he has suffered I don't know what to say to him. That's the situation, I'm useless. Making certain discoveries at my time of life is sad, believe me.'

Pietro had tears in his eyes. In his hours of discouragement in banishment or exile the mere thought of Don Benedetto had been sufficient to restore his calm and confidence, and now the poor old man was reduced to this state. What was he to say to him that would not seem to be inspired by compassion?

'For the rest,' Don Benedetto went on, 'it is not those who say mass and profess themselves to be ministers of the Lord who are closest to him in the intimacy of the spirit.,'

Hearing the old man talking of God as in the old days, Pietro suspected that there might be a grave misunderstanding in his mind that might falsify the whole meeting.

'I lost faith many years ago,' he said quietly but distinctly.

The old man smiled and shook his head. 'In cases such as yours that is a mere misunderstanding,' he said. 'It would not be the first time that the Lord has been forced to hide Himself and make use of an assumed name. As you know, He has never attached much importance to the names men have given Him; on the contrary, one of the first of His commandments is not to take His name in vain. And sacred history is full of examples of clandestine living. Have you ever considered the meaning of the flight into Egypt? And later, when He had grown up, did not Jesus several times have to hide himself to escape from the Pharisees?'

This religious apologia for the conspiratorial life brought back serenity to Pietro's face and gave it a childish cheerfulness.

'I have always felt the lack of that chapter in the *Imitation of Christ*,' he said with a laugh.

Don Benedetto went on in the same sad tone with which he had begun. 'I live here with my sister, between my garden and my books,' he said. 'For some time past my mail has obviously been tampered with, newspapers and books arrive late or get lost in transit. I pay no visits and receive few, and most of them are disagreeable. All the same, I'm well informed about many things, and they are demoralizing. In short, what should be given to God is given to Caesar and what should be left to Caesar is given to God. It was to such a brood that the Baptist spoke the words: "O generation of vipers, who have warned you to flee from the wrath to come?" '

Marta came in and said good evening to Pietro. She did so in a faint voice and with a frightened smile that seemed to have been prepared outside the door and then kept fixed with pins. She put a jug of wine and two glasses on the table and hurried back to her room.

The old man continued, 'There is an old story that ought to

be brought to mind whenever belief in God is doubted. Perhaps you will remember that it is written somewhere that in a moment of great distress Elijah asked the Lord to let him die, and the Lord summoned him to a mountain. Elijah went there, but would he recognize the Lord? And there arose a great and mighty wind that struck the mountain and split the rocks, but the Lord was not in the wind. And after the wind the earth was shaken by an earthquake, but the Lord was not in the earthquake. And after the earthquake there arose a great fire, but the Lord was not in the fire. But afterwards, in the silence, there was a still, small voice, like the whisper of branches moved by the evening breeze, and that still small voice, it is written, was the Lord.'

Meanwhile a breeze had arisen in the garden, and the leaves began to rustle. The garden door that led into the sittingroom creaked and swung open.

'What is it?' Marta called out from the next room. Pietro shuddered. The old man put his hand on his shoulder and said with a laugh, 'Don't be afraid, you have nothing to fear.'

He rose and shut the door that had been opened by the evening breeze. After a short pause he went on, 'I too in the depth of my affliction have asked, where then is the Lord and why has He abandoned us? The loudspeakers and the bells that announced the beginning of new butchery to the whole country were certainly not the voice of the Lord. Nor are the shelling and bombing of Abyssinian villages that are reported daily in the press. But if a poor man alone in a hostile village gets up at night and scrawls with a piece of charcoal or paints "Down with the war" on the walls the Lord is undoubtedly present. How is it possible not to see that behind that unarmed man in his contempt for danger, in his love of the so-called enemy, there is a direct reflection of the divine light? Thus, if simple workers are condemned by a special tribunal for similar reasons, there's no doubt about which side God is on.'

Don Benedetto poured a little wine into a glass, raised it and held it against the light to make sure it was clear, since it came from a new barrel, and sipped it before filling the two glasses.

'I don't know if you can imagine what it is like to reach

225

certain conclusions at my age, on the brink of the tomb,' he went on. 'At seventy-five it's still possible to change one's ideas, but not one's habits. A retired life is the only kind that fits in with my character. I lived in seclusion even when I was young. Revulsion from vulgarity always kept me away from public life. On the other hand, inaction irks me. I look around and don't see what I can do. With the parish priests there's nothing I can do. Those who know me personally now avoid me, are afraid of meeting me. The few priests who have left the Church in the past fifty years in the Marsica diocese have done so because of scandalous breaches of celibacy. That is sufficient to give you an idea of the spiritual state of our clergy. If news spread in the diocese that a priest had abandoned the priesthood, the first thing that would naturally occur to the minds of the faithful would be that another one had eloped with his housemaid.'

'I had to call on Don Angelo Girasole this afternoon,' Pietro said. 'He gave me the impression of being a very decent man, a good clerk in an administrative office.'

'You're quite right,' Don Benedetto said, 'but Christianity is not an administration.'

'The others, those who believe they have historical vision, are worse,' said Pietro. 'They believe, or pretend they believe, in a Man of Providence.'

'If they allow themselves to be deceived it is their own fault,' Don Benedetto interrupted, livening up. 'They were warned about two thousand years ago. They were told that many would come in the name of Providence and seduce the people, that there would be talk of wars and rumours of wars. They were told that all this would come to pass, but that the end was not yet. They were told that nation would rise up against nation and kingdom against kingdom; that there would be famines and pestilences and earthquakes in divers places; but that all these things would not be the end, but the beginning. Christians were warned. We were told that many would be horrified and many would betray, and that if someone, whoever it might be, should say here is a man of Providence, there is a man of Providence, we must not believe him. We have been

226

warned. False prophets and false saviours shall arise and shall show great signs and wonders and deceive many. We could not have asked for plainer warning. If many have forgotten it, it will not change anything of what will come to pass. The destiny of the Man of Providence has already been written. *Intrabit ut vulpis, regnabit ut leo, morietur ut canis[1].*'

'What a fine language Latin is,' said Pietro. 'And what a difference there is between that honest old church Latin and the modern sibylline Latin of the encyclicals.'

'What is lacking in our country, as you know, is not the critical spirit,' Don Benedetto said. 'What is lacking is faith. The critics are grumblers, violent men, dissatisfied men, in certain circumstances they may sometimes even be heroes. But they are not believers. What is the use of teaching new ways of talking or gesticulating to a nation of sceptics? Perhaps the terrible sufferings that lie ahead will make Italians more serious. Meanwhile, when I feel most disheartened, I tell myself I'm useless, a failure, but there's Pietro, there are his friends, the unknown members of underground groups. I confess to you that that is my only consolation.'

Pietro was taken aback by the despondency in his former master's voice. 'My dear Don Benedetto,' he said, 'we have not met for fifteen years, and after this perhaps we shall not meet again. You are an old man, my health is uncertain, the times are hard. It would be wrong to waste this short visit exchanging compliments. The trust you have in me terrifies me. I genuinely believe I'm no better that my former school fellows. My destiny has been more fortunate than theirs because I was helped by a whole series of misfortunes and cut the cord in good time. For the rest, you must forgive me for not sharing the optimism of that only consolation of yours.'

'There's no salvation except putting one's life in jeopardy,' Don Benedetto said. 'But that is not for everyone. After his first meeting with you at Acquafredda Nunzio, that poor soul in torment, came here and told me everything. He told me again about his position, which I already knew. Under a

[1] He will come in like a fox, reign like a lion, die like a dog.

dictatorial régime how can one exercise a profession in which one depends on public offices and yet remain free? he asked me. What good fortune that at least Pietro is saved, he said.'

'Saved?' said Pietro. 'Is there a past participle of saving oneself? Alas, recently I have had plenty of occasions to consider what is undoubtedly the saddest aspect of the present degeneracy, because it concerns the future. My dear Don Benedetto, perhaps the future will resemble the present. We may be sowing contaminated seed.'

Don Benedetto signalled to him to be silent. 'There's someone at the door,' he said in an undertone. 'Come into the next room.'

They rose and went into Marta's room. At that moment there was a knock at the door.

'Go and see who it is,' Don Benedetto said to his sister. 'Don't let anyone in. Never mind who it is, say you don't know whether I can see him. And please, before you open the door bring the wine and the two glasses in here.'

There was another knock at the door, and Marta opened it. It was Don Piccirilli.

'Good evening,' he said. 'Am I disturbing you? I was told that Don Angelo Girasole was here with Don Benedetto, and I should like to see him too.'

'You have been misinformed,' Marta said. 'Don Girasole is not here.'

'Didn't a priest arrive here in a carriage from Fossa a short while ago?' Don Piccirilli said.

'No priest and no carriage have been seen here,' Marta said. 'You have been misinformed.'

This conversation took place at the front door. Marta showed no inclination to let him in.

'I hope I'm not being troublesome,' Don Piccirilli said, 'but as I've come all this way I should like at least to say good evening to Don Benedetto.'

'I don't know whether he can see you,' Marta said. 'He may be resting. I'll go and see.'

In the next door room she found her brother alone. Pointing to the window that gave on to the garden, he indicated that his first visitor had left. 'Now we must try and keep Don Piccirilli here as long as possible,' he said to his sister in an undertone. 'Bring us some wine immediately!'

He went to meet the newly arrived guest.

'What are you doing standing there in the doorway?' he said reproachfully. 'Come in, come in, don't stand on ceremony. You must tell me what you think of the wine from a new barrel.'

CHAPTER 25

Matalena was preparing flour for bread making on the ground floor of the inn, and Don Paolo was keeping her company. At Pietrasecca bread was baked once a fortnight in a communal oven. It was a ritual with strict rules. The woman's head was wrapped in a cloth rather like a nun's veil and she was passing the flour through a sieve over an open bin. Thus she separated the white flour from the chaff and the best from the ordinary flour. The chaff went to the chickens and the pig, the ordinary flour was used for bread and the best for pasta. The woman's face and hands were covered with dust from the flour that rose from the rhythmical movement of the sieve. Chiarina, the goatherd's wife, was having difficulty in lighting the green wood under the copper in which potatoes were being cooked that were to be added to the flour to make the bread heavier and more lasting.

The sieving stopped when a strange young man, looking halfway between a cafone and a workman, came into the bar and asked for Don Paolo. He had a letter in his hand. He seemed rather surprised and embarrassed at the sight of Don Paolo, and was on the point of apologizing and going away again.

'Don Benedetto told me he was sending me to someone in whom I could have full confidence. To tell the truth, I didn't expect to find a priest here,' he said.

'Never mind,' said the priest. 'Don Benedetto will have had his reasons.' The youth handed over the letter of introduction.

It consisted of these few words, written in Don Benedetto's fine, tremulous hand: '*Ecce homo*, my friend, here is a poor man who has need of you, and perhaps you also have need of him. Please listen to him to the end'.

Don Paolo took the young man to his room and made him sit beside him.

'If you had come here as one goes to a priest,' he said, 'I should certainly have asked you to apply elsewhere. How long have you known Don Benedetto?'

'We belong to the same village,' the young man said. 'Every family at Rocca knows every other. Everyone knows everything, or nearly everything, about everyone else. When you see someone going out you know exactly where he's going, and when you see him coming back you know where he has been. My family has a vineyard near Don Benedetto's garden half-way up the hill above the village. We use water from his well to spray sulphur on the vines, and he borrows our stakes for his tomatoes, beans and peas. My mother always consulted him about my education. His advice may not always have been good, but his intentions always were. He has always liked me, ever since I was a boy.' After a pause he added, 'He told me to tell you everything.'

As he spoke the young man's personality became better defined. At first sight, particularly because of his plain, patched clothing, the earthy marks on his face and hands, and his untidy, ruffled hair, he created the impression of being half-workman, half-cafone, but on closer inspection he turned out to have extraordinarily lively and intelligent eyes, and his manners were controlled and polite. Also instead of using dialect he spoke very correct Italian with complete ease. After some hesitation he started telling his story.

'I was a delicate and sickly boy, and also I was an only son,' he said. 'So my mother decided that I should not work on the land. "Our family has always worked the land, and we're still where we always were," she said. "For generations we have hoed, dug, sowed and manured the land, and we're still poor. Let the boy study. He's not strong and he needs a less tough way of living." My father didn't agree. "Working the land is hard, but it's safe," he said. "Education is for the sons of gentlemen. We have no-one to back us." Our backing was Don Benedetto. "Since the boy wants to study, let him," he said. He helped my mother with his advice. As long as I was at grammar school my family could still regard itself as being prosperous. Apart from the vineyard, my father had two fields on which he

231

grew wheat and vegetables and a shed with four cows. While I was a student the money orders my mother sent me to pay for my keep never arrived regularly, but they arrived. But during my three years at high school the family situation went from bad to worse, because of two bad harvests and an illness of my father's. On top of this were my heavy expenses. The result was that one of the two fields had to be sold to pay off my father's debts. Two cows died in an epidemic; the two that were left were sold at the fair, and the shed was let. "No matter," my mother said, "When our son has passed his exams he'll be able to help us." I passed the state exam three years ago and the following October I went to Rome, where I registered in the faculty of arts. Actually my mother didn't know where to find the money to keep me in Rome until I got my degree.'

'Why did you choose the faculty of arts?' Don Paolo asked. 'It's not the best from the point of view of earning a living.'

'Don Benedetto said that was what I was best at. In Rome I led a life of severe privations. I lived in a small room without electric light. My midday meal consisted of white coffee and bread, and for dinner I had soup. I was permanently hungry. I was comically dressed and had no friends. The first time I tried to approach other students they laughed at me and made stupid jokes because of my provincial appearance. Two incidents of that kind were enough to make me completely unsociable. I often wept with rage and mortification in my little room. I resigned myself to a life of solitude. After the warm family atmosphere to which I was used I was ill at ease in the noisy, vulgar, cynical students' world. Most of the students were interested in sport and politics, both of which offer frequent opportunities for rowdiness. One day I saw a typical piece of rowdiness from the tram. About a dozen students belonging to my faculty beat a young workman till the blood flowed. I can still see the scene in my mind's eye. The workman lay on the pavement with his head on one of the tramlines while the students who had surrounded him went on kicking and hitting him with sticks. "He didn't salute the flag," they shouted. Some policemen arrived on the scene, congratulated the aggressors on their patriotic action and arrested the injured man. A crowd had gathered, but no-one protested. I was left alone on the stationary tram. What cowardice, I muttered to myself. Behind me I heard someone mutter, "Yes, it's a real disgrace." It was the conductor. We said goodbye to each other that day, but that was all. But as he was often on duty on the line that went down my street, we saw each other every so often and got into the habit of greeting each other like old acquaintances.'

There was a long pause as if he had lost the thread. Then he went on, 'I met him in the street one day when he was off duty. We shook hands and went into a tavern for a glass of wine. Each of us told the other about himself, and so we struck up a friendship. He asked me to his home, where I met other persons, nearly all of them young. There were five of them altogether and they constituted a cell, and those meetings were cell meetings. All this was strange and new to me. Thanks to the tramwayman's introduction, I was admitted to the cell, and I regularly attended the weekly meetings. Those were my first personal contacts with townspeople. The other members of the cell were workers or artisans, and they liked me for being a student, and I enjoyed those meetings too. The purely human pleasure they gave me meant that I did not at first realize the gravity and significance of the step I had taken. At the meetings badly printed little newspapers and pamphlets were read in which tyranny was denounced and the revolution was proclaimed as a certain, inevitable and not distant event that would establish fraternity and justice among men. It was a kind of secret and prohibited weekly dream in which we indulged, and it made us forget the wretchedness of our everyday lives. It was like a secret religious rite. There was no link between us apart from those meetings, and if by chance we met in the street we pretended not to know one another.

'When I went out one morning I was arrested by two policemen, taken to the central police station and shut up in a room full of other policemen. After some formalities they started slapping my face and spitting at me, and that went on for an hour. Perhaps I might have put up better with a more violent beating, but the slapping and spitting were intolerable.

When the door opened and the official who was to interrogate me appeared, my face and chest were literally dripping with spittle. The official railed at, or pretended to rail at, his subordinates, made me wash and dry myself, took me to his office, and assured me that he had studied my case with benevolence and understanding. He knew I lived in a small room, he knew the milk bar where I had my midday bread and coffee and the inn where I went for my soup in the evening. He had detailed information about my family, and he knew about the difficulties that endangered the continuation of my studies. He could only guess the motives that had led me towards the revolutionary groups but, he said, that impulse could not in itself be regarded as reprehensible; on the contrary, in fact. He said youth was inherently magnanimous and idealistic, and it would be disastrous if it were otherwise. However, the police had the socially necessary but perhaps distasteful role of keeping a close watch on the magnanimous and idealistic impulses of the young.'

'In short,' Don Paolo interrupted, 'he suggested that you should put yourself in the service of the police. And what did you reply?'

'I agreed.'

Matalena appeared at the door and said, 'Dinner's ready. Shall I lay for two?'

'I'm not hungry this evening,' the priest replied. He rose from his seat because he was tired and lay on the bed.

In a soft voice the young man continued, 'I was given 100 lire to pay the rent of my room, and in return I wrote a short report, like an academic essay, on "How a cell works, what its members read and what they talk about". The official read it and praised it. "It's very well written," he said. I was proud that he was pleased with me, and I undertook to remain in contact with him in return for an allowance of 500 lire a month. That enabled me to have soup at midday as well as in the evening and to go to the cinema on Saturday night. One day he also gave me a packet of cigarettes. Actually I had never smoked, but I learnt to out of politeness.'

'And what did you write in your next reports?' Don Paolo asked.

234

'They went on being very general, and he began to be dissatisfied with them,' the young man said. 'I always sent him a copy of the printed matter that was distributed in the cell, but that was not enough for him, probably because he received the same material from other sources. Eventually he advised me to leave that cell and join a more interesting one, and I had no difficulty in doing so. I told my friends that I wanted a transfer to a cell in which there were other intellectuals, and it was arranged immediately. In the new cell I met and struck up a friendship with a girl, a dressmaker. She was the first woman I had ever met. Very soon we were inseparable, and it was then that I began to have the first twinges of conscience. With her I began to have glimpses of a pure, honest and decent way of living the possibility of which I had not previously imagined. At the same time an insuperable abyss opened up between my apparent and my secret life. Sometimes I managed to forget my secret. I worked for the cell with genuine enthusiasm, translated into Italian and typed out whole chapters of revolutionary novels that we received from abroad, stuck manifestos on the walls at night. But I was deceiving myself. When my new comrades admired my courage and my activity they reminded me that in reality I was betraying them. So I tried to get away from them. Also I told myself that I too had a right to live. No more money was being sent to me from home. When I was hungry and the rent was due I lost all restraint. I had no other resources. I regarded politics as absurd. What did all that stuff matter to me? I should certainly have preferred to live in peace, to have two or three meals a day, consigning both "economic democracy" and "the necessity of imperial expansion" to the devil. But that was impossible. I had no money to buy food or pay the rent. But that kind of cynicism collapsed when I was with my girl. We were very much in love. To me she did not represent a way of thinking, in fact she argued very little but kept silent and liked listening to others; to me she was a way of being, a way of living, a way of giving oneself in an unparalleled human and pure way. I could no longer think of life without her, because she was really more than a woman, she was a light and a flame, she was concrete proof of the possibility of living honestly, cleanly, unselfishly, seeking harmony with one's fellows with the whole of one's soul. It seemed to me that only after I met her had I become spiritually alive. But I did not blame my parents. They were good, honest people, but they were traditional. That girl did not follow rules, but her heart. She seemed to me to invent her life as she lived it. But in the face of her ingenuous confidence in me how could I not remember that I was deceiving and betraying her? Thus our love was poisoned at the roots. Being with her, though I loved her so much, was an insupportable pretence, a torment . . .'

'Why, when your relations with the police became morally reprehensible to you, did you not break with them?' Don Paolo asked.

'I tried to get away from them and cover my tracks several times,' the young man said. 'Once I moved, but they had no difficulty in tracking me down to my new address. For a time I tried to quieten my conscience by writing harmless, phoney reports that told them nothing. At that time I was beginning to receive a small monthly allowance from my mother again. I tried to deceive the police by telling them I had left the cell because my comrades no longer trusted me. But they had other informers who satisfied them of the opposite. Finally I became obsessed with the idea that my situation was irremediable. I felt condemned. There was nothing that I could do. It was my destiny.'

The young man spoke with difficulty, almost struggling for breath. Don Paolo avoided looking him in the face.

'I don't want to make my behaviour seem less ugly than it was,' he went on. 'I don't want to make my case more pitiful. This is a confession in which I want to show myself in all my repulsive nakedness. Well, then, the truth of the matter was this. Fear of being discovered was stronger in me than remorse. What was I to tell my girl if my deception were revealed? What would my friends say? That was the idea that haunted me. I feared for my threatened reputation, not for the wrong that I was doing. I saw the image of my fear all round me everywhere.'

The young man paused. His throat was dry. There was a

bottle of water and a glass on the table, but it did not occur to Don Paolo to ask him to help himself.

'I knew I was being trailed by the police who no longer trusted me,' he went on. 'I kept away from my friends to avoid having to denounce them. The police threatened me with arrest if I associated with suspects without informing them. I lived in terror of being arrested again. I tried to live in complete seclusion, with the result that every meeting with my girl was a torment. But in spite of that she was always patient, gentle and affectionate with me. On Christmas Day last year we went together to a little eating-place outside the walls . . .'

Don Paolo went on listening to a story every detail of which he already knew. The unusually cheerful lunch. The invitation to go home with the girl. The buying of flowers, fruit, sweets, and a bottle of Marsala. The arrival of the police and the escape on to the roof. The long wait on the roof. But the young man did not finish. He hid his face in his hands and burst into tears. After a while he resumed his story.

'I went home to Rocca dei Marsi. I told my parents that the doctors had insisted on my returning to my native climate. I spent the winter at home without seeing anyone. Sometimes I went to see Don Benedetto, who gave me books to read. In the spring I started working in the fields with my father, winnowing, pruning the vines, hoeing and reaping. I went on working as long as I could stand on my feet, to the point of physical exhaustion. Immediately after dinner I went to bed, and in the morning, at dawn, it was I who woke my father. He looked at me with admiration. He said, "It's obvious that you come of a race of peasants; if you come from the land you cannot free yourself from it." But if you come from the land and have lived in a town you're no longer a peasant and you're not a townsman either. Memory of the town, of my girl, of the cell, of the police, was a perpetually open wound, a wound that still bled and was beginning to putrefy and threatened to poison the rest of my life. My mother said town air had ruined me and put sadness in my blood. "Let me work," I said, "perhaps work will make me better." But in the fields my girl would often appear before me in my mind's eye. How could I forget her?

Having glimpsed the possibility of another way of living, a clean, honest and courageous way of living, having seen the possibility of open and frank communication and dreamed of a better humanity, how could I resign myself to village life? On the other hand, how could I undo the irremediable? In my solitary brooding, that left me not a moment's peace, I passed from fear of punishment to fear of non-punishment. The idea that I was haunted by the wrong I had done only because of the continual risk of being found out began to frighten me. So I began to wonder whether, if better technique enabled one to betray one's friends with the certainty that one would never be found out, that would make it more supportable.'

Don Paolo looked him in the face, in the eyes.

'I must confess,' the young man went on, 'that my religious faith has never been very strong. I have never believed very deeply. I was baptized, confirmed and received holy communion like everyone else, but my faith in the reality of God was very vague and fitful. That was why I put up no resistance in Rome to accepting the so-called scientific theories that were propagated in the cells. These theories began to strike me as too comfortable. The idea that everything was matter, that the idea of right was inseparable from that of utility (even if it were social utility) and was backed only by the idea of punishment, became intolerable to me. Punishment by whom? The state, the party and public opinion? But supposing the state, the party and public opinion were immoral? And then, if favourable circumstances or an appropriate technique made it possible to do evil with impunity, what was morality based on? So might technique be capable of destroying the distinction between right and wrong by eliminating the risk of punishment? The idea frightened me. I began to be seriously afraid of the absurd. I don't want to weary you with these digressions, which may seem abstract to you; nor do I want you to suppose that by moralizing I'm now trying to put myself in a more favourable light. No, those ideas became the very substance of my life. I no longer believed in God, but with all the strength of my mind I began to want Him to exist. I had an absolute need of Him to escape from the fear of chaos. A night came when I

238

could no longer stand it, and I got up to go and knock at the door of a Capuchin monastery in our part of the world. On the way I met a monk whom I already knew, one Brother Gioacchino. I said to him, "I want so much to believe in God and I can't manage it, won't you please explain to me how it's done?" "One mustn't be proud," he replied, "one mustn't claim the right to understand everything, one mustn't try, one must resign oneself, shut one's eyes, pray. Faith is a grace." But I could not let myself go. I wanted to understand. I couldn't not try to understand. My whole being was in a state of extreme and painful tension. I couldn't resign myself. I wanted God by force. I needed Him.'

The young man fell silent, as if exhausted.

'You must be thirsty,' Don Paolo said. 'Drink some water.'

'Eventually I went to see Don Benedetto,' the young man went on. 'I went to see him, not because he was a priest, but because to me he'd always been a symbol of the upright man. He has known me since childhood, as I said. When I went to see him I told him that actually he did not know me yet, because he had no suspicion of what was hidden inside me. My confession lasted for five hours. I made a tremendous effort and told him everything, and in the end I was lying almost unconscious on the ground. I seriously believed I was dying. On that first occasion the words came out of me as if I were bringing up blood. When I had finished only a vague gleam of consciousness remained. I felt like an empty sack. Don Benedetto sent his sister Marta to tell my mother that I would be sleeping at his house that night, and that for the next few days I would be helping him working in his garden. We worked together for the next few days, and every now and then he stopped and talked to me. He taught me that nothing is irreparable while life lasts, and that no condemnation is ever final. He explained to me that, though evil must not of course be loved, nevertheless good is often born of it, and that perhaps I should never have become a man but for the infamies and errors through which I had passed. When at last he had finished with me and said I could go home I had no more fear and I seemed to have been reborn. I was struck by the air coming from the mountain. Never before had I breathed such fresh air in my village. Having stopped being afraid, I stopped brooding and started rediscovering the world. I started seeing the trees again, the children in the streets, the poor people labouring in the fields, the donkeys carrying their loads, the cows pulling the plough. I went on seeing Don Benedetto from time to time. Yesterday he sent for me and said, "I should like to spare you the repetition of a painful experience, but there's a man near here to whom I want you to repeat your confession. He's someone in whom you can have complete confidence." He gave me the necessary information, added some advice, and here I am.'

By now it was dark, and the young man's exhausted voice faded away in the shadows. After a pause the other man's voice emerged from it.

'If I were a leader of a party or of a political group,' Don Paolo said, 'I would have to judge you according to the party rules. Every party has a morality of its own, codified in rules. Those rules are often very close to those with which moral feeling inspires everyone, though sometimes they are the exact opposite. But I'm not (or am no longer) a political leader. Here and now I'm an ordinary man, and if I am to judge another man I can be guided only by my conscience, respecting the very narrow limits within which one man has the right to judge another.'

'I did not come here to ask for pardon or absolution,' the young man said.

'Luigi Murica,' the other man said quietly, 'I want to tell you something that will show how much I now trust you. I'm not a priest. Don Paolo Spada is not my real name. My name is Pietro Spina.'

Murica's eyes filled with tears.

Meanwhile Matalena of her own accord had laid the table for two, and she now insisted on their coming down for dinner. 'Convalescents mustn't miss meals,' she said. 'And if they have visitors the least they can do is to invite them.'

She had put a clean tablecloth and a bottle of wine on the table. The two men dined in silence. The wine was the previous year's and the bread was a fortnight old. They dipped the bread in the wine. When they had finished Murica wanted to go straight back to Rocca, and Don Paolo went up to his room to fetch a coat and go with him for some of the way. Matalena did not conceal a certain amount of jealousy at this sudden friendship between a stranger and her priest.

'You talked for such a long time,' she said to Murica. 'Do you still have things to say to each other.'

'I confessed,' the young man said.

When the two men parted in the road leading down to the valley Murica said, 'Now I'm ready for anything.'

'Good, we'll meet again soon,' Don Paolo said.

The priest delayed returning to the inn. He sat on the grassy edge of the road, oppressed by many thoughts. Voices could be heard in the distance, shepherds calling to their flocks, the barking of dogs, the low bleating of sheep. A slight odour of thyme and wild rosemary rose from the damp earth. It was the time of day when the cafoni put their donkeys back in their sheds and went to sleep. Mothers called their children from the windows. It was a time favourable to humility. Man returned to the animal, the animal to the plant, the plant to the earth. The stream at the bottom of the valley was full of stars. Pietrasecca was submerged in shadow; all that could be seen was the cow's head with its two big horns at the top of the inn.

CHAPTER 26

Don Paolo met Cristina on a visit to the cemetery. She was touched by the fact that he too had brought flowers to put on her father's grave. On the way back he accompanied her as far as her garden gate. The girl looking thin and unwell; she wore a long, plain black dress loosely tied at the waist with a cloth belt.

'You must forgive me for what I said the last time we met,' Don Paolo said. 'I was presumptious and rude.'

'No, it was entirely my fault,' Cristina replied.

They parted, promising to see each other again soon.

After the excitement caused by the declaration of war Pietrasecca had returned to normal. Women and old men ate their soup in silence in the doorways of their hovels without looking about them, and when they were spoken to they responded wearily. Some mothers were receiving a small allowance for sons who had been called up and prayed that it would last. Schoolboys engaged in battles with stones outside the inn, 'Italians' on one side and 'Africans' on the other. Sometimes, to the horror and indignation of the schoolmistress, the Africans won.

Apart from that, there was no point in worrying, because what was bound to happen was bound to happen. War had been bound to come, and it had come. If there was going to be a plague, there was no way of avoiding it.

Magascià's wife had been told in great confidence by Matalena that Don Paolo had confessed a young man who had come to see him from the valley. So he must have received permission. Therefore the woman came to implore him to confess her husband, who had not been reconciled to God for twenty-five years.

'He has no confidence in the priests in this part of the world,' the woman said. 'If you don't do him this grace, he'll die in sin and go to hell.'

The priest had relapsed into a state of extreme weakness. He had caught a bad cold the day before, he had a headache and had not slept all night. So his reply to the woman was an absent-minded no, and he thought no more about it until old Magascià appeared in person in his room. Tall, bearded and massive, with his hat in his hand, he filled up almost the whole of the doorway. His empty left sleeve hung from his shoulder and was inserted into his jacket pocket. Don Paolo was sitting in a chair near his bed and was going to say something, but the old man knelt at his feet, made the sign of the cross, kissed the floor, and with his face to the ground beat his breast three times. '*Mea culpa, mea culpa, mea culpa,*' he muttered.

Without raising his head and lowering his voice still more, he went on mumbling incomprehensibly for some minutes; all that Don Paolo could hear was a sibilant sound accompanied by brief sighs. When this stopped the man remained prostrate on the ground, his huge form filling up half the room. His enormous frame made him look like a geological phenomenon, a fossilized antediluvian monster; his beard and hair were like wild vegetation; only the fear that his attitude expressed revealed him to be a man.

He remained prostrate and silent for some time. Then he raised his head and asked in a normal voice, 'Have you given me absolution? May I go?'

'You may go,' the priest replied.

Magascià rose and kissed his hand. 'By the way,' he said in an undertone before leaving. 'I need advice on something I dare not mention to anyone else. Isn't murder pardoned after twenty-five years? If one is found out, does one have to go on trial just the same?'

'What murder?'

Magascià couldn't understand why the priest now simulated ignorance, but as he urgently wanted an answer to his question he repeated in his ear, 'The murder of Don Giulio, the Lama notary.'

'Oh, I see, I'd forgotten already,' the priest said. 'But I'm not a lawyer. I don't know the answer to your question.'

The news that Don Paolo had received permission to hear

confession spread like wildfire. All that Magascià said was, 'He understands everything and forgives everything. Matalena's right, he's a saint.'

'He's a saint who reads sinner's hearts,' said Matalena.

People started coming along to find out for themselves, and very soon Don Paolo's room became public property, as it were, with people continually coming in and going out. Some wanted to arrange an appointment for their own confession. Children came up the stairs and stayed in the doorway without daring to approach the priest, who could not hide or defend himself. He rose, went to the window or the door, struggling like an animal caught in a trap.

Though he was feverish, he was on the point of taking flight, walking out, but was stopped at the door by the arrival of Mastrangelo, supported under the armpits by his wife Lidovina and his sister-in-law Marietta, because one of his legs was bandaged and he could hardly walk. As he could not kneel, the two women made him sit on a chair near the father confessor. They kissed his hand and left. Mastrangelo began to speak, putting his mouth to the priest's ear so that no-one else should hear. His breath was foul, it stank of many years' wine drinking and made Don Paolo feel dizzy.

'My wife had eighteen children, but God took sixteen of them back,' Mastrangelo said. 'Two remain. There is flesh that is chastized from birth, and there's no help for it. My sister's wife Marietta has been chastized in a different way. She was poor, but healthy. Before her wedding day everything was ready, the banns had been put up, and Nicola, the bridegroom, came to see me and said there was a secret he must tell me. The war had chastized him, he said. He showed me what had happened. He was no longer a man. To save his life they had had to operate on him in the military hospital. The wretched man was alone in the world, he had no mother or sisters, he had no-one to wash his shirt or make his bed or cook his soup, so it was natural that he should want to marry. Also he had a vineyard and a medal. If Magascià died, the salt and tobacco monopoly would go to him because of the medal. Magascià was already an old man then, and it was only reasonable to expect him to die soon; it isn't my brother-in-law's fault that he's still alive. Well then, Nicola and Marietta got married, and it was only after the wedding that Marietta discovered the misfortune. Nicola said to her, "Your brother-in-law Mastrangelo knew everything." Marietta sent for me immediately and started to weep. "You're the ruin of me," she said, "now I'll kill myself for shame." Nicola left us alone. Before going away he said, "Since God wished to chastize me I have no right to be jealous; but on condition that honour is saved and no-one knows." Marietta has had six children, four of them still living. You may not know it, but making children is rather like drink. You swear that this glass is going to be the last, but then you get thirsty again and have another. I'll have this one and that will be that, you say, but who can control thirst? Sometimes it's the woman who's thirsty, sometimes it's the man, sometimes it's both. At first relations between the two sisters were very difficult, but in the course of time they settled down. We accepted it all with resignation, as God had sent it to us. Honour was satisfied, there was no scandal, no-one suspected anything. But one day Nicola confessed to Don Cipriano, and Don Cipriano made him change his mind. He explained that the chastizements of God that we had already suffered were nothing in comparison to those we deserved and were yet to be inflicted on us, and that those that we did not suffer ourselves would be suffered by our children, who were the children of sin; and that those not suffered by our children would be suffered by their children, and so on unto the seventh generation. But, if God knows the truth, how can He go on chastizing us? Haven't we suffered enough?'

The penitent fell silent and looked at the father confessor with staring, bloodshot eyes, awaiting his reply. The tipsy voices of some morra players floated up the stairs from the ground floor. On the window-pane two dusty, motionless flies were attached to one another, surprised by death in the act of union. Outside it was raining. Don Paolo shuddered. Mastrangelo seized his arm, shook it, wanting an answer, 'Was Don Cipriano right?' he said. 'Are Marietta's children and their children cursed already?'

'Cursed by whom?' said Don Paolo.

'Aren't they cursed by God?'

'God does not curse,' Don Paolo said. 'He has never cursed a living soul.'

'Won't they be children of misfortune?'

'Perhaps they may be,' Don Paolo said. 'But like everyone else, neither more nor less.'

Mastrangelo called Lidovina and Marietta, who came upstairs again and helped their man out, supporting him under the armpits and interrogating him with their eyes to find out the result of his confession.

Other penitents, men and women, were sitting on the stairs, waiting their turn to confess. An acute, pungent, smell came floating up, as if these people relieved themselves in their pants and never washed. There was also another smell, a new and unusual one in an inn – the smell of incense. Matalena had hurried to get the keys of the church from Cristina and had taken a little incense from the supply in the sacristy. Don Paolo put on his coat and took refuge in the street. The penitents, disappointed and disheartened, watched him from the door.

'Wait, wait,' Matalena told them. 'He only wants a little fresh air. He won't be going far in this rain.'

After about an hour he reappeared but, instead of coming back to the inn, he made for the Colamartini house.

Cristina opened the door. The girl seemed thinner and more unwell than before.

'We were just talking about you,' she said.

She showed him into the big room in which the whole family was gathered, her grandmother, her aunt, and her mother.

'But you're wet through,' Cristina exclaimed when she saw him in the light of the room. 'And your teeth are chattering with cold.'

She made him give her his coat so that she could hang it up to dry and made him sit by the fireplace.

'Stretch out your feet towards the fire,' she said.

In the room there was the usual stuffy smell, modified by the odour of preserved fruit and aromatic wine. The three old women were silent. Don Paolo tried to avoid their eyes.

Through a big window he could see the rain-drenched garden. The flowers had turned to seed, and the seeds had fallen to the ground. Cristina's aunt and mother rose and withdrew to the next room. Cristina murmured something into her grandmother's ear and followed them.

'Weren't you the last person to whom my son spoke before coming back from Fossa?' the old woman said to the priest. 'What did he say?'

'He said, "It's the end." He didn't want me to go with him. It was in fact the end. That's all he said to me,' the priest replied.

The old woman, who was dressed in black, was sitting on an armchair covered with old red velvet near a window that looked out on to the garden. She was small, shrivelled and wrinkled; she looked at the priest with glassy, inscrutable, abstracted eyes, and when she spoke she revealed her empty gums. The rain beat on the blurred windows.

'They left us alone because they want me to confess,' the old woman said. 'But I don't want to confess. Must I tell you the truth? I lack the repentance necessary for confession. Why should I repent?'

She held her hands crossed on her breast; they looked like old tools worn out by long, hard use. Her shrivelled arms looked like two dry branches waiting to be broken off and thrown on the fire.

'Why should I repent?' she went on. 'For eighty years I have cared about one thing only, a good thing, the only good thing, the reputation of my family. I have never thought of anything else, or cared about anything else, or done anything else. For eighty years. Am I to repent now?'

In her eyes, which suddenly opened wide, there appeared a hopeless anguish, a long repressed fear, a dismay so fixed and irremediable, an expression of despair so primitive that Don Paolo was taken aback.

'Is it the end?' she asked. 'Is it the end of everyone or only of the Colamartini?'

'It's the end of all the landowners, I think,' Don Paolo said.

When the old woman realized that the priest was looking her

in the eyes, she closed them. The shape of her completely fleshless and almost hairless head recalled that of a sparrow. Such a fragile thing, but so tough, so stubborn, so tenacious, so pitiless, so durable that it had lasted for eighty years. Cristina had told her that if she did not repent and confess she would go to hell, and she had replied, 'Very well, then, I shall go to hell.' But, since an opportunity of consulting a priest had arisen, there was a detail on which she badly wanted information.

'How long do those who do not repent and go to hell have in the presence of God on the judgment throne? Do they at least have time enough to tell Him the truth?'

Don Paolo had to admit that he had no definite information on this subject, but he said commonsense would seem to suggest a reply in the affirmative. 'That is what is done at every decent tribunal,' he said. That was sufficient for the old woman.

Cristina returned in time to accompany Don Paolo to the door, but before he left she wanted to show him a small room next to the kitchen in which there was a loom on which she worked in her rare moments of leisure during the day and until late at night.

'We do not know how we're going to manage,' she said. 'You know that we lost all our savings in the failure of the bank? We get nothing from our remaining land. The tenants don't pay the rent.'

She had had the idea of earning something by weaving, but had changed her mind.

'Wool is expensive,' she explained, 'and nowadays no-one wants hand-made cloth any longer; it's a luxury. The few orders I've had so far have been from friends who gave them to me out of sympathy, I think.'

'Have you given up the idea of taking the veil?' Don Paolo asked.

'How could I do it now?' she replied. 'In this house I'm both the mistress and the maid, with three persons to look after. The most vigorous of the three, my grandmother, can't even dress herself.'

'You do not realize how worried I am about you,' said Don

Paolo. 'It distresses me that I'm not able to help you.'

'Thank you,' Cristina said with a slight smile veiled with sadness. 'It will help me if you no longer bear me any ill-feeling. Will you promise me that? Besides, believe me, material difficulties are the least of our worries. Spiritual troubles are much more painful. Some family matters I'd never heard of before are now the subject of continual arguments and disputes.'

'And Alberto?' Don Paolo said.

'He has joined the militia,' Cristina said. 'He's certainly not cut out for military life, but it was the only thing that offered. If he does well, he'll at least be able to provide for himself.'

Cristina showed the priest a piece of weaving she had finished the day before, a small red and white rug with graceful geometrical patterns which she had copied from an old one.

'Do you know that my brother Alberto greatly admires you?' she said. 'He told me about your plot for the second revolution. Isn't it dangerous? Isn't it condemned by the Church?'

'In our time there are many ways of serving God,' Don Paolo said with an evasive gesture.

'That is also Don Benedetto's view,' Cristina said. 'Do you know that he came here with Signorina Marta for the funeral? Alberto and I had a long talk with him. We asked his advice on certain family matters, and eventually, I don't remember how, the conversation turned to the question of obedience to civil authorities, and that led to Pietro Spina. "You mustn't think badly of him," he said. "I know him, he was my pupil. Socialism is his way of serving God" '.

'Did he actually use those words?'

'Yes, I remember them distinctly. He also said of Spina, "He was touched by God when he was a boy and was thrown by God Himself into the shadows in search of Him. I'm sure he is still obeying His voice." In short, Don Benedetto talked to us about him as if he knew him very well. After what he said I felt very confused.'

'I can well believe it,' Don Paolo said. 'But perhaps what he said was not to be taken literally.'

The priest was about to leave when Cristina said she would like to confess to him at a time and place convenient to him.

'Oh, no,' he replied, taken by surprise. Then he added in embarrassment, 'Please don't take it amiss, but above all I lack the detachment desirable between penitent and confessor.'

Cristina blushed. 'You're right,' she said. 'It would be difficult for me too.'

'I very much enjoy talking to you, but as an ordinary man,' Don Paolo went on. 'I too am going through a difficult period, and seeing you more often would help me.'

'I don't have a single free moment all day long,' Cristina said.

'Very well then, I shall come this evening after dinner,' Don Paolo said. 'I shall keep you company while you work at the loom.'

'All right,' said Cristina, a trifle hesitantly.

That evening the priest ate his dinner cheerfully and with a good appetite. Matalena too was radiant because of the afternoon's confessions. Her inn was becoming a sacred place. Two lamps were burning in front of the image of Our Lady of the Rosary.

'The carpenter will be coming later for the measurements,' she told the priest. 'The work will be at my expense, of course.'

'What measurements?' Don Paolo asked, touching iron.

'The measurements for the confessional. Diocleziano's a good carpenter, but he has never made a confessional before. I'll put it in your room, where the small table is now. What do you think of the idea?'

'I think you're going out of your mind.'

'You don't want to use a confessional? It's a pity, but as you wish. It was chiefly for the sake of the girls. I told them to wait until the confessional was ready. But if you prefer doing without . . .'

Matalena brought him an apple and a handful of walnuts.

'Just to let you know, those who queued up this afternoon will be coming back later,' she said.

'What do they want?'

'You know very well, they want to confess. Now that you've started.'

'I haven't the slightest desire to confess them.'

'Shall I tell them to come back tomorrow? The trouble is that most of them work during the day.'

'Just tell them never to come here again.'

'Impossible. They'd say it was my fault, they'd blame me.'

'You are not responsible for my actions.'

'They'd say, "Why others and not us?" They'd say, "It's all Matalena's fault." They'd never forgive me.'

'Let them say what they like. I shall not confess them, that's certain.'

'If that's the case, talk to them yourself when they come. Then they'll believe it's not my fault.'

'I shall be out when they come.'

'I'll make them wait till you come back.'

'Matalena, listen to me,' said the priest, raising his voice. 'I shall not set foot in this house until they've gone.'

This alarmed Matalena.

'If you don't want to, no-one can force you to,' she said. 'I'll tell them you're tired tonight and that perhaps you'll change your mind in the morning.'

The priest did not answer. But when she saw him pick up his hat and make ready to go out she was seized with remorse.

'It's raining,' she said. 'It's bad for you to go out in this weather. Stay here, I'll see about getting rid of them. I'll see you're not troubled. At most we'll talk about it again tomorrow. Where are you going in this weather?'

'Where I like,' said the priest.

But when she saw him making for the Colamartini house all her anxieties vanished and she smiled with satisfaction. The spell was obviously working.

Don Paolo found the door half-open and Cristina already at work at the loom, busily trying to untangle some warp cords which had got in a knot.

'Can I help you?' Don Paolo said.

'Do you know anything about it?'

'Try me.'

The girl gave up her seat to him, as if it were a game.

'The trouble's in the register,' the priest said with confidence as soon as he had tried the shed of the warp cords.

Cristina was left open-mouthed with astonishment.

'You understand weaving?' she asked.

'I used to help my mother when I was a boy,' he replied with a laugh. 'She was an expert. She did it more for pleasure than for profit. I did it as a hobby too.'

'Was it a loom like this?'

'Eventually my mother bought one exactly like this, but before that she had another of an older, bulkier, more complicated type. Have you ever seen one of them?'

'There's one up in the attic.'

'In that case you'll know that with the old type of loom you had to have an assistant whom you told to pull up a new sequence of threads whenever that was required by the design. I was my mother's assistant, and I would not allow anyone else to take my place. While we worked my mother used to repeat the parables in the Bible to me as if they were fairy stories. When I come to think of it, if I have remained more or less a Christian, perhaps it's because of those fables.'

'What are you saying?' Cristina interrupted, both shocked and amused.

'For once the truth slipped out of me,' Don Paolo said seriously.

'And you worked at the new loom, even though your help was no longer required?'

'On the new loom my mother gave weaving lessons to a girl who was a friend of the family. I liked her, and for the sake of her company I took lessons too.'

'So what it amounts to, if I may say so, is that you're backsliding in the same way again,' Cristina exclaimed with a laugh.

Don Paolo laughed wholeheartedly too. Something had lit up in his face and eyes as if he had taken off a mask. One memory led to another, and he went on talking about his boyhood. While Cristina went on with her work he talked to her about the discoveries and surprises of his early reading, his first friendships, his first travels. There was no stopping the flow of his memories. Thus they spent the evening in a peaceful, affectionate atmosphere such as neither had experienced for a long time.

'Now it's time for me to go,' Don Paolo said eventually. 'You have been working hard all day and it's time you went to bed.'

'Yes, you had better go,' Cristina said. 'Matalena might be jealous.'

She shook hands with him at the door and said, 'I shall see you again soon, I hope.'

CHAPTER 27

'After all we have been through,' Don Paolo said to Murica, 'we can no longer talk of politics as others do. When you come to think of it, to us it has become something quite different.'

'Wasn't it always like that?' said Murica. 'Could purely political aims and calculations have caused either of us to join an underground movement that has not the slightest prospect of immediate success?'

Murica went ahead of the priest to make way for him between the brambles that lined the slippery path that led down to the bottom of the valley.

After a while he stopped and said, 'I must tell you something that concerns you. In a short piece you wrote about two years ago you spoke of men painfully attaining consciousness of their own humanity. Romeo sent me a copy. It gave me food for a great deal of thought even then, but perhaps it's only now that I'm able fully to understand your meaning.'

'That's something that can also happen to the writer,' Don Paolo said. 'There are infinite gradations of consciousness, just as there are of light.'

The path led quickly to the stony stream bed. A trickle of clear water wound its way between the rocks and boulders. The two walked one behind the other, and every so often they had to stop because the path was interrupted by holes. The jawbone of a donkey with the molars still attached was whitening in a ditch.

'When I come to think of it,' Murica said, 'it's obvious to me now that in the movement I was from the outset in the false position of a gambler who stakes much more than he possesses. But perhaps that's a more frequent occurrence than I assume.'

'If you felt unready to face the risks, why didn't you leave after the first few meetings?'

'The fact of the matter is that that is an argument that was beyond me at the time,' Murica said. 'But I think about such things a great deal now, and I want to talk to you about the conclusions I have come to so that you can tell me whether you agree. Well, then, it seems to me that one can rebel against the existing order for two opposite reasons – if one is very strong or if one is very weak. By a strong man I mean someone superior to the bourgeois order, who rejects, despises and fights it and wants to replace it by other values, by a more just society. That was not my position. I felt crushed by bourgeois society, I was at its margin, a provincial student, poor, shy, awkward, and lonely in a big city. I felt incapable of facing the thousand minor difficulties, the daily humiliations of life.'

'In such case contact with a revolutionary movement can be a source of strength,' said Don Paolo.

'No,' Murica replied. 'Since it's an underground movement, it offers the deceptive advantage of secrecy. The resentments of those who are offended and humiliated are offered satisfaction, but covert satisfaction. Their outward behaviour remains unchanged. Their repudiation of legality remains internal, as in a dream, and for that very reason assumes extreme, reckless and foolhardy forms. They conspire against the state, just as in a dream they may throttle their own father, whom they continue to obey and respect in the daytime.'

'Until something happens that reveals their double life,' Don Paolo said. 'Then there's panic and terror.'

After a few minutes' silence Don Paolo said, 'When you were arrested were you beaten?'

'I was slapped and they spat in my face,' Murica said, 'but from the first moment I was completely terrorized. Just imagine it, when they asked me for my particulars I couldn't remember the date of my birth, or my mother's maiden name. In short, my challenge to the law was disproportionate to my strength. I had staked more than I possessed.'

For a short while the two walked on in silence along the path that flanked the stream, and then the valley widened and the road came close to the path.

'Let us stop here,' said Murica. 'If we go on they may see us from the road and recognize us.'

'Do you have the feeling that you're still being watched?' Don Paolo asked.

'I don't know,' Murica said. 'Now that I feel strong it doesn't matter to me. I was thinking of you.'

'Don't worry about me,' Don Paolo said. 'But you're perfectly right, after all we've been through we have no more reason to be afraid. It's the police who ought to be frightened of us.'

Between the road and the stream there was a field with a sheepfold. This was the season when the flocks were brought down from the mountains to winter on the plain.

'When does Annina arrive?' Don Paolo asked.

'Perhaps tomorrow,' Murica said. 'She writes to me every day.'

'She's a marvellous girl,' Don Paolo said. 'I'm certainly jealous of you.'

'My father was in favour of our getting married immediately,' Murica said.

Near the flock of sheep an aged shepherd was lighting a fire of twigs, a young man was blowing on it and a boy was looking for dry branches. The old man's name was Bonifazio, and he told Don Paolo that he had dreamed about St Francis. 'He was smiling and wanted to give me a lira,' he said.

'And did he?'

'No, he searched in his pockets, but they were empty.'

Don Paolo laughed, and gave him a lira.

'Do you know the old story about the lake of Fucino?' Bonifazio said. 'It's not a story to be found in books.'

As Don Paolo didn't know the story, this was the shepherd's way of saying thank you for the lira.

'Well then, Jesus was going about looking for work as a carpenter,' he said. 'He travelled from place to place and eventually arrived in this part of the world. "Have you any work for a poor carpenter?" he asked everywhere. "What's your name? Have you a recommendation?" the employers asked him. To all the jobless who had no recommendation whom he met on the road he said, "Follow me." And they all followed him. "Don't look back," he told them, and no-one looked back. When they were all on the mountain Jesus said, "You can look back now." In the place where land and houses had been there was a lake. Now the lake has been drained,' Bonifazio went on, 'and if the masters' wickedness goes on the land will sink beneath the waters again.'

'Your story is certainly worth a lira,' Don Paolo said with a smile.

'Next time I'll tell you another,' said Bonifazio.

Don Paolo said goodbye to Murica and hurried back towards Pietrasecca. When he was halfway he came across a woman crawling along the roadside. She looked like a bag of rags and dust, a swaying, tottering bag. Don Paolo's first impression was that she was mad, but she explained that her son had gone to the war, and to get rid of an obscure premonition she had made a vow in a fit of religious fervour to go on her knees from Pietrasecca to Lama to obtain from Our Lady that the boy should come back safe and sound. The wretched woman had been on her way since morning, her voice was hoarse, her face unrecognizable, her sick, haunted eyes befuddled with dust and tears. She looked as if she were going to collapse at any moment. Don Paolo, not being convinced of the unbreakability of the vow, tried to persuade her to rise and walk, and he actually tried to lift her by her armpits and put her on her feet by force, but in vain, for she resisted with nails and teeth. Having made the vow, she must fulfil it or her son would be sure to die. She was astonished that the priest did not understand such a simple and well known fact.

'What kind of priest are you?' she yelled at him.

Don Paolo left her to her fate and continued on his way. It had grown colder. The top of the mountain behind Pietrasecca was already white with snow. The village was plunged in the shadows mounting from the valley. Only the Colamartini house, which was a little higher up, was still lit by the sun. Cristina appeared at a window on the top floor, and her face was like a crystal receiving the rays of the setting sun. Don Paolo could see nothing of the whole village except that incandescent face.

As soon as the sun had disappeared it was freezing. Matalena was awaiting the return of her priest, sitting spinning in the doorway of the inn. 'It will soon be snowing,' she said, looking up into the sky.

Snow came two days later. Don Paolo awoke to find the landscape transformed. The snow had been falling all night and it went on falling steadily, silently and thickly, like something expected and inevitable.

A few people turned up at Matalena's inn that evening to celebrate the first day of snow. Cristina arrived a little later too; suffering had made her eyes bigger, but she was no less beautiful because of that. Looking at her was a delight.

Don Paolo sat by the hearth, with cafoni, women and children in a big circle all around him. On one side of the fire there was a dog and on the other Teresa's baby, who was to have been born blind but had been saved. The child was in a wicker basket on the ground and looked like a cauliflower, and its face, reddened by the reflection of the fire, looked like an apple. Don Paolo was asked to tell stories, and Cristina specified sacred stories. In the end it was impossible to refuse, so he opened his breviary and looked up the *index festorum*. Then he started telling in his own way the story of the martyrdoms of which the breviary speaks.

The story was always different but always the same. There was a time of trials and tribulations. A dictatorship with a deified leader. A musty old Church, living on alms. An army of mercenaries that guaranteed the peaceful digestion of the rich. A population of slaves. Incessant preparation of new wars of rapine to maintain the prestige of the dictatorship. Meanwhile mysterious travellers arrived from abroad. They whispered of miracles in the east and announced the good tidings that liberation was at hand. The bolder spirits, the poor, the hungry, met in cellars to listen to them. The news spread. Some abandoned the old temples and embraced the new faith. Nobles left their palaces, centurions deserted. The police raided clandestine meetings and made arrests. Prisoners were tortured and handed over to a special tribunal. There were some who refused to burn incense to the state idols. They recognized no god other than the god that was alive in their souls. They faced torture with a smile on their lips. The young were thrown to wild beasts. The survivors remained loyal to the dead, to whom they devoted their secret cult. Times changed, ways of dressing, eating, working, changed, languages changed, but at bottom it was always the same old story.

The heat of the fire made everyone drowsy. Those who were still awake listened, gazing at the fire. Cristina said, 'In all times and in all societies the supreme act is to give oneself, to lose oneself in order to find oneself. One has only what one gives.'

The fire went out, the customers said goodnight, and Don Paolo went up to his room. He picked up the notebook in which he had written the 'Conversations with Cristina' he had begun during the early part of his stay at Pietrasecca, re-read the first few pages, which were full of tenderness and affection for the girl, and then he re-read and tore up the following pages, which had been dictated by disappointment and resentment. Several months had passed, and not for nothing, either for him or for Cristina. Before going to bed he added a few lines.

'Cristina,' he wrote, 'it's true that one has what one gives. But to whom and how is one to give?

'Our love, our disposition for sacrifice and self-abnegation are fruitful only if they are carried into relations with our fellows. Morality can live and flourish only in practical life. We are responsible also for others.

'If we apply our moral feelings to the evil that prevails all round us, we cannot remain inactive and console ourselves with the expectation of an ultra-terrestrial life. The evil to be combated is not the sad abstraction that is called the devil; the evil is everything that prevents millions of people from becoming human. We too are directly responsible for this . . .

'I believe that nowadays there is no other way of saving one's soul. He is saved who overcomes his individual, family, class selfishness and frees himself of the idea of resignation to the existing evil.

'My dear Cristina, one must not be obsessed with the idea of security, even the security of one's own virtue. Spiritual life is not compatible with security. To save oneself one has to take risks.'

259

It went on snowing all night.

In the morning the priest was still asleep when Matalena called him. Outside the inn a small crowd of cafoni and boys were standing round Garibaldi, Sciatàp's donkey, on the crupper of which was the body of a wolf that had been killed that morning on the mountain behind Pietrasecca. Its skin was grey, hairy, stained with blood and mud; its teeth were white and strong, and two bloody patches on the shoulder and flank showed where the bullets had entered. In accordance with custom, the dead wolf was shown from house to house so that alms might be given to those who had killed it.

Luigi Banduccia still had his gun on his shoulder and described what had happened. This was the fourth wolf he had killed. On the nape of the beast's neck he showed a love mark, the deep bite made by a she-wolf. Love-making by wolves is a serious matter. Banduccia could identify from a distance the different kinds of wolf howl: the howl of danger that the wolf utters when it is attacked with weapons; the howl of prey, which means that it has found an animal to tear to pieces and summons its companions, because wolves do not like eating alone; the howl of love, which means that it needs a female and is not ashamed to announce the fact.

Cristina's grandmother was unwilling to give anything for the dead wolf, but Cristina, who had had a special regard for wolves since childhood, tried hard to persuade her.

'Dead wolves don't bite,' the old lady said.

That same day Magascià brought Don Paolo an urgent note that he said had been given to him by old Murica of Rocca dei Marsi. It was signed by Annina, who had just arrived at the Murica house, and it said that Luigi had been arrested. Don Paolo wanted to leave at once, but Magascià answered evasively; he was tired, and his donkey was not so young either.

'Very well then, I'll go on foot,' the priest said. 'A little fresh air will do me good.'

'Is it so urgent?' Matalena said.

'It's a case of conscience,' said the priest.

'Is it someone from your diocese?'

'Someone from my diocese and my parish.'

260

Matalena had never seen the priest so agitated. He left with the briskness of a boy. He may have been surprised himself at his own energy. Fortunately the route was downhill.

CHAPTER 28

The ring of mountains that surrounded the Fucino basin was completely covered in snow; in places it had actually reached the lowest foothills. Don Paolo wore a black coat that came right down to his ankles and had a black woollen scarf round his neck. To rid himself of his ecclesiastical disguise all he had to do was to unbutton his coat and remove his scarf. But the most ingenious feature of his attire was the ordinary felt hat he had brought back from Rome that could equally well be adapted to ecclesiastical or lay purposes, depending on how it was shaped or worn.

The road, which acted as a boundary between a stony hillside planted with vines and an expanse of recently ploughed fields, sloped gently downhill. When the snow finished he could walk more quickly. At a bend in the road he came to a trap waiting by the roadside.

'Don Paolo?' the driver asked him. 'Get in, Annina sent me.'

The priest got in, and they set off at a trot.

'I've been expecting you,' the man said simply. 'I've been expecting you for a couple of hours.'

'I came on foot,' Don Paolo said.

The man's beard was several days old, his shirt and suit were dirty and neglected, and he had a stricken appearance as if he were ill.

'Is there any news of Luigi Murica?' Don Paolo asked. 'Is he still in prison?'

'He died yesterday.'

'*Consummatum est*,' Don Paolo said.

'The news does not seem to surprise you.'

'No, in one way or another I feared it would happen.'

There was a great calmness in the air, the calm of the countryside at the approach of winter.

'Were you friends?' Don Paolo asked.

'We were friends,' the man replied. 'One spent time willingly with him. He was a good man, and made others want to be good too. He also talked to us about the revolution. He told us that the beginning was being together without being afraid.'

'We must stay together,' Don Paolo said. 'We must not allow ourselves to be divided.'

'Luigi had written on a piece of paper: "Truth and brotherhood will prevail among men instead of lies and hatred. Labour will prevail instead of money." When they arrested him they found that piece of paper, and he didn't disown it. So in the yard of the militia barracks at Fossa they put a chamber-pot on his head instead of a crown. That is the truth, they told him. They put a broom in his right hand instead of a sceptre. That is fraternity, they told him. Then they wrapped him in a rèd carpet they picked up from the floor and blindfolded him, and the militiamen formed a ring around him and punched and kicked him backwards and forwards between themselves. That is the kingdom of labour, they told him. When he collapsed to the ground they trampled on him with their nailed boots. After this first stage of the legal proceedings against him he lived for a whole day.'

'If we live like him, it will be as if he were not dead,' Don Paolo said. 'We must stay together and not be afraid.'

The man nodded.

At the approach to Rocca he pointed out the Murica house in the middle of the fields. Don Paolo went to it along a grassy path. He took advantage of the short walk to laicise his appearance. The Murica house was a big, squat, single-storey building, half dwelling, half stable. The windows were closed and shuttered and the front door was wide open, in accordance with the custom. People paying the obligatory visit were coming and going. Pietro went in hesitantly. No-one took any notice of him. As soon as he crossed the threshold he found himself in a big room with a cobbled floor that normally served as a kitchen and store for agricultural implements, but now it was full of people. Some women dressed in black and yellow were sitting on the floor near the fireplace, and some men were standing round the table, talking about land and harvests.

Pietro spotted Annina at the far end of the room, sitting on a stool, alone, pale and distraught, shivering with cold and fear among all these strangers. She was not weeping, for to weep she would have had to be alone or with people she knew. But as soon as she saw Pietro she broke down and sobbed. The dead man's parents came in from a neighbouring room, dressed in black. His mother went to Annina, wiped away her tears, wrapped her in a big black shawl and made her sit beside her on a bench near the hearth.

'Who's she?' the other women whispered to one another.

'She's the bride,' someone replied, 'the bride from town.'

The father sat at the head of the table, together with the other men. Relatives arrived from a neighbouring village. Some boys arrived. The mother, as is the custom, spoke in praise of her dead son. She described how she tried to save him, how she had sent him away to study, to save him from the fate that his weakness, his delicacy, his sensitivity had made her foresee. She had not saved him. The air of the city was not made for him, and the land had reclaimed him. He had started working on the land, helping his father. One might have supposed that he would soon tire of it and turn against it, because working on the land every day was a real chastizement of God. He had woken his father in the morning, harnessed the horse, chosen the seed, filled the barrels, and looked after the vegetable garden.

Every now and then the mother paused in her eulogy to poke the fire and add a dry branch to it. Marta, Don Benedetto's sister, and cafoni from the neighbouring countryside arrived, and others rose and left. Old Murica stood at the head of the table, offering food and drink to the men round him.

'He helped me to sow, hoe, reap, thresh and grind the corn of which this bread is made. Take it and eat, this is his bread.'

Others arrived. The father poured out wine and said, 'He helped me to prune, spray, hoe, and gather the grapes of the vineyard from which this wine came. Drink, for this is his wine.'

The men ate and drank, and some dipped their bread in their wine.

Some beggars arrived. 'Let them in,' the mother said.

'They may have been sent to spy,' someone murmured.

'Let them in. We must take the risk. Many, giving food and drink to beggars, have fed Jesus without knowing it.'

'Eat and drink,' the father said.

Finding himself in front of Pietro, he looked at him and said, 'Where do you come from?'

'From Orta,' he said.

'What is your name?'

Annina went up to the old man and whispered a name in his ear. He looked at the young man with pleasure and embraced him.

'When I was a young man I knew your father,' he said to Pietro. 'He bought a mare of mine at a fair. I heard about you from the son who has been taken from me. Sit here, between his mother and his bride; you too must eat and drink.'

The men around the table ate and drank.

'Bread is made of many grains of corn,' said Pietro, 'so it means unity. Wine is made of many grapes, so it means unity too. Unity of similar, equal, useful things. Hence truth and fraternity are also things that go well together.'

'The bread and wine of Holy Communion,' an older man said. 'The wheat and the grapes that are trampled on. The body and the blood.'

'It takes nine months to make bread,' old Murica said.

'Nine months?' exclaimed the mother.

'Wheat is sown in November and reaped and threshed in July.' The old man counted the months. 'November, December, January, February, March, April, May, June, July. Exactly nine months. It also takes nine months for the grapes to ripen, from March to November.' He counted them, 'March, April, May, June, July, August, September, October, November. That makes nine months too.'

'Nine months?' his mother said. It had never struck her before. It took the same time to make a man. Luigi was born in April. Quietly she counted the months backwards to herself, 'April, March, February, January, December, November, October, September, August.' Nine months from August to April.

More acquaintances arrived, and others left to make room for them. Marta said to the mother, 'Do you remember when Luigi was a little boy and you were still young and went for walks on the hill carrying him in your arms? Don Benedetto used to say that you were like the vine and he the grape, that you were like the stalk and he the ear of corn.'

Bianchina appeared in the doorway and Pietro went towards her. The girl was distraught and could hardly manage to speak.

'Pietro,' she said.

'Why do you call me that?'

'Aren't you Pietro Spina?'

'Yes, I am.'

'You must disappear as quickly as possible, you've been found out.'

'How do you know?'

'Alberto Colamartini told me, he's in the militia now. They're going to Pietrasecca to pick you up tonight or tomorrow morning. You haven't a minute to lose.'

Pietro consulted Annina. He took her advice and asked old Murica to lend him a horse for a few hours. The old man went to the stable and led a handsome colt, only just broken in, into the field.

'A little fresh air will do him good,' he said and handed him over to Pietro.

'What can I do?' Bianchina asked.

'Do what Annina tells you,' Pietro said. 'I'm going to Pietrasecca, where I left some papers I must burn. If there's time I'll come back here and go in the Pescasseroli direction, to Alfedana or Castel di Sangro. Don't worry about me. I'm not afraid. Forgive me for the deception. I'll send you news as soon as I can.'

'It wasn't deception, it was only a secret,' Bianchina said. Her eyes filled with tears.

CHAPTER 29

The colt had neither saddle nor bit, but merely a hempen halter round its neck. The moment it felt a man's weight on its back it whinnied and set off in a wild gallop across the fields. Pietro was taken by surprise. he had not ridden for many years, and to avoid being thrown he had to cling to the animal's mane and neck. But after the first furious dash it quietened down a little and allowed itself to be guided towards the Pietrasecca valley, trotting along a path parallel to the road. In spite of the steep slope, the colt negotiated the first stretch of the valley without pausing for breath. When it came to the snow on the road it slowed down.

Every so often Pietro looked back, but there was no sign of pursuit. The farther he got into the valley the more he was struck by its new aspect. A great deal of snow had already fallen, and the unbroken grey of the sky showed that there was more to come. The colt was panting, steaming and foaming, but kept up a brisk, steady pace. Pietro looked at the white walls of the chain of mountains. They had never looked so high and forbidding.

When Pietrasecca came into view he changed the shape of his felt hat and buttoned up his coat. His eyes were fixed on the mountain behind the village with its two unequal humps, like those of a dromedary. Between them there was a deep hollow known as the Goat's Saddle, which was the only way of crossing to the opposite slope. In summer it took four or five hours to reach the first house on the other side. But in winter? Apart from that, was there any other way of escape? Or, as an alternative was there any way of hiding himself?

At Pietrasecca he tied the colt by the halter to a ring on the wall of the inn and was just going in when he heard someone hurrying towards him. It was Cristina. She looked so utterly dismayed that it frightened him.

'Alberto has told me,' she managed to stammer out.

'Are you unwell, perhaps?'

'Please tell me the truth, are you Pietro Spina?'

'Yes, I am,' he replied. 'I ask your forgiveness.'

Matalena emerged from the inn and interpreted in her own way the emotion by which both of them were obviously affected.

'Wait here for a moment,' Pietro said to the girl. 'I have something for you.'

He hurried up to his room and took the notebook from the table drawer. On the cover he scribbled: 'My dear Cristina, here you will find my defence, and something also that concerns you personally – something beyond the conventional fictions, the hidden truth, the truth of the heart. Pietro Spina.'

He came down to the kitchen and handed the notebook to Cristina, who was waiting outside the door, looking livid and as if paralysed. The girl hurried away, almost running, without saying anything. At that moment Sciatàp passed by. Pietro called him and asked him to take the colt back to old Murica at Rocca dei Marsi, for which he would pay him a day's wages in advance.

'Thank you,' said Sciatàp.

In winter this was a totally unexpected windfall. Matalena was present at the scene, and she saw the man who to her was still Don Paolo going upstairs to his room again. Nothing had happened to rouse her suspicions. Cristina's display of emotion was in accordance with Cassarola's predictions. Matalena emerged smiling from the bar to go and buy some salt and, since she was in a good humour and in no hurry, she stayed and gossiped for a bit with Magascià's wife and some other women.

'How's Don Paolo?'

'He's very well. Now I'm sure he'll be staying the whole winter.'

'When is he going to start taking confessions again?'

'It won't be long now. He's waiting for a definite answer from the Pope.'

When she got back to the inn, still totally unaware of what

was going on, she started cooking dinner. How long was it exactly since she'd seen the priest going up to his room? About an hour and a half, perhaps two hours. As soon as dinner was ready she went up to tell him. The room was dark and empty. Matalena turned on the light. There was some money on the table and a note of apology and thanks. She could not believe her eyes. What sort of joke was this? Had her priest gone mad? With her heart in tumult she went down into the garden, and recognized his footsteps in the snow. She followed them all the way to the stream, from where the trail led, not down towards the valley, but up towards the mountain. Matalena met the deaf-mute and asked him by signs whether he had seen the priest. He replied, also by signs, that he had seen him hurrying in the direction of the mountain. Magascià appeared on the scene and confirmed this incredible information. The priest had been dashing along like a madman. By now he must be a long way away.

'He has gone mad,' Matalena exclaimed. 'Why didn't you stop him?'

Without waiting for a reply she hurried back and went to the Colamartini house. She knocked several times, but there was no answer, so she went round to the back of the house and went in by a back door which she found open.

'Donna Cristina,' she called up the stairs several times. But there was no reply.

Cristina was in her room, alone, in a state of extreme anguish. The sheets of Pietro Spina's notebook trembled between her hands.

'Our priest has gone mad,' Matalena yelled, bursting into her room.

'Mad?' Cristina exclaimed.

'He left suddenly, and he's gone up towards the mountain,' she went on. 'Was it you by any chance who reduced him to that state?'

Cristina dashed to the window and looked out in the direction of the mountain. There was no sign of any human being on the white slope leading up to the Goat's Saddle. He must have taken the safer and longer route, the mule track that first followed the stream and then climbed in big zigzags to the pass.

'If he had only had his dinner,' Matalena whimpered. 'If he had only taken some warmer clothing. But he left it in the wardrobe in his room.'

The course of the stream at the bottom of the valley was so hidden by boulders and shrubs that Cristina could not possibly see how far the fugitive had gone. The air was not clear either.

'It'll soon be dark,' Matalena went on whimpering. 'Even if he reaches the Saddle he'll be caught in a blizzard.'

Cristina was still standing at the window, gazing in the direction in which the fugitive must have gone. In his bad state of health, with his ignorance of the locality, without special clothing or food it was an adventure that might cost him his life. She seemed suddenly to make up her mind.

'Go,' she said to Matalena.

As soon as she was alone she hid the diary under her pillow. From a wardrobe in the corridor she fetched some heavy clothing, a warm sweater, two scarves, a pair of thick woollen socks and a pair of gloves, and wrapped them up in a bundle. She went down to the kitchen, took a loaf of bread, a piece of cheese and a bottle of wine and put them in the bundle. To avoid being seen or heard she took the big bundle and went out through the back door which Matalena had used. She made a small détour behind the church and the cemetery and slid about ten yards down a steep slope to the path that followed the stream and then started climbing beside it in the direction of its source. When she was sure that no-one from the village was following her or had seen her she started to run. If she were to catch up with the fugitive there was no time to lose. There were traces of footsteps in the snow, and as she hurried along she tried to guess which were his. They grew rarer and rarer, but did not leave the side of the stream. This was a sure sign that he had taken the mule track, the longer route to the Goat's Saddle, instead of the short cut up a steep slope about three hundred feet in height.

Even in summer tackling it was an enterprise best left to foolhardy boys and goats, and in winter it was almost impossible. Cristina jumped the stream without hesitation and started climbing it. She used hands and feet, clinging to branches, bushes and boulders that protruded from the snow. Several times she stumbled and fell badly with her face in the snow and slipped back. Luckily there was less snow where the slope was steepest, because the wind had swept it away. But she sank in the deep snow that was still soft between the rocks, and had to use all her strength to struggle out of it. She was hampered by her skirt and the bundle, but for different reasons she could rid herself of neither. In a place where a big projecting rock formed a kind of dry cave she flung herself to the ground, exhausted and almost breathless. Mist was mounting from the valley. Trails of grey cotton wool filled the ravines, hid the houses, covered fields, hedges and walls. The earth had a shapeless, empty look, as if it were uninhabited. Cristina rose and continued the ascent. Up here the snow was harder and progress easier, but also it was easier to slip. Sweat poured from her, and her hands, torn by the thorns to which she had had several times had to cling to avoid plunging into the abyss, were bleeding. Her heart was hammering so much that she had to hold her chest. When she reached the top of the slope she found herself in a wide, nearly rectangular, space known as the Witches' Field. Beyond it the mountain continued sloping gently upwards. The snow all round was intact. Nobody had passed that way. Going on towards the top, apart from being exhausting, was pointless. It would be more sensible to go round it, so as to cut across the route taken by Spina. She went off in this new direction. Soon she completely lost sight of the Pietrasecca valley. In front of her and all round her there was nothing but the white rumps and summits of other mountains. A freezing wind was blowing that cut her face. Twilight was approaching, and so was a blizzard. She reached the point where the hollow begins that divides the mountain into two humps, forming the Goat's Saddle. There was no trace of any human being on the snow. The ground was much cut up by boulders and landslides caused by floods and, with snow up to her waist, Cristina could not see very far. She went on climbing towards the Saddle. Perhaps she thought that when she got

271

there she would be able to see both slopes and spot Pietro more easily, or at any rate be seen by him. But a moment came when she could go no further and let herself collapse in the snow.

So that he should not pass without noticing her, every so often she called out his name with all the strength of her lungs. She called him by his new name, his real name, 'Pietro, Pietro.'

If he had passed he would certainly have heard her. She brushed back her hair, cleared the snow from her face, her eyebrows, her ears and her neck. And every so often she went on calling, 'Pietro, Pietro.'

Eventually a voice in the distance answered her, but it was not a human voice. It was like the howling of a dog, but it was sharper and more prolonged. Cristina probably recognized it. It was the howl of a wolf. The howl of prey. The summons to other wolves scattered about the mountain. The invitation to the feast. Through the driving snow and the darkness of approaching night Cristina saw a wild beast coming towards her, quickly appearing and disappearing in the dips and rises in the snow. She saw others appear in the distance. She knelt, closed her eyes, and made the sign of the cross.